MANDINGO

'*Mandingo* shocks, shakes'—*Sunday Times*.

'What remains vivid in the memory is his picture of an extraordinary and almost unbelievable pocket of the not-too-distant past'—*Evening Standard*.

'All the more horrifying because it is so calmly and quietly written. . . . Not for the squeamish or self-complacent'—*Time & Tide*.

'A novel of flaring colour'—*News Chronicle*.

'Terrifying climax'—*Sheffield Telegraph*.

G000149787

MANDINGO

KYLE ONSTOTT

UNABRIDGED

PAN BOOKS LTD : LONDON

First published 1959 by Longmans, Green & Co Ltd.
This edition published 1961 by Pan Books Ltd,
33 Tothill Street, London, SW1.
ISBN 0 330 20263 4

2nd Printing 1962
3rd Printing 1964
4th Printing 1965
5th Printing 1965
6th Printing 1966
7th Printing 1968
8th Printing 1968
9th Printing 1969
10th Printing 1970
11th Printing 1970
12th Printing 1971
13th Printing 1972
14th Printing 1973
15th Printing 1974

Dedicated to
VICKY and PHILIP
of course

Printed in Great Britain by
Cox & Wyman Ltd, London, Reading and Fakenham

AUTHOR'S NOTE

IN THE early 1830s the economy of the Southern States of the USA was largely based on trading in human flesh. What happened there led to the struggle between North and South that broke out thirty years later.

From today's vantage point the developing situation may be viewed objectively. Actually, the finger of blame should be pointed at no one geographical group of people. Although those who promoted the abolition of slavery were ethically in the right, Southern planters in general are shown to have been victims of circumstances rather than diabolical tyrants as they have sometimes been painted.

The land, once the most valuable asset of the plantation owner, deteriorated through lack of knowledge of conservation methods. In turn, the potential return from the sale of agricultural products gradually lessened. In an attempt to drain the final dregs from the impoverished soil, slave labour was utilized. But, finally, the land became so nearly exhausted that the planters turned to the more lucrative enterprise of propagating slaves for marketing to landowners in other areas. Then, as a sordid outgrowth of a last endeavour to maintain financial security, speculation in the slave market became the outstanding interest. More emphasis was placed on the propagation of slave stock than on the production of any other commodity. The excuse was used that the practice was intended to better the physical characteristics of the offspring. But physical oddities and freaks were as much in demand as were the robust.

The average plantation owner was considerate of the welfare of his human property. But he was considerate not as one concerned with the needs of another—rather, the planter's concern was based on maintaining and increasing the value of a marketable chattel.

K. O.

CHAPTER ONE

THE OLD man heard the closing of the front door and the limping step in the hall. He was pleased that his son should have the good sense to send the Negroes to quarters and come into the house out of the cold, drizzling February rain.

Hammond walked across the room, picked up his father's glass of toddy and took a swallow.

"Take more, take more," urged Maxwell. "Do you good, son. Gittin' too cooled off fer me anyways. Got to have me another'n, and I kin ever git that triflin' Memnon to stir me one. Mem!" he called. "Mem! Memnon!"

Hammond started toward the dining-room to get Memnon when the boy opened the door with apparent alacrity.

"Didn't you hear me callin', Mem, you god-damn black varmint? Stir me a toddy, hot, mind you. Now! Not nex' week," Maxwell commanded.

"Yas, suh, Masta," said the slave and started to go.

"I talk to you, I cod you, I beg, an' I cuss you," the master said sternly. "Only I cain't whup you—with this rheumatiz. You young masta got to do that."

The slave was used to the threats of his old master, which, so far, had always come to nothing. None the less, Agamemnon rolled his eyes toward the younger Maxwell, with dilated pupil and a show of white.

"Whenever you reckon, I'll take keer of him," Hammond promised his father. "Whut you think, boy? When I whups, I whups—takes the meat right off your bones. Eh?"

"Naw, suh, please, suh, Masta, suh," replied the Negro. "I be spry. I ain't goin' to sloth no mo'." While he reckoned the impatience of his senior master to be mere bluster, he was by no means sure that the forthright younger man did not mean business. Memnon knew that he was lax, slothful, and procrastinating, and he resolved henceforth to be more diligent—at least for a time. His duties were small enough, to mix toddies for the older man, to replenish the fire, to serve at table, remove his master's clothes at night and help to put them on in the morning; and he was indulged, fed white man's viands, kept in clean, whole clothes, given at least one ardent woman with whom to sleep, with a frequent alternative. He was valuable, being strong-thewed, broadshouldered, yellow-skinned, free from scars, disfigurements, or blemishes. He knew he was not for sale, though he was past thirty and would bring a larger price now than later, but it was unthinkable that his young master would risk scarring him up with the whip and reducing his market worth, especially since he knew the pride the Maxwells took in having their stock, human and quadruped, clean-limbed and sound.

Despite the cold rain and the father's entreaties, the son returned to his work, determined to clear more land, split the rails to fence it, chop wood for the house fires, but above all to keep the Negroes employed and exercised. Agamemnon prepared the toddy that Maxwell had ordered, saw to it that it was hot, as commanded, and when he saw that the fire was burning low in the fireplace, brought fresh chunks of water-oak and adjusted them upon the dog-irons.

Maxwell, surprised at the slave's access of industry, could only grunt at what he assumed was a sign of reformation. His joints racked, and he lifted one hand with the other and examined the swollen knuckles. Yet, in spite of the pain and effort it cost him, he braced himself and staggered to his feet occasionally to totter to the window to scan the weather, just to prove to himself that he was able to do it and to alter the tedium of watching the fire and waiting for Hammond's return.

On one of the excursions, near to evening, he noted that the downpour had subsided to a mere drizzle and scanned the sky for a patch of blue in the hope that the rain would cease altogether. Between the boles of the bare miscellany of trees, maples, tupelos, oaks, chestnuts, hickories, and elms, that behind a zizgag stake-and-rider fence lined the long avenue to the main road, he descried a moving object. He could hardly credit that a visitor was arriving at Falconhurst on so wretched a day and through such mire as the rains had made of the roads.

He could not be sure. "Mem!" he bellowed. "Memnon! Memnon, you hear? Memnon, you yaller mongrel! Come here! Come here, I'm sayin'!"

Drowsing before the fireplace in the kitchen, Mem roused himself and shuffled unhurriedly across the open passageway, through the dining-room and into the living-room. "Yas, suh, Masta. You a-callin'?"

"Course I'm a-callin'. Come here to this winder. Look out. Whut you reckon that be movin' up that laneway?"

Mem looked. "Look like horse with gen'man a-ridin'," he said.

"Course it a gen'leman and of course he ridin' a horse," Maxwell said contemptuously. "But who it goin' to be? Who comin' to Falconhurst in all this weather and through all this mire?"

Memnon had no idea. His interest was no less, however, than his owner's. "Now we'll have doin's," he declared optimistically. The arrival of any white man at Falconhurst was an occasion.

The horseman emerged into the open and it could be seen that he wore a frock coat and a slouch hat, as might have been expected, that he was thin to emaciation without being very tall, that his bay mount was tired, muddy, and from his action probably a gelding, for which Maxwell felt a contempt.

Three children ran beside the horse, lifting their feet high in an effort to surmount the mud. The man monotonously cracked a whip to urge the children's haste, but he usually and intentionally missed them. Now and again one was seen to flinch when a blow stung its legs or buttocks, and for three or four strides to hasten its pace.

"Jest a nigger buyer," scoffed Maxwell more to himself than to his servant.

Despite the contempt in his voice, he hastened to the double front doors and went out on the verandah, followed closely by Agamemnon, to await his guest. The profession of dealing in Negroes was deprecated, but the scorn for it was not so intense as to warrant a denial of hospitality to its practitioners. The disdain was for the calling, not for the man. If it was an evil, it was a convenient evil. Dealers saved planters from the necessity of a trip to market with one or two slaves; they were not too particular about the viciousness of Negroes they bought for early resale and were good agencies for the riddance of 'bad' Negroes; and better yet, they paid cash on the barrelhead for their purchases. Moreover, they were white.

Visitors to Falconhurst were rare; they brought news. And Maxwell's dislike for dealers was more of a convention than a conviction. He was aware that his own rung of the social hierarchy was not that of a gentleman—not a fine gentleman at least, merely a gentleman by courtesy, far, far above a dealer but not quite a full gentleman.

The stranger dismounted stiffly from his horse, briefly rubbed his lean flanks to relieve the fatigue of the saddle, doffed his hat, and said, "Howdy, suh. Name of Brownlee—Brownlee."

9

The Negro children who accompanied him retreated to the off side of the horse, and, open-mouthed, looked warily at their master's reception.

"Name of Maxwell, suh, Warren Maxwell," the host returned the greeting and identified himself.

"I was informed of your name, suh. It's well and, pardon me, suh, favourably known in these parts."

"Ought to be, suh. We been right here at Falconhurst sence befo' the rebellion of 1776." The reply was not ungenial, but it served to underline the difference between gentleman planter and slave dealer. No gesture of handshaking was made by either man. "Cast the bridle to the boy, suh, who will stable your horse and bed down your servants. Then, come right in. Dinner is mighty nigh ready."

Agamemnon caught the reins, but only to turn the chore over to another black boy who had appeared, more bold than the other Negroes, from behind one corner of the house. Brownlee had an eye for a Negro and quickly noted that this slave boy had only two toes—the great and the little one—on his left foot. Every eye in the quarters appraised the visitor from cover. His arrival was reason for speculation and low-toned talk.

Maxwell was specific in his orders to the black. "Take the gen'leman's horse straight to the stable. Take off his gear and wash him down good—warm water, mind you, not too hot, but warm. I ketches you washing a horse with col' water this time of year, I'll hide you sure."

"Yas, suh, Masta," the boy replied conventionally.

"And take these little niggers with you and bed 'em down in another stall and give them some pone, all they'll eat of it. Cook will issue you some black-strap to make it tasty. Tell her I said to."

"Cook won't give black-strap to no nigger withouten your say," protested the boy.

"Tell her I say. If she don't heed you, have her ask Memnon."

"Yas, suh, Masta; have cook ast Memnon," the boy repeated to impress the command on his own mind.

Maxwell consulted Brownlee, "Reckon I better have your niggers chained up?"

"I reckon it ain't necessary on a cold day like this. They too tired to run. Of course you cain't tell whut goes on in a nigger's haid," he reconsidered. "Wouldn't do no harm."

Maxwell turned again to the boy. "And chain the niggers to

10

the side of their stall—the wench separate from the bucks. Use them small little anklets that they cain't slip out of and fetch the keys up and turn 'em over to Memnon."

"Turn keys over to Memnon," the black repeated.

"When that mud on their legs dries out, crack it and rub it off, too," interposed Brownlee. "Pardon me, suh, for giving orders to yo' servant," he apologized to Maxwell.

"My servants are yo' servants, suh, so long as you honours me with your company at Falconhurst," Maxwell reassured his guest. "Anything else the boy kin do fer yo' property, suh?"

"That will accommodate me nicely, suh, nicely."

"Memnon, go down after dinner to the stable and see that this boy—whut's your name, boy?" the master broke off.

"My name Preacha', suh, please," the confused boy stuttered.

"Whut's that? Talk plain."

"Preacha', suh. My name Preacha'."

"Preacha'? I don't like it. It don't mean nothin'. I like names out'n history or names of heathen gods."

"My mammy wanted that I should be a preacha'—a reverend."

"I'll reverend you. We'll change your name right now—let's see—Barbarossa. We haven't had a Barbarossa fer a long time. Remember that—your name is Barbarossa."

"Barbarossa, Barbarossa, Barbarossa," the baffled boy muttered in determination to remember his new designation.

Maxwell continued his orders to Memnon, "See that this Barber do all whut I told him. If he neglect that horse and if he don't take good care of them niggers, he kin depen' on a hidin'. Understand, boy?"

"Yas, suh, Masta."

"That's all," said the master.

The newly christened Barbarossa led the horse toward the stable, followed by the three children. "Barber, Barber, Barber —something or t'other. My masta done change me from Preacha' to Barba'," and he snapped his fingers, "jest like that," he said to himself, but aloud. Then he laughed delightedly at his own joke. "Barba', Barba', Bar——"

"I trade in niggers," Brownlee announced to Maxwell.

"So I reckoned, suh, so I reckoned," replied the host. "We got to have traders if we're goin' to have niggers. We cain't eat 'em."

"I know some gen'lemen don't like traders, but everybody's got to live. Whut would you planters do withouten we traders?"

"We'd have to plough the niggers under, I reckon. I got

11

nothing agin' traders. I've sold to lots of 'em; they're welcome right in my house and at my table—that is, sence my wife passed away. She was a Hammond, daughter of old Mista Theophilus Hammond of the Anglebranch Plantation down near Selma. Mista Theophilus wouldn't have no truck with traders—a fine gen'leman. He never sold a servant—not one. Bred good niggers too. I remember twenty year back when servants was cheap, Theophilus Hammond pay two thousand dollars fer a yaller quadroon stallion—a lot of money them days."

"Sure was. Why even today you can pick up a mighty noble hand, housebroke and everything, fer fifteen hundred or two thousand. Jest before Christmas I sold a big, sound, robust buck, six foot one and shoulders like that," Brownlee stretched his arms, "right off the block in New Orleans fer fourteen hundred—yeller, too, good enough to cover anybody's wenches."

Mr Maxwell refused to relinquish his aristocratic father-in-law. "Of course, Mista Theophilus (being in the family I calls him by his first name), used to sell off a bad nigger, if he got one; or he'd sell to accommodate a friend with a good houseboy or a fancy, yaller sew-er; or he'd rarely, rarely, part with a young buck to get money to run Anglebranch Plantation and feed the other hands till cotton time. But he never made a practice of selling his stock at all. Didn't trust traders and wouldn't sell to 'em."

"I come a right smart bit out of my way to pay my respects to yo'." Brownlee bowed and Maxwell returned the bow in so far as his rheumatism permitted. "And see didn't yo' all have a few servants you wanted to git shet of."

"No, cain't say we have. I sent a fine coffle of prime young bucks Natchez way, right after pickin' time. If yo' had of come along about then we could have talked, but I ain't got nothin' prime to offer yo' right now."

"They don't got to be prime, suh. I'll prime 'em when I git 'em to New Orleans," Brownlee urged, betraying his eagerness.

"If yo' come this way again in the late fall, I might have a dozen or fifteen nice, strapping boys fer yo', or a wench or two if I kin get 'em knocked up and showing. Don't pay to sell a wench open. Buyers like to git two fer the price of one."

"Don't know if'n I could afford to relieve you of a dozen at a time. Limited capital, yo' know, mighty limited, but I'll be here —count on't."

The wind was playing through Maxwell's shock of red hair, and he suddenly was aware of the chill in the air that would worsen his rheumatism.

"Right like to rain some more; I kin feel it right in my jints. Wind a-comin' up, too. One good comes out of this consarned rheumatiz—learns me to prognosticate." He rubbed the swollen joints of one hand over the equally swollen knuckles of the other. "I'll always remember 1831 as a wet year, the year the rheumatiz got me. And now in February, it's started out wet again and the rheumatiz mirrors the weather, seems like."

"Roads like thick gumbo, all the way across Alabama, ever sence I left the Georgia line. Horse mired up to his fetlocks and the young niggers muddy half up to the crotch. Had to stop oncet and take the little wench up on the crupper; and lashing the two boys slowed 'em down more than it hurried 'em up. Nigh glad I had so scant a coffle because they a-goin' to be all skinny, even if not sick, before I kin fetch 'em to market." Mr Brownlee sighed, removed his square-lensed spectacles, wiped his bloodshot, porcine blue eyes on a soiled blue bandana which he drew from the tail of his frock coat, after which he took off his black slouch hat and wiped with the bandana his bald scalp with the tufts of curly black hair above the ears. His small face had been smooth some three or four days ago, but now it was scantily peppered with black.

"Now, howsomever, at last yo' kin rest your bones and fatten your niggers. We hope you'll squander some time with us, least-wise till after the spell of weather."

"No, thankee, I reckon I better git along this same evenin', more 'specially that yo' cain't spare me no niggers. The nigger crop is real slim ever'whure. And the prices are going up like balloons in the wind," complained Brownlee.

"No hurry at all," argued Maxwell. "Not many gen'lemen honour us at Falconhurst."

"Got to git along. Got to git along. I values your hospitality, suh, but I got to git along."

"Come morning and I might, I jest might, fix my mind on letting yo' carry away a buck or two. We are all run over with young niggers, got to kick 'em out of the way to walk, but they jest too young to dispose of to advantage me."

"I need niggers, I do indeed, suh," emphasized Brownlee. "If there is a chance to dicker and yo' prices are not too powerful, I'll settle down and discommode you all fer the night."

"Nothin' at all, nothin' at all. Yo' cain't discommode me one

13

bit. Charmed to enjoy your conversation. Of course yo' remember I say I might sell, not that I would sell. I'll have to counsel with my son. Turn the whole plantation shebang over to him to run, account of my rheumatiz. But come into the house, suh, come right in and set," urged Maxwell, spitting into his hand and hurling to the ground a cud of tobacco he had been harbouring in his jaw. "Dinner will be ready soon as Ham rides up."

Brownlee paused on the gallery which fronted the house to remove on the footscraper some of the mud that was drying on his boots.

"Never mind that, never mind," said Maxwell as he held open the door. "We ain't got no finery, jest rag carpets all over and plenty of nigger grease to clean things up. A little mud don't matter at all."

"Seem to me a purty fine mansion," Brownlee looked about him. "Mighty comfortable."

"My grandpappy built a log house in the clearing right here. My pappy built this nine-room clapboard, which was good enough, a plain and common house in his day, purty fancy, fact is, then, fer these parts. I was jest aiming to build a better'n— could well afford it too—somethin' like Mista Tom Jefferson's place back in Virginia—fitten to live in like a gen'leman—when my wife upped and passed away seven years back. My wife was a Hammond, daughter of ol' Mista Theophilus Hammon' of Anglebranch Plantation."

"Fine family; fine, fine family," interposed Brownlee.

"I aimed to build a mansion, as I'm a-telling you, when she come down, some female trouble, a growth. And when she went to her reward, it jest nearly tore the bowels right out'n me. I ain't got over it yet. I jist dropped everything. This old house good enough fer the boy and me. Course, if Hammon' marry some fine lady like his mamma (and I'm a-countin' on it) he'll prob'bly build her a fine home over on the other knoll and let this place go to quarters. We're cramped fer quarters anyhow; two families with an extrie wench or two in ever' cabin, and the extrie boys bedded down on straw in the stable. It ain't healthy. Come an epizootic and it would ruin us."

A genial fire in the wide fireplace warmed the sitting-room into which Mr Maxwell welcomed his guest, who gingerly eased his lean body into a large rocker. The host baked himself in front of the fire, alternately facing it and turning his back to it in an effort to relieve the rheumatic pains that racked his joints.

14

"Memnon! Memnon!" he called. Before the boy arrived he questioned his guest, "How do you like your corn?"

"Uncontaminated, please, suh, uncontaminated."

"A glass of unwatered whisky fer the gen'leman and a toddy fer me—hot, mind," the host gave his orders to the Negro.

Brownlee eyed the slave appraisingly. "Right smart boy," he declared. "Ain't fer sale, I reckon."

When Agamemnon returned with the drinks, Brownlee seemed even more interested in the boy than in the whisky. As the Negro approached to hand him the brimming water goblet, Brownlee reached out and grasped his leg, felt his muscles critically. "Kneel down," he commanded and ran his hands over the shoulders, opened his mouth and ran his fingers perfunctorily along the sound teeth. " 'Bout thirty, I should say."

"Not that old," observed the master proudly.

"Seems like about thirty, teeth and all. 'Bout a quadroon, I reckon."

" 'Bout that. His dam a mulatto, his sire a white man."

"Fully housebroke, I reckon?" the buyer persisted.

"Yes, but triflin'. Cain't git no work out'n him."

"Sell him to me and I'll cure that quick."

"And he back talks too. I been laying off to hang him up and have him hided fer quite a spell, but whut with the rheumatiz and all, I put it off and put it off."

"No, no, Masta, suh," the boy began a plaintive wail. "I's spry nigger; don't hide me; I'll be good. No, no, Masta, I'll——"

"Dry up," the master warned. "See whut I mean?" he addressed himself to Brownlee. "He's al'ays puttin' his mouth into white folk's talk. He's a kind of pet of my son, and Ham has ruint him. My son don't mind if I peel his rump, but he too busy to do it hisself."

"Reckon you don't want to sell him then?" interposed the trader.

"No, I reckon not."

An irregular step sounded on the creaking floor of the hall and Hammond Maxwell limped in. "Sorry, suh, about keeping dinner," he explained to his father. "I rid around agin to see how the river is comin' up after the rainin'."

"Don't spoil your dinner with concernment." Maxwell turned to address his guest, "This son of mine is much too ponderous. His only fault, only fault, suh, is that he loves this damned leeched-out plantation and its blacks more than he loves white

15

ladies. Mr Brownlee, suh, this is my son Hammond; named for his grandsire, suh, Theophilus Hammond."

"Right charmed by the honour of your company," responded Hammond cordially.

"Thankee, suh. Right charmed my own self," said Brownlee, rising and extending his hand.

"Mr Brownlee goin' about the country purchasin' negras fer the New Orleans block. Cain't make a sizeable coffle and so he drop by Falconhurst to look over our stock. Do yo' reckon we kin accommodate him with a buck or two?"

"Don't reckon we kin deny a gen'leman in need. Might hap we kin spare something," Ham encouraged Brownlee, his hospitality overweighing his contempt for the profession of his guest. "But dinner awaits us. May I escort you, suh, into the other room?"

"Yes, it's gitting on to one and you must be wolf-hungry, Son, after all mornin' in the saddle," declared the father, as he led the way into the dining-room.

It was an immense, bare apartment, its size only modified by the height of the ceilings. Against one wall stood a wide sideboard of the Empire period, mahogany, over-ornate, but with some claim to distinction of taste. Its surface, however, was so cluttered with rococo silver and glass as to destroy what dignity it might have possessed.

The large rectangular table in the middle of the long, tall room was covered by a cloth of heavy damask in a checkerboard pattern of red and white. In the very centre of the table stood a tall revolvable silver or silver-plated caster with cruets of condiments and jars of various kinds of pickles. From its upright handle were suspended two pairs of tongs and around its perimeter dangled a fringe of silver teaspoons.

On one corner of the table stood a tall, glass pitcher of thick, yellow milk. Places were laid for three. The pinkish willow-ware plates were enormous, ornamented with pictures of Chinese temples and pagodas. Each was flanked with a bone dish of the same ware. The substantial knives and forks were of steel, their bone handles streaked with yellow from too long boiling in dish-water. The empty coffee cups that stood at the right of each cover, each handle meticulously turned to the exact right of each cup, were on the same oversized scale as the plates. Tall goblets of heavy pressed glass, each holding upright in its bowl a red napkin starched and ironed to display its fringed border, stood behind the cups. Except for the pickles in the caster jars, and salt in

16

capacious open dishes of heavy, red glass, no food was visible.

Although there were no flies to be brushed on this chilly day, two sleek boys stood, one on each side of the table, waving fans of frayed peacock-tail feathers monotonously and tirelessly to and fro. The trader began his evaluation of the boys the moment he set eyes upon them. Here was something choice, something fancy. What a price these two would fetch at private treaty in New Orleans! He knew exactly the men who would be interested. The bumper of whisky he had drunk enlarged his imagination. Perhaps these rustics had no comprehension of the value of such a brace in the right market, of the purposes for which they could be sold, of the uses to which they could be put. Either, alone, was a jewel. Together, as a span, twins, they would bring four or five times what they would bring singly.

As he glanced from one to the other, he was not able to detect a trace of difference. The contours of closely shorn skulls were exactly alike, the same round faces with full cheeks, the same noses only slightly flat with nostrils somewhat large, the same neat ears, the same large full mouths turned upward at the corners, the same large eyes with irises so black that it was impossible to detect that they had pupils. The facial skins were alike in colour and in texture—a light amber through which shone a rosiness round the cheekbones. They appeared burnished, but it was with health and the soft soap that had been recently applied to render them fit for service in their master's dining-room.

Down to their small, arched, bare feet they were made alike, height, arm length, leg length, flatness of chest, roundness of buttock. It was not by design that they were uniformly clad, because the small boys on Falconhurst after six or eight were all dressed alike in rough shirts and rougher pants, which were their only garments. Before six or eight, often up to ten, boys wore nothing at all, although girls were clothed a little earlier. The boys' clothes were uniform also, in their age and drabness—it could not be called colour.

Brownlee's survey of the room and his evaluation of the twins were rapid. It took no more time than for Agamemnon to withdraw the horsehide covered chair, and to seat his rheumatic master at the head of the table, after which he pulled out Brownlee's chair and seated him. Hammond dispensed with the Negro's assistance and sat down at the side of the table opposite Brownlee, whose liquorish eye continued to steal glances at the boys.

17

Agamemnon fetched from the kitchen an immense platter of stewed chicken enveloped with dumplings, tender as tissue. This was followed by another platter on which rested slice after centre slice of fried ham surrounded by the red gravy in which it had been cooked. A third platter contained eggs, more than a dozen of them, fried on one side only.

Next to be handed round was a heaped-up dish of boiled potatoes, followed by tender spring greens on which reposed a large piece of bacon.

Agamemnon filled the glasses with the creamy milk from the pitcher, then filled the cups from a battered tin pot of strong, black, and hot coffee, upon which he floated cream so thick that it oozed from the pitcher only semi-liquid. He then passed a pitcher of light-coloured molasses with which the coffee was to be sweetened.

"Eat hearty, suh, eat hearty," urged the host. "Might as well clean up the vittles. The leavin's are jest scraped to the servants anyways."

"Scrumptious meal, suh," declared Brownlee after his fourth cup of coffee.

"Nothin' extrie, nothin' extrie. Jest the general run of dinner," Maxwell deprecated the compliment paid to his food, and led the way back to the sitting-room.

"Now about those servants you offerin' to sell me," Brownlee persisted, sinking into his chair before the fireplace.

"Well, let's see," Maxwell said. "Whut you reckon, Ham?"

"Well, s'pose we drags out that Preacher and that lean, brown boy named Emperor?"

"Changed Preacher's name to Barbarossa," corrected the father. "That's good. They all right, an' you say."

"They brisk and lively? How big are they?"

"One about fifteen hands, three inches, I reckon. You saw him. He barned your horse. The other taller, mayhap close to seventeen hands—but they got a spell of growin' in 'em yet. Yes, they right vig'ous and frisky. They'll make good hands," the elder Maxwell affirmed.

"They ain't unsound, but they not sound neither, not quite exactly prime," Hammond warned.

"I was jest calculatin'," replied the trader, "That Preacha' is kin' of cripped, ain't he? Toes off one foot?"

"Not cripped. It don't slow him down none," said Hammond. "Of course, if you don't crave him——"

"It's all right, it's all right. A nigger's a nigger—of course, at a price."

"Of course," Hammond agreed.

"What ails the other'n?" inquired Brownlee.

"A burned scar; don't ruin him none, but Papa and me, we don't like to shovel feed into a boy that don't strip down purty. Falconhurst negras are right sound and we wants to keep 'em so. We right proudish over havin' good stock without'n blemish or blight. Our only reason fer cheapening these boys."

"If'n he kin cut cane and pick cotton, I kin use him—of coursen, with allowance fer price."

"Memnon, gather up them two boys, Preach and Emp; shuck 'em down; and give 'em a hunk of hard soap. Tell 'em to go down to the river and wash all over good, and then come on back here and tarry in front of the gallery." Hammond gave instruction. "And sen' fer my hoss."

"You ain't goin' out, Son. It's rainin' right down."

"Got to see after that passel cutting stove wood up beyond that fur clearin'. Not a hand would cut a stick if I wasn't there to drive them."

"Don't want you to ketch your death, Son, a-workin' in this kin' of weather—cold and rain."

"Don't fret yourself, Papa," said the boy. "I'm warm dressed and waterproof."

"Whut am I goin' to rate Mr Brownlee fer them boys?" the senior asked.

"Whutever's right and fair," the boy replied. "You've had more truck in that kind of messin' than ever I had." He bent over and kissed his father, bowed to the trader and was gone.

The father sighed, arose and trudged painfully to the cloudy window on which he wiped a space through which to watch his son mount his horse.

Despite Brownlee's anxiety to inspect his prospective purchases, Maxwell chose to enjoy awhile in anticipation the pleasure he knew would be his in conducting the transaction. He surmised how ardent the trader was to buy, and was confident to wait until his fish had fully swallowed the hook.

"Hammond think this a cotton plantation," he observed. "Falconhurst ain't a cotton plantation at all. It a nigger farm, that whut it is, a nigger farm. It's been cropped and cropped fer cotton year after year till there ain't no more cotton in the dirt."

Brownlee was but little interested in Alabama cotton economy.

19

Every little while he arose and paced to the window and looked at the two nude Negroes waiting patiently beneath a tupelo tree that partially shielded them from the wind-driven train.

"That burn on that buck is middlin' bad," he observed.

"Jest looks that way through that wrinkled pane. That winder light is all wavy. Ain't nothin' at all, scarcely. But Hammond jest cain't abide a nigger on the place that ain't perfect. Funny that way. Mayhap it reminds him of his own stiff leg which he got from that pony gelding when he was six years old. His mamma didn't want he should have a pony so young. She warned me, but I've got a stubborn streak too. Besides the little feller wanted a pony, wanted it bad. I never could suffer that child to crave nothin' and to not git it. I cain't yet. That spotted pony seemed gentle when I traded for it, but you can't never trust a gelding, horse or nigger. They villainous and double-hearted. The varmint throwed the boy off the third day he had him, bucked him right off withouten no reason at all. I didn't think the boy was hurt none, but I toted him into the house (didn't trust him to no nigger) and laid him down on that very lounge there in the corner, eased his cryin', undressed him gentlelike as I could, and rubbed him down with whisky. Lucretia Borgia, the cook, that is, suckin' them two twins—the two you saw in the dining-room—her and I give the babies to Ham fer a bribe to let her rub him with whisky ever' day. Didn't do no good, howsumever. His knee stiffened up. Cain't scarcely bend it at all."

Brownlee was less interested in Hammond's stiff knee than in the Negroes in the dooryard. "We better look after them boys out there. Standing nekid in this drivin' rain is liable to give 'em lung fever or somethin'."

Maxwell led the way through the hall to the front doors, which Agamemnon opened for him, guiding his way down the single step to the verandah. The Negro brought rocking-chairs, but only his master sat down. Brownlee, in his concern to get down to business, continued to stand and Agamemnon to hover about his master for the primary purpose of overhearing the negotiations.

"Git them boys up here onto this gallery and sop that rain offn 'em," Maxwell ordered Agamemnon, drawing a soiled bandana from his pocket and heaving it toward him. "Mr Brownlee craves to finger 'em over."

The two young Negroes approached the gallery with misgivings. They had never been permitted to come so close to the house, and, now that they were summoned, they were aware of their muddy feet. Both shivered as much from fear as from cold. Preach's teeth chattered but the mouth of the lanky Emperor was so much overshot that his teeth failed to meet and the convulsions of his jaw made no sound.

Agamemnon, degraded to the place of valet to a field hand, chose the lighter-hued Emperor as the lesser evil and dabbed at him gingerly with the handkerchief, after which, with a glance askance in the direction of his master, he tossed the wet handkerchief to Preach who proceeded to wring it out and wipe the standing drops from his body. To dry himself on the wet rag was impossible.

Brownlee took charge of Emp, made a preliminary pass of his hands over the goose-pimpled back and skinny legs, after which he turned his attention to the big cicatrix which was firmly healed and could not be forced to open or bleed for all the pummelling and pinching the trader gave it. Emperor had been inured to pain by the burn and the treatment it had undergone, and he did not flinch.

"Purty ganglin'," deplored Brownlee. "Narrow-shouldered and stooped over."

"I know he ain't ready to sell yet. Needs a year on him. Besides he aint't been fattened and primed," countered the owner.

"Terrible pig-jawed, too."

"Don't want thim to chew the cane down, do you?" Maxwell replied.

"Kneel down here in front of me, boy," the dealer ordered. "No, not that a-way—back to me."

Emp turned around and, despite the absence of visible wales, Brownlee carefully explored the muscles beneath the skin for ridges that would betray the healed-over marks of the whip.

He then pulled the boy upright onto his knees, tilted his head back and ran his fingers along the teeth, which despite the malformed lower jaw were as sound as if their cusps had fitted together normally. Getting Emp to his feet, he pulled and twisted his fingers, and, finding none broken, stiff or badly twisted, signalled him by a grasp of the calf to lift the feet, one at a time, to the arm of the chair that he might examine the toes.

"How much you want fer him, suh?"

"Ought to be worth six-fifty," Maxwell ventured, tentatively.

"Too much. Cain't use him at that price. Cain't git more than seven fer him in New Orleans."

"Six twenty-five, then?"

21

"Wait; let me look at the other'n. Maybe we kin deal on the the two of 'em."

Preacher was cold and shaking, but he slouched forward for his examination. He was no longer afraid and showed no more feeling of his indignity than his fellow had displayed. He knew that he was mere property which had changed ownership before.

Brownlee pursued his inspection much as he had inspected Emperor.

"An Angola," he disparaged.

"Don't know no more about his breedin' than about the other'n. Angola or not, he's peart and vig'rous."

"But Angolas don't sell good. Buyers afraid they'll come down. The least ailment carries 'em off, and a good hidin' lays 'em by fer a month. Course, fer myself, I don't care; but buyers are slow to bid 'em in."

"I reckon you don't want nothin' but Mandingos and Fulahs," said Maxwell contemptuously.

"Well, they're good niggers, 'specially Mandingos."

Brownlee speeded up his examination of Preach, sensing Maxwell's growing irritation, but his canvass was none the less minute.

"Whut you want fer this one?" asked Brownlee.

" 'Bout seven hundred, I reckon, more or less," Maxwell had reached the price part of the trade, which he enjoyed bickering about.

"Cain't give it and git out whole. How much fer the two of 'em?"

"How much I ask you fer the yaller one? Six hundred twenty-five, weren't it? And seven hundred fer this one. That's, that's, let's see. I'm kind of slow cipherin' in my head. Thirteen twenty-five, ain't? Make it twelve hundred and a half fer the span of 'em. Cheap enough."

"Cain't cut 'er," parried the trader. "Make it, say, about——"

"Ain't no good. Twelve fifty's my best price. Take 'em or quit 'em. It's jest accommodation. I ain't anxious to trade."

Brownlee perceived a finality in Maxwell's statement which the latter had not intended to put into it. Brownlee seemed about to retire.

"Oh, make it even twelve hundred," Maxwell conceded.

"They unsound," argued the dealer, running his hand over Emperor's scar. "I'm sorry, but I jest cain't git out at that price."

"Tell you whut!" proposed Maxwell, as if the concept had just occurred to him. "S'pose you trade in them three young 'uns of yourn out in the stable on these two bucks."

"Wouldn't trade 'em in. Might trade even," parried the trader.

"Let's see 'em," Maxwell turned to Memnon, "You got the keys to 'em. Git 'em."

While Agamemnon was gone on his errand, their master gave the two boys permission to go into a cabin and get warm. "Try Dido's cabin. She got a good fire about this time; cookin'."

"You cain't git shet of them little saplin's in New Orleans," began Maxwell. "I reckon you know that and bought 'em up cheap. Keep 'em three, four, five year and they'll be real sale-worthy."

"Whure'll I keep 'em? Cain't keep 'em cheap in New Orleans. I bought 'em to sell. Want to git my money and buy more niggers."

"Jest whut I mean. Trade 'em to me fer them two young bucks that are able to work and jest right fer the market. I'll grow the young 'uns here whure feed is cheap and you kin come back and buy 'em off'n me when they're growed up and ripened. Course I aims to look 'em over before there's a swap."

There seemed to Brownlee to be no flaw in Maxwell's argument. Memnon appeared from the direction of the stables, followed by the two boys. He led the small girl by the hand. Exhausted by their morning journey, they had been asleep and were now but half awake.

"Shuck 'em down," ordered Maxwell.

Memnon peeled the garments from the two boys, and the girl, releasing the single button, pulled her dress off over her head.

Maxwell made no such detailed examination as Brownlee had made of the older boys. He delegated most of it to Memnon. The boys were of approximately the same age, both bronze mulattoes. Obviously not twins, they were similar in make and shape, well rounded but sturdy and hard of muscle, considering their youth. Maxwell remarked about their resemblance and Brownlee answered him, "Same pappy prob'bly. I bought 'em from the same breeder—hard up but wouldn't sell his grown stock."

Maxwell perfunctorily felt their thighs and calves, scrutinized the navel of one that he suspected of having a hernia, commanded Memnon to open the mouths that he might examine the teeth, and declared himself satisfied.

The girl was not pretty but she was animated and appealing.

23

She enjoyed the attention given to her and responded instantly to any command. Maxwell appraised her quickly. Yellow, approximately quadroon, she had small bones, lightly fleshed. Her breasts were just beginning to swell but she was far short of nubility.

"Well," Maxwell said, "how will we trade?"

"Even—your two fer my three."

"No, I want a hundred dollars to boot."

"Even."

"Fifty."

"Cain't do better than even. Them two bucks of yourn is unsoun'."

"I don't run down your stock."

"Nothin' to run down. All three sound as gold pieces."

"I never make a trade without boot. I'll tell you whut I'll do, I'll match you—ten dollars or five."

"Hell, I'll give five," conceded the trader.

"Done!" declared Maxwell, sustained in his resolution to obtain some hard cash in each transaction.

"All's to do now is to make out bills of sale."

"And plank down the money boot. But now she's mine, I'll tell you that wench ain't soun'. She jest gant and peaked."

"She's yourn to doctor up however you wantin'."

"Memnon, you take the pore little thing over to Dido. And put some dry rigging on them two boys of Mr Brownlee's and take 'em back to the stable." Turning to the trader, Maxwell asked, "Want them boys chained up—afraid they'll run tonight? They're yourn now. I wash my hands of 'em."

"Bring 'em back here afore you straw 'em down. I want to give 'em a talkin' to. When I gits finished with 'em they won't run," replied the new owner.

"Bed these two little black bucks in the stall with the other saplings. Let 'em git acquainted. Feed 'em strong and give 'em plenty of clabber. Don't worry about them running tonight; they too petered out to run tonight, and tomorrow they'll know Falconhurst grub so good that you couldn't chase 'em off."

"That all, Masta, suh?"

"That's enough. Fetch that Barbarossa and Emperor right here to their new master. I'll go in to the fire. Gitting cold and raining yet." Maxwell rose and entered the house.

"I'll go with you," Brownlee said to Memnon. "I don't want them two nekid bucks out in this rain."

24

Agamemnon led the way to Dido's cottage, followed by the nude striplings, the trader bringing up the rear.

They found Preach and Emp sitting on the puncheon floor on either side of the fireplace over which big Dido was cooking dinner in a pot, a baby clinging to her breast. Four other children, dispersed about the small windowless single room of the cabin, gathered with back to wall to stare at the strange white man. The two nude boys roused to their feet and moved away from the fire to make way for their betters. Their faces were grim.

Brownlee addressed them: "I'm a-dickering with Mista Maxwell to buy you two boys."

"Yas, suh," they answered in unison.

"How would you like to go with me—to be my niggers?" he said with a kindly tone.

"I likes it here. Masta's good to me," said Emp, and Preach burst into fresh tears.

"I'll be good to you, too."

"You goin' to take us to New Orleans and sell us fer cane han's," protested Emperor.

"Nonsense, no sich thing. If I gets you, you goin' to be stock niggers. Of course we goes by way of New Orleans, whure I got to buy me some more hands; but I got a big plantation up in Kaintuck and I got eighteen or twenty wenches comin' ripe that got to be serviced."

Brownlee waited for his information to penetrate the hard skulls. He watched their spines stiffen, their heads lift, and animation suffuse their faces. "Reckon you kin do that kind of work for me?"

"Sure kin," said Emp, and Preach echoed his words before he could get them both out of his mouth. They looked at each other, hardly able to credit their prospective good fortune.

"I craves the both'n you," said Brownlee, "if I kin set the price right. We'll know, come mornin'."

He turned to leave the cabin. "They won't run tonight. Don't bother to chain 'em. Put dry clothes on 'em and bed 'em down as usual," he instructed Memnon.

Brownlee walked slowly from the quarters toward the house in the waning light. He chuckled to himself about the lie he had told those boys to fortify their willingness to go along with him. A Negro that changes ownership against his will is likely to give trouble to his new master. Brownlee conceived that his paltering with the boys would hasten their steps across country quite as much as the threat of the whip around their legs.

He entered the darkling house only to find his host huddled over the few embers in the fireplace, in a violent temper, reviling Agamemnon for permitting the fire to die.

Dark had well set in before Hammond came. He was tired but cheerful.

"Evening, Papa," he said, bending to kiss the old man's cheek. "Evenin', Mr Brownlee. Did Papa gold-brick you into buying them boys?"

"Mighty nigh," answered the trader.

Maxwell sensed that his confession must be made. "Spittin' out the right of the matter, it wasn't a sale," he began.

"No?" inquired Hammond.

"No, it was a sort of swop, so to speak—although I got boot," he hastened to add, and reiterated, "I got boot, by golly."

"Whut sort of swop?" asked Hammond.

"Well, Mista Brownlee had three little striplings when he rode up, a couple of young bucks nigh on to fifteen hands high, about, and a nice little yaller wench."

"I seen 'em chained up down in the stables. And you, I s'pose, swopped the two big bucks fer 'em?" The tone of the question betrayed vexation.

"But I got boot, I got boot," protested the father. Brownlee abstained from argument.

"How much boot?"

"Only fi' dollars—but boot is boot."

Maxwell sensed Hammond's displeasure and rubbed his arthritic knuckles as if to invite sympathy. His face clouded as if he were about to weep. "I thought I was makin' a good trade. Mayhap I'm losin' my grip, mayhap even my mind."

"No, now, Papa. You're all right." Ham saw the distress his criticism had caused. He rose from his chair, shuffled across the room, gently grasped one of the distorted hands and soothed it with light friction. "No, no; you made a good trade. It's jest that instead of gittin' money out of two niggers, here you've gone added another—and got no money."

"Fi' dollars."

"Yes, five dollars. You jest cain't lay eyes on a likely little nigger without havin' it. Falconhurst is crawling with young niggers—two deep—nowheres to grow no cotton and no hands big enough to work it."

26

"As I always says, Falconhurst ain't no cotton-growin' planta-tion. Jest a nigger farm, a nigger nu'sery," the elder man justified himself.

"Papa, if you want another little servant, you a-goin' to have another little servant. Ain't nobody goin' to try to balk you, least of all me. You all are still the master of Falconhurst, Papa, and I'll stack your gumption in a nigger trade up against what little I've learned from you, anytime." Hammond patted and relin-quished the hand and returned to his chair. The older man felt good; the pain had miraculously gone. Hammond's approval and the evidence of his affection were all the medication he required.

"You in charge of Falconhurst now, Son. I don't want to do nothin' without'n your nod."

Agamemnon threw open the door to the dining-room and sounded the supper bell. There was much sameness about the meals at Falconhurst, but there was always plenty of plain and filling food—chicken, pork, and hot bread.

"Pitch right in and hit that fry, suh," Maxwell adjured his guest. "Don't be backward. An' make a long arm and reach some of that watermelon-rind pickles. Lucretia Borgia makes it right tasty-like."

"Don't crowd the gen'leman, Papa. Don't crowd him. Does seem like though that Mista Brownlee don't eat nothin' at all."

Before he could answer, Brownlee was compelled to wash down his mouthful of food with coffee that had hardly cooled in his saucer. "Wonderful meal, gen'lemen!" he gulped. "As good vittles as ever I et."

Lucretia Borgia insinuated herself into the room with the excuse of bringing hot coffee to refill the emptying cups. She had wanted to get a look at Brownlee ever since she learned of his arrival. "That Memnon, he don't step fas' enough," she said by way of explanation. "He let ever'body run out of coffee. Triflin', that's whut."

"Sure is triflin'," assented the master. "Takes you jackin' him behind and me in front to git any work out'n him."

"Lucretia Borgia is the only nigger on the plantation worth killin'," Hammond added. "Does more work than any three on 'em."

The black eyes of Lucretia Borgia sparkled; her mouth grinned, displaying an expanse of powerful teeth; and her second chin bobbled in appreciation of the compliment. Approximately a quadroon, Lucretia Borgia, always addressed by her full name, was buxom and broad-beamed, rather than fat, as she appeared at a casual glance. She planted her large, bare feet on a broad base, swaying from side to side as she walked with a kind of majesty around the table. She was good-natured from the good treatment she received and the good food left from her master's table. She chuckled her way into her master's graces and had her will of the whole plantation.

"She cook all these good vittles?" inquired Brownlee.

"She not only cook, but she boss the feedin' of the hands, over-looks the spinnin' and the loomin' in the quarters, and up to comin' three years ago brought a good sucker about every eight-teen or twenty months. Shore a fas' breeder. She the dam of these triflin' twins," Maxwell piled praise upon praise. He knew how to inspire her to even greater efforts. "I guess she bred out, though she ain't too old. Jest brung babies too fast and clean bred out."

"Naw, suh; naw, suh, Masta," Lucretia Borgia burbled her tidings. "I knocked up again."

"No? Well bless my soul," said Maxwell, in amazement. "Have you got a silver dollar, Ham? Give it to Lucretia Borgia. How that come about?"

"I don't know, suh; but I is."

"Here's your dollar," said Ham. "And when that baby come there'll be another dollar, two dollars if it twins agin." Lucretia Borgia curtsied coyly as she took the coin from his hand and expressed elaborate thanks.

"So that Napoleon boy I give you had a nigger in him after all? A long time comin' out," commented Maxwell.

"I reckons I didn't git it from 'Poleon. That squirt no good. This baby is Memnon's, I figures. Masta Ham tole me to try Memnon agin, and I been pesterin' with him fer about a month."

"By golly, it might be twins, if it Memnon's. He was a twin his own se'f and he is the twin-gittin'est nigger I ever had."

Memnon grinned to hear himself discussed so favourably. But his grin faded as his owner continued.

"I'd send the lazy son-of-a-bitch to market if he warn't such a sure stock boy. All he good fer is to pester the wenches. Cain't even keep a fire goin', and his toddies is always cold agin he gits 'em to you."

"I didn't know Memnon was running down again, Papa. Whyn't you tell me? Jawin' him don't do no good. I reckon I'd better call him out to the stable, when I gits time. A good patch

28

of hide offn his rump with a good rubbing down with *pimentade* will spry him up," volunteered Ham.

"Pimentade?" inquired Brownlee. "Whut's pimentade?"

Ham explained. "Hide tore offn a nigger, rub it over with pimentade and skin will grow right back without a mark. It sovereign fer skinning. You mix it out of salt, cayenne, and lemon juice. Course, it stings. The niggers dread the rubbin' more than the hidin', but it sho' straighten 'em out."

"Salt, cayenne pepper, and lemon?" Brownlee made a mental note. "Sounds convenient. Have to try it."

Ham pushed back his chair and the party rose to return to the sitting-room. Ham said, "Mayhap, and you don't feel yourself pushed in the mornin' to git away, I'll find the time to brush this boy down and you kin watch him squirm and wiggle and hear him holler when the pimentade goes on him. It's sovereign. Seems peculiar you never heared about it. The idy come from Domingo. Them Frenchies are smart, that way."

"Don't aim to git goin' too early. I'll kindly wait if you goin' to correct the boy anyway; wouldn't want you to take the trouble jest fer me to see. I sees lots of niggers larruped, but I always admires to see it. It's kind of comical-like—that is if it has to be done anyways. One kin always learn something."

Maxwell took a more moderate view. "We don't flog much on Falconhurst. Only two cases all last year that I recollect—both fer stealin'. But when we flogs we flogs good—we lays it on well."

"Only way," declared Brownlee.

"Only way, suh. Course, we don't use a snake to nip hunks out of the meat and ruin a nigger. No, suh. I had me made a couple of paddles, a big one and a littler one fer saplin's and wenches, made out of sole leather with holes drilled through 'em. Hang 'em up, jest by the ankles, never by the toes 'lessen you twist 'em, with the legs spread wide as you kin spread 'em, and a rag stuffed in they mouth. Give that big paddle to a strong young buck and tell him to go to work. Why, you git the skin offn a nigger's rump in no time at all, and finish up with a good dosin' of this here pimentade, as Ham was tellin' you. Then go away and let the nigger hang and smart fer an hour or two, you got a good servant, a good servant, suh, from then on. Yes, suh, no nigger don't want a second dose like it."

"I've hearn of them holed paddles. Never saw none. Yes, suh, it must be right purty to watch."

"No, not so purty—unless your taste run that way. Ham and

29

me, we don't enjoy floggin's, and don't have more than we kin help. Course, goin' to keep niggers, you got to take the hide offn one, oncet in awhile. Especially house niggers. You're good to 'em, feeds 'em up on the kind of vittles you eats your own self, breeds 'em to your likeliest wenches, and they gits slack, gits triflin'. They don't mean no harm, but they's nothing more aggravatin' than a slack house nigger, nothin'."

"They takes advantage," interpolated Brownlee, who never had possessed a servant in his own house.

"Sure do, and has to have it corrected out of 'em. Take this Memnon boy, here, a good buck but lazy, lazy as they come. Spiled, spiled. I reckon you right, Ham. Reckon you better pull a piece of hide offn him, sometime when you got an extra hour or two, no hurry about it. I kin spare him any time you likes."

"All right, Papa; I'll take care of him, tomorrow or next day. Lucretia Borgia kin mix toddy and fire up fer you while he's hanging up to dry, cain't you, Lucretia Borgia?"

"Sho' kin. Sho' kin." Lucretia Borgia enjoyed carnage.

"Maybe it might be a good idea to have Lucretia Borgia spank Mem ever' morning when she spanks the twins, that is after I gits through with him," declared Ham.

"Ever' morning?" inquired Brownlee.

"Yes, suh, ever' morning I soften up they bottoms some fer the devilishness they do yestiday. Cain't keep track of what the devilishness is, but I know they does it. Yas, suh. That way, with a little warmin' every day, they won't grow up and use up Masta Ham's time a-skinnin' 'em down every month or so. I aims that Alph and Meg to be spry niggers, fitten fer Masta to keep right in the house to wait on him good."

"I done told you, Lucretia Borgia, I don't know how many times, that I won't never whup them boys without'n your leave. Un'erstan'? I promise you," declared Hammond.

"Whup 'em whenever you feels like, Masta Ham," Lucretia Borgia answered. "But jest don' sell 'em. Don't sell 'em unlessen you gits a great big price fer 'em, please, Masta."

"No, I won't never sell 'em either. Papa and me wants 'em fer ourselves. Don't we, Papa?"

"You done sold so many of my children right out from under me."

"Well, they was mine, wasn't they?" Maxwell bridled.

"Yas, suh, Masta. They's yours."

"And I got good homes for 'em, ever'one of 'em."

"Naw, suh, Masta. I ain't moanin' 'bout whure they went. I knows they gittin' good Christian raisin' up. But——"

"But what? Lucretia Borgia, you outgrowin' your pants—tellin' me whut to do with my own little niggers. Remember I bought them children from you, paid you a silver dollar fer ever' damned one of 'em and two dollars fer them twins, and I'll do with 'em whut I damn please."

"Papa, Papa, don't git yourself all riled. It ain't good fer your rheumatiz," Hammond admonished.

Maxwell turned as quickly as his rheumatism would permit and stumped vexedly into the sitting-room. Brownlee followed. Hammond remained in the dining-room. He was disturbed at the turn the conversation had taken, thought the arousal of Lucretia Borgia's apprehensions about her beloved and badgered sons just a little gratuitous, debited his father's unnecessary testiness if not to age at least to rheumatic pain. It was unlike his father to bully the Negroes.

Hammond at length followed Lucretia Borgia across the open passageway and into the cheerful hot kitchen where the twins were gourmandizing on the left-overs from the main table and where he found Lucretia Borgia in unwonted tears. At his show of surprised compassion, she heaved from her bench, threw her heavy arms about his neck, and wept herself dry while Ham supported her vast bulk of hot flesh.

It required only a little compassion with the merest trace of diplomacy, which was all Hammond possessed, to turn Lucretia Borgia's misery to the happiness which was her birthright. Her health, her indomitable vigour, and her status in the plantation hierarchy, first as a cook and then as a breeder of amber twins, conspired together to provoke such gusto. Ham, without quite understanding his purpose, merely steadied Lucretia Borgia's tottering pedestal. He comforted her until the fountainhead of her tears was dry, after which he joked with her.

Ham's jokes lost nothing by their lewdness nor their lack of euphemism. They concerned Memnon's supplanting, or rather supplementing, Napoleon, the yellow youth whom Lucretia Borgia had chosen as her paramour, the comparison of their anatomies, and the circumstances of the woman's pregnancy.

The twins listened in silence, only half-comprehending at all why it should provoke such laughter from their mother and smiles from their master. They kept their eyes fixed on the single battered platter from which both ate with their fingers, lifting

31

and rolling them now and again in the embarrassment of their failure to understand some of the terms their elders were using. There was no shame at what they understood, for they had listened to stark talk and overt bawdiness at the table of their masters, who would have thought it absurd to modify their conversations to protect so impersonal a commodity as the innocence of a couple of young slaves.

CHAPTER TWO

HAMMOND'S MOTIVE in going to the kitchen was as much to get away from Brownlee's conversation as to succour Lucretia Borgia. He had endured about all of Brownlee that he was able, but he was about to return to the sitting-room when out of the black night there emerged an even blacker apparition in the person of Belshazzar, the son of Black Lucy.

"Miz Lucretia Borgia," he blurted, "my mammy say tell Masta Big Pearl sick. She awful sick."

Belshazzar addressed himself directly to the cook, ignoring the master.

"Whut ail Big Pearl?" Hammond demanded with an unintentional gruffness which paralysed the child into dumbness.

Hammond grasped Belshazzar's shoulder and repeated his question, "Whut ail Big Pearl?"

Big Pearl was the very gem of Falconhurst. Tawny as burnished copper, strong as a block and tackle, straight as a beam, and barely nubile, Big Pearl was as magnificent a pure Mandingo as had ever wielded a cotton hoe. She was elephantine equally in her proportions and in the grace with which she progressed. She did not walk or run or amble—Big Pearl progressed. She was the plantation showpiece, docile as a kitten, biddable as putty. She delighted in being stripped and paraded and handled and bargained for, confident that the tremendous offers for her would be declined. She had never known an ill day in her life. To Hammond the heavens seemed to have fallen.

"Whut ail Big Pearl?" he asked a third time.

Belshazzar, frightened into dumbness was re-frightened into speech. "Me? I don't know, 'um. Big Pearl got a misery."

Hammond, shuffling in his carpet slippers and limping on his stiffened knee, strode off across the blackness to Lucy's cabin. He walked so fast that Belshazzar had to break into an occasional run to keep up with him. The nearness of his master protected him from the dark.

Hammond heard the girl's groans, pierced at intervals by a wailing scream. He pushed open the cabin door. All was in confusion. Children cowered in fright against the walls in the background. Flames roared in the fireplace. Lucy bent, solicitous but in helpless despair, above the bed where her daughter Big Pearl threshed in her agony, making the cold night hideous with her cries.

Hammond was moved to compassion. He approached the bed, pushed the towering Lucy aside and, sitting down beside the girl, took her hand in his. "Big Pearl, whut's the matter? Whut ail you?"

"I got a misery, Master Ham, I got a misery in my belly, Masta—but it better now." The moaning ceased and Big Pearl lay calm. "It better now," she repeated weakly.

Hammond returned to the house and, sinking into a chair, ordered Memnon to fetch him a toddy. His apparent fatigue and anxiety caused his father to voice his solicitude.

"I's all right," Hammond replied, not very convincingly.

"How Big Pearl? Whut ails her?" Maxwell inquired impatiently.

"Big Pearl better now, I reckon. Guess it weren't more than the belly-ache. Worst over, time I got there," the youth explained. "I poured her out a big dose of castor oil and give her a little laudanum. Reckoned that the bes' thing."

"Sure is," Maxwell affirmed.

"Then I called Lancelot and had him tote Big Pearl down to the old pest house on his back. Big as that boy is, all he could do to tote that young wench. Don't think it's nothin' but too much hog meat from that fresh killin', but don't want to take a chance in no catchin' epizootic with a plantation full of young niggers."

"You don right, Ham. Got gumption, you has," Maxwell said approvingly. "I ain't heard of nothing goin' around, but the pox or the vomit would clean us right out. You done jest right."

"Good as I could. Had Lancelot make up a big fire in the pest house, and left him a-settin' by it to watch her. If Big Pearl ain't better by morning, I'll put a boy on a mule and have him ride to the veterinary in Benson."

" 'Tain't safe, 'tain't safe, I'm afeared, to leave that Lancelot

33

boy with that wench all night. He mighty full-blooded and vig'ous. We doesn't want no accidents of that kind with that choice wench."

"I warned him I'd hide him if he pestered her," said Hammond.

"Virgin yet, ain't she?"

"I reckon so. I ain't felt to see since last pickin' time. Lucy pretty moral and she goin' watch her."

"I don't know whut's the matter with you, Ham, lettin' a nice smooth wench like Big Pearl go virgin so long—goin' on fifteen years."

"Kinda shirkin' your duty, ain't you, son?" interposed Brownlee, leering.

"I done tol' you at least fifty times," Hammond answered his father, "I can't stan' the musk of a real nigger. The yaller ones is bad enough."

"Course, there's one way to kill musk ever' whit," said Brownlee, "good deal of trouble, but it kin be done."

"Whut way?" inquired Hammond interestedly. "Rub 'em with some essence? That jest puts one stink on another and makes 'em worse."

"No; I mean soak 'em good, about five minutes, in 'manganate of potash water, not too strong, jest kind of red."

"Why, that's that coarse powderlike stuff in that dusty bottle out in the medicine shelf. Never knew whut it was fer," said Hammond.

"That's whut it's fer," declared Brownlee. "Everybody in New Orleans use it on they house niggers. A 'manganated wench will keep absolutely sweet two whole days; a buck begins to shed his musk again after 'bout a day. I reckoned everybody knowed about that."

"Shore never heared on it," Maxwell said.

"We'll have to try it," Hammond resolved. "How much do you use?"

"Jest enough to make the water red—not purple, and soak the nigger in it, head and all, all but his nose, about a good five minutes. One tub of 'manganate is enough fer a dozen or more niggers—no call to waste it. But never don't let it set to use over and over. It loses its stren'th in time."

"Shore gotten to try it," Maxwell said. "I don't hold much with these new-fangled idees. But that cain't do no harm. Think me to try it tomorrow, Ham."

"Papa sure don't believe in new-fangled stuff," complained Ham. "Papa don't want I should even go fer that new way of ploughin' across the gullies instead of alongside 'em, that Mista Tom Jefferson up in Virginia wrote about. But I'm goin' to do it, come plough time, anyhow."

"Too late, too late. Falconhurst is done fer cotton. If I had a-started earlier, when Mista Tom first talked about it, things might have been different. But it's a lot of trouble, and too late anyway. Falconhurst does all right as is."

"Don't git riled up so, Papa. It ain't good fer your rheumatiz."

"Damn my rheumatiz! Don't do this and don't do that. It gits worser, whatever I do or quit doin'. Toddies do more fer it than anythin', seems like. But tonight's the worst it's ever been."

Ham shook his head in despair. "I only wishes you could git one of them nekid dogs the Mexicans got. They do say that sleepin' with your feet agin one of them dogs dreens the rheumatiz right of a man and into the dog."

"I've hearn about 'em, but I never seen one. I doubt that there really is sich a thing as a nekid dog."

"They is. They have 'em," Brownlee declared.

"Must be right comical," conjectured Maxwell.

"Course, any dog shaved down so that the feet kin git right agin its skin is jest as good—or a nigger. A nigger will dreen off the rheumatiz through the feet jest as good as any nekid dog."

"Do you reckon so?"

"Shore do," Brownlee was confident. "Why, I knew a man name of Bronson over in Natchez that tried it. So cripped up he couldn't hardly walk. Hd tried sleepin' with his feet agin the belly of a nigger and in no time at all Bronson was a-walkin' and a-straddlin' his horse as good as ever. The old rheumatiz jest dreened right out'n him into the nigger. Nigger all cripped in no time, jest like Bronson was before."

"Might be worth tryin'," said Ham.

"Might be," repeated Maxwell hopefully. "Get me a nigger, Hammond; I'll begin this very night. Have him washed up good. A buck is better than a wench—a wench is sorta disturbin' when you got the rheumatiz and cain't do nothin'."

"We'll use one of the twins, and I'll give Lucretia Borgia some of that black powder to put in the wash water to kill the muskiness."

"Sort of hate to ruin one of them twins with rheumatiz," speculated Maxwell.

35

"We kin dreen it right out of him into some other nigger if he gits too bad. He's right here in the house and handy," Hammond said, rising to go to arouse Lucretia Borgia to give her instructions about the preparation of her son for his master's use.

"Course, you got to have the nigger sort of curl up around your feet, and you got to press hard and force the rheumatiz right out'n the soles," Brownlee counselled expertly.

Maxwell rubbed his knees and massaged one hand with the other. The pain subsided from time to time, but it never entirely left his joints. He had become so inured to its presence that when it was least he was unaware of it, until a sudden pang shot through the various parts of his body which forced him to restrain himself to keep from crying out. "The worse of it is," he lamented, "Ham's young—too young to tote the whole plantation on his shoulders. I got no mind to complain about the way he does— does right good; but at eighteen I was out and around, sowing my oats, and up to all kinds of devilment."

"A smart, sturdy boy like him. It won't hurt him none to be nailed down for awhile," Brownlee hazarded. "I never got out to raise no hell. It never hurt me."

"He never even got no schoolin' to speak of. His mamma learned him to read a little and I tried to after she died. She could read real good, better'n I kin. Then I sent him to the Institute over at Jackson fer a term three or four years ago, but couldn't stand havin' him away—wouldn't let him go back. Always afraid somethin' would happen to him—after that gelding pony. I was fool enough to put him on when he was little, threw him off and stiffened his knee. You cain't never trust a gelding; give me a whole horse or none. Schoolin' is a great thing fer a boy. He needs it—more and more as time goes on, more than in my day."

"Don't know; don't know. Sometimes schoolin' ruints a boy— makes 'em big-headed," Brownlee opined. "Jest cain't stand a big head. I didn't never have no edication and didn't never need none. Course, I had got to learn to cipher a little, and am right good at it now. But I never was ruint by book learnin'."

Maxwell was still doubtful about the havoc wrought by education. "Guess Ham got enough to git along with, but I wish't he had more of it. I wish't I hadn't been so hoggish fer him, a holdin' of him back."

"It sense that counts—not learnin'," Brownlee consoled. "And Hammond got sense."

"I helt him back that a-way, and I'm still a-holdin' him back.

36

Besides the plantation and two hundred niggers, he's got me and my rheumatiz on his shoulders. Young as he is, I wonder if he wouldn't be better off if I was dead. Of course, if my pains don't better, I won't last long, and I'd like to see him married off before I die—course to some nice, well-bred young lady—I want to see it. I want to see 'em breed another boy to take over Falconhurst when Ham gits the rheumatiz or whatever and to carry it along through the generations. Course, Falconhurst is played out fer cotton; but who needs cotton with niggers goin' up and up?"

" 'Lessen them abolitionists at the North sets all the niggers free," Brownlee interposed, at once derisive and sceptical.

"Triflin' loafers, interferin' in other folks' business. Slavery was ordained by God, and there ain't nothin' they kin do about it except talk and stir up trouble between slavery territory and free territory, between South and North. Cain't they understand that you got to have niggers to grow cotton, and you got to grow cotton to feed them Northern spindles? They tryin' to 'bolish they own jobs and they own profits?" Maxwell rose to his feet in the excitement of his own eloquence.

"They dangerous, howsumever," said Brownlee. "Take them Quakers, and take that Garrison and that newspaper he started to print last year, that *Liberator*, as he calls it. Seen any o' them papers?"

"Don't want to see none. To read about 'em in *The New Orleans Advertiser* turns me sick. Better not nobody fetch one of them *Liberators* to Falconhurst."

"Better not let the niggers see 'em, anyway. Puts idees in they heads," Brownlee warned.

"My niggers cain't read. Best law ever passed, that law agin learnin' niggers to read."

"Some does it even agin the law," Brownlee said.

"An' they liable to have a risin' to fight, too. No nigger readin', no nigger risin'. Why, that Garrison hadn't printed that *Liberator* of his six months when that nigger risin' up in Virginia happened last year. Wonder they never could ketch that Nat Turner nigger."

"They ketched him. Didn't you know? They ketched him and hung him along about harvest time."

"Hung him?" Maxwell was incredulous.

"Hung him."

"Jest hung him? Didn't burn him or nothin' after killin' all

37

them white folks? Had ought to of burned him. Ought to of made a 'xample of him."

"Had ought to have burned that Garrison at the same post and to stoked the fire with *Liberators*," Brownlee agreed. "Garrison jest set the nigger on. Strange you never hearn about it."

"I missed some *New Orleans Advertisers* around pickin' time. Ham didn't have no time to ride to Benson and the postmaster throwed 'em out. Reckoned we didn't want 'em."

"All up and down the Seaboard, folks are still a-talkin' about Nat Turner. They skeared of more risin's. All through Virginia and the Carolinas, and 'specially Georgia."

"They don't know nothin' about how to treat niggers. Treat 'em right, feed 'em, don' overwork 'em, and they don't uprise. Owners too greedy to git work out'n 'em. A nigger responds to good treatment better'n a dog. I don' have no trouble with mine, and Ham don't."

Hammond entered from the dining-room, guiding with hand on shoulder one of the Borgia's twins. The boy had been roused from bed, bathed and soaked in a potassium permanganate solution, despite which he still was not fully awake. He was entirely naked and seemed unconcerned about the purpose of his arousal or the fate in store for him. He had confidence in Hammond and feared no abuse.

"Here's your Mexican dog," Ham greeted his father. "Used that red stuff on him and there ain't a trace of musk about him; smell like'n as if he was white."

"Come here, boy. Set and drink your toddy, Ham, ere it git cold." Maxwell sniffed at various parts of the boy and declared himself satisfied. "Must be strong medicine that kill nigger-stink like that. Smell of him, Mr Brownlee," and he pushed the child towards the trader's chair.

Brownlee in his turn sniffed and continued to sniff the boy all over, handling and embracing and patting him and clinging onto him, as if he doubted the efficacy of his own prescription. Brownlee too, at last, was convinced, but reluctant to surrender the young Negro servant. The Maxwells were insensible to Brownlee's dalliance with the child, until, in the belief that the boy was lingering for attention and failing to note that the trader was grasping him, Hammond commanded the boy to be seated.

The chairs about the fireside were occupied and the boy retreated to one at the rear of the room and gingerly propped himself into it, unsure of what was expected of him.

"Meg, whure your manners? You knows better than set in a chair," Hammond said sternly.

The boy immediately found his feet. "I ain't Meg; I Alph."

"You Meg if'n I call you Meg. You knows who I means. You a nigger, and niggers sets on the floor in white folks' houses."

Hammond saw that the child intended no disrespect and changed his tone. "Come over here and set whure it wa'm," he half commanded, half invited, "there at one side of the hearth."

The boy complied, squatting toad-fashion between his legs, comfortable and serene. He made an effort to listen to the conversation of the whites but couldn't keep his eyes open. What he heard was neither interesting nor intelligible to him. He wondered what his masters drank that smelled so good. At length he toppled over upon his side, curled up, and slept warmly.

"One more toddy, and we'll all retire to bed," said Maxwell. "I crave to git me into bed with my feet agin his belly; crave to try it," whereupon he summoned Mem.

Memnon had been in and out of the sitting-room all the evening, renewing the fire, serving drinks, replacing candles. Unobtrusive and alert, he forgot nothing. He was bent upon proving that the whipping promised him for tomorrow was unnecessary. His imagination already felt the smart of his buttocks, and he pictured the contempt that the other Negroes would feel for him. His disgrace would be as poignant as the impact of the paddle.

"Reckon I ought to go down to the pest house to see how Big Pearl come on afore I goes to retire?" Hammond asked his father.

"Let Big Pearl be. You weary, Ham. Night's cole outdoors. Git yourself some sleep, and stop your frettin' about all them niggers. You ain't they mamma. You ain't called to coddle and nurse 'em, the way you doin'. They all right. Let 'em alone."

"Howsumever, I 'sponsible fer 'em. I'm right fond of our niggers, and right proud of 'em. Every one of 'em sound as a hickory. And that Big Pearl—I'd sure grieve to lose her."

"Course, a good nigger is a right smart loss, these times and these prices. But why this here Pearl more than some othern?"

"Whyn't you show Big Pearl to Mista Brownlee, Papa?"

"First place, she ain't fer sale. Second place, she make other niggers look puny. Third place, it rainin' and I didn't want to shuck her down out in that rain and wind."

"Youen's show nigger, eh?"

39

"Mandingo, pure Mandingo," Maxwell explained. "Don't find many Mandingos pure no more."

"I likes 'em black," Brownlee declared.

"Me? I likes 'em lusty, whutever they colour. Course, it all right fer white men to pester black wenches—a protection to white womanhood, I always says. But everybody wantin' yaller niggers; puny, frail, weak, white owners spends all they sap a-tryin' to git light-coloured babies, that ain't fitten to grow into strong cotton hands. They all dreams of gittin' fancy yaller wenches that they kin sell young fer a monst'ous price. If they had a lookin'-glass they know they couldn't sire nothin' but ugly, knotty runts. Course, I ain't meaning such owners as Ham, here, sturdy, and purty an' vig'ous, but Ham ain't runnin' through the cabins a-coverin' all the wenches a-tryin' fer yeller offspring. No, suh."

The personal aspect of his father's conversation Hammond found embarrassing. He sought to turn it back into its channel. "You sayin' about Mandingos, Papa," he began.

"So I was, so I was. I was talkin' about Big Pearl. I'll come back to that," said Maxwell, refusing the interruption. "Ham ain't got but two or three babies all told—but they all turned out little bucks. They fancy, light-yallers, all right, but all bucks. His oldest one—comin' on four, now—is as healthy and purty and straight a saplin' as ever I see. Course, it gits extrie feed and everythin'."

"Ham look like he be a right vigorous stud," said Brownlee.

"Didn't look fer that first one to amount to nothin' at all with Hammond jest fourteen years old when he got it. Dropped the day after his fifteenth birthday. Proudest boy ever was; thought he was a man fer shore."

"You purty mad, I reckon, when you found out about him pesterin' your wenches at that age," said Brownlee. "Course, I know they all do it, but nothin' come of it."

"Wasn't my wench. She was his'n. One his mamma left him. She begin a-waitin' on him when he was about eleven or twelve —when he shed his nurse-mammy."

"Wonder he wasn't a-ruint."

"Ruther have a boy a-pesterin' a smart, little clean wench than have him a-drivin' hisself crazy a-hankerin' to. I'd been stronger —and smarter too—if my old man had a-give me a wench of my own before I was sixteen, a-goin' on seventeen."

"Seventeen? I was nineteen and even then she wasn't mine

or my pappy's. She belonged to the man my pappy was overseein' fer, a ugly sambo, I reckon, leastwise lookin' back I think she was part Choctaw. Course, I sneaked some before that," conceded Brownlee. "Out in the patches when the hands was noonin', whenever I could shun my paw."

Maxwell showed little interest in the trader's youth. Brownlee was a poor recommendation for boyhood continence. "In them days pappies didn't know how hankerin' fer a wench could stunt a boy and drive him lunatic." The intimation was that Brownlee's shortcomings were chargeable to his father's negligence. "Pro'bly the reason young men at the North are so sapless and witless— nothin' but white gals to pester with when they boys."

The trader was more interested in the goblet of corn whisky which Agamemnon was bringing than in Maxwell's comments. Mem's gait was unsteady, his eyes emitted a glassy glint. His hand trembled on the tray as he handed the drinks about, although he refrained from spilling them.

"Come here, you black scoun'rel. Kneel down here and let me smell you," Maxwell commanded.

Memnon found refuge in tears. "I didn't drink none. I didn't do it, Masta, suh. I didn't do it. I on'y jest taste to see was it hot. On'y jest taste, suh."

Memnon knelt by Maxwell, afterwards he crawled on his knees toward Hammond, who sniffed him but casually.

"That mean jest twenty-five more squashings with that paddle tomorrow." Hammond addressed his father, ignoring the Negro. "And a big drench of ipecac tonight last thing."

"No, Masta, suh, no," the darkie begged *sotto voce*, not daring to speak out lest he aggravate the sentence, and yet unable to keep silent. "I jest tasted." Memnon knew that in so factual and objective a mood Hammond was relentless; if his master had reviled and threatened him, he might have softened him with his repentance. Hammond did not even deign to address him. His resolution was not even tempered by his anger.

When Memnon saw that Hammond was unmoved by pity, he rose to his feet and slunk from the room, but he was entirely sobered. The whisky he had drunk to smother his anticipations of the morrow's chastisement had lost its lethe. All the agility and promptitude he had displayed throughout the evening to avert the disaster had been cancelled out. The ipecac was a punishment that exactly fitted the crime. The very thought of it caused him to retch in anticipation. When he returned to the

41

house from his excursion out into the windfilled darkness, the yellow of Mem's face had taken on a greenish hue. He was sick at his stomach and sick at heart.

"As I was a-sayin' about the Mandingos," Maxwell resumed his monologue, oblivious of the interruption, "they right satisfyin'—powerful, biddable, healthy. Cain't un'erstand this Big Pearl a-fallin' sick."

"How you know she pure Mandingo?" Brownlee inquired.

"Look at her! Look at her! Don't have more than to look at her," answered her owner. "But I knows her history—all about her, too. Ol' Colonel Wilson of Coign Plantation, up the road a-piece, about fifty or sixty miles, needed some han's and rid to Charleston to buy a passel of bozals. Course, it was back in the time when the Colonel was young and could ride, the days before Mista Tom Jefferson stopped 'em from bringin' in brutes. Everything was law-abidin'."

Hammond had heard the story before, and diverted himself by tickling Alpha's feet and watching his reflexes. Brownlee was mildly interested in Maxwell's tale, and even more in Hammond's play with the young boy.

"Colonel Wilson foun' 'em unloadin' a whole cargo of prime Mandingos, two or three hunerd big, docile, upstandin' brutes, and he picked himself out four or five good ones. Colonel Wilson know a good nigger. They never cost much then—five, six or seven hunerd apiece. Two of 'em, a big buck and a stout wench, was about the purtiest things I ever see. That wench must have been nineteen hands, or near it, and the buck even taller; and they wasn't jest tall, but they was thick, not fat but hard, hard as mahogany.

"Course, Colonel Wilson bred the two of 'em together and got a wench child—a big sturdy wench over sixteen pounds the day she was dropped; but 'bout that time the vomit broke out at Coign and the old wench died and all the other Mandingos, all except the big buck and the baby."

"Bad luck," said Brownlee.

"Turrible, turrible. But the baby growed; and when she big an' ready to breed, Colonel Wilson didn't have no Mandingo 'ceptin her pappy to breed her to, and he was bounden to keep his Mandingo blood pure. So what he do? He put the wench right back to her pappy."

"Didn't he know no better than that?" Brownlee asked. "Why, that awful; that incest; that goin' agin the Bible. I knowed a white

42

man up in Tennessee oncet that pestered his own nigger daughter and had a wench child, that was jest a little puny, that cried all the time, never did grow none, and was weak-minded. Jest lay and slobbered. About three years old, the old man, seein' that it wasn't never goin' be worth nothin', took pity and knocked it in the head. Your Colonel Wilson ought to know better'n that."

"Well, he didn't. The wench brought him the biggest, most vigourest young saplin' you ever see. Most grown now, but the Colonel won't market him. Goin' to keep him fer seed."

"I swan!" said Brownlee.

"Seein' as how it worked so good the first time, Colonel Wilson put the young wench right back to her pappy agin, and this time got a wench baby, Big Pearl. I bought her and Lucy—that her mammy—offen the Colonel while Big Pearl was a-suckin' yet.

"That's how I knows she is pure Mandingo. Her and Lucy and Colonel Wilson's two—the old buck and the young one—are the only simon purentee Mandingos I knows about anywhures. Beautiful niggers, all on 'em."

"Real dangerous, I call it," said Brownlee. "I wouldn't risk it. Whut you goin' to do with your wench? No more Mandingos to mate her up with."

"When Hammond gits the time, I aims to have him ride to Coign Plantation and plead with Colonel Wilson to borrow the old bozal buck to us fer a month or two. I aims to breed Big Pearl right back once more to her pappy, and her grandpappy. The buck is sixty or sixty-five years, maybe seventy, come now; but I reckon he got sap in him yet."

"Don't risk it, Mista Maxwell, suh. Don't risk it. That awful."

Brownlee's horror only confirmed Maxwell in his determination. "Works fine in horses and cows and hogs and dogs and sich. I don't see why it won't work with niggers. Course, you got to have fine stock; no good with puny stock."

"You breedin' in too fur, Mr Maxwell. Thought you knowed more'n that about niggers."

"Ham thinks it all right. Don't you, Ham? If he gives the nod to it, we goin' to try it."

Hammond had stopped playing with the sleeping child. He was tired, resting, hardly listening. "Papa, you been talkin' that plan fer three years. Thought your mind was set, jest waitin' fer me to go to Coign to fetch the buck. I'll find the time in a few days. Don't reckon there's nothing to lose except Big Pearl's time, if the foal should turn out puny or something."

The Seth Thomas which ticked and ticked on the mantelpiece coughed and clanged eight rapid strokes of its bell, as if its duty were unpleasant and it wished to get it over with as quickly as possible.

"That danged clock," observed Maxwell. "Keeps right time—about; but it's an hour slow in its chiming. Kin fix it—ever git time."

Hammond stretched. "Reckon it time to go up. 'Bout nine ain't it, Papa?"

Memnon brought the drinks for Maxwell and Brownlee as ordered.

His presence reminded Maxwell of his misdemeanour. He cautioned Hammond, "You won't ferget that ipecac, Son?"

"No, Papa. I mix it, I git upstairs."

Memnon paled at the thought. "I ain't needin' no medicine now. I's puked that corn, ever' bit of it."

"You's goin' to puke some more. You's goin' to puke up all your innards with that dose I'm plannin' to pour into you," Hammond threatened. "And you better go to sleep with them bucks in the stable, 'stead of in the hall by my door."

"Cain't cure a nigger from drinkin' corn, 'lessen you locks it up away from him," Brownlee observed.

"I'll cure this one; last thing I do—cure him or kill him."

Memnon was silent. There was no rebuttal to fate itself. Hammond yawned and rose, reluctant to leave the warm fireside to go into the cold hall. He planted a perfunctory kiss upon his father's cheek, bade Brownlee a polite goodnight and pleasant dreams, and noting the inviting target of Alpha's protruding rump, reached down and gave it a resounding smack. Alpha's muscles were constantly bruised from Lucretia Borgia's daily spankings, and the blow, intended only as a caress, was painful. The boy, only half aroused from sleep, cried out, reached around and rubbed his buttock and slept again. "Don't fergit your foot-warmer; it's a cold night, Papa," Ham joked.

"Dite gone up a'ready?" Hammond inquired of Memnon.

"Dite go up early," Memnon replied.

"Come 'long, then," said Hammond and limped out, followed by the apprehensive Negro.

Maxwell listened to the uneven steps of his crippled son upon the stairs. He censured himself again for having entrusted his heir to the uncertain temperament of a gelding.

"Who that?" Brownlee inquired.

44

Maxwell's mind was upon the accident, long passed. "Whut you mean, suh?"

"Who that? That Dite?"

"Oh, that. That Hammond's bed wench."

"Purty, I reckon," the trader voiced his imagination.

"Right likely. Mustee, I guess."

"Light, eh? And young?"

"Fourteen, mayhaps fifteen now. Why?"

"I was jest a-thinkin', jest a-thinkin' whut a fine lot of niggers you all got. Got 'em all over the place, and won't sell none."

CHAPTER THREE

WHEN HAM entered his bedroom his concubine rose to welcome him. She had taken off her clothes and stood covered only with a quilt wrapped around her and hanging from her shoulders. "You late, suh," she said casually.

"Yes, a little. Big Pearl sick. Whyn't you lay down?"

"Waitin' to know an' if you wants me in the bed or on a pallet."

"On the floor, I reckon. I tired tonight," Hammond said as he sank into a chair before the fire and surrendered to Mem's ministrations. Then he reconsidered, "No; git into bed and warm them sheets up until I strips and after that you kin take to your pallet."

Aphrodite dropped her quilt and stood naked as she turned down the covers, adjusted the bolster and plumped herself upon the feather bed. Mem stripped Hammond of his clothes, hoping his master had forgotten the ipecac. As Ham stood before the fire Aphrodite lay looking at him with servile affection.

Hammond's body, barring some areas on his back and around his belly, was enveloped in blond hair, hardly heavier than down, but of considerable length. Standing, the stiffness of his knee was not apparent. His shoulders were not broad, but they were hard and strong and, clothed with hair, seemed larger than they really were. His body was more than normally long and his legs somewhat short. Long hours in the saddle had developed his thighs, which bulged and rippled as he changed his position in the firelight.

"Fetch me a big gourd, that big, yeller bottle agin the wall on the shelf, and a jug of hot water. We goin' to have some fun."

Mem knew that protest was futile. "And stir yourself," Ham added as Mem started on the errand.

Mem did as he was told, and his gorge rose as he watched Ham pour the staggering dose from the bottle into the gourd, add water, and stir the mixture with his finger, which he wiped on the hair of his thigh. The gourd he set upon the hearth, propping the handle against the mantelpiece. "We'll keep it hot," he said, taking one final turn around before the fire. He was reluctant to leave the heat and to get into his bed.

At length he crossed the room, fell on one knee, stretching the stiff leg behind him, as he bowed his head and hastily repeated his simple prayer: "Now I lay me down to sleep; I pray the Lord my soul to keep. If I should die before I wake, I pray the Lord my soul to take." It was a mere meaningless formula, hastily uttered without a concept of sleeping or dying, of keeping or taking souls. He hesitated as if taking thought and added, "Dear God, bless my mamma up in heaven; bless my papa and dreen his rheumatiz into Alph; bless They servant Hammond; bless Big Pearl and make her git well; bless Dite; bless Lucretia Borgia and the twins——"

"Mem, Masta, suh, Memnon. Ask God bless Memnon. Please, Masta; please, suh," the Negro interrupted the orison, assuming that white petitions received more prompt attention than black ones.

His master humoured him and interposed for him, "Bless Memnon and learn him not to steal and make him a good nigger after his hidin' tomorrow; and, God, bless Falconhurst, and all the niggers on the plantation." It was little enough to ask. Falconhurst was a goodly place, and its personnel a goodly company.

Dite vacated the bed and assumed her place on the pallet beside it, and Hammond crawled upon the high bed and snuggled down between the sheets her body had warmed.

"Leave the can'le, boy. You'll be comin' back to drink that drench, right after you waits on Mr Brownlee and your masta. If I a-sleepin', wake me up."

"Yas, suh, Masta," said Mem; and then he ventured, "I jest take the gourd along and drink that stuff before I lays down."

"You'll come back here, like I tol' you. You drink it now, you'll puke up so you cain't wait on the gen'lemen. Wrap that twin around Papa's feet good."

Mem escaped without making a promise. Ham knew he would come back, and Mem knew it.

46

Hammond lay and looked into the fire. His day was not finished until he had done his duty by Memnon and he did not intend to sleep until the Negro's return.

"Masta, suh, is you 'wake?" Dite asked tentatively, reaching up from her pallet to place her hand on the bed.

"Whut you wantin', Dite?"

"Masta, I knocked up." She had postponed telling him, in the knowledge that the tenure of her position would be limited by her advancing pregnancy. She had won her present status by another slave girl's pregnancy and would lose it by her own. She could never be deprived of the distinction of having shared her young master's bed, however long in the past it might grow to be. To be the mother of a master's child would engender envy from the other wenches, and envy made for status.

However, it was unlikely that the present relations, once interrupted, would ever be resumed. She could pretend that she would be reinstated after her child was weaned, but her figure would thicken, her breasts would sag, and Dite would be old. On a plantation of the size of Falconhurst, there was a succession of young wenches maturing at frequent enough intervals to render at least unlikely the summons of a once discarded wench back to her master's couch.

Hammond was dozing and was slow to reply. "I been a-lookin' fer that. How long ago?"

" 'Bout two months. I don' know 'xactly."

"I ben kind of hopin' you wouldn't be 'til that wench of Dido's got bigger. She right purty."

"That Tense nigger?" Dite knew her successor now.

"Yes, that her name, somethin' like that. Hortense, I believe."

"That triflin', skinny, brown thing? She ain't fitten fer you, Masta."

"She light yaller; she ain't brown," Ham defended.

"She not light like me."

"Yes, she darker'n you. You 'mos' white. But her colour light enough. She right nice," he argued.

"She ain't got hardly no meat on her at all."

"She puttin' on meat. I was lookin' at her the other day—hippin' out good and tittie-in' up real full-like. Course her udders ain't full growed yet. That why I wishes you wait awhile, another six months."

"You don't reckon that Tense no virgin, does you?" Dite clinched her disparagement.

47

"Why, I reckon she is. Dido right moral-like."

"Dido moral, yes. But with that big brother of hern sleepin' right in the cabin, Tense's maidenhead shore gone, plumb gone," Dite declared hopefully. "I was a virgin, wasn't I, Masta?"

"Shore was. Shore was. You wasn't no older than Tense that time. You was plagued and skeared of me till I had to slap your face and hold you down. You was real comical-like. Remember?"

Dite remembered that first, terrified but treasured night with Hammond well enough, remembered his ruthlessness and his tenderness, her own evasion and enforced submission.

Hammond made a mental note to caution Dido again about her protection of Tense and to send that young buck of hers to the stable to sleep. He lay quiet awhile. Mem had had ample time to see Brownlee and Maxwell to their beds. He wondered whether Mem's stubborn recusancy would extend so far as to fail to return for the draught mixed for him. Ham was already resolved to chastise the Negro as hard and as long as he dared without destroying his value; further disobedience could not aggravate the punishment. Ham wondered whether Mem would be astute enough to realize this.

In fact the chores of putting the two elder men to bed had been minor ones. Brownlee had been shown to a room without a fireplace. It was upstairs over the ell of the house and was cold. It was habit, however, not the cold that determined the removal only of his outer garments and prompted him to crawl into bed wearing undershirt, drawers and socks, none of which had been laundered or even removed since he left the Carolinas.

Brownlee's vocation made him unduly sensitive to any treatment he could interpret as a slight. He so interpreted the absence of heat in the room assigned to him and especially the absence of a wench to keep him warm.

"Memnon, fetch me a wench to pleasure me tonight. Did you fergit that, too?"

"No, suh, Masta Brownlee. My Masta never tol' me nothin' about no wench fer you."

"I tell you whut. Fetch me a likely, young, clean, light-skin wench, an' I'll try to beg you off your hidin' tomorrer mornin'. I'll tell Mista Hammond that you not no bad nigger at all. I'll tell him his pappy cranky——"

"Naw, suh, don't tell Masta Ham that. You make him mad. He know Ol' Masta ain't cranky. He think Ol' Masta all time right."

"You fetch the wench, and leave the res' to me."

"Yas, suh; yas suh, Masta Brownlee. I will, suh." Memnon was uncertain whether he would keep his promise, but there was no harm in giving it. He was torn between his desire for mediation in his difference with his masters and the fear of acting without authority. The bribe the dealer offered was a tempting one, but he doubted Brownlee's will as well as his ability to divert Hammond from his policy.

And what wench? If the dealer's intercession was worth bartering for, was it not wisdom to supply him with the best in the quarters? Would his gratitude be the greater? Should he fetch Dido's Tense, whom Memnon surmised that Hammond had staked out for his own uses? A night spent with this white man could do a wench no harm.

Mem was not used to making decisions; decisions were made for him. He pondered the alternatives all the while he was putting his old master to bed, which, except for adjusting the boy to the old man's comfort and so draping the bed coverings that the urchin could breathe, was a mere routine. Alph's unwaking torpor was so sound that he did not alter the position in which he was draped rather than placed. He could have been tied in a bow knot without knowing it.

Maxwell, sodden with his toddies, and somnolent with the unwonted lateness of his bedtime, was wellnigh as complacent as the child. He sprawled on the bed while Memnon removed his clothes, the silence broken only by an oath or two when Mem had some difficulty in pulling his shirt over his head.

The light of the fire suffused the room, and the candle was hardly to be missed when Memnon took it with him and closed the door.

There remained for Mem only to go to Hammond's room to swallow the vile drench which awaited him there. The very thought of it caused him to shiver with nausea. He knew the violent sickness it would cause all through the night.

Memnon hesitated before he entered Hammond's room, fearing the dressing-down that was in store for him. Instead Hammond appeared to be in the best of humours. He even chuckled as he commanded, "Fetch me that gourd and that bottle. Wouldn't come back to drink the dose I mixed, eh? We'll jest mix it stronger," and he emptied half the contents of the bottle into the already potent mixture and handed it to Mem.

"That white gen'man say fetch him a wench. Whut wench I

goin' to git fer him? Tense? Got to fetch her right away afore white gen'leman git mad and go to sleep," Mem sought to divert Hammond from the project in hand.

"You let that white gen'leman alone, and you let Tense alone. Hear? That nigger trader don't need no wench. I don't want that kind of dirty, nigger trader blood mixed up with my niggers."

"But he say——"

"And I say drink that gourd and git out'n here. And mind you strike the fires early in the morning. Lots to do come tomorrow. Now drink that gourd."

Memnon held the gourd by the handle and slopped the contents as he sank on his knees by the bed to beg for mercy. "Masta Ham ain't goin' to hide Memnon tomorrow? Is you Masta, suh? Memnon your little boy. Memnon wait on you and take care of you and mix toddy fer Ol' Masta. Who goin' to serve you and mix toddy while Mem git well from the larrupin'? I be good nigger, I be spry nigger, I won't taste the toddy. I won't do nothin'. Please, Masta, suh, don't hide Mem!"

"You goin' to mix toddy and do jest whut you been doin'; that's who. Needn't think that sore ass I'm goin' to give you git you out of workin'. You'll go on and work jest the same. Now drink down that gourd and go to the stable like I tol' you, and let me go asleep."

Ham's calm, which Memnon took for complacence, was the calm of anger. He was fed up with the boy's evasion and disobedience and the mention of the wench for Brownlee did Mem some harm.

Memnon's hand trembled as he lifted the gourd to his mouth. He sipped the nauseating mixture.

"Drink it down. Drink it down quick—ever' drop of it."

Memnon drank. "Please, Masta Ham, suh, that enough. Cain't drink no more."

"Ever' drop. And drink it fas'."

Memnon tried again—and swallowed it all. He felt himself sicken and rushed from the room. At the bottom of the stairs he fell prone on the floor, broke into a cold sweat. He lay there retching, too sick to rise.

When Lucretia Borgia rose at her accustomed time, shortly before the dawn, she came upon Memnon in the hall.

He was still too sick to explain anything to her. She lifted him to his feet, and half guided him, half carried him into the kitchen.

50

She called the first boy she could find, who happened to be Napoleon, and set him to cleaning the stairs and hall. She loaded Meg's arms with firewood and herself carrying an even larger load strode through the hall and up the stairs, to prepare fires before which her masters could dress in comfort. The elder Maxwell was still asleep, snoring; but Alph's head protruded from the covers at the foot of the bed, and he proudly boasted, "Mammy, I got rheumatiz. It hurts awful, jist like Masta."

"Hush up yo' mouth and keep it hushed. You wake Masta and I goin' rheumatiz you fer sure," Lucretia Borgia whispered, but she rejoiced in the improvement of Maxwell's ailment and even more that one of her sons had absorbed his pains. She did not doubt the truth of Alph's claim.

Meg stood beside his mother while she unloaded her arms and started the fire. Then he followed his mother into Hammond's room at the other end of the hall.

Hammond was awake. He had told Memnon to make the fire early and the chill of the room had deterred him from rising immediately. He was refreshed from his fatigue of the previous night and had reached down to rouse Dite and had given her leave to come into his bed. Lucretia Borgia, entering the room, ignored the contortions that were taking place beneath the covers. Meg, however, while his mother unloaded the wood from his arms and laid the fire, could not keep his eyes from rolling toward the bed. He was not entirely innocent; he had overheard bawdy talk; he knew approximately what his master was doing.

As Lucretia Borgia laid the fire she noted that the ashes were cold and she sent Meg down the hall and into Maxwell's room to fetch a brand. He met his brother coming out, limping and rubbing with one hand the knuckles of the other. Meg's envy of Alph's ailment made him pause, forgetting for a moment the errand on which he was bound.

"Masta's misery dreened right through my belly," Alph declared. "It hurt awful, and my han's jist killin' me."

"You jest puttin' on, nigger. Hain't nothin' ails you, 'ceptin' you don't crave no spankin'. You thinks Mammy ain't goin' whup you 'cause you got rheumatiz, you a fool. Mammy all riled 's mornin'!" Meg warned and went into Maxwell's room while Alph went slowly down the stairs exaggerating his limp.

Maxwell ignored Meg's squatting by the fire until he had ignited a piece of kindling and had crossed the room to leave with it, when the old man demanded, "Wha' Memnon?"

51

"Memnon, he sick," answered the boy with diffidence and made an effort to be gone.

"That nigger ain't sick. He jest cravin' to git offn that touchin' up he goin' to git. He goin' to git it a'right. Nigger ain't sick," Maxwell said aloud but to himself.

"Yassum, Masta, suh." Meg would have agreed with any statement the master made. He was not exactly afraid of the stern old man, but he was ill at ease. He had never been upstairs before and what appeared luxury to him appalled him. White living was so complex. White men took more trouble to be comfortable than comfort was worth.

"Take that bran' along. Then, come back here and he'p me on with ma boots," ordered Maxwell, and Meg was relieved to get away.

Back in Ham's room Lucretia Borgia still squatted before the fireplace. "That nigger jest nasty hisself all over," Meg heard his mother chuckle to Ham, who, without waiting for the fire, was getting out of bed.

"Wha' fer you stay so long? Cain't you see you makin' your masta dress hisself withoutn no fire?" Lucretia Borgia scolded.

"Ol' Masta say I come back and he'p with his boots."

"Then mind; mind, you hear? An' take care you polite," his mother cautioned.

Meg's eyes were riveted upon Hammond. He had seen many naked Negroes, but it had never before occurred to him that white folks removed their clothes. He had assumed that white gentlemen were disembodied angels, but they were flesh he saw, beautiful pink flesh covered with golden hair. So far from disillusioning the boy, the revelation augmented his reverence for white mastery. He obtained but a lingering glance, but it was enough to excite a physical love. He had seen Dite in Hammond's bed, and in his jealousy Meg hated the girl.

He returned to Maxwell's room and knelt before his seated master. Maxwell threw his socks to the boy and stuck his feet toward him. Meg put them on the old man, after which he struggled with the boots, preoccupied the while with thoughts about the pleasure it would be for him to perform the same office for his younger master. He dreamed of becoming Hammond's body servant. His imagination ran to the removal of Ham's clothes, to putting him to bed, and bathing him.

CHAPTER FOUR

Hammond's first morning chore was to go to the pest house to see Big Pearl. As he entered the door she sat upright and reached with her arms toward him. He sat on the side of her bed and she grasped his hands and began to whimper.

"Whut ails you, Big Pearl? Whure you hurts?" Hammond inquired with a kindly tone.

"Don't hurts nowhure now. Misery done left me," Big Pearl replied, clinging to him. "Masta, suh! Masta, suh!" she wept.

"Don't cry, Big Pearl. You all right."

"Yessum, suh. I knows I all right, you here—Masta, Masta."

"Whut you cry about?"

"You goin' to leave me, and then my misery come back. Masta, Masta, stay here, stay right here, please suh, Masta!" Pearl begged passionately.

"How was she all night, Lance?" Ham turned to the big buck who has risen on his entrance.

"First off, when you leave, suh, Big Pearl go off to sleep right nice. I set right here by fire all the night. Then she wake up and begin to howl and beller, and she keep that up until you comes in that door, suh."

Ham felt Big Pearl's forehead. It seemed cool. He noted, however, a slight convulsive movement of her body when he laid his hands on her. He was baffled. There were no symptoms of the vomit or of smallpox. Possibly this was the evil effects of in-breeding.

Not because he thought it would do the girl any good, but because he did not know what else to give her, he poured out a dose of laudanum and held the glass for her while she drank it. She fixed her eyes on Hammond in an expression of gratitude that was adulation.

"I tell you, Lance, you put a bridle on that grey mule and ride to Benson and git that veterinary. You know Doc Redfield. You know the way to Benson, don't you?"

"Yes, suh, Masta, I knows him. He the white gen'man whut cure Nimrod las' year."

"You'll find him around the tavern or over at the grocery store, drinkin'. Tell him come right out to Mista Maxwell's Falconhurst Plantation. Kin you remember that?"

"Yas, suh, Masta." Lance was elated at being chosen to go on such an errand. He could boast of it around the quarters and recount the sights he should see in the town. "I got to have pass, though, Masta. I don' want to be ketched up fer no runnin' nigger."

"I'll write you out a pass. Stop at the big house, and git it. And be careful of that mule. Go easy like, and don't sink in the mire."

"Yas, suh. I be careful. I careful nigger."

"Better take a pocketful of pone, if you should git hongry," Ham warned, always thoughtful of the welfare, if not of the comfort, of his hands.

The opiate began to have its effects upon his patient, and Hammond went to the house to eat his breakfast. Meg heard him come in and limp down the hall. Without waiting for orders, he galloped into the kitchen and excitedly pulled at Lucretia Borgia's skirt. "A toddy fer Masta, a toddy fer Masta Hammond, a toddy. It fer Masta Ham," he insisted with impatience. His mother paused in her preparation of the breakfast to mix the toddy.

Hammond entered the sitting-room and stopped to extend his hands to the fire and to turn before it ere he sat down, more from habit than from chill.

"Better drink a toddy, Ham," his father admonished. "Do you good."

Hardly had Hammond sunk into his chair when Meg rushed through the door, glass in hand. His impetuosity vanished, and he grew diffident as he approached his young master. He bit his lip as he extended the unordered libation to his god, uncertain as to how his ministration would be received.

"Whut's this?" Hammond asked.

"Do you good," repeated Maxwell.

"Whure did this come from?" Hammond said rather than questioned, nodding toward Meg. "This nigger better than the other one. Don't have to tell this 'un." Ham smiled at the boy.

Meg was abashed at the praise for which he had longed. He hung his head and chewed his lower lip as he returned a sickly grin. Then emotion overcame him and he began to cry.

"Whut ails you, boy? Nobody ain't goin' to hurt you. You good boy," Hammond consoled him.

Meg knew it was sacrilege, but he was unable to restrain himself. He could no longer stand. His knees folded under him and he fell kneeling with his face between Hammond's legs. "I your nigger, Masta, I your nigger, Masta, suh. Say I your nigger, Masta Ham; jest your little nigger. Nobody's nigger, but jest yourn," the boy begged between his sobs.

"Course, you my nigger. Whose nigger you afeard you goin' to be? Course, you my nigger and you Ol' Masta's nigger, too." Hammond, uncomprehending, sought to comfort the boy.

Meg looked Hammond full in the face to swear his allegiance. "You so good, Masta, I loves you, Masta."

Lucretia Borgia appeared with the breakfast bell. Breakfast was late, but Lucretia Borgia had not been idle. She saw the tears on Meg's face. She knew that something unusual had occurred. "That little nigger been troublin' you gen'lemen? I'll skin him, I skin him till he cain't stan' up."

Hammond smiled at her and said, "You'll mind your business, Lucretia Borgia. That my nigger. I wants him skinned, I'll skin him. Keep your han's offn him." The rebuke was jocular and Lucretia Borgia knew her son had not offended.

Alph was duly posted beside the table, weilding his peacock-feather brushes. He managed to move enough to display his limp. Lucretia Borgia pulled the chair to seat Maxwell, and Meg was alert and ceremonious in his withdrawing of Hammond's chair. He hastened to pull the napkin from its glass, to shake it open and place it in Hammond's lap.

Lucretia Borgia served the breakfast, but in all that pertained to Hammond's needs Meg forestalled her. Ignoring Maxwell and Brownlee, he filled Ham's glass with milk, heaped bacon and eggs upon his plate, shifted the platter on which the cornbread was served so as to extend it with the largest piece on the side nearest Hammond.

There was an unstated rule that Negroes should not eat from dishes reserved for whites. Yet Meg now whispered to Ham, "Masta, kin I eat whut you doesn't?"

"Oh, I see; that why you help me so good. You wants my leavin' vittles?" Hammond joked with the boy to his father's disapproval.

The accusation was unfair and the boy could only deny it with, "Naw, suh, Masta. I wan's you should eat all you kin, but, please suh, let me have yo' leavin's."

"Course you kin. You my nigger, ain't you?" Ham had intended no rebuff to the child.

"Right offn yo' plate? Please, Masta, suh, kin I?"

"Righ offn my plate."

Maxwell kept his eye upon Alph's limp. The more Alph limped the more Maxwell was assured of his own improvement.

Hammond had noted his father's bearing without comment until he could be sure that he was better. His increased dexterity was apparent. He could raise his knife to his mouth with sureness and without flinching.

"You chipper, kind of, this mornin', Papa," Ham at length remarked.

"Better, Ham, better. I goin' to git well, now I's found the cure. See that little buck, Alph, limp? The pizen is all dreenin' away. I goin' to git well and take this plantation offn your back. I'll straddle a hoss agin first thing you knows."

"Don't you worry none 'bout me. I all right an' Falconhurst all right."

"I knowed a nigger belly sovereign for rheumatiz. I tol' you," Brownlee took credit. "That man Bronson over at Natchez——"

"Wonder how Big Pearl come on," Maxwell declared. "You better go down after breakfast and see how she do, Ham."

"Done went. She some better, but Lancelot say she carry on all night."

"Better git Redfield," Maxwell advised.

"Done sent Lancelot."

"Damndest thing, Mista Brownlee, on this plantation. Cain't suggest nothin', not a thing, but it already been 'tended to. This Hammond think of ever'thing an' do it afore I gits around to talkin' about it. Jest have to nurse my rheumatiz, drink my toddies and stop my yappin', I reckon."

"Reckon Lance git through to Benson? Mire is terrible deep and thick," Hammond pondered.

"Ought to of put him on a mule," Maxwell suggested.

"I did a'ready. Ol' Grey."

"I thinkin' about that mire," said Brownlee. "Purty bad comin' in yestidy, worse this mornin'. Still, this wind and sun dries out them roads right fast. Course I goin' to wait to see you thresh that nigger."

"Don' reckon he fitten to thresh this mornin'. He sick," Ham explained.

"Playin' off, more 'an likely." The trader was disappointed.

"No, he sick. I was mad an' I poured too much ipecac into him. He awful sick."

"Deserved it, deserved it. Wasn't more than right," said Maxwell.

"Wouldn't hurt to whup him too, I reckon," Brownlee urged. "You promised him, you know. Ought to always keep a promise of a larrupin' to a nigger."

"I'll keep my promise all right, but not while he sick. No hidin' of sick niggers at Falconhurst. Besides, 'll do him good to relish his whuppin' a few days afore he git it. Let him ponder how sore he goin' to be."

"Cain't wait, cain't wait to see it, much as I'd like it. Always admire to see 'em squirm and hear 'em holler. Sometimes right comical."

Meg sidled to Ham's side. "Kin I see? I won' cry."

"See? See whut?"

"Memnon git hided," whispered Meg.

"Course you kin," Hammond promised. "Do you good. Learn you whut to expect."

"You spoils your niggers at Falconhurst, suh; spoils 'em till they putrid. No Saturday workin'! No threshin' when they sick! Veterany fer belly-ache! 'D think the niggers owned you stead of you ownin' niggers," Brownlee voiced his disapproval.

"That, kind of fact," Hammond agreed. "One way our niggers does own us, and we owns them. They feeds us and we feeds them. Nothin' I craves more than good niggers, fat and well and happy—and a-growin'."

When the whites had moved into the front room Meg appeared before Ham and asked, "Does you want a toddy?"

"No, too soon after breakfast," Ham replied. But it was not too soon for Brownlee and Maxwell.

Meg retired a little crestfallen, but complacent. To serve his master was a joy, to serve anybody else a chore. He fetched the drinks and served them with politest unction; and when he passed his young master on his way out of the room, Hammond caught him a playful but sharp blow with his hand across the boy's seat. It caused Meg to drop his tray, and tears gathered to his eyes. As he stooped to retrieve the tray, he looked into Ham's face and blossomed into a wide and satisfied grin.

"Send that other'n here soon as he feeds," Maxwell commanded.

Meg acknowledged the command and hastened into the diningroom lest the table should be cleaned. He picked up Hammond's plate with the food he had left on it, hurried into the kitchen and began to eat from it.

Lucretia Borgia saw. "Nigger boy," she said, akimbo, "you knows better'n eat offn white dish!"

"My Masta said."

"Whut your masta say?"

"He said I could—right offn his plate. I ast him an' he say yes."

"I say no. Now scrape that feed onto that crack' platter and you two eat like you always does."

"My masta say," Meg persisted.

"Nigger, I'll smash you," and Lucretia Borgia stepped toward him with upraised hand.

A glare of defiance shot from Meg's eyes. "Nigger, don't tetch me. Don't you ever tetch me. I bust this platter on your haid. My masta want me whup, he whup me hisself. No nigger ain't goin' whup me."

Lucretia Borgia was taken aback, halted.

"My masta say I eat offn his dish, I eats offn his dish. Ain't no nigger goin' to stop me," the boy declared between bites. "My masta say you not whup me, you not whup me, d'you hear?"

Lucretia Borgia hesitated to disobey Ham's commands, no matter how casually given. She felt her authority vanishing.

"I Masta Ham's nigger now, jest Masta Ham's," Meg gloated. "Masta Ham hang me up and skin me alive, he want to; he kill me, he want to. I Masta Ham's nigger," he impressed Lucretia Borgia. "Masta Ham whup me this mornin', whup me hard, harder than you kin," he announced, triumphant.

"Whut you do, nigger? Whut you do, makin' Masta trouble?"

"I not makin' my masta no trouble. I crave him to whup me and my masta done it." Meg had finished Ham's food and had picked up the plate to lick it clean.

Alph had listened with trepidation to Meg's quarrel with their mother. He sensed that his brother's victory would redouble her tyranny over him. Meg turned to him and with contempt in his voice told him, "Ol' Masta say you come in to him, soon as you feed."

"Whut he want?"

"He want you; that whut he want. Cain't you do whut your masta say without as'in ques'ions?" Meg was truculent. "You Ol' Masta's nigger, I guesses. Old Masta's sleepin' nigger. But I got the bes' masta. Ol' Masta ain't young and strong like Masta Hammond, an' purty. Now, go along to your masta."

Alph's limp, which he had forgotten, recurred to him. He rubbed the joints of his hands and limped away. He crossed the dining-room to the sitting-room. He waited, unsure of the demand for him. He had nothing but Meg's word that he was wanted. The gentlemen were talking.

"Ain't no call fer niggers from the Texies yet; but they sure to be as time goes," Brownlee declared.

"I sure wish I could go there—not to stay, but jest to look around. If Papa hadn't got rheumatiz, I'd sure be off. There's fortunes to be made in the Texies, I know."

"An' surer fortune, fewer dangers, an' more comforts right here at Falconhurst. I knows boys. When I Ham's age, I crave to wander, too, jest like Ham. Hemmed right down here by my rheumatiz, he ain't had no blowhole fer his spirits. Even when he take a coffle to New Orleans, has to quicken right back home. With my rheumatiz betterin', he kin git around some, go to N' Orleans, even to N' York, at least kin go sparkin' some of these nice young ladies of good families, pinin' at home fer some handsome blade to come and marry 'em."

"Don't talk no more, Papa. I ain't goin' to the Texies, but I'd sure like it. I goin' to stay right here; you kin lay to it. Mayhap, I'll git around, go into town some, go to New Orleans and dress me up some. But, an' I stay here, whut I wants is a fightin' nigger to have me some sport with."

"You stay home and mind Falconhurst, Son, you kin have the bes' fightin' nigger in all Alabam. Don't pay to have a fighter, lessen you has a good one. You'll have a good one—the best."

Alph waited, ignored. At length he asked, "You send fer me, Masta, suh? I's here."

Maxwell resented, or at least disapproved of Hammond's trifling with Meg, was stern in his reply to Alph. "You knows better, boy, than to stick your mouf into white talk. Now, keep your britches on and wait whure you at, an' shut your mouf."

The frightened boy rubbed a tear from his eye.

"Ain't nothin' in fightin' niggers in this part of the country. Young fellers that fight niggers in country taverns ain't got no money to bet on 'em. They thinks a hundred dollars is money. Ought to see a nigger fight in N' Orleans. Bets of a thousand dollars nothin'; some of them sports backs their bucks fer five thousand," Brownlee expounded.

"Young gen'men who fetched their niggers to Benson to fight ain't got much money to back they boys, you right, but they most generally brings along a good young nigger or two to bet with.

All got niggers, or they pappy has," protested Hammond. "Young niggers good as money right in the bank."

"Gamblers in N' Orleans trains they niggers to fight, not jest strappin' bucks out of the cotton gang. They trained how to fight. They exercised and fed and petted up for the purpose," Brownlee continued.

"That whut I mean," said Hammond. "That whut I means to do. Git a fine, strong, young buck and learn him to fight, scientific like."

"An' them N' Orleans niggers knows they has to fight, an' they does. They owner tells 'em before they shove 'em in that if they loses the fight they goin' to brand 'em good or take 'em to the doctor to be cut. An' they niggers knows they means it. They fights an' fights an' don' give up. They claws and they chaws and they gouges like anythin'."

"N' Orleans a right sportin' like city, I reckon," said Maxwell.

"I see one fight between two French gen'lemen—that is between niggers belongin' to 'em. Big, young, yaller bucks they was, right purty, and trained down hard as hickory. Them niggers fit and fit all over that place for more 'n an hour and a half, first one a-whuppin' and then the othern. Them Frenchmen right game! Wouldn't neither one on 'em give up. Finally one nigger couldn't move no more. Everybody thought he daid; might as well be, all chawed up. The winnin' boy not much better off. Don't know whut them Frenchies done with them boys; wasn't much they could do, I reckon. Blood jest a spurtin' over everything—even ruint the fine coat of one of the Frenchies. Five thousand a side, but even the winner never made much. His nigger 'most worth that. I made fifty dollars that fight."

"I'd admire to see it," longed Ham.

"When you come N' Orleans way, let me know. If I there, I knowin' all about the fights. They kind of secret-like, but I kin git you in."

"Sure will, sure will."

"Ham ought to go roun' some and see things like that. Mayhap he kin buy a good fightin' buck in N' Orleans," Maxwell acquiesced.

"Course, oft times they turns half a dozen niggers all together 'tilln one comes out on top. Don't never bet on that, howsumever; cain't hardly never predick' the winner."

"The gent'men at Benson ain't never tried that," Ham declared.

"Look around, look around," suggested Maxwell. "Git you a boy. Has we got any fitten to train? Big Vulc?"

"He won't do. He coward."

"Well, look aroun'."

"Whut that boy waitin' fer? Whut fer you wantin' him, Papa?"

"I want to see how bad he cripp'ed by this rheumatiz. Want to see how much dreened out of me. Come you here, boy."

Alph obeyed.

"How bad you cripp'ed?" asked Maxwell. "Whure you hurtin'?"

Alph hung his head. "All over, Masta, suh. I got misery all over me," and Alph believed it.

Maxwell grasped the boy, felt his leg, twisted the knee until the child grunted with the pain. He manipulated the elbow so hard that the boy cried out. He pulled the fingers and bent them upward. He placed one hand on the boy's back and with the other forced the head backward, contorting the spine until Alph screamed with pain. Alph was limber and flexible. He offered no resistance. He was pleased and interested in the attention bestowed upon him and sensed no indignity. By the time Maxwell finished his survey, the boy's pain was real, even if before it had only been feigned or imagined.

"Don' twis' the little feller so, Papa. You hurts him. You'll ruin him," protested Hammond.

"You too tender with these niggers. You ruin 'em your own self," said the old man. "But he got it all right! He got it! Wouldn't think so much pizen could dreen out'n me in jest one night." Maxwell was satisfied. "Be gone," he told the boy.

"Masta, suh, kin I be your nigger?"

"You is my nigger. Whose nigger you reckons you is?"

"I mean, your nigger, jest like Meg Masta Ham's nigger? Your own nigger? Please, Masta, sir."

"I'll do whutn I wants to you; that whut you mean?"

"I wants to bring yo' toddies and eat yo' leavin's—right offn yo' plate—like my brother do. I wan's you should whup me too, whup me harder'n Masta Ham whup his nigger. My brother brag over me sompin' awful." Alph's was no passion for service or punishment, such as Meg's. It was a mere desire not to be overshadowed and shamed by his brother, for which he was willing to pay a grudging price in work and pain.

"You my bed nigger. Ain't that 'nough? The other'n"

(Maxwell assumed not to be able to tell the twins apart) "ain't Mista Ham's bed nigger."

Alph was in a measure satisfied with this ascendancy over his brother.

"Don' fergit to have your mammy soak you in that red water before evenin'. You gittin' musky agin," Maxwell warned.

While Maxwell was speaking Doc Redfield rode up the lane on his dun-coloured gelding. A hundred yards behind him came Lance, riding barebacked the mule which had been grey when he set out two hours ago, but which was now so mud-daubed as to appear as dun as the veterinarian's horse.

Meg appeared out of nowhere to grab the horse's bridle when the doctor dismounted, but at Hammond's command transferred it, as soon as he came up, to Lancelot, who led it along with the mule to the stable to be dried and curried. Meg did not vanish again, however, but lurked, listening, on the gallery, removed from the group. His eyes were fixed on Hammond. His mouth was open, and he appeared ready to spring in response to a gesture which was never made.

"Don't know why I been sent fer," Redfield said genially. "Always said Mista Warren Maxwell was the best veterinary in the county. Takes better care of nigger'n any man I know. I'd starve 'f I depend on him fer a livin'." He was a small man with a pointed chin, quasi-bearded, his face spattered with a mixture of red, black, and grey whiskers, which indicated that he had not shaved for some two weeks.

Hammond extended his hand to Redfield, who remarked, "Don't seem no time at all sence you was a boy, no bigger'n that thar little nigger, a doggin' your pappy's heels ever'whure he went. Comin' to be a man, ain't you? Spec' you thinks you is one?"

"Is a man, is a man. Ain't got time to be boy. Runs the whole plantation with me sick. Let me knock you down to Mista Brownlee, Doc Redfield. Mista Brownlee around buyin'," Maxwell explained.

"I've hearn of Mista Brownlee, before. Servant, suh."

"Yo' servant."

"Reckon you better be gittin' down to that pest house. Ham will see you down there. I too cripped up to go. Stop by and have a drink of corn before you depart."

"I'll go along," said Brownlee. "I'd like to see that big wench of yourn."

Maxwell stood on the porch, reluctant to be left behind and yet without the will to join the party. Meg followed his master without appearing to follow.

Hammond told Redfield about Big Pearl's weird symptoms as they walked. "Reckoned better git you first thing. Don' want no epizootic aroun' here with all these young niggers. Might be vomit or pox."

"Not vomit this time of year. Your pappy know better'n that. Cain't be pox. Jest a little congestion of the guts, I reckon. We'll see."

"I know I hadn't ought to git you out in this kind of mud, but——"

" 'S all right; 's all right. I got to go out to the Widder Johnson's anyhow; Falconhurst ain't hardly none out'n my way. You know Widder Johnson?"

"Course, of course; out on Six Mile Road."

"Right likely plantation she got out there—small, of course, only a hunderd and sixty—but she makes right smart of cotton, and she got a passel of fifteen, twenty, good niggers Johnson left her."

"Her servants kindly old like, though," objected Hammond. "Ain't breedin' none hardly."

"Some is. That whut she call on me fer, to git her shet of a triflin' old cripped up wench, all deef and near blind. By rights ought to put an end to her long time past, but the widder kind of tender that way."

"Agin' the law ain't it—kind of?"

"Well, I sort of guess; but who goin' to take a hand in the pore widder's own business? Never hearn of the law a-meddlin' with sich things."

"Goin' to shoot her? Kindly disturb the servants, won't it?"

"Antimony. Somethink new. Leastwise I never hearn of it till lately. Come from a New Orleans doctor. Lets 'em down easy like. They never knows, an' the other niggers never knows."

"Never heared of it and I reckon Papa never heared of it."

"Ever need none, I got plenty. Jest send a nigger with a note. You kin give it your own self. Don' need me. Course, with a lady, like the widder, it's different."

"Don't never hope to need it. Our hands all purty young and sound," said Hammond.

"Never kin tell. Might git a-hold of a bad nigger—a trouble-stirrer."

"Might," Ham admitted without interest.

They had walked slowly down the hill toward the river in the sunshine toward the cabin used as an isolation ward.

"River still a-comin' up," commented Hammond. "Guess it won't rampage now, though. Rain stopped."

"Due to be fallin' soon, with no more rain."

"Don't hear Big Pearl carryin' on," said Hammond, opening the door.

Big Pearl lay on the bed in the corner, her eyes fixed in space. All her splendid energy was gone; a kind of languor enveloped her.

"How you come on, Big Pearl?" Hammond inquired.

Big Pearl raised her arm and extended it toward him. "I all right now, you come. Misery go right off." She grasped Hammond's hand and held it with her still powerful grip.

"Got the doctor to come, Big Pearl. He give you medicine to make you well. Leave him look at you now," explained Hammond.

"Don't need no doctor," replied Big Pearl. "Not no doctor's kin' of misery I got. My Masta stay with me, I gits well. Masta leaves, I dies; I shore dies."

Redfield placed a hand on Big Pearl's brow. He looked at her tongue. He took her pulse. He shook his head in quandary and puffed out his cheeks with wisdom. He turned down the covers and lifted Big Pearl's dress, kneaded her abdomen. She denied pain in the region.

"How old this wench?" Redfield demanded.

" 'Bout fourteen; most fifteen," said Hammond.

"Shore powerful, that age. Look at them laigs—like oak trunks, but right shapely," commented Brownlee. "Shore do admire to see a big, neat wench."

"Virgin?" asked Redfield.

"Reckon so," said Hammond.

"Reckon so? Don't you know?" said the doctor with contempt. "Whut you doin'? Shirkin' your duty? Or is yo' pappy tryin' to keep you a virgin, too?"

Hammond blushed. "She too musky fer me."

"But it a masta's duty to pleasure his wenches—the first time. A strapping, good-put-together wench like this makes a man fergit the musk. Sure, she virgin. You ought to be plagued of yourself, boy."

"But bein' virgin didn't give Big Pearl no misery," Hammond declared in astonishment.

"Course it do. You know whut ails that wench? She's hipped. That's whut she is—jest hipped," declared Redfield positively.

"Kin you cure her?" Hammond demanded, baffled.

"I cain't, but you kin. She craves you to pleasure her."

"That don't make her sick, don't make her beller and scream all night."

"Yes, it do. Yes, it do. She fall off, maybe she die, an' you don't pleasure her; take that maidenhead, anyway. Don't you see how she grabs a hold of you and hangs on? Ain' got no temperature, ain' got no pulse, tongue clean. Nothink the matter with the wench 'cept she cravin' you. Hipped, plumb hipped."

"I is, too, sick, Masta Hammon', suh. I sick," protested Big Pearl. "I isn't either cravin' you to pleasure me, Masta, suh— 'lessen you cravin' to. I knows I black. I knows I got musk, I knows I not fitten fer you, Masta. I ain't bad, Masta, I ain't bad." She rolled over on her belly and face down upon the bed sobbed long sobs of shame, of yearning, of blasted hope.

Hammond ran his arm tenderly under Big Pearl's body to turn her toward him and spoke to her in a low, confidential voice.

"You ain't bad, Big Pearl. Nobody say you bad. You been sick, but you well now. Come along. Git up, and go back to Lucy. You'll be all right. We'll see, we'll see."

Big Pearl gave a lurch and was on her feet, pulling down her dress. She stumbled over Meg, who sat on the step outside the door, listening for what went on. He picked himself up and scurried behind the cabin, lest he be seen by his master. Big Pearl galloped up the hill toward the quarters as if possessed. The three men watched her run, noted the power, vigour, suppleness and sureness of her gait.

"I tol' you that big wench jest hipped," said Redfield.

They wandered slowly back up the hill, the dealer and the veterinarian impeded by shortness of breath, Hammond by the stiffness of his knee joint. Some fifty feet behind them loitered Meg, innocent of eavesdropping but straining an ear to hear every word.

"This Widder Johnson, say she got likely servants? Whar-abouts she live?" Brownlee speculated upon calling on her.

"Won't do you no good, goin' there. She ain't got none fer sellin'." Redfield was positive.

"Ain't worth your while," Hammond added. "Her niggers plumb played out, all too old fer anybody to want. If it ben't fer her yarb doctorin' and midwifin', she and her niggers would all starve to death."

"Reckon so?" asked Redfield. "I 'speck she kind of rich-like—well, not rich, but tol'able, tol'able. Johnson left her right well off."

"Mayhap, mayhap. I don't rightly know. She right savin'," Hammond conceded.

"I ben a-thinkin' mayhap I'd pop the question today. My wife departed this life three or four year ago now, and seems like I don't git ahead none. The widder a-hintin' how she needs a man and all. Thought maybe it a good idy to hitch up an' leave off vetinarin'. Kinder nice to settle down planter and not have to do no work."

"I reckon we cain't let a nigger git puny no more. Won't have no veternary to call on. As soon trust a sick nigger to Lucretia Borgia to doctor it as to git that Doc Simpson; kills more'n he cures."

"Course I'll go on takin' care of Falconhurst hands. Cain't quit entire, and not have no reason to go to town. Besides, don't want the ol' woman to leave off her doctorin' and midwifin'," Doc reasoned.

"Papa will be glad."

"Maybe the widder won't have me, but she ben a-hintin' fer quite a spell—leastwise I takes it as hintin'. I ain't done no sparkin', either. To speak true, it's kinder hard to spark the widder; she so fat and them warts all over her face and that black moustache of hern makes lovin' her up kinder loathy like. She right good-natured, though, right hearty."

Brownlee thought of his sour, scrawny wife waiting for him in New Orleans. Redfield's description of Mrs Johnson was enticing to him, despite warts and moustache. The pleasant plantation well stocked with likely servants was even more enticing. If only he were single, he would enjoy entering into competition with the veterinarian for the widow. If only he had access to some of that poison that Redfield talked about. It would work as well on a white woman as on a Negro. What had the doctor called the substance? Where could he buy it?

The party had arrived at the house. Maxwell they found ensconced in a comfortable chair in the sunshine on the long gallery. Alph sat on the floor at the feet of his master and both were sipping at toddies so hot that they could take only small swallows.

"Git our more cheers. Memnon, more cheers," Maxwell greeted them heartily. "Come in and set and drink some corn."

The taste of whisky was unpleasant to Alph, but to sit at his master's feet and drink it was a triumph, notably a triumph over his brother whose master showed him no such indulgence. As Meg approached, he rolled his eyes in his direction, smacked his lips and devoted himself assiduously to swallowing the hot liquid.

Memnon appeared dragging a chair awkwardly. He was haggard and fearful of the whipping in store for him. Meg leapt with alacrity into the house and, struggling under its weight, brought the most comfortable rocker from the fireside and shoved it behind Hammond. Memnon returned to the house for another chair for Brownlee, after which he went to the kitchen for drinks all around.

Meg retreated against the house, his eyes on his brother, watching enviously each sip from his glass. But, when Memnon appeared with the drinks on a tray, Meg all but upset him, grabbed the lone toddy and carried it to Hammond, knelt by his chair and gazed at his face. "Hot enough, Masta?" he whispered solicitously. "Sugared enough?" He was ignored. "That Memnon cain't stir 'em good, Masta. Masta had ought to let me."

Hammond addressed his father, "I reckon as how we'll have to break this young buck in fer to take a-hold in place of Memnon. Mem seems a-failin'-like. This little buck right peart."

"Mem be all right after that hidin' you goin' to give him, Son. Matter with him is he flinchin' that trouncin'."

"Goin' to flog that Memnon?" Redfield was surprised. "Thought he a pet of yourn? Whut you ben up to, Mem?"

"A-slothin', an' a-thievin' and a-lyin'. Treated too good; my own fault. A little touchin' up here an' there an' he'll be better'n new," Maxwell said casually.

"Never knowed you to flog a boy before. Don't do much threshin', do you?" Redfield asked.

"No, don't do much. Don't like it. Skears all the young niggers so, they stops they growin' fer a day or two. An' the trouble with sendin' 'em to you—besides you a-chargin' two bits a lash —is you welts 'em up with the snake. Nobody wants to buy a welted nigger."

"Everybody who sends a nigger to me fer to flog wants him checkered up a little—that's whut they pays me fer. Send him home withoutn no marks on him and they don't believe he trounced good. Wants 'em sent back to 'em raw like."

"Don't want snake-wales on backs of my niggers," Maxwell declared.

"Wants 'em to remember good, got to gouge a little meat offn they backs. Niggers fergits correction right quick," opined the veterinarian.

Soon the sunshine and toddies and absence of pain made Maxwell drowsy and he nodded off to sleep. He did not know when Redfield took his departure.

Brownlee arose and stretched. "Reckon I'll wander down and see about them bucks o' mine," he said.

"They fed and watered and looked after, Mista Brownlee, suh," Hammond assured him.

"Sure, sure enough, I knows; but I like to keep an eye on 'em."

He had to have another look at Big Pearl. He was a connoisseur of fine niggers, he believed. No really fine ones had ever passed through his possession, a few big, sturdy bucks, but all had something the matter with them, not truly prime. He aspired to deal in the fancy market—housebroken young bucks, nubile yellow wenches, twins, dwarfs or giants, oddities or monsters, hermaphrodites or freaks—but he had never had the capital for such speculation.

He was not certain of Lucy's cabin. He thought he knew it. He had seen Big Pearl's flight to her home. The door stood open to admit the light, and he entered. Big Pearl sat on the side of the bed, and out of the shadows appeared a monstrous, tall, rawboned, lantern-jawed woman, a large naked child astride her hips. Except for the exposed pendent breast with which the baby toyed, Brownlee might have believed her a man in woman's clothes.

"Whut you wants, white man?" Lucy greeted him, irritated at his intrusion and frightened with the knowledge of his trade.

"I wants to see Big Pearl agin," Brownlee explained. "Shuck her down fer me to look at."

"Masta Hammon' know you come?" Lucy demanded.

"No, but I reckon he won't care if I looks over the wench. Come on, Pearl, shuck down," and the white man started toward the girl.

Lucy intercepted him, forced the baby into Big Pearl's arms and strode through the door, around the corner of the cabin and across the clearing toward the house, bellowing at the top of her mighty voice, "Masta, Masta, suh, white man rapin' Big Pearl; white man rapin' Big Pearl. Masta, Masta, you done tell white man rape Big Pearl?"

The commotion startled Maxwell awake. He staggered helplessly to his feet, calling for Ham. His effort was wasted, since Hammond could not fail to hear Lucy's alarm. So long and firm was Hammond's step as he strode through the door, loosening his gun in its holster as he came, that his limp was imperceptible. At his heels came Meg, eyes bulging, arms flailing. Alph, stupefied by the toddy Maxwell had prescribed for his rheumatism, opened his eyes, made as if to rise, and fell over on to the gallery floor, asleep again.

Before Hammond could cross the open space, Mr Brownlee appeared from behind the cabins, bland of manner, assuming an unconcern he did not feel.

"Whut the meanin' of this? You rape my wench?" Hammond demanded.

"No harm done, no harm done. Jest lookin' around your quarters a little. Never went near that nigger's cabin—'cept jest to stick my head in the door." Brownlee knew he lied but he had downed three large goblets of whisky during the morning, and he tried to breeze it out.

Ham was coldly angry. "If you wasn' a white man, I'd kill you. I'd shoot you right through the belly." Hammond fumbled at his gun but did not draw it from its holster. "That Lucy never lie before, an' she not lyin' now."

Brownlee cleared his throat as if to speak again, but found nothing to say.

"Git your geldin' and your two cripped bucks and git out of here. The roads are bad, but Redfield made it from Benson and you kin make it that fur."

Brownlee half-shrugged. It was not the first time he had been ordered away from a gentleman's plantation and he was not sadly embarrassed, but as Hammond walked away, the trader saw him dust his hands together and heard him say something about 'white trash'. The epithet scalded him.

The dealer turned toward the stable. He saddled his own horse and rounded up his slaves. There was no time for farewells. As he walked his horse past the gallery where the Maxwells stood silent, he called, "I reckon I jest ride by the Widder Johnson's whure they murderin' that ol' wench. The sheriff might be in'erested in that goin's on."

The Negroes at a slow trot kept abreast of the horse. The shorter, black one was thoughtful and kept his eyes to the ground as if watching his foot with its two toes. The gangling yellow boy was in happier mood. "Goo'bye, Masta," he called as he passed the gallery, "goin' to Kaintucky." He was silenced by the sting of the lash about his legs.

The sheriff would ignore charges brought by an itinerant Negro buyer against Mrs Johnson and Doc Redfield for the killing of a slave. It was a minor crime at worst. The wench was old, Negro testimony meant nothing to the court, and Brownlee's accusation would have no validity against the denials of guilt from substantial citizens like Doc Redfield and the Widow Johnson. None the less Hammond was relieved to see Brownlee's horse as he reached the road turn to the left toward Benson rather than to the right toward the widow's.

CHAPTER FIVE

"Bᴜᴛ I don' crave to git married, Papa. Whut I craves is a fightin' nigger," Hammond was saying. The elder Maxwell's desire for a grandson, white, an heir, was persistent.

Supper was over and the two slouched over toddies before the fire. The night was balmy, but the fire was comfortable. Meg had rushed in to remove Hammond's boots, forestalling Memnon in that duty. He knelt in front of Hammond and tugged, and when a boot suddenly slipped off it threw the boy backward. He peeled off Hammond's socks, and, instead of drying the feet with his hands, as Mem had done the previous night, Meg leaned forward and wiped them on his kinky hair. Before he shoved the slipper upon the second foot, he embraced it and rubbed his cheek against the white flesh. He half expected disapproval, but Hammond failed to notice the gesture or the questioning, diffident smile that followed it.

"Besides, I don' know no young white ladies," Hammond went on.

"Why, why, there's Miz Daisy Prescott, over to Sommerset Plantation. Right good family—the Prescotts; and she'd jump to git you."

"Yes, I knows Miz Daisy Belle. Right respectable and all; real purty an' you likes 'em dark. But Miz Daisy Belle older'n me; she goin' on an ol' maid. Must be twenty-one, twenty-two year ol'."

"An' then there's your cousin, Miz Blanche Woodford, an' you likes 'em light and you likes 'em young. Cain't be more 'n sixteen

70

and has hay-colour hair, at least did have last time I seen her. You remember her?"

"Cain't say I do," Hammond denied.

"Yes you do. Went to Crowfoot Plantation with yo' mamma to visit her Cousin Beatrix when you little. Miz Woodford your mamma's cousin, a Hammond, too—gal of ol' Orestes Hammond who was brother of Theophilus, your mamma's papa."

"How you keep it all in your head, who kin to who?"

"It's 'portant. Got to know who you kin trust. Blood outs. Orestes Hammond no such man as ol' Theophil—a drinker, kind of, drunk hisself to death. Howsumever, he a Hammond—good blood. Major Woodford, Miz Blanche's papa, of a good family too—his mother a Sitwell. Got Crowfoot Plantation from her side; added to it and built a new big house, hisself, howsumever."

"Whure is Crowfoot?"

"Over beyant Briarfield which is beyant Centerville, near as I kin tell. Everybody in them parts knows Major Woodford and Crowfoot."

" 'Bout fifty mile, ain't it?"

"Nearer sixty, maybe sixty-five."

"Not the place whure a boy had the billygoat hitched up to a cart and let me ride?"

"That the place. Now you remember. That boy was Richard —older than you. Then comes another boy, younger than you, name of Charles I believe. Then Miz Blanche. And there was still another'n, a baby boy or gal I disremember, but it died. Blanche is the youngest livin'. You real taken with that billy!"

"I don't remember the gal."

"You right young then—about five. Before—before I put you on that geldin' pony."

"Long piece to go to git a wife," sighed Hammond.

Alph came in and took his place on the floor between Maxwell's chair and the fire. He was naked, ready for bed.

"Boy, did you soak?" Maxwell asked him.

"Yassum, Masta, suh," replied Alph, rolling his eyes questioningly, as if he did not expect to be believed.

"I ain't never had no truck with a white lady. I wouldn't know whut to do," Hammond confessed.

"Why, if you sees one you wants, you asts her papa, kin you ast her. He say yes, and then you up and asts her. All there is to it."

"I don't mean that. I means goin' to bed. Goin' to bed after you marry. How you ack?"

71

"Don't fret about that. You'll ack all right. No trouble. The gal won't know how to ack either, supposin' she a nice gal."

"Treat 'em jest like they was a nigger wench?"

"Jest like a wench. That is, not exactly. A nigger knows whut you goin' to do. White lady doesn't—not the first time. She modest. She makes out to cry. Mayhap, she scream and holler."

"And won't let you?"

"You loves her up and kisses her, and she let you all right at las'."

"Kisses her? I no good at kissin'."

"You gits so you likes to kiss 'em, kinder. I knows you doesn't kiss your wenches. White ladies, you has to."

"I kissed my mammy when I was little."

"Course, of course. I means you don't kiss your bed wenches. You jest pleasures 'em and lets 'em go. You asts a white lady; you doesn't tell her. White ladies doesn't like pesterin', but they submits, they submits to their husband. It's their duty, their married duty. Sometimes they slow, and you has to promise 'em somethin', a new bonnet or somethin'. But they submits. Leastwise, your mamma did."

"An' you cain't have no more wenches? Whut you do when your wife git ol', twenty-five, maybe thirty?"

"Course have wenches, jest the same. You doesn't talk about 'em, frontin' your wife, but she know you have 'em. She want you should have 'em. Saves her from havin' to submit."

"A white lady better'n a wench?"

"Better? No, wouldn't hardly say she better. But you got to have a wife in order to have children—white children."

"I knows. I knows that."

"Another thing. You cain't shuck down afore you gits in bed with a white lady. Always keeps on your shirt and drawers. Plague a white lady mos' to death to see a man nekid."

"Kindly unhandy like, ain't it?"

"Not as unhandy like as the riggin' she wears to keep you from seein' her. Wears a chimmy that button plumb up to her neck an' comes clean to the flo'; covers her right up all over."

"Not in New Orleans. They white ladies there that strip all off, ever-thing. I seen 'em last trip——"

"Whores. They's whores. That different. Not much better than niggers. Some of 'em not even as good," declared Maxwell in disgust. "Lets you see their brestes nekid, even lets you finger 'em."

72

"They right purty—white skin and all."

"Don't you let me ketch you pesterin' around no white whores, Son. You gits crabs from 'em, and clap and everythin'."

"I didn't, Papa, I didn't, but I seen 'em."

"When you go to New Orleans again, come fall, you better take Dite, or some wench, along. We knows our niggers clean; won' give you nothin'."

"Cain't take Dite. She'll be jest about foalin' in the fall."

"She knocked? You has worse luck with your wenches 'n anybody. Only been pesterin' Dite three, four months. Dite might bring a right likely sucker, though. Your other git has been right prime. You growin' older and stronger; your git ought to be even better'n ever."

"Ain't none of 'em with stiff knee. First thing I looks fer in my suckers."

"Ain't likely—not in first crossin'. Liable to find some stiffness in your grandchildren, not in all of 'em, course, mayhap not any."

"Kindly like to keep my own, the wenches anyhow, fer breeders."

"Good idy. That Hammond blood had ought to give a nigger some quality. But don't turn your son to 'em—that knee sure to show up comin' from both sides."

"Ain't got no son, yet, Papa. Not no white son."

"You goin' to have. You goin' to have," predicted Maxwell in confidence.

"Mayhap, I'll ride to Crowfoot Plantation to see Cousin Blanche Woodford next week or week after—before ploughin' time set in. Kin you git along?"

"Fer that, sure enough kin. Won't have to do nothin'. Jest give the niggers a rest, kinda, before ploughin'. Anything has to be done, I'll save it up fer your back coming."

"Long trip—jest to see a lady, see if I'm a-wantin' her or not."

"And on your way back you kin turn off to Coign and ast old man Wilson fer the loanin' of that old Mandingo fer Big Pearl and Lucy. Reckon they still got him at Coign."

"Take a day more, mayhap, two, accordin' to if the roads is good."

"Take your time. I'm set—kinder like—on that Mandingo. And you might look around some fer that fightin' nigger you a-wantin'."

"I had thought of that," said Hammond.

"Thought of that, mayhap, more than of gittin' you a wife."

73

"A wife is discouragin'—kinder like. But I guess that ever' man has got to have one."

"A man o' property anyhow. You a man of considerable property, will be; an' it looks like you'll have more—unless you wastes it all on fightin' niggers an' sportin' around."

"I doesn't sports, an' you knows it. This fighter I'm a-layin' off to git ain' no sport. It jest a way I sees to pickin' up some good young niggers without costin' nothin'. Course, fightin' him means takin' him to Benson and around to other towns Saturdays, gittin' a chance to see folks—but that not sportin'."

"Ifn you buys you a fightin' nigger, buy you a good one—one that kin win. A losin' fighter worser than no fighter at all."

"That whut I means," explained Ham. "Most of these men who fights niggers ain't got no fighters. They thinks jest any big buck outn the cotton gang good enough to fight with, an' he big enough."

"An' train him. Harden him and practise him an' learn him how to fight."

"That whut I goin' to do—if only I finds me a buck that suits me an' kin buy him."

"Mayhap git one in New Orleans, like Brownlee tell about, in the fall when you go there, an' you don't find one sooner."

"No, suh, Papa. Don't want none o' them bad niggers, like them sports uses fer fightin' in New Orleans. Ruin all the good niggers on the plantation."

The clock interrupted the talk by coughing out the wrong hour. It was eight o'clock, with allowance for error a quarter after eight.

"I don't hold none with keepin' late hours, like last evenin'. Better go up," said Maxwell, yawning. "Let Memnon take you first; he kin come back fer me an' the little buck."

"Goin' to drink another toddy?"

"Reckon not. I had enough."

Memnon was summoned. He picked up Hammond's boots to take them upstairs. "Ain't fergot about that floggin' you promised this buck, is you? He all well again. Ain't you, Memnon?"

Memnon did not commit himself.

"Cain't do it tomorrer. Tomorrer Sunday. Don't want no floggin' on Sunday."

"Don't fergit it. I hones to hear him yelp a little," said the older man.

"I'll make him yelp. I got to have me an all-over washin'

tomorrow. Didn't do no bathin' the week before—begins to feel sweaty-like."

"All this washin' ain't healthy—not in winter time. You washes all the sap outn you. Swimmin' in the river now and agin' in summer time don't do no harm agin you careful to dry good, but washin' in hot water in winter is real dangerous."

"Won't hurt me none. Never has. I be careful," Hammond promised.

"Too clean. Too clean like. Got so young folks is so fine-haired they cain't stan' a little sweat."

"I'd wash more even, if it wasn't so hard to manage this leg in that round washtub. Cain't squat."

"Only thing about your leg I glad fer, Ham. Keeps you from washin' so much. All my fault; all my fault, your mamma always said."

Hammond kissed the tobacco-stained cheek of his father and limped away, followed by Mem carrying the boots. The older man listened to hear the uneven steps upon the stairs.

As the young man approached the head of the stairs, the candle Mem carried illuminated a small figure rising from the top step, which turned out to be Meg.

"Whut you doin' up this hour?" Hammond asked.

"I waitin' to serve you, Masta, suh."

"To serve me?"

"Yas, suh, Masta. I wants to strip your britches off and see you to bed, Masta, suh, please, suh."

"You too little. Git along to the pallet with your mammy."

"I's strong, suh, Masta, even if I little. I your nigger, suh, Masta. Ain't I yo' nigger?"

"All right. All right. Give him the candle, Mem, and them boots."

Mem had prepared a plea to be let off his whipping and had been waiting to get Ham alone to prey upon his sympathy. He was consequently disappointed at Meg's interference. He was safe through tomorrow, and might be able to get in his speech while he helped Hammond with his bath in the morning. However, obsessed by the prospect of being punished he was unable to wait.

"You not a-goin' to whup Mem tomorrer, Masta?" Mem spoke of himself in the third person when he sought compassion.

"No, mornin' is Sunday. We'll have to put it off."

"Mem still sick, Masta. That nasty dose you give him make Mem real sick."

"That whuppin' you in fer make you sicker."

"Mem good nigger, Masta. Mem try to be good nigger," he pleaded.

"Mem goin' to be a good nigger or a dead nigger, time I gits finish' with him."

"Please, Masta, let Mem off. Don' whup Mem, please, Masta Hammon'."

"But I promised you. An' I promise you a fresh wench or new shoes, you expect me to keep my promise, don' you?"

"Yas, suh, Masta, you always does."

"An' I promise you a lambustin', and you goin' to git lambusted good."

"Don't hurt Mem, Masta, suh. Don't hurt Mem. Mem loves you, Masta. Mem Masta's little boy," he begged.

"Mem's Masta's big triflin' nigger. Won't hurt much—jest a little touchin' up here and there. Jest a few patches of hide offn your backside with that pimentade rubbed in to heal it up. You'll be settin' right down in a chair withoutn no cushion in a week or two."

"Pimentade? No pimentade, Masta. Please, suh, no pimentade. That make a nigger squeal worser than the larrupin'."

"Plenty o' pimentade. That stuff cheap. Now, go down an' take care of Papa. See to his feet right next to that Alph's stomick."

"Goin' to whup that Memnon hard, ain't you, Masta?" Meg would not let the subject rest.

"I reckon he need it, hard," said Ham, resuming his progress down the hall.

"Kin I help, please, Masta, suh?"

"Help whut?"

"Help you in whuppin' Memnon?"

"You too little. Cain't sling that paddle. Have to have Vulcan or Pole or one of 'em."

Dite on her pallet beside the bed was awakened by the candlelight and the talk. She rose upon her elbow and asked, "Whure you want me, Masta, suh, in the bed or on the floo'?"

"Better git in bed a little. Mayhap I wants you."

Hammond knelt on Dite's pallet to pray and Meg knelt beside him and listened. When Hammond arose from his knee and crawled upon the bed, Meg was aware of the girl lying beside him. He looked with abhorrence at her face upon the pillow, and hatred took possession of him. He desired not merely to kill

Dite but to annihilate her. He wished that she had never been born, better yet that she had been born black and ugly, at very least that she were out in the quarters and not beside her master in his bed.

Meg pinched out the light of the candle and, finding no excuse to remain, went out of the room and closed the door. He spread himself out on the carpet in the hall as close as he could get to the door. Only when he heard Dite getting out of the bed to sleep on the pallet was he reconciled to sleep.

Hammond lay awake weaving fantasies about his projected journey in search of a wife, whom he was by no means certain he wanted. The errand would be pleasant, even if its objective was dubious. It would offer a respite from the responsibilities and the round of daily duties. He was in a state of somnolence between waking and sleeping when he heard a low-voiced altercation in the hall.

"Git out o' here, nigger. Your mammy waitin' fer you. You cain't sleep here. This my place." It was Memnon's voice.

"No, suh, nigger; I goin' to sleep right here by my masta's doo'. Don' talk so loud; you wake Masta Ham, he be mad," Meg whispered. "I Masta Ham's nigger."

"You isn't nobody's nigger. You ain't hardly no more'n a sucker."

"I is too Masta's nigger."

"Masta Ham jest a-coddin' you, lettin' you make like bein' his nigger. Now, go down to the kitchen an' let me go asleep."

There was a sound of scuffling and the impact of a blow on flesh. A whining cry followed. It sounded as if it came from Memnon, but it must have been he who had slapped the child. Hammond leapt from his bed and made his way to the door.

"Whut you mean, you scoun'rel, woppin' my little buck?" he demanded of the dark where he could just distinguish moving figures. "Now git outn here and keep quiet."

"I never hit him. He wopped me right in my mouf, Masta, suh," Mem pouted.

"Never mind. Let Meg alone. Git outn here and stop your bellerin'. Meg, you lay down and go to sleep." Hammond closed the door and crawled back into his bed.

Dawn had hardly broken when Hammond was awakened by a small figure in front of the fireplace. Ham stretched and yawned.

"Wants your wench?" suggested Meg, kicking Dite with his

77

bare foot. "Wake up, nigger. Masta crave you in his bed. Ain't know nuffin'?"

"Min' your business, Meg. I wants Dite, I gits her. I don't feel like no wench this morning."

"Yas, suh, Masta," and Meg resumed his squatting position before the fire, coaxing it to flare. He continued so, long after the flames were bursting brightly from the wood, adjusting the chunks across the dog-irons and readjusting them, killing time until the room should warm up and his master should see fit to arise. Dite got up, put on her dress and left the room without a word.

Hammond emerged from the bed, sat on the side of it, rubbed and scratched himself. "Pile plenty chunks on. Keep 'is room hot. I goin' to wash after breakfas'," he admonished.

"Yas, suh," answered Meg, kneeling in front of his master and holding his long drawers for him to slip his legs into. A dexterity in adjusting his master's garments seemed to be a part of the boy's nature, since nobody had taught him a valet's duties. He dressed his master as if he were dressing a baby, tenderly, carefully.

Breakfast was hardly finished when Meg announced, "Your tub ready, Masta, suh. Water all carried."

"Whut water?" asked Hammond.

"Water fer you to wash."

"All right. Run along an' eat. Mem ready to wash me?"

Meg put his arm before his eyes and began to cry silently as he slowly walked toward the door.

"Whut a matter, nigger? Whut you cry about?" Hammond was baffled.

"I wan's to wash you, Masta, suh. Memnon gits to do ever' thing. I not your nigger at all," Meg cried overtly.

"You too little," declared the master.

"Kin do better'n Memnon."

"Aw right, aw right. You kin wash me," Hammond promised.

"You lettin' that nigger boss you. He be ownin' you, first you knows," objected the elder Maxwell.

"He right. He better'n Mem. He little, but let him try," Hammond placed his hand on the boy's shoulder, and said, "He my nigger you know, Papa." Meg looked at him with the pleased solemnity of a prime minister.

When Hammond returned to his room, before the fire stood a washtub half filled with water from which arose small wisps of steam. A metal pail of water, with which to temper the heat of that in the tub, was on the fire. Towels were laid out on the bed. An irregular piece of home-made soap was on the floor. Fresh underclothing, socks and shirt were methodically arranged upon a chair.

Meg piled another knot of wood upon the fire, lest the warm room should cool off. He slipped his master's clothes from him as deftly as he had put them on.

Hammond's knee precluded his squatting in the water. It was necessary for him to sit in it, letting his legs protrude. Meg supported him with his whole strength as Hammond eased himself into the tub. Then the boy got down on his knees and soaped his master's body, crawling around the tub from Hammond's shoulders to his knees and legs and feet. Meg splashed himself and the carpet in rinsing the lather away.

He struggled to help Hammond rise, dripping, to his feet, sopped the water from him with a towel, and led him to the bed where the master lay and was rubbed with a dry towel warmed before the fire.

Hammond shoved his legs into his long drawers and submitted to being dressed. He felt refreshed, renovated, clean. Meg slipped himself into his own garments, buttoning the shirt askew in his haste to accompany his master down the stairs. He ran to the kitchen and, without waiting for help, mixed a toddy, which he carried to Hammond in the sitting-room. He stoked and replenished the fire, and drew a low rocker in front of it, brushing its upholstery in an unspoken invitation.

"Nigger tryin' to tell me whure I kin set down," Hammond commented to his father.

"I tol' you that you be his nigger first thing, an' you give him his head. Plagued if I don't reckon but he got more gumption than you, a white man washin' hisself right dab in winter."

Hammond was restless in the afternoon. There was no work that required doing. He thought of riding to Benson, but the roads were wretched and there would be nobody in the tavern, unless perhaps Brownlee had been delayed by the mire, and Ham had no desire ever to see Brownlee again. To sit by the fire and drink toddies with his father would be to rehash again plans already formulated and recollections of trivialities best forgotten.

As a relief from ennui, Hammond would with gusto have undertaken the unrelished task of giving Memnon his whipping, but the day was Sunday. For the Maxwells, Sunday was not a day of devotion but a day of rest, to which the servants looked forward. A few of the older slaves, purchased from plantations where there had been religious services, might still recall some of the customs of their youth and say Sunday prayers in their cabins. The Maxwells didn't know. They did not object to religion in the quarters, but did not encourage it. They did object to their Negroes learning to read. Besides being against the law for slaves, it gave them ideas they were safer, and, for that matter, happier without. At Falconhurst, no Biblical justification of the institution of slavery was required. Nobody disputed it. No admonition of servants to obey masters was needed. Why suggest to them that there exists an alternative?

Maxwell, by ignoring God, avoided the necessity to dispute authority with Him. Why introduce into plantation economy a being superior to the white master?

Hammond ordered his horse and rode over the plantation. He found the river falling and the dangers of overflow past. The horse picked its way upstream to where Saint Helens Creek emptied into the Tombigbee. Ham noted three of his young Negroes fishing with hooks and lines, reined up his horse to talk to them. They had caught four small catfish, but the current was too swift and the sunshine too pale for good fishing.

One of the Negroes had stepped on a moccasin with his bare foot, but the snake had slithered into the water without trying to bite him. Hammond warned the boys to be more careful. His father had paid six hundred dollars for that boy four years ago, and the bite of a moccasion might have killed him.

A deer crossed Hammond's path, a pregnant doe, and disappeared in the brush. Later he saw a wildcat with two kittens playing on a log. He drew his pistol and shot at the mother, but was sure he missed her. He saw innumerable quail and some jacksnipes. The horse shied at a rattlesnake, sufficiently disturbed to coil in alarm. Wild life was so copious on the Maxwell property that it failed to excite Hammond's interest.

He rode back across the fields he intended for cotton, but found them too sodden for ploughing, as he knew they would be. He was impatient to get to that work, which could not be undertaken for another month.

He returned to the stable and gave the horse to a hand with instructions about cleaning and currying it. Meg had seen him set out and was waiting at the stable for his return.

"A toddy, Masta? Kin I stir you a toddy, suh?" the urchin begged, following his master toward the house.

"I reckon so," replied Hammond, bored and impatient for something to do.

He saw Big Pearl crossing the open space between the cabins, balancing a bucket of water on her head. She was as lithe and graceful in her way as the blacksnake that had scurried across his path down by the river. Big Pearl saw Hammond, too, and, embarrassed by Doc Redfield's diagnosis of her ailment, hurried forward to avoid a direct meeting.

But he called to her and asked, "All right agin, Big Pearl?"

She couldn't hang her head lest she spill the water, and could only answer, "Yas, suh, Masta, I's well. Didn't nothin' ail me, I reckon, nothin' but jest bellyache."

"Lucy in the cabin?"

"Yassum, she'm to home," Big Pearl was reluctant to have her master and her mother discuss her illness, which she knew was his intention, but there was no way to prevent it.

Hammond turned toward the cabin. Meg would have followed him, but the master wouldn't permit it. He told him to go to the house and stir his toddy. Belshazzar adjourned his hopscotch before the door to follow his master into the cabin, where Lucy was picking over fresh, wild greens, the first of the season, she had gathered for supper. Meat was in a pot on the fire.

"Evenin', Masta, suh. Come right in. Come right in. Evenin', suh. Bel, you git your triflin' self out'n here. Cain't you see Masta come? Let me move that kittle offn the cheer sosan you kin set down." Lucy was flustered at the honour of a visit from her young master. She grabbed a broomstick and began poking nervously at the fire.

"Evenin', Lucy. Big Pearl all right agin?"

"Wasn't nuffin, wasn't nuffin at all," Lucy disparaged. "Just tomfoolery, I reckon. Wenches gits that way."

"Big Pearl craves I should pleasure her?" Hammond asked without his embarrassment being noticed.

"She sho' do. She sho' do. You isn't goin' to, is you?" Lucy couldn't credit her fortune.

"And you thinks I had ought to?"

"An' yu craves to, I be mighty 'bliged. Of course, Big Pearl craves her master."

"Well, git her ready. Wash her good—all over."

"Sho' will scrub that wench, Masta, suh."

"And put some red stuff in the water that you gits from Lucretia Borgia. She tell you how."

"Red stuff?" Lucy failed to understand.

"To kill the musk. Big Pearl powerful musky."

"Sho' is. An' then I sends her over to you at the big house?"

"Nev' mind. I comes back here in little while."

Hammond left the cabin with a kind of loathing. He flinched at the task he had undertaken, doubtful of his ability to complete it? Would he falter when the time arrived? It would be a shock to his manhood, if he should fail. As a connoisseur of fine animals he was proud of Big Pearl, but he had never thought of her as human. There was something bestial about the chore. He was being used as a mere service jackass, like a stud nigger. Yet his father expected it of him, the wench would feel cheated of her right. Lucy would lose caste if he neglected the daughter she had preserved so carefully for him, the other Negroes took it for granted as a master's right, and, insofar as a master had any obligation to a slave, a master's duty. To omit it would not impair his authority, nor excite contempt, except his own; it would beget only wonder, question.

Hammond was hardly out of Lucy's cabin, when the orgy of preparation for the long-anticipated event began. A tub was brought in and Big Pearl and Belshazzar were sent to the well for water, enough of which to bathe the huge girl required three trips for each. There was no time to heat it, since the master would return in 'a little while', and Lucy didn't know whether he meant in five minutes or at his leisure, and she had feared to ask. She ran to the kitchen of the big house for soap and the red stuff to kill the musk, and Lucretia Borgia took her deliberate time in getting it for her.

"Hurry up; hurry. Young Masta gwine to rape Big Pearl, an' I got to git her scrubbed clean," Meg heard Lucy tell his mother. "Hurry up, please, mam, Miz Lucretia Borgia."

When Big Pearl got her feet into the washtub there was little room for the rest of her. If she should sit or squat, the water would slop out. Lucy used a dishrag gourd as a sponge, soaping it and scouring Big Pearl's body. Then, since Big Pearl could not be soaked in the permanganate of potash solution, Lucy achieved the same results by repeatedly squeezing her sponge over the girl's shoulders, keeping the body wet.

Big Pearl was too excited to sense the coldness of the water. She listened to Lucy's injunctions and threats without hearing them.

"You ack a lady now. Do everything like Masta Hammon' say

—jest like he say—ever'thin'," Lucy instructed her. "Don' you dare ask Masta fer nuffin'—nuffin' at all. Young Masta know whut he want to do to you and know whut he goin' to give you. If you not a lady, I thresh you. An' remember to say thankee to Masta Ham. Whether he give you nothin' or not, say thankee." Lucy repeated her cautions with variations over and over.

While Big Pearl dried herself, Lucy scurried to Dido's cabin to spread the news and to borrow a quilt. Her excitement was unconcealed. "Dido," she implored, "let me have your new quilt. Masta Ham gwine to rape Big Pearl right away, an' my quilt dirty. I knows you choice of it, but for Young Masta, an' I knows you let me have it."

"Better take along this bolster, too. Yourn 'most ragged," Dido suggested.

Lucy hurried home with the bedclothes, and Dido lost no time in heralding the tidings about the neighbourhood, not neglecting to boast that her bedding was better than Lucy's.

Lucy made the bed anew, ordered Belshazzar to empty the tub and to be gone and not come back until Hammond should come and go. She replenished the fire and sat down to wait. She was more nervous than Big Pearl, and as happy.

"You cold?" she asked the naked girl.

"No'um," Big Pearl replied. "Reckon he come?"

"He come. Give him time," said Lucy. "You too hasty. White man take his time," said Lucy, getting up to smooth an imagined wrinkle from the quilt. "Right kind of Dido, borrowin' her new quilt to me."

The mother resumed her seat upon a bench by the fire and looked at her daughter. "You real purty, Big Pearl," was her verdict. "Coarsen you ain't yaller an' you big. Always was big, bigger'n any sucker I ever had—'ceptin' that one buck, borned before you, that Ol' Masta Wilson kept fer his own self when Masta Hammond's pappy bought me an' you. I wonders did Ol' Masta Wilson sell that little buck or is he still at Coign Plantation. Course he big now. He two or three crops older'n you."

"Who pleasured you, Mammy; the first time, I means?" Big Pearl asked.

"My masta, course," replied Lucy candidly. "Ol' Masta Wilson. He gettin' ol'. I speck he dead now, he so ol'."

"You reckon Masta Ham let me take up—after he through with me?"

"Prob'ly, prob'ly. As is, you wastin'. Could have a nice sucker

83

a'ready. Prob'ly give you to Big Vulc or some of 'em fer awhile. Vulc a right likely nigger, stylish an all. Pole better lookin' but he no good. Lucretia Borgia ain't had no sucker fer goin' on three year now. Pole young an' strong, but he jest ain't got no sap."

"You don' reckon Masta Ham aim to take me into the big house fer his bed wench, does you?" Big Pearl said hopefully.

"Whut foolishness you talk! Masta don' crave no big gyascutus like you fer his bed. He wants 'em light and little, like Dite. Dido say he lookin' at Tense, only she too little yet awhile."

"You says you own self that I purty."

"You purty, but you big and you right dark. Make a good breeder, mayhap, fer Masta. No bed wench. Ain't you satisfy?"

"Yassum."

When Hammond emerged from the big house, more eyes were watching him than he suspected. Lucretia Borgia saw him through the kitchen window and grunted with envious jealousy. Meg's jealousy was even greater. From behind bushes and around cabin corners, black faces peered, and all knew his errand and envied Big Pearl the honour they knew he was about to do her.

Lucy and Big Pearl both rose when they saw the master. He entered the cabin, removed his coat and laid it on a box which served as a table. Unbuckling his holster, and laying his gun beside his coat, he said, "All right. Lucy, you kin go over to Dido's or somers, but watch that door and keep them niggers outn here."

"Big Pearl, you ack like lady, now. Do whut Masta say or he whup you. Dat a good strong broomstick right by fire, and you needs it, Masta."

"Don' you fret, Lucy. Big Pearl ain't goin' to need no broomstick to her."

"Better not; better not need none," threatened Lucy, closing the door behind her.

Later, when Hammond left the cabin, he was at once exhausted and exhilarated. The ordeal had been more difficult but more pleasant than he had expected. He had a sense of duty performed. His back tingled with the raking of Big Pearl's powerful fingers through his shirt and his shoulder pained from her bite.

When Lucy returned she found Big Pearl still on the bed weeping and laughing.

"Whut you cryin' fer, nigger? Masta Ham hurt?"

"No'um, no'um. Masta Ham awful nice. I jest loves Masta Ham."

84

"He have to whup you?"

"No'um, no'um. Masta never whup me once. Masta Ham sho' is kin' white man."

"Masta Ham say about you takin' up?"

"Didn't say nothin'. Mayhap he goin' to crave me for his bed wench," Big Pearl speculated.

"Mayhap he don'. Mayhap he goin' to give you to one of the niggers and raise him a sucker outn you."

Hammond had no fear of his father's disapproval; rather, he feared the chuckle of approbation. He decided to postpone the narration of his exploit, to draw the sting from the old man's triumph by passing the incident off as a plantation routine when the father should eventually learn of it. But he reckoned without Negro gossip. Lucretia Borgia and Agamemnon had both blabbed to Maxwell, who had already noticed Meg's restless perturbation, which he attributed to a scolding or switching which Hammond had probably given the urchin.

The father was taking the final swallows from his glass when the son entered the room. "Memnon," he called. "Better drink a toddy, Son. Do you good."

But without waiting for Memnon to answer, Meg slipped a hot glass into Hammond's hand.

"Now, stir one fer your masta. Mustn't never give me nothin' 'thout givin' some to your masta, your ol' masta," Hammond explained.

Hammond held his drink in his hand, letting it cool, but by the time Meg returned with Maxwell's drink, Hammond was sipping his own. "This too strong, boy, too much corn," he complained. "Taste."

Meg took the glass, looked at it and then at Hammond. "Right outn yo' glass?" he asked, incredulous.

"Taste it," Hammond said again.

Meg raised the goblet dubiously to his lips. He never had liked the smell of the concoction, and the flavour he relished even less. He had been told to taste, however, and he took three small swallows before Hammond grabbed it from his hand. "I tol' you to taste," the master reprimanded. "I never tol' you to drink it down. Now fill it up with hot water. Yourn all right, Papa? Not too much corn?"

"Mine good. That saplin' of yurn stirs 'em better'n the big nigger, seem like."

The pleasure that the praise, which he overheard, gave Meg

was tempered by the fear of having his services diverted from the son to the father. He was back with Hammond's drink and waited for approval.

"This better. This good," said Hammond.

"Never did like much corn in yo' toddy, Son. Whisky do you good after your tussle. Big Pearl powerful strong," Maxwell led into the subject.

"She big, all right."

"How you likes black meat?"

"Same as yaller meat, an' you closes your eyes. Reckon white meat ain't no different, 'ceptin' fer musk."

"Jest the same. Jest the same. Right pleased you found out. Tired, Ham?"

"A mite, jest a mite. I feels good."

"Be a-pesterin' Big Pearl regular, first thing," Maxwell predicted.

"Mayhap," admitted Hammond. "Worst thing is havin' to— the first time."

"All your own doin'. Nobody didn't make you. Niggers cain't make they owner do nothin' he don' want to."

"They expects it, howsumever, kind of. You says so your own self. A good masta has to pleasure 'em. If'n he kin, that is. An' I kin."

"An' you kin, an' you wants to, it a good thing. Makes 'em feel you takin' an in'erest in 'em. Makes 'em feel they belong to you. Even bucks sets more store in a wench that her masta has pestered. I wisht you enjoyed it more."

"I doesn't disenjoy it. Oft times I likes it right well. Take this Big Pearl now, she dark and she big, but she right hearty. Right hearty."

Father and son exchanged a smile.

CHAPTER SIX

"GO DOWN to the river and wash yourself good all over, and come to me at the stable," Hammond dispassionately instructed Memnon the following morning at breakfast.

Memnon began to whimper, "Masta goin' to whup Memnon. Don' whup Mem, Masta, suh, please, suh. Mem sick, Masta. Cain't whup a sick nigger, Masta."

"I said wash an' meet me. I never said about whuppin'."

Ham usually omitted his toddy after breakfast, but this morning he felt a need for one. Meg prepared the drinks, one for each of his masters, before he sat down to his own breakfast in the kitchen with Alph. He ate hurriedly and nervously. He feared Hammond might go to the stable without him.

He stood outside the door with the leather paddle in his hand when Hammond came out.

"Give it here," commanded Ham.

"But I goin' along," protested the boy doubtfully.

"Who said?"

"You said," affirmed Meg. "I'm goin' to rub the stuff—the—— You said I could."

"The pimentade? Well, come along. I reckon I did say."

The first adult buck they met was Napoleon, who had been supplanted in Lucretia Borgia's affections by the more fertile Mem. He was a stout yellow boy somewhat more than Hammond's own age, all of nineteen, possibly twenty.

"Come along, Pole; I needs you," Hammond said.

Pole saw the paddle and began to protest, "Don' whup me, Masta. I ain't done nothin', Masta?"

"Don't fret yourself. Ain't minded to trounce you, Pole."

"Going to hide Memnon. I goin' to rub the stuff," Meg elucidated.

"Not, an' you cain't keep your mouth shutten," warned Hammond. He was preoccupied, reluctant about the task in front of him. He ran his eyes over Pole, however, in contemplation of the price he would bring the following fall in New Orleans—fifteen to eighteen hundred dollars, possibly two thousand if the demand for Negroes continued to grow. Pole was lazy and not very alert, just bright enough to get out of work and to avoid punishment. However, he was husky, upstanding, well proportioned, with good, almost pretty features, and an active dimple. Hammond noted that Pole was soft, his muscles flaccid; it was none too early to begin to prime him.

The double doors of the stable stood open, and bluebottle flies buzzed in the sunshine. A surrey and a gig stood with shafts upraised in the shadows of the cavernous interior. The corners of the main room held cobwebs in which pieces of hay, dust and other debris rested lightly. Hammond noticed that some little-used harness, hanging on the wall, was dusty and in need of oil.

The puncheons, running crosswise on the floor, were worn with the traffic of years, and the cracks between them were filled with

87

dirt. The studding which supported the building was warped with the top-heavy weight of hay in the loft and was no longer quite plumb, if it had ever been. Scabrous patches of whitewash still adhered to the walls near the ceiling, but they were grey from the accumulations of dust.

Hammond's stallion nickered for attention when it caught his odour, and Hammond went back to the stall to rub the horse's nose. The mares and mules in the box stalls behind the stallion ignored Hammond's presence, although the sounds of their switchings and stampings and mumbling made their presence known. The doors of the other box stalls which served as dormitories for young bucks, stood open.

"Drive them niggers outn this barn and tell 'em be gone clean away from here," Hammond instructed Pole. "Look in the stalls, and clean 'em all out, ever' one on 'em. Whure that Mem nigger? Reckon he don' crave no touchin' up, here and there? Reckon he hidin' out?"

"Here come Mem now, Masta, suh. Here he come," Meg announced from outside the building.

Assorted in all stages of adolescence, Negro boys, black, brown, ochre, and all but white, squat and tall, fat and lathy, scurried, sauntered or sidled past their master in the exits from the building. One ugly, gangling pubescent had kinky hair of a brown bordering upon rufus, grey eyes, and a saffron face spattered with freckles. Hammond ignored their passing, but this unpleasant combination attracted his attention and he made a note to sell him. It didn't pay to feed and mature an animal so hideous, even though he might be sound. Why hadn't he thought to offer the little buck to Brownlee? What was such trash doing at Falconhurst anyway?

Memnon moped into the doorway.

"Where you been? I tol' you to wash an' come here?" Hammond greeted him.

"Been a-washin', like you say—all over, good. Masta, I sick. I don' crave whuppin' at all. Mem don' need whuppin', Masta, please, suh, please suh."

"That rope right wore out. Reckon it will hold?" Hammond addressed himself; and then said to Napoleon, "Put it through that off pulley."

Pole got on a box and inserted the rope into the end pulley of a series affixed, about a foot and half apart, to the centre beam in the ceiling.

"You isn't goin' to hang me up, Mista? I kneel down good, I ben' over, I hol' still, an' you doesn't hang me. Don' please." The now naked Negro was terrified.

"That pulley stick. It won't turn," said Pole.

"Not used in long time," said Ham. "Pick the dirt outn it and grease it. Goin' to use the two end ones and stretch him."

"Don' stretch me that fur, Masta. My legs won' reach that fur. Use a middle pulley, Masta, please."

"Mem, git out that jug of pimentade and the crock and sponge. You put it away last time it was used in that little corner room."

"You ain't goin' to pimentade me, Masta, too? That burn awful. Oh, Masta, Masta, please, no pimentade." Memnon wept, but got the dust-encrusted jug and went back for the crock, which held the dishrag-gourd sponge, over which had settled dust mixed with fine webs. He set them gingerly down on the floor beside the box on which his master sat.

Pole had cleaned and oiled the pulley until it functioned with a whining squeak.

Meg attacked the jug of pimentade, struggled with the corncob which served as a stopper and finally extracted it with his teeth. He began pouring the liquid over the soiled sponge in the crock until Hammond checked him.

"Don't pour that yet. Shake the jug first. Stir up the pepper that settles to the bottom," he instructed Meg.

The jug was too heavy for the boy to manage and Hammond lifted it and shook it himself. Meg, however, tipped it and gurgled its contents into the crock, such as he didn't spill on the floor. He soaked the gourd and wrung the liquid out of it and soaked it again. He held the saturated sponge before him ready when it should be needed, oblivious of the sticky mixture that dripped down the front of his clothes.

"Close them doors, Meg," Hammond ordered. "Don't want them bucks hangin' around to hear this paddle slappin'. Scare 'em till they green."

Gloom and dusk settled over the great room with the shutting out of the sunlight that had poured through the wide doors.

"Now lay down," Hammond commanded Mem. "No, on your back and closer this way." He formed a loop in the end of the rope and drew it tight around Mem's ankle. "Now, Pole, you pull."

Memnon stopped protesting. He clambered along the floor with his hands and arms in an effort to protect his back from the

89

roughness of the floor as Napoleon on the other end of the rope hoisted him in the air. His fingers could just reach the floor and relieve a small part of the tension on his foot when Hammond called to Pole, "That's enough. Tie it."

The boy hung upside-down by one foot, the other threshing the air.

Pole stood on a box and thrust another rope through the pulley farthest from Mem. Hammond looped it around Mem's other foot and Pole pulled it and tied it, thus spraddling Mem's legs to the greatest width it was possible to open them.

Hammond grabbed Mem around the waist and added his weight on the ropes. "Reckon they strong enough," he commented.

"Oh, oh, my foot hurt. Oh, oh, Masta," Memnon screamed, but Hammond wadded up his bandana and, stuffing it into Mem's mouth, stifled his noise. Memnon could have removed it, but he was glad enough of the gag. His cries were involuntary.

"He sure look funny, a-hangin'. Wisht Miz Lucretia Borgia see him now," said Napoleon.

Hammond ran his hands over Mem's thighs and buttocks, and found them soft. He had known that they would not be firm, for Mem did no hard work. He felt the belly, which offered no resistance to his grasp.

He put the paddle in Pole's hand and instructed him, "Now, stand off from him, so like. An' aim fer his bottom. Git it down on his legs, it won't hurt none, but don't slam his back. An' stay away from the front side. Don't hit him in the belly. Un'erstan'?"

"Yas, suh, Masta; I reckon I does."

"I'll tell you when to start an' stop you when I ready fer you to stop." Hammond retired to a box against the wall. He didn't feel just well. "Go ahead," he gave the word.

Pole took his stance and raised his paddle, measuring the distance from his target. He tried to conceal his exultation, but couldn't control the play of his dimple. He tapped Mem's rump lightly, hardly touching it. Then three sharp spats which caused the pendent body to sway only slightly. Mem's groans were audible, but he was unable to cry out.

The next blow set Mem swinging and begot a moan that the handkerchief in his mouth couldn't stifle. Thereafter the paddle fell at regular intervals, slowly but steadily, a blow followed by a wait until the victim came to rest, and another blow. The impact of the heavy leather upon the flaccid flesh produced a dull sound.

Muffled sounds, incomprehensible and distorted, got past the handkerchief. Mem's body writhed and he took his fingers from the floor and flailed his arms.

Hammond's queasiness turned to nausea. He told Pole to wait. He went out and closed the door behind him.

Mem's swinging body came to absolute rest. The swaying weight had stretched the ropes so much that Mem could reach the floor with his palms and relieve the tension on his ankles.

Pole guffawed, "Nigger, 'Cretia Borgia had ought to see you now. Reckon you not much good to Lucretia Borgia, now, never goin' be no good agin. You sure a purty sight. Goin' to be purtier when Masta come back."

Hammond came back into the barn, the colour gone from his face. "Better give him some more," he said stoically and sat on the box.

Pole resumed his pummelling. The respite increased the pain. In the interval the bruised flesh had begun to grow sore. Hammond wanted to stop the blows, but couldn't. If he had not sickened he would have commanded Napoleon to desist, but he was ashamed of his weakness. He had to prove his own ruthlessness, which he thought of as his courage. He had to prove to himself that he could whip a nigger. As soon as he dared, he put a stop to the beating. Pole rested the end of the bat on the floor; Hammond took it from his hand and hung it on a nail in the wall.

Meg had stared at the whipping, transfixed, enraptured. He harboured no hatred for Memnon but this was a nigger's fate, a concept he had acquired from Lucretia Borgia, who was syco-phant enough to avoid punishment but ready to submit to it if it should be her master's whim. But for the grace of Hammond, it was Meg who hung there bruised and raw. Yet it sobered him. He resolved to evade the chastisement which he had before invited.

"All right. Go to work," Hammond nodded towards Meg. He was serious; except that this was duty, he was contrite. He sensed Mem's agony and terror. He imagined the furious smarting the application of the pimentade would beget; and he would have withheld it but for his faith in its power to heal. He was not wanton, but, having caused the injury, he must heal it.

Meg had to reach up to apply the sponge, and when he squeezed it, as much of its liquid ran down his arm as on Mem's injuries. Mem writhed at the excruciating burn of the acrid mixture and tried to scream. Hammond himself untied the ropes, lowering Mem to a position on his shoulders, so that Meg had to stoop somewhat rather than to reach upward. Mem's head was forward, but he changed his position so that his left cheek was on the floor. He had chewed the handkerchief into a wet wad and spat it out without volition. He could have removed it with his hand, but was glad enough to have his cries silenced.

Hammond told Pole to release the ropes and let Mem down. Pole untied one rope and released a leg, and Mem's face dragged slowly along the floor as the weight on the other rope brought it vertical. The free leg flailed weakly. Pole released the second rope and Mem's body fell on its back to the floor. He was too exhausted, too weary, too relieved to turn on his belly. He made no effort to extricate his ankles from the slackened ropes.

Hammond opened one of the doors and Meg pushed back the other. Light flooded the barn and the line of the sun fell diagonally across Mem's body.

Hammond turned toward the house. Meg followed him, turning his head backwards, reluctant to leave the carnage. They met Maxwell, who had started on rheumatic legs towards the stable. He had paced the gallery impatiently until he had heard Mem's scream and could restrain himself no longer.

"How is he?" the father asked.

"He all right—goin' to be."

"Any fuss? Everythin' all right?"

"Ever'thin' all right," answered Hammond briefly.

"Bleed much?"

"Not much."

"How are you, Son? Had ought to a done it myself."

"I all right, Papa. I tired is all. I reckon I tender. I reckon I wasn't cut out fer threshin' niggers."

"It got to be done—sometimes."

Hammond climbed the stairs, Meg at his heels. He sent the child away, entered the room, threw himself upon the bed face down, and found relief in tears.

CHAPTER SEVEN

"WELL, I SWAN! Warren Maxwell's boy. I'd a-knowed you anywhures. Look jest like yo' papa," said Major Woodford genially and shouted: "Beatrix come and see Sophie Hammon's boy. She don't hear me; don't hear right good. She'll be in later. You ain't been here in years? Guess not. Kindly neglectful, ain't you? Whut do we owe the honour of seein' you now to? You right welcome, mighty welcome, any time. But whut do we owe the honour to?"

"Well, I over these parts to borrow an old Mandingo buck offn Mista Wilson over at Coign Plantation. Papa got two prime Mandingo wenches, an' he want Mista Wilson's buck to mate up with 'em. Papa Mandingo crazy, seems like. Thinks they no niggers like Mandingoes."

"They good, all right. Not many pure ones around. I guess they purty hard to ketch in Africa. Didn't many ever come to America. Plenty in Cuba, folks say, and Jamaica."

"But no way to fetch 'em in."

"Not now. Fool law. I recollect that big buck of Mista Wilson's. Must be old though. Goin' down to Coign to borrow him, eh?"

"An' rode by Crowfoot to call—sorta. You my nighest of kin —that is, Cousin Beatrix is."

"That's right, I reckon. You an' your papa the only Maxwells left. Used to be a big family of 'em; and the Hammonds have sort of petered out—one thing and another, I reckon my wife and children are your nearest blood. Married?"

"Not yet." Hammond blushed.

"Ought to git married. Keep the blood from running out," argued Major Woodford.

"That whut Papa say. I lookin' around. Don't know many white ladies."

"Woods full of 'em, and you kin jest about take your pick. Steady young man, and next in line to heir a good plantation. Quite a ketch, an' I knows anything."

Hammond was ill at ease as he talked. The elegance of the Crowfoot parlour, the ornate American-Empire suite of walnut, the imitation Aubusson carpet, the great square piano with its massive legs, the curtains of yellow damask at the long windows, although they were worn, the muddy portraits in heavy, gilt frames, impressed the boy so much that his diffidence increased. His host, after so many years of living with it, still counted the cost of the house and its furnishings, which he had acquired when cotton crops were good and when his Negroes were young and before it was necessary to mortgage both the plantation and its slaves. His taking Hammond into the elaborate room had been by design and it had brought about the effect he intended.

93

The Major rose from the pink sofa and stuffed his thumbs into the pocket of his vest, thus throwing open his tailcoat and revealing the heavy, gold chain with its seals that hung across his well-rounded stomach. "Let's go and find Miz Woodford, your Cousin Beatrix that is. She'll shore be right glad. Won't tell her who you air; let her reckon."

He bustled on his short legs, with a show of haste but no speed, toward the sitting-room, his hand on the arm of Hammond, limping beside him. They found his wife reading a Bible in which she traced the lines with her forefinger and moved her lips. She failed to notice their approach until they came near to her and started when she saw the unexpected guest. She looked Hammond up and down and then looked questioningly into the face of the Major, closing her book and raising her ear-trumpet with a single gesture.

"Who you reckon this is?" shouted the Major into the funnel-like contraption.

The woman looked Hammond up and down with what to him appeared like hostility, indifference at best. "I don't know. Should I ought to know? Ain't ever seen him before as I know of," she finally said in a loud voice without resonance.

"Sophie's boy, Hammond—Hammond Maxwell," explained the Major.

"How? I cain't hear," she said, searching the Major's face.

"Hammond. Hammond Maxwell. Your Cousin Sophie's boy," the Major shouted.

A smile spread slowly over her face as she rose, dropping the book from her lap. "Well, I declare! Hammond, Cousin Hammond. I'm glad to see you, right glad," she exclaimed, throwing her heavy arms around his shoulders and planting a kiss upon his embarrassed mouth. "Whure did you ever come from?"

"From home," Hammond answered.

"I declare!" she said, standing back a step, but keeping a firm grasp on his shoulders with her outstretched hands. "I jest declare! Sophie's boy. I had ought to have knowed. The very image of Uncle Theo. Ain't he like Uncle Theophilus, Major?"

"More like his pa. Jest like Warren," the Major said in a loud voice.

Beatrix made a face and shook her head in disagreement. "He's a Hammond, pure Hammond. Ain't nothing Maxwell about him as I kin see. Pull up a seat and talk," she gestured toward a chair and resumed her own, kicking the Bible aside.

Hammond was disappointed in his cousin. She was a heavy-made woman of indefinite middle age, her dull, dark chestnut hair combed severely back from her sallow, moth-patched face and amber eyes. Her thin upper lip, short and covered with dark down in which no stiff hairs had yet appeared, drew back to reveal wide-spaced teeth which were also brown, and which protruded over her lower jaw. Her brown woollen dress, well stayed, was neat and severe.

She held her instrument in Hammond's direction, but he at first talked around it rather than into it. She picked up only half he said, even after he had repeated, but it made little difference, since she was bent more upon what she herself had to say than upon what Hammond said.

"How'd you leave Cousin Warren?" she asked, and Hammond explained the state of his father's health.

"When did you come?"

"Jest rode in. Slept last night at the tavern in Centerville."

"Too bad. Might as well of found Richard and slept with him. He's in Centerville a-readin' law," she gloated. "Goin' to be a lawyer. Whut are you a-aimin' fer?"

"Don't know. Jest a planter, I reckon," Hammond said.

"Ought to be a lawyer and go into politics, like Richard. Reckon he'll be governor or somethin' someday."

"More likely to turn out a gam'ler or a nigger stealer," interposed Major Woodford in a normal tone.

"Whut say?" His wife turned her horn toward her husband.

"Nothin'," the Major shook his head.

"More 'n likely somethin' about Richard. You got a grudge agin poor Richard. Richard ain't real strong. Got to make allowance. Always did favour Charles. Charles is my second boy," she explained to Hammond.

"Charlie ain't a nigger thief—yet," the Major said in a voice Beatrix couldn't hear.

"Charles is younger 'n you. Richard older 'n you. Sophie had you jest between 'em."

"I know," Hammond shouted.

"And Blanche, Blanche is younger yet. Jest sixteen. She my youngest. Whure is Blanche? She ought to be ready fer church."

"She about ready, I reckon. Prob'ly a-primpin' extry if she know Hammond here," laughed the Major.

"The kerriage ready?" asked Beatrix.

"Will be," the Major nodded toward her.

"Charles come to go with her?" the mother inquired.

"Cain't count on him. He promised to be back in time, but you cain't never depen' on him. Don't like goin' to church, nohow."

"Somebody got to go with Blanche. Can't have her go alone with jest that nigger coachman."

"Why not? She safe with ol' Wash."

"Don't look right. Church would talk," declared Beatrix. "Don't see whut Charles have to go to Centerville to see Richard fer ever Sat'day, and cain't git home to take Blanche to meetin' on Sunday. Them boys cain't git along together at home."

"To Centerville to see Dick?" Major Woodford scoffed. "Charlie don't care no more 'bout Dick in Centerville than he do at Crowfoot. He go to Centerville to see the nigger fightin' ever' Satiday."

"You hadn't ought to let him," complained his wife. "Leads to gamblin'."

"Gamblin'. Whut he got to gam'le with? Few dollars pocket money, mayhap. Cain't keep a boy from gam'lin' a little," said the Major with complacence.

"Gamblin' is a sin, jest like dancin' and playin' cards and carryin' on. Brother Ben Jones say so the las' sermon I could hear him preach," she quoted her authority. "I don't go to church no more. Ain't no use. Cain't hear right good, so I jest sets at home and reads the Bible and lets the chil'ren go. But gamblin's a sin. Don't say nothin' in the Bible about nigger fightin', but the gam'lin shore is bad. Whure they is nigger fightin', there sure to be gam'lin', an' I don't want my boy Charles corrupted. Charles is sich an innocent, good boy, but you'll git him wil' like Richard an' you don' keep him home away from them fights."

"I cain't keep him home withoutn I put him in spancels. Always cravin' I give him a young buck to make a fighter out of. I don't do it, do I? I don't want my hands ruint, chewed up and scarred and blinded. Give him a nigger to fight, have to have another to bet—maybe lose. You cain't say I aids and abets him in his lowness," the father excused himself.

"Charles don't come, whyn't you go to meetin' with Blanche?" the wife suggested.

"You know, well as I do, I got to go to that nigger meetin'. You know the law that you cain't have no nigger church, 'lessen a white man there to hear that they don't preach no risin'."

"Mayhap, Cousin Hammond would crave to carry Blanche to church meetin'?" Cousin Beatrix suggested.

"Hammond tired," objected her husband. "Ridin' all day yestiday, and up early this morning to git here."

"I not tired hardly. I be right charmed to go, an' I knowed how to ack," volunteered Hammond.

"Ack jest like in any church. We're Baptists."

"Whut I mean, I ain't ben to church sence Mamma die," confessed Hammond.

"Course, you got to stay and look after your nigger meetin'," Beatrix sought an excuse for him. "Jest as good. God sees you in nigger meetin'."

"We don't have nigger church at Falconhurst. Papa think it keeps the hands all stirred up," Hammond explained.

"He right," agreed Woodford. "I'd sell that preacher and stop that foolishness if it wasn't fer her."

"Why you usen to hold meetin' fer your servants," Beatrix remembered.

"Not sence Mamma die."

"Had a good meetin' house an' everything."

"Use it now to sleep niggers in. Got to be so many," said Hammond.

"Whut the use of slavery an' it ain't to save pore heathen souls, to bring the niggers to Jesus and learn 'em to lay their burdens at His feet? Ain't right, ain't right, I say, to keep 'em from learnin' about the Lord."

"Warren always was a free thinker," the Major sighed in a low voice. "I got to have religion, women about."

"Whut you needin' is a good Christian wife, Cousin Hammond," Beatrix prescribed. "Make you go to church. Save your soul an' bring you to Jesus."

"Whut the matter with that Charles? We late a'ready. He cain't ever do nothin' he promise," complained Blanche as she entered the room, tying her bonnet with ribbons beneath her chin. Seeing Hammond, she stopped short and expressed her surprise with "Oh!"

"Come here, darlin', and kiss your Cousin Hammond, Hammond Maxwell, Cousin Sophie Hammond's boy," her mother bade Blanche. "Ain't seen him sence he was a little lad an' you was a baby. Come to visit us from Falconhurst Plantation. Goin' to carry you to church. Come here an' kiss him welcome."

The girl blushed but was without reluctance. She advanced and the boy encircled her stays and pecked an embarrassed kiss

97

upon her small petulant mouth. "Never knowed I had no cousin like you," she said.

"There's Wash with the team," Major Woodford said, looking out the window. "Better git along, don't want to be late fer the meetin'. Reckon Charlie ain't comin'. We'll talk some when you gits back."

Blanche kissed her mother, who did not rise. The Major led the way through the wide hall to accompany the pair as far as the front gallery, where he stood watching Hammond awkwardly hand the girl into the wide back seat of the surrey and get in beside her. The old chocolate-hued coachman, in his dilapidated livery, appraised the newcomer with approval without turning his own head or appearing to look. He noted the affability of his master and the animation of the girl, and he surmised in them the hope to bring the visitor into the family.

For Hammond, sitting so close to a white girl was a fresh experience. He thought Blanche pretty, in fact beautiful. He wanted to think so. She was indeed fresh and she was young, and her costume emphasized what allure she had. Her flowing dress of cream-coloured woollen challis with a painted pattern of small moss roses was held in at the tightly laced waist by a sash of pink ribbon and enveloped her from neck to ankle. Her stays forced her bosom upward and there was a hint of copious and upright breasts beneath the folds of her frock. The wide brim of her flowered hat was bent against the sides of her face by streamers that tied beneath her chin.

What Hammond could see of Blanche herself satisfied his inexperience. He approved the smallness of her mouth. He thought her small, pinched nose precious, her light blue eyes divine, although their narrow spacing annoyed him. How was Hammond to know that the curls that showed beneath the hat were made with a curling-iron? That the alternate blanching and blushing of her cheek was occasioned by his own presence? He failed to note the bulbous fingers with the bitten nails that protruded from Blanche's short, fingerless black lace mitts. He was allured by a fresh scent, something like rose geranium, and wondered whether all white ladies smelled so sweet.

But he would have to get used to whiteness of female flesh. Its pallor seemed to him not quite healthy. He knew the beauty of blondeness, but failed to appreciate it. He knew, moreover, that if he was to have a wife he would have to tolerate that she was white.

"Folks won't believe that you-all my cousin," observed Blanche.

"Why won't they? I am."

"I knows you are, but I ain't never talked about you, didn't know nothin' about you at all."

"Thought everybody knowed we cousins. I did. Papa been talkin' 'bout you and Cousin Beatrix ever sence I was little boy."

"Reckon Mamma disremembered how good-lookin' you-all are, and all."

"I jest a little puke last time she seen me. I don't remember you at all. All I remember is your brother Richard an' his billy goat hitched up. Let me ride in the little cart," reminisced Hammond.

"You remember a billy goat and disremember me. You think that nice?" the girl pouted.

"You jest a baby, that time. How I know you goin' to grow into the beautiful lady you are? I won't never fergit you again," Hammond essayed gallantry.

"You-all jest sayin' that. You doesn't really think I purty."

"Shore do. Awful purty an' awful sweet," Ham avowed.

"Folks at church will think we aimin' at gittin' married," Blanche suggested.

"Why will they think that?" Hammond asked, relieved to find Blanche was easing his talk for him.

"Us coming to church together. Won't know we jest cousins. Young man carry a girl to church, everybody reckons they goin' to git married. That's the way it is."

"Mayhap we is," Hammond declared.

"Is whut?" pressed Blanche.

"Mayhap we is goin' to git married. How you like to?" Hammond buzzed nearer the web.

"You got a nice plantation? Big house?"

"House ain't much. Leastwise ain't fine like Crowfoot, but we got a big passel of niggers. Ain't nobody got finer niggers than my papa," boasted Hammond.

"Niggers!" Blanche scoffed.

"I kin build a house, any kind of house you craves. Jest been a-waitin' until I marries to build a house—a fine house. House we got is good enough fer jes Papa and me. Papa was gittin' ready to start buildin' when my mamma up and die."

"I ain't thought about gittin' married—much," said Blanche, reverting.

"How'd you like to?"

"Is you-all askin' me? Is you proposin'?"

"Shore am. Don't know how else to do it. I'm bashful, kindly."

"We ain't knowed each other long, seems like, but——"

"We're cousins, ain't we? That makes a difference."

"I reckon it do," she agreed. "Did you ast Papa? He say it all right? Or did you aim to run off?"

"Ain't asted him yet. Ain't had no chanst; but I will. Hadn't thought about us running off—unlessen he say no."

"Papa purty choozy. I don't know whut he say."

"Ifn he say yes, do you say yes?"

"I reckon I do."

Hammond made no move, and Blanche added, "But don't kiss me yet. Ast Papa first. Unlessen it jest a cousin kiss. Guess that all right."

Desire in Hammond was not absent, but it was to embrace, not to kiss. However, when he placed his arm about the girl's body she glued her lips to his and refused to let go. And they were locked in each other's arms, oblivious of the swaying of the carriage over the rutted roads, when they rounded a wooded corner and met Charles, returning, horseback, from Centerville. They failed to see him until he was upon them.

Charles grabbed hold of the bridle of the off horse and Wash stopped the team. "Whut this mean—you a-huggin' o' my little sister? Right out fer everybody to see, too."

Blanche was flustered, caught. "This Cousin Hammond, Charles, Cousin Hammond Maxwell. Maxwell right, ain't it? I disremember. It all right fer cousins to kiss some, ain't it?"

"Papa know you out alone with this man?"

"Course he know. You didn't keep your promise to come home an' carry me to church meetin', and Cousin Hammond say he carry me."

"Papa don't know you out kissin' him and lovin' him, I reckon," said Charles. "You crawl outn that carriage and I git down offn this hoss and thresh you."

Hammond made as if to comply and Blanche pulled him back into the seat. "Don't pay no 'tention to him. Who he think he goin' to whup, anyway? Couldn't whup a pup."

Blanche was probably right. Besides being young, Charles was frail, long of leg and of arm, narrow of shoulder, hollow of chest, anaemic. His eyes were crossed and it was impossible to be sure just where he was looking. Despite his boniness and the stoop of his shoulders, he was at home in the saddle and sat his horse well.

100

"I don't hanker fer no fuss, Cousin Charles," Hammond said, "but ifn we fights, we fights. Your sister and me, we goin' to git married, and I craves to be friends."

"And if you tells Papa about us kissin', I tell whut you do to me," Blanche threatened.

"That two or three years back; nobody ain't goin' to do nothin' about it now. Besides, you as much to blame as I was," Charles replied.

"I's a-warnin' you, don't tell." Blanche knew her blackmail would be effective as it had been before. "Don't you tell nothin' either, Wash."

"Ain't nothin' to tell. I drivin' this team," replied the coach-man. "Ain't got two sets of eyes."

"Well, drive ahead, and trot them hosses," ordered Blanche. "We already late fer that meetin'."

The carriage moved forward and Charles wheeled his horse towards Crowfoot.

"This road——" began Wash.

"Never mind, nev' min'. No back talk. I said trot 'em," said Blanche peremptorily.

Some two hours later the tired horses drew the carriage up the avenue of elms and halted in front of the Crowfoot mansion. As Hammond and Blanche alighted, they saw upon the gallery Major Woodford in hearty conversation with a big, moustached man of middle age and authoritative, ponderous manner. A Negro led a heavy saddle-horse toward the stable.

"Come in, come in," urged the Major. "You remember Blanche, Colonel Butler. Her and her cousin ben to church meetin'."

"Course, course, I remember her. How she growed up. And purty, too. An' I was younger——" flattered the large man.

"This is my wife's cousin, Mista Hammond Maxwell, come a visitin'. Colonel Jim Butler. Colonel Butler is speakerin' around some about electin' Gen'al Jackson again, come next fall. Goin' to speak over Centerville tomorrer night."

"I hopes you goin' to vote the Gen'al in agin, Mista Maxwell, suh," said Colonel Butler. "Course, there ain't no question about it."

"I cain't vote—yet," answered Hammond, blushing for his youth.

"Well, support Gen'al Jackson, in that case; 'lectioneer fur him. Jest as good." The Colonel dismissed the subject closest to

101

his heart. "Maxwell? Maxwell? Ain't no relation to ol' Warren Maxwell, over by Benson, I reckon?"

"Warren's own boy," interposed the Major. "Wouldn't suppose Warren would git a boy like this one, would you?"

"Kindly see a resemblance now. Well, I declare. I didn't know you two war akin."

"Run in and take off your bonnet and git ready fer dinner. Dinner nigh ready," the Major prompted his daughter. "Us gents will santer about."

"Mighty purty, mighty purty," said the Colonel, watching Blanche depart. "Kindly sweet on her yourself, ain't you, Mista Maxwell? Come a visitin'? Sparkin', I'd call it."

Hammond wished that he didn't blush so readily.

"Let's us go over to the spring house and git us a drink of corn before we eats," suggested the Major. "Wife don't allow me to drink it in the house. She's temp'ance."

"Maybe we better not offend Miz Woodford," Colonel Butler objected.

"No offence at all. She knows I keep it. Jest won't have it in the house, that all. Damned preacher idy. Her jurisdiction don't go as fur as the spring house."

"A swallow would taste right good. Jest a swallow," said the Colonel as they walked along.

"Colonel Butler callin' means you got to bed with your Cousin Charles," the host explained to Hammond. "Reckon you don't mind. Bed wide and Charlie clean. Washed all over yestiday to go to Centerville."

"Pleasures me all right, an' Charles don't gainsay," declared Hammond.

"Kindly caught us off balance, so many visitors at oncet. Gen'ally plenty of bedrooms, but old Mista and Miz Satherwait coming by fer the night. They church cronies of Beatrix's, goin' to Mobile, I believe. Mighty pious."

"I do not wish to intrude," said Colonel Butler. "I kin go on toward Centerville."

"Won't hear on it. Won't hear on it," said Woodford. "Plenty of room. Jest means them boys doublin' up, they and their wenches."

"Don't reckon I need no wench," said Ham.

"Course you do, course you do, after your trip. Unlessen your pappy ain't broken you in yet," urged the host.

" 'Lessen Warren Maxwell changed a lot, I reckon his boy know

102

whut a wench is fer," said the Colonel, downing his second whisky.

"Don't know ifn Charles knows or not. He has hisn, but don't seem to git her knocked. Charles kind o' puny," the Major said. "Backward like," he added. "His grandpa died of gallopin' consumption, an' Charles is made fer it. Coughin' around all the time."

The whisky sharpened the appetites for dinner, which was served in a room which impressed Hammond as much as the parlour. The dining-room was in daily use, however, while the parlour was reserved for occasions. Here, too, the Empire motif had degenerated in its excess of ornament. The heavy white napery and the flowered borders on the thin china contributed a festive note to an otherwise solemn occasion.

An immature yellow girl swung the peacock brush and kept her eyes fixed on Charles. Colonel Butler, the oldest guest, invited to pronounce the blessing on the food, lowered his head and mumbled something that wound up in an "Amen". The servant in command in the handing about of the food was a brown man of middle age. He was assisted by old Wash, the Negro who had driven the young people to church.

"Whut did Brother Ben Jones talk about in his sermon this mornin'?" Mrs Woodford wanted to know from the end of the table and raised her horn to her ear.

"Somethin' about gamblin' and things. Had a text about casting lots fer a coat with no rent money in it. I don't know. Didn't make no sense," said Blanche in a loud voice directed toward her mother. "And," looking toward Charles, "Brother Jones say that them as keeps fightin' niggers goes straight down to the bad place, 'cause you cain't fight niggers unlessen you gam'les on 'em."

"Jest whut I always sayin'—whut I said this very morning. Bless God," Beatrix nodded.

"I don't see how as fightin' two niggers together do no harm, so long as you jest bettin' niggers. Don't need to bet no money," objected Charles.

"Seems like all the young men wants fightin' niggers these times," interposed the Colonel. "Reckon it only natchel to want to do whut everybody doin'."

"Reckon Hammond don't mess in that kind of sportin'?" Major Woodford angled for an opinion.

"I ain't had no fighters my own self, but I been into Benson and look at 'em. Right takin'. I don't see no harm."

"Me neither," said Charles, looking gratefully toward Hammond.

"Course, the fightin' in Benson ain't like the trained niggers they gotten in New Orleans," said Hammond.

"You ever been in New Orleans?" asked Charles.

"Yes, but I never seen no fightin' there—only at Benson."

"See, Papa. Cousin Hammond ben places, mos' ever' place. And you won't let me go nowhures," whined Charles.

"An' you ever had a fightin' nigger, I'd never speak to you agin, Hammond Maxwell," declared Blanche.

"Now, daughter," cautioned her father.

Hammond merely lowered his head and raised his eyes in a confident smile across the table.

"Well, I wouldn't," pouted the girl weakly.

"We'd still be cousins, I reckon," Hammond bantered.

The conversation shifted to the cotton market, the Negro market, General Jackson, fried chicken, bad roads, and Texas. Beatrix wore a fixed, uncomprehending smile and followed each speaker with her face, but she gave up any effort to hear what was said. The other members of the dinner party soon tired of shouting and talked in a natural tone.

Colonel Butler, when the diners had risen, walked over to his hostess and at the third try made her understand his appreciation of an excellent meal.

Major Woodford took Colonel Butler into the parlour, ostensibly to talk to him, but really to exhibit the room's grandeur, which the Colonel dismissed as "mighty fine, mighty fine." The Major was already converted to Jacksonian democracy, and the Colonel, knowing no other subject, agreed with the Major's comments until he could no longer control his desire to sleep and dozed off, sprawled in his chair.

Major Woodford, chafed at his guest's lack of interest in his house and conversation, wandered into the sitting-room and interrupted the flirtation between Blanche and Hammond, who shouted intermittently at blank-faced Beatrix.

Blanche rose and said pointedly, "I reckon you and Papa wants to talk."

When she was gone, Hammond cleared his throat, which was dry with doubt. He stared at the Major and summoned at length, "Cousin Blanche and me, we likes each other right well."

"Ain't gittin' ideas so fast, son, air you?" smiled the Major. "Ain't knowed her more than three, four hours."

"Well, we cousins, you know," countered Ham. "Real sweet girl, seems like, and real purty."

"Raised good. One thing I say, Beatrix is good mother—strick but good."

"To tell true, I kindly lookin' around to marry me a wife. Papa think I ought to marry and settle down an' sire me a son."

"Good advice to a young man. Stops 'em from runnin' wild," agreed the Major.

"An' I sweet on Cousin Blanche. I wants your leave to spark her a little," said Hammond tentatively.

The elder man had his fish on the hook and proceeded to play it. "Reckon you didn't spark none this mornin', goin' to church?"

"To tell true, I did say that I liked ridin' with her. Kinder ast her ifn she liked me," admitted Hammond, who was unsure of what Charles might have said about encountering them on the road.

"That gal raised so innocent-like, she don't know who she like. She like anybody young-like who wear britches." Her father by his intonation turned his sarcasm into a boast.

"I want's to marry her, all right. I loves her. Knowed it first thing when I seen her in that purty dress."

"Didn't ast her?"

"Well, kind of sort of like. She say ast you. She say she like to marry me, but I has to ast you."

"I hardly knows whut to answer," meditated the father. He grew gravely sentimental. "I knows Blanche old enough to marry, but she sech a baby, seem like. Innocent and pure as a baby."

"Sure is," agreed Hammond.

"An' I don't know nothin' about you—'ceptin' your breedin'. A good mamma, an' a good enough papa, I reckon. Not very religious, but a good man. I ain't got no religion either, 'cept fer the women folk. I don't know how you treat my little gal."

"Treat her good. Best in the world. Good as I knows how."

"Don't know how she like livin' so fur away from her mamma and all. You ain't got a very fine house at Falconhurst, has you?"

"Aims to build a new place, soon as I marry."

"Kin you? Whut I mean, kin you afford it?"

"Shore kin. Papa kin. Ever'thing hisn, but I runs the place; has whut I craves."

"Doin' real well, eh? Makin' good crops of cotton?"

"Not cotton so much; niggers. Falconhurst dirt, like all Alabama dirt, is purty much niggered out. Whure Papa gits his

105

money at, his cash crop, is in buyin' strong young niggers an' raisin' 'em fer the New Orleans market."

"Mor'gage on Falconhurst?"

"Oh, no 'um."

"An' the niggers. No mor'gages on them neither?"

"Naw, suh. Don't owe a cent on any nigger we got, nor on anythin'." Hammond was shocked at the idea of debt. "An' ever' nigger we got is sound and healthy, better than two hundred of 'em."

"Well, I have to think about it—talk to my wife some. I reckon we goin' to give you a yes about our daughter. Serious matter, marryin'. Reckon we might as well chance you as any of the rest."

"I sure thank you, suh."

"Remember, I ain't said it yet, but I reckon I will," and the Major paused. "I reckon, an' I helps you out, you goin' to help me out, too."

"Any way I kin, anythin'," Hammond pledged.

"I purty bad pressed fer money, the bank a-pressurin' me an' all—jest until after the crop is sold. That's all. I pay you back after the cotton crop."

"That ain't planted yet," said Hammond.

"But it goin' to be, and it shore to be good this year. Had three bad years a'ready. Time I was havin' a good crop."

Hammond was unable to follow the reasoning but was unwilling to lose the girl. "I understand you wants my papa to borrow you some money. I ain't got none, my own self."

"Well, yes. That is kindly it."

"How much you want?"

"I needs about five thousand dollars—to pay the in'erest on whut I owes the bank, an' to ready Blanche fer her marryin', that is."

"A heap of money, five thousand dollars. I doubts Papa got that much in cash to spare."

"He kin borrow, cain't he? Credit's good. You say he don't owe nothin'."

"Reckon could. But he won't. Afeared of owin'."

"It jest till cotton pickin'," the Major emphasized.

"Whyn't you loan from the bank your own self?" asked Hammond. "You got a good plantation and a passel of niggers."

"It plague me to tell it, but Crowfoot already blistered fer more 'n it worth, and ever' hand I got is mor'gaged fer all they will fetch. Jest a-holdin' on by my teeth. Bank liable to smash down on me any day. Seem like your papa could help out an old friend and a cousin-like to boot," the Major whined.

If Hammond had but known it, Crowfoot hospitality, open and freely offered as it was, always was accompanied by its owner's solicitation of a loan. Not that Woodford wouldn't have accorded a loan to another as freely as he asked one from a guest, if only he had been more affluent. Frugality he did not know. Stinginess, or even caution, he was unable to comprehend. To beg had become a habit. Every guest was evaluated as to the size of the loan which could be extracted from him, and Hammond Maxwell seemed like fair game for a sizeable touch. Moreoever, he had Hammond on the hip; he was in a position to refuse him the hand of his daughter.

The Major had no intention to withhold his consent to the match, which was just what he had been hoping for. What he misjudged was the depth of Hammond's infatuation with Blanche, which he mistook for passion. The boy wanted a wife, or rather his father had talked him into taking a wife, and he was drawn to Blanche because he knew no more suitable candidates. He had fallen in love not so much with the girl as with her challis frock, a garish house, a glamorous life, and, above all, with Hammond blood, which he had heard extolled the whole of his life.

Already Hammond had given a passing thought to what imperfections might lie beneath the gay challis. The house and the life had lost some of their allure for him in the knowledge that the house was mortgaged and the life was steeped in debt. All this graceful living was a bubble about to burst. And, as for Hammond blood, here sat his deaf, sallow, brown-toned Cousin Beatrix, and had observed the pimple-spattered, hollow-chested, squinting Charles across the dinner table, both Hammonds.

He had not changed his mind about marrying Blanche, but if his suit should be rejected he would suffer no anguish. He had not contemplated a marriage by purchase, but that is what Woodford's proposal implied, since the debtor would have neither the desire nor ability to repay a loan. That was clear, even to Hammond.

Five thousand dollars, the price of four or five strong bucks. He wondered whether he wanted Blanche so badly.

Hammond temporized. "Five thousand dollars. Couldn't you git along with less? Pay part?"

"I figures I needs that much. Mayhap could shade it a little, but it would pinch me," conceded the Major.

107

"Papa might hap advance you half that much. I'll have to ast him. Reckon he will. Does most whut I ast him."

"I could give him my note of hand. That had ought to be good."

"Had ought to be, yes; till cotton harvest," Hammond joined in the pretence that the negotiation was a loan.

"Then I kin reckon on it?" Woodford sought finality. "When s'pose he send it?"

"Soon as I gits home, an' I kin git him to do it."

"I reckon as how you kin marry my daughter, then," the father blatantly reverted to the previous theme. "Seem like a fine, gen'rous, upright young man, that kin take good care of a gal."

"I take care of her, you kin lay to that."

"Blanche and Hammond goin' to marry," the Major shouted at Beatrix, who was lost in her own contemplation.

She cocked her trumpet and asked, "How?"

"Blanche and Hammond goin' to git married," her husband screamed again. "They in love."

"Why, Cousin Hammond on'y jest come."

"That don't make no difference. Don't take a man long to make up his mind fer a purty piece like that Blanche."

Beatrix began to weep; she arose and kissed Hammond, continuing to weep in his arms. "You'll be good to her?" she demanded. "I've raised her up in the fear of the Lord, and she'll make you a good, faithful wife. Maybe she'll bring you to Jesus."

Hammond got loose from Beatrix as soon as he could, but was forced to endure the shake of the Major's pudgy hand and the enthusiastic pat on the shoulder. "How it feel to be plighted?" Woodford tittered.

"Purty good," Hammond shrugged from his doubt. "Purty good," he repeated for emphasis.

"And Hammond goin' to borrow me twenty-five hundert dollars," Major Woodford added in a stentorian whisper into the horn.

Beatrix nodded that she had heard, and murmured with polite indifference, "That nice. That nice." No lady was concerned with money.

That night Blanche and Hammond sat aside from the company, which now included the superannuated and devout Satherwaits, and planned their life together.

Blanche found it necessary to count on her fingers to set a

propitious date for the wedding and chose the eighth of May, something more than two months hence. Hammond said nothing about a ring to bind the betrothal and Blanche found it necessary to remind him. He was oblivious of the engagement ring, which no woman ever forgets; but, brought to his mind and explained, he promised to comply with custom.

Blanche was elated at her prospects. All the local swains were callow; worse, they were poor. Her betrothal was additionally romantic, even glamorous, because it was with a stranger, a man from strange parts, a man of the great world who had been to New Orleans, and a man whom she had toppled off his feet at their first meeting. All these attributes were items to boast of in Centerville and Briarfield.

Hammond, for his part, was complacently pleased with his bargain, for a bargain it had been. He could well put up with the petulance which Blanche habitually displayed until she got her way, in the silent solace of the knowledge that she was bought and would be paid for. In due course, she would be his to dominate as he chose.

The bedroom to which Charles and Hammond eventually retired was the only one on the ground floor, a big room furnished with pieces, largely of walnut, that had been left over from the furniture of the old house when the new one was built, pieces good enough for destructive boys. It was cluttered with a broken spinning-wheel, and an extra dresser with a cracked mirror, a heavy round table piled with dust-covered clothes that were outworn or outmoded, two crippled chairs as well as containing usable if badly designed bedroom furniture, quite as good, however, as that in Hammond's room at home. The carpet was woven of rags, but so were all the carpets at Falconhurst. There were no curtains on the wide bed with a frame for a canopy. Except for the junk, which the room had ample surplus space to accommodate, the informal room was not uncomfortable.

When Hammond entered, Charles was stripped to the waist, reclining on the bed, his stockinged feet upon the floor too tired or too lazy to take off the rest of his clothes. His bearing toward Hammond had veered completely since the morning encounter upon the road. His affability was prompted by Hammond's statements that he had visited New Orleans and that he did not disapprove of fighting niggers, a subject upon which Charles desired to draw his guest out."

"Which side the bed you crave?" he asked.

"Don't make no difference," Hammond replied.

"I always sleeps this side. Dick sleep over there when he home."

"Your papa say Cousin Dick readin' the law in Centerville," said Hammond. "Must be right smart, fixin' to make a lawyer. Takes a heap of studyin'."

"Dick ain't a-goin' to be no lawyer. Readin' law is jest his excuse. Dick fixin' to be gam'ler."

"He older than you, ain't he?"

"Yas, he older, and Mamma's favourite. Gits ever'thin'. I don't hardly git nothin'. Even has to wear Dick's old clothes, cut down. Papa pore, plumb pore," Charles confessed. "Dick better-lookin' than me, too. Makes a difference."

"You ain't through your growin' and makin' up," condoned Hammond. "You right big, leastwise tall fer your age."

"An' Dick looks straight. He ain't gotch-eyed like me."

Hammond's compassion could summon no satisfactory answer, and the subject was dropped in Charles' fit of coughing.

"You a-sparkin' Blanche?" her brother demanded abruptly. "Aimin' to marry her?"

"Well, yes, kinder," acknowledged Hammond.

"I likes you, even if you are my cousin. You my frien', ain't you? Well then, let Blanche alone."

"Your papa say I kin. He say it all right. Why you hostile?"

"I tells you I your frien'. She pizen. Blanche is pizen."

"She your sister. You hadn't ought to talk that a-way," Hammond sought to shame Charles.

"She my sister, and I knows her, knows all about her. I tell you she won't let you have no fightin' nigger."

"Who say I craves to have no fightin' nigger?"

"Everybody craves nigger fightin', anybody that got any sap. I un'erstands you at dinner that it warn't no wrong." Charles' confidence was shaken.

"To say true, I does crave me a fighter, an' Cousin Blanche ain't goin' to restrain me from gittin' me one. I lookin' around— kinder. I find one someday."

"I thought you had lots of good bucks. Folks say you rich."

"Ourn ain't fightin' niggers though. I wants a buck that kin whup all the rest 'n them."

"I jest craves to see 'em fight, no matter they wins or loses," said Charles. "That whut I doin' this even' whiles you all talkin'. Takes me a couple of bucks up beyant the wood lot whure Papa couldn't hear 'em, and I fights 'em. Course, I wouldn't let 'em

110

bite or gouge; jest scuffled and pounded 'em. Didn't want Papa to find out. You won't tell?"

"Course not. Ain't none o' my put in. Ain't my niggers," Ham washed his hands.

"Don't want Papa should know—Blanche leasten of all. She hold somethin' I do a long time ago over my head. She pizen, I tells you. Why you reckon them wenches don't come?" Charles answered his own question. "That Sukey afeared of you."

He strode to the outside door to call the girls and found them huddled together on the edge of the gallery, waiting to be summoned. "Git yourself in here, and shuck down," he ordered them.

Hammond was embarrassed, torn between his misgivings about the propriety of receiving a wench into his bed in this household on the one hand and the exhibition of his lack of virility on the other. "Reckon I don't need none tonight. I kind of tired," he temporized.

"It all right. Papa say it all right. Papa say give you a wench," Charles urged, while the two girls shed their simple clothes, perfunctorily.

"This Sukey kind of tall and stringy like, but Dick think she right good. She Dick's when he at home. Ain't no virgins on the place, 'ceptin' some blacks that ain't right ripe yet."

"Sukey all right. Ain't you, Sukey?" Hammond declared, without enthusiasm.

"Yas, suh, Masta," Sukey admitted, diffidently.

"Coursen, she ain't so round like as yourn, ain't fleshed out," Hammond admitted.

"This here Katy gittin' too fat. Got to cut down on her eatin' some," commented Charles, running his hand over the girl's flank and pinching her ample calf. "An' if you ruther trade——" he suggested hospitably, but failed to conceal his reluctance and Hammond declined.

Katy was low and wide, moonfaced, short-necked, and fat. She waddled provocatively when she walked. She enjoyed her status as her young master's concubine and Hammond thought her presumptuous in her display of familiarity.

While Hammond knelt by the right-hand side of the bed to utter his prayer, Charles and Katy climbed into the deep feather-bed on the opposite side.

"You reckon that prayin' ever' night do you no good?" asked Charles when Hammond had mumbled his amen.

111

"I don't reckon it do, but I promised my mamma, 'fore she died," Hammond answered. "Don't you ever pray?"

"I gits 'nough of that trash mornin's after breakfast. Ever'body kneels down, even the house niggers, even Papa; cain't nobody git outn it. You'll see. You marries Blanche, you'll be kneelin' down ever' mornin'," Charles threatened and was ignored.

Sukey waited for her unhurried lover to enter the bed so that she might pinch out the candle. He would have dismissed the wench and have gone to sleep, but for the violation of hospitality. Charles, on the other side of the bed, would see in such behaviour a contempt for the best entertainment Crowfoot had to offer. Hammond performed what he looked upon as a duty without pleasure and with little satisfaction.

Sukey sensed Hammond's apathy, but, none the less, thanked him for his favour, as Dick had taught her to do.

"Git out now and let me turn over and git some sleep. This bed too crowded," whispered Hammond.

"You means you don' want me no more?" Sukey asked in surprise.

"Not tonight," groaned Hammond.

"Whure I go? Whure I sleep?"

"Whure you wants to, on'y be gone outn here," said Hammond with a show of impatience. "Go back to the quarters, an' you wants, or on the floor."

"I be cold. Masta Richard, he don' never throw me out of bed," Sukey complained.

"Well, wrap in a quilt. Think I wants to lay and smell you all night?"

To return to the quarters would be to admit to the other Negroes her fall from the grace of her lover's bed. She couldn't bring herself to do it. Perhaps, if she remained, the white man would avail himself of her again. She crossed the room to get a quilt from a stack of bedclothes on a chair, evoking Charles' impatience.

"Fer Christ sake, Suke! Whut's the matter? Lay down and behave yourself."

Sukey obeyed. She flung herself naked on the carpet and shivered through the night, protected only by her dress and Katy's, which she was able to reach and pull over her.

Hammond was disturbed through the night by the bedfellows of whom he could not so easily rid himself as he had done of Sukey. He was aware of the couple's nestling in each other's arms; he felt the stretching and relaxation of the ropes that supported the mattress; he heard the little squeals of delight; sensed the clipping and kissing that was going on.

Ham's disturbance was not physical, however, not mere noise, nor lack of space, nor movement. It was disgust, bordering upon nausea, that a white man should assume an amatory equality with a Negro wench. It was beneath the dignity of his race—somehow bestial. A wench was an object for a white man's use when he should need her, not a goal of his affections, to be commanded and not to be wheedled. It disturbed Hammond that Charles should kiss Katy with passion. How could white lips endure the contact with the yellow skin? How could Charles so demean himself, aware of another white man lying beside him?

Scarcely had the dawn broken when Hammond arose. Sukey lay on the floor, her legs drawn up to keep warm, and Hammond spread a quilt over her. His pants went on easily, but he had to struggle with his left boot, as was usual when he put it on without assistance. Sukey had relaxed her position and stretched out before Hammond left the room by the gallery door to keep from waking the household.

The outdoor air was fresh and crisp and the morning star had paled but was still visible. Hammond ambled about in a critical mood. He observed gates off hinges, a field of dry thistle seeding the adjacent land, wheelbarrows overturned in the weeds and left to the elements, a fruit orchard blighted and unpruned, a worm fence with half the rails broken. No wonder Woodford was in debt and needed money.

Hammond wandered back toward the house and sat down on the gallery, waiting for the family to stir. Sukey came out the side door and greeted him on her way to the quarters. It was not long before Katy followed, and Charles soon appeared.

"Whats to git them wenches gone afore Mamma gits up," he explained. "I reckon she know, but——"

"Course, she deaf," said Hammond. "Maybe——"

"That Blanche, she know and she blab. She make trouble however she kin. You ain't goin' to marry her? I likes you and I'm a-tellin' you," Charles warned again.

"Yas, I'm goin' to marry your sister!" Hammond declared positively.

"You kin crawdaddle outn of it," Charles suggested. "Tell her you pore. She don' want no pore man. You too good fer her, tha's all."

"You don't know if I good or not. I reckon she right pure and good and simple. Seem like to me."

"You honest. She ain't. She won't let you keep your fightin' nigger, I tell you, jest to be honery."

"I reckon she git used to it."

Mrs Woodford presided at the breakfast table with her hollow voice and her horn. Blanche appeared late in long riding-habit —the most striking costume in her sparse wardrobe. She had timed her entrance to occur after the rest of the party was seated when all eyes would be upon her, although she was interested only in Hammond's appraisal.

"Plannin' to ride some this mornin', darlin'?" asked Beatrix, cocking her horn.

Blanche nodded and shouted, "Hammond and me goin' a-ridin' right after breakfast."

"You'll wait fer prayers, of course," said her mother. "Mista and Miz Satherwait is here, and I'm sure Colonel Butler is a godly man. Hammond will kneel down with us."

"Cousin Hammond don't have to say his prayers," Charles announced. "He knelt down las' night."

Beatrix beamed on Hammond. "I hope, Son, you kneeled with him. I knows Cousin Hammond comin' to Jesus."

"I'm afeared I cain't go a-ridin', Cousin Blanche, or wait fer prayer neither," Hammond excused himself. "I got a long ride ahead and got to git me started. I craves to git me to Coign Plantation afore noon or a little after, and to git on my way to Falconhurst before nightfall."

Blanche intended merely to pout, which she believed she did very prettily, but found herself crying and abruptly left the table. Hammond pushed back his chair and followed her into the sitting-room, trying to appease her.

"You don' love me! You don' love me! I wouldn' marry you if they never was another man!" percolated into the dining-room and appalled the girl's father, who hastened into the sitting-room to settle the quarrel which threatened his calculations.

Charles's satisfaction was dampened by his fear that Blanche would never permit the boy to escape from her. Beatrix looked from one to another for an explanation of what was going on, but amid the embarrassment of the party nobody gave her one.

"Now, now, Blanche, darlin'," the Major consoled his daughter; "Hammond got to return to his plantation. He a busy

114

man. You s'pose he propose marriage the first day, an' he could stay an' spark?"

"But, Papa!" protested Blanche, drying her eyes. "It ain't fair, ain't decent. Nobody will believe me. Nobody think I got me a beau at all."

"We'll show 'em, won't we, Hammond? The quicker Hammond git home and talk to his papa, the quicker he git back and you gits married," said the Major.

"He already say he come the eighth of May," sobbed Blanche. "I wants he should stay now."

"I has got to git home and buy me that di'mon' ring," wheedled Hammond. "The quicker I buys it, the quicker it come."

This argument appeased the girl. She blew her nose and wiped her eyes. Hammond stooped and kissed her awkwardly and the three returned to the dining-room.

The Major beamed. "Jest a lovers' fuss," he proclaimed proudly. The tears of reconciliation still sparkled in Blanche's eyes as she again took her seat at breakfast.

As the party rose from the table, Charles placed his arm about Ham's shoulder and whispered a reminder, "You goin' to ast Papa kin I come to visit you at Falconhurst?"

Despite his distaste for the boy, Hammond's invitation was genial. "Major Woodford," Ham said, "Charles here wantin' to ride Falconhurst way. He right welcome, an' you lets him."

"I reckon he purty young to go gallivantin'," replied the Major. "Cain't trus' him."

"I ain't never been nowhures. Cain't go nowhures. I ain't no little boy no longer," argued the boy. "Cousin Hammond, he ben to New Orleans an' all over. I most as old."

"Don't ack like," said his father. "Mayhap and ifn you sends that money, I let him go."

"Course, he come, he got to do like I say," specified Hammond.

Hammond ordered his horse, and went into his bedroom to fetch his saddlebags. He stole a brief aside with Blanche in the parlour, from which the pair emerged embarrassed, the girl's hair dishevelled and tears in her eyes. Wash held the stallion by the bridle. The Major repeated his directions how best to get to Coign and warned of mire in the road through the swamp for about four miles.

Hammond dreaded Beatrix's kiss, which he knew that he couldn't avoid, braced himself and got it over. Beatrix wiped her eyes. Hammond shook hands all around. To Colonel Butler and

115

the Satherwaits the farewell was perfunctory; Charles was nervous, and Hammond wondered at the boy's anxiety to get him gone; Major Woodford held on to Hammond's hand, pumping it. "Reckon I better write a letter to your papa about that money?" he suggested aside. "I ain't very handy writin' letters."

"Won't do no good," Hammond told him. "Papa do whut I say. He send it—sure."

A final seemly kiss for Blanche, ardent enough to confirm his affections, brief enough not to violate propriety, and Hammond was in the saddle. The group stood back to be out of the way of the wheeling horse. What was intended as a brave smile, the stuff of heroines, appeared on Blanche's face.

Hammond walked his horse, looking back and waving, till he reached the public road and turned south. The rest of the party could not escape Beatrix's morning prayer meeting, and the Satherwaits had no desire to.

"A nice young gen'leman, and right well fixed, seems like," opined Mrs Satherwait. "A good wife will bring him right to Jesus."

"I aims to," said Blanche possessively.

CHAPTER EIGHT

THE HORSE under him again, the saddle between his legs, felt good to Hammond. The horse was fresh and broke into a slow canter. Hammond was not aimless, but he was in no haste except to escape from the cloying affability of Crowfoot. The sunshine poured down upon him.

Well, he had accomplished his errand, had got what he had come for. He was satisfied. Marriage was an obligation to his Hammond blood, which should not be permitted to perish. Blanche was petulant and would need to be humoured. But what was a white lady for but to humour? This one was certainly pretty, at least what parts of her he could see. He reflected on the challis dress. How small Blanche's waist! How full her breasts, and she so young! Hammond had little misgivings about her shape. What still bothered him was the expanse of pale flesh. But he would no doubt get used to it.

The road was good and he let the stallion have his head for a stretch, but the girth seemed loose and he drew up, dismounted and tightened it. The road led through a wood and Hammond felt strangely lonely. It was a new sensation; he had never been lonely. He had no desire to return to Crowfoot, but rather a longing to get back to Falconhurst, to see his Negroes and put them to work.

It was his father's errands quite as much as his own that took Hammond from home; it was his father's desire, even more than his own, that he be married; his father's passion for pure Mandingos was taking him to Coign Plantation. Riding out of the woods into a clearing, Hammond saw turkey buzzards against the blue of the sky; he watched the ease and grace with which they soared and glided. Farther on, down the wind from a clump of trees, his nostrils caught the stench of carrion.

He had come five, possibly six miles on his unhurried way without meeting anybody, but was sure he was on the right way to Coign when behind him he heard a horse at a hard gallop. He turned in the saddle and the other horseman raised his arm and beckoned him to wait. It was Charles.

"I'm a-goin' with you," Charles declared, out of breath.

"No, you not. You turnin' around and a-goin' right back to Crowfoot. You runnin' off."

"No, I not. Papa done say I kin," protested the boy.

"Say you kin whut?" Hammond demanded.

"Say I kin go home with you to Falconhurst. Don' you want me?"

"I wants you, all right. You welcome. But you lyin'."

"Papa did so, he said," Charles was vehement. "I ast him, and he say I should ketch up and go along with you. I swear he say it, I swear on the Bible."

"You hadn't ought to run your horse like that. He all over foam and he breathin'," admonished the older boy.

"I had to ketch up, didn' I?"

"I still thinks you lyin' to me."

Charles made an effort to focus his eyes to look Hammond in the face. "I swear," he said.

Hammond still did not credit the youth's oath, but his dislike for him had moderated, and Charles' company took the edge off his loneliness.

They reached their destination some hours later, after a leisurely journey spent mainly in discussing the desirability of owning fighting niggers. Coign sat on an eminence that was hardly to be called a hill. 'The Coign' in letters of Gothic, surrounded by filigree of wrought-iron, stretched about the two gates

117

of the same material, which stood open. The gilded knobs at the tops of the pickets which made the gates were so tarnished that they were nearer black than golden. Beyond the gates stretched a straight avenue of walnut trees, their branches meeting and interlacing, between the sturdy trunks of which could be seen the pillars of a Doric portico. Ham had not anticipated such magnificence.

The walnut trees ended abruptly on a lawn, but the driveway continued around the lawn in a symmetrical oval. The expanse of grass and weeds was broad enough to permit one coming up the avenue to stop at its end and enjoy the complete façade of the brick Georgian mansion, including the wings which flanked it at either end.

This was a mansion indeed. Chaste, and even austere, the house was uncluttered with ornamentation, and the eye was left free to appraise the delicate, yet sturdy, proportions of the whole edifice. Four tall chimneys took flight from the ends of the main part of the house, but failed to relieve the sombre picture. The white paint scaled from the heavy cornice and from the window frames of the wings, but under the roof of the portico it was unmarred.

A rheumatic old mulatto, neatly dressed and shod, appeared from around the corner of the house to take the horses. "Good evenin', gentlemen. Your horses are fatigued. I'll see to them," he said, bowing but without obsequiousness, and gesturing, palm upward, toward the door.

Hammond, followed by Charles, stepped on the porch and raised the brass knocker. Tender spears of yellow grass grew in a crack between the flagging of the floor. The wait was long and Ham was startled by his own voice when he remarked, "Nobody here, seem like, but only that ol' buck." He had reached toward the knocker a second time when the door swung silently open.

"Gentlemen!" the servant who opened it greeted the youths. "Mista Wilson is sleeping, but is due to wake. Will you not come in?" he asked cordially but without enthusiasm, and led the way across the wide hall into a large drawing-room, where he invited them to wait. He adjusted the curtains to admit more light, then withdrew.

This ancient butler had Caucasian features and was all but white. His jowls sagged and there were heavy bags beneath his eyes, but he had been handsome and was still distinguished in manner and courtly in bearing. He wore a livery of dark blue

118

satin, well rubbed but nowhere frayed, knee breeches and pow-
dered wool, drawn back and braided. Stockings of white silk
clothed his long legs.

The elegance of the room into which the boys were ushered
left them ill at ease. They whispered when they spoke. The walls
were of walnut with grey damask panels outlined in tarnished
gold. The draperies were of unfigured peacock blue velvet. The
Kirmanshaw carpet which covered the centre of the floor left a
wide border of polished oak. The furniture, if not Hepplewhite,
showed the Hepplewhite influence, and the chairs were covered
in a damask of yellow faded to old gold.

Above the marble mantel hung a large portrait of a tall man
of middle years but with sagging jowls and baggy eyelids, like
those of the butler. His long right hand rested upon the shoulder
of a young black Negro who looked up at him with admiration,
and on his left was depicted a handsome but leggy hound with
his eyes also fixed on his master. There were no other pictures or
ornaments. The portrait might have been by Benjamin West,
but was somewhat too late for his American period.

The boys did not hear the approach of Mr Wilson when at
length he came, their backs were toward him. He greeted them
with the single word, "Gentlemen."

Old, feeble and palsied, Wilson still seemed a monarch. But
here was another version of the portrait and the butler.

"Gentlemen," he repeated, "I demand your pardon. I was
sleeping and my servant refused to wake me. Your pardon, suhs."

"Mista Wilson, suh?" Hammond asked.

"The same, suh, at your service."

"I Hammond Maxwell, son of Mista Warren Maxwell of
Falconhurst Plantation."

"You?" the old man asked. "You?" He placed his hand on the
boy's shoulder and led him toward a window, stepped back and
looked him up and down and focused on his face. He nodded his
head and extended his hand. "Well, well. I'm glad to see you,
son." He looked at Charles and asked, "And this young man?"

"Charles Woodford, Major Woodford's son, of Crowfoot. I'm
goin' to marry me his daughter, the Major's daughter that is, and
this Charles ridin' home with me to Falconhurst."

"I am acquainted with the Major—slightly that is; very estim-
able, I believe," the old man guarded his statement. "I'm glad to
see you, suh," he said to Charles; he turned to Hammond, "Con-
gratulations on your approaching marriage. Warren Maxwell

119

will be pleased. You are an only son, I believe? Or is there another?"

"Ain't no other. Ain't nobody but Papa and me," said Hammond.

"He is fortunate to have even one son," sighed Wilson. "My eldest son was killed, shot to death in a duel. The younger boy died of the fever. Two boys and four girls, all dead. One of the girls perished in childbirth, the others died young. Warren Maxwell is fortunate."

The old man felt behind him for the seat of the chair on which he was about to drop. "How is your papa?"

"He tol'able, except his rheumatiz purty bad. Betterin' though," explained Hammond. "I reckon he right dismal with me away. He worry when I leaves Falconhurst."

"Well he may, well he may. All boys are damned fools, especially if they have any spirit. No knowing what they're doing when you take your eyes off them. You're young?"

"I'm eighteen," Hammond remonstrated. "Nigh on to nineteen. And Papa don't think I a damned fool. He trust me, but he like me with him—jest craves me."

"Don't wonder, don't wonder at all. Must be twelve years or more since I saw Warren. He was much younger than I, much younger, but I liked him. Used to be crazy about black wenches, I remember, or any other colour for the matter of that, but the blacker the better. I envied him his youth and vigour. I was already ageing."

"Reckon he still craves 'em, only his rheumatiz——"

"Last time I saw him, he came here and talked me out of as fine a big Mandingo wench as I ever saw and her female child, about three years old and big enough to be five—handsome. I didn't want to sell them, but Warren had to have them—just crazy about Mandingos."

"Still is. That's whut I come fer," declared Hammond.

"Wonder whether he still has that wench and that child? The little one must be big enough to breed, almost."

"Still got ol' Lucy, and Big Pearl we calls the young wench. They fine. Lucy still breedin' and the young one ready. That whut I doin' at Coign Plantation."

Wilson levered himself upright with his hands on the arms of his chair. "Let us retire to the library where there is a fire, and we can talk better there," he suggested. "The evenings get chilly and at my age one likes the heat."

He led the way and Charles put his hand on his arm to guide him.

"Never mind," Wilson resented the aid. "I can still walk alone, a little feebly, but I can still walk."

Despite his protest at Charles's assistance, the aged man submitted to help from the butler who grasped his arm and steadied his way across the hall. Except for the clothes, and that the butler was younger, the two were singularly alike.

"No good from trying to fight him off," smiled the elder appreciatively as the younger man eased him into a chair. "Bent upon having me helpless. That comes of having a son for a servant; he does what he wants to me and won't take orders. Thinks he knows more than his master."

"You need help, suh," said the servant.

"I know it," resigned the master. "Chairs, gentlemen."

"Do you want your paisley, suh?"

"No, no, let me alone, Ben," replied the pampered old man. "But you might bring us a bottle of that Madeira, please; you know the kind, the Malvasia. The young gentlemen might enjoy it."

"Yes, suh; right away, suh."

The old man nodded in the direction of the slave, and explained, "I wasn't older than you, Mr Maxwell, when old Ben was born—the first male I ever got and about the best. My get had all been girls before that—at least I believed them mine, although my older brother often poached on my domain and I wasn't sure. Ben's dam was a griffe wench my father had given me for my own use; I think she was his own get. I raised Ben and trained him and he has been faithful. One gets fond of a slave after seventy years. I think Ben is seventy-one or seventy-two. I'm eighty-seven. If you want a good servant, get him yourself and break him to your ways, and you know what you have."

"I kind of plan to sell off my bucks and keep my own wenches. Course, they all little yet, and not many," said Hammond.

"Hold on to a nice, likely buck, too," the old man advised. "It's comforting to have your own when you're old."

Cases of calfbound books, a few with spines stained or cracked, lined the room, and above the bookcases the varnish over the white panelling had yellowed to tones of old ivory. Behind the four capacious chairs that ranged before the fireplace stretched a substantial table with account books, an inkwell, feather pens, a sand box, three or four of the calfbound books for which there

121

were vacancies in the cases, and a standing candelabrum at each end. This seemed to be the old man's retreat.

"Whut I come here fer was——" Hammond began.

"To pay me a visit, I hope." Wilson forestalled him from stating his errand. "This old tomb needs the sound of young voices. I could well wish that you might stay a week, a month, a year, as long as you will and listen to the garrulity of an old man."

"We has to git along towards Falconhurst," said Hammond.

"Yes, yes, tomorrow or the day after, or the day after that. Meanwhile, to worry will do Warren good, teach him patience, give him to know what it means to have a son, how precious a son can be," and Wilson bent forward at the cost of some energy and reached out to pat Hammond on his stiffened knee.

"I don't crave that Papa should fret none about me. Papa count on me."

Ben returned with a dustladen bottle and three glasses on a tray which he set carefully upon the table. He wiped the bottle on a napkin, tenderly, inserted the corkscrew and pulled the cork, raised the bottle gently to his nostrils to appraise the bouquet, and poured the wine into the glasses. He passed the salver first to his master, next to Charles, lastly to Hammond, with a manner like that of a sovereign bestowing decorations.

His owner passed the wine back and forth under his nose, savoured a short sip of it and nodded to the slave. He raised his glass toward Hammond and proposed a toast, "To Warren Maxwell and to his son who is like him," and then, as a polite afterthought, he added, bowing in Charles' direction, "And to Major Woodford and his son, suh." He tasted the wine again, and smacked. "How do you like it, gentlemen?"

"It good, but I not knowin' whut is it. I never had none like this afore now," said Hammond candidly.

"It is Madeira—Malmsey; one learns to like the sweet stuff," Wilson said. "You may have some, Ben. Get you a glass."

"Thank you, suh."

Hammond was anxious to transact his business. He liked his ancient host but felt himself remiss to squander time. He failed to fathom the old man's motive in his avoidance of the discussion of the mission, which was in fact merely to prolong Hammond's stay. Wilson had not expected guests, but his pleasure in entertaining them was dampened by the dread of their early departure.

Hammond tried again. "Whut I come here fer, Mista Wilson,

122

suh, was you got an ol' Mandingo buck an' Papa craves you to borrow the buck to him to breed them two wenches."

"The two you got from me? Warren knows that old buck was the sire of both of them, the young one in-bred to him already."

"Yas, suh, Mista Wilson. Papa know that, but he don't know nobody else who gotten a Mandingo, a pure one. He craves to try it again, craves you to borrow him the buck. Won't take long, and Papa will pay you."

"Nonsense. Pay? Nonsense. But I haven't that buck. He's dead. A bull gored him about three months ago and old Xerxes died."

"Papa had laid store," said Hammond, betraying his own disappointment.

"Warren Maxwell and his Mandingos! He is Mandingo mad!"

"Mighty sweet niggers; I likes 'em, too," Ham defended his father.

"Of course you do; you've been taught to," said Wilson. "But there are Mandingos and Mandingos. I have known Mandingos that weren't worth killing, although they are admittedly hard to kill. They are tough. I was fortunate with the bozals I got and in the progeny they produced. The original pair were big handsome varmints; old Xerxes was the original buck. They were related somehow. They tried to tell me their kinship, but never could make it clear; possibly it wasn't clear even to them."

"That makes Big Pearl more bred-in even than Papa knowin'; even Lucy was bred-in, seems like."

"No telling how far back the incest may go. I think it's time to stop it. Of course, I know that it results in progeny of exceptional excellence or of more exceptional degeneration. There is no middle ground. It produces paragons or monsters—nobody knows why," Wilson expounded.

"But, Big Pearl and Lucy?" Hammond refused to be diverted. "Whut we goin' to do?"

"I'd look about for a good Mandingo buck of another strain, one quite unrelated," suggested Wilson, but without conviction. "Where? I don't know."

"Folks says they is plenty in Cuba," despaired Hammond.

"In Cuba, yes. But smuggling Negroes is dangerous, unless you are in the business as a business and bribe the authorities to let your contraband through. It doesn't pay to smuggle a single buck; and, anyway, you should see the buck."

The subject bored Charles. "Ain't you got no buck niggers at

123

all? A buck's a buck. Don't make no difference. Whut you craves is a sucker, ain't it?"

"The sire makes a great deal of difference, young man," said the old man. "Never breed a Mandingo to a member of another tribe. Keep the stock pure. A hybrid cross with a Mandingo, a Mandingo mule, as I call it, is treacherous, untrustworthy. Half the bad niggers you hear about have Mandingo blood somewhere, and the wenches are as bad as the bucks—worse."

"That whut Papa say. That why he craves your old buck fer them wenches."

"He's right. A pure Mandingo is playful as a kitten, strong as a bull-elephant. A half Mandingo is a viper, a viper, suh. Now, I'll tell you, I have the brother of that Pearl—do you call her?"

"Big Pearl, yas, suh."

"I have the full brother of Big Pearl, from Lucy bred back to Xerxes. He is about three years, nearly four, older than Pearl. Handsome an animal as ever you saw—bigger, finer all over than Xerxes. If you want to take him along with you and let your papa look at him and try him, you're welcome to do so. That is, if he wants to go, and he will want to."

"I'd have to keep him until May, when I come back to Crowfoot fer my weddin'."

"That's all right. Keep him as long as you like. When you are through with him, write him a pass, give him a package of pone and turn him loose. He'll come home. There's only one thing."

"Yas, suh."

"He is mortgaged, in the amount of fifteen hundred dollars, I think—it may be only twelve hundred—and a couple of year's interest. The whole of The Coign is mortgaged and every stick of furniture and every slave. The mortgages are all mature and interest is delinquent, and I am just living here on the sufferance of the Jew, who refuses to kick an old man out and is waiting for me to die to foreclose upon his property. Jew Wertheimer of Mobile, no matter what folks may say about Jews, is a white man. If that Mandingo buck should die or even be crippled while he is your possession, you'd have to pay off the mortgage on him. I wouldn't want the Jew to stand the loss, after his leniency to me, and I should be unable to pay him."

"Of course, that all right. Papa do that, of course. I'll give you a writin' about it."

"No writing required, just a clear understanding. If Warren

Maxwell's boy isn't good for a dead nigger, my faith in human nature dies and I might as well die with it. I haven't lived eighty-seven years without learning to know men, especially when I know their breeding—and you can't deny yours. Maybe you'd like to see him."

"I'd thank you, suh. Sure would like to see that Mandingo."

"Is he a fightin' nigger?" Charles asked.

"Cain't you never think about nothin' but fightin', Charles?" demanded Hammond.

"Ben, oh Ben," Wilson called, pounding on the floor with the poker to summon the butler, who appeared immediately. "Round up that Ganymede and bring him in here."

"Whut you call that boy, Mista Wilson? Ganymede, whut kind of name is that?" Hammond asked.

"I usually call him Mede. I carry him in the books and on the mortgage as Ganymede."

"That whut I take you to say. Whut it mean?"

"Well, to tell it without blushing, Zeus, the sovereign god of the Greeks, saw a boy named Ganymede and fell so in love with him that he sent a great eagle to steal the boy and to carry him off in its talons to Mount Olympus where the boy served Zeus as a cup-bearer, that is he poured his wine, and for other purposes."

"Other purposes? Whut other purposes?"

"Well, other purposes—whatever Zeus wanted."

The door opened and Ben asked, "Ready for Mede, suh?"

"Yes, let him come in," replied the master.

Mede bounded in and filled the room, which was not large enough to give him scope. His legs seemed made of springs. He moved like a stallion and yet maintained the dignity of a potentate. Though some six feet two or three inches, he looked taller than he was. He seemed incapable of fear, and his subservience to his kindly master derived from devotion.

"Mede, come here," was hardly uttered when the boy was across the floor, standing docile but nervous in front of the old man's chair.

Hammond noticed that his skin was not dead black but a deep, warm brown, like polished walnut, with vague hints of red in the cheeks. His eyes were spaced wide in his broad face, but within the temples, flush with the cheeks and without much overhang to the brow of the low forehead. The bridge of the nose was not quite flat and the enormous round nostrils were animated by the

125

boy's breathing. The large, regular teeth were yellow and bone-like behind the wide opening which formed the thick-lipped but not protruding mouth. The lower jaw was massive and square. A mat of kinky, coarse wool grew low and formed a straight line across the forehead. The effect was barbaric, like some rough hewn sculpture, a great unfinished carving, with a head so powerful and primitive as to inspire fear—except for the eyes, black, longlashed, and benevolent. The eyes rested on their master with adoration.

"Mede, step out of your clothes and show these gentlemen what you have." The command was modulated into a request. "They won't mind a little musk, if Ben didn't give you time to wash yourself."

"Masta, are you planning to sell me?" Mede asked with interest but without alarm.

"No such luck," scoffed the master. "You know damned well, Mede, that I wouldn't sell you without asking you."

"You need money, Masta, and I'm worth a good price. It's all right with me if you want to sell me." Mede was kneeling to unbuckle his shoes.

"I'll do the worrying around The Coign about getting all of us something to eat, boy, and I won't have to sell you either. I don't eat my slaves. The reason I'd like to sell you is to know what is going to happen to you, to get you a good master before I die."

"I knows that, Masta."

"God damn it, stop that nigger talk. You grew up to speak English," the first harshness the master had shown.

"I know, Masta," Mede corrected himself contritely.

"That's better."

"Yes, suh. Let the old niggers, Ben and the others, worry about new masters. I'll bring too much money on the block for a new masta to treat me bad." Mede cast aside his shirt and stepped out of his pants.

Hammond nodded his head in approval. "A right purty boy," he said. "Looks like Big Pearl, too, even bigger. Right purty," he repeated.

Soundness was not in question, but Hammond rose to run exploratory hands over the boy's shoulders and arms, stroked his thighs and smiled his admiration. Hammond knew a fine Negro when he looked at one.

Wilson realized the pleasure Hammond took from seeing so magnificent an animal, and, connoisseur himself, sensed Hammond's speechless admiration. Ham merely looked at the old man and nodded.

"Thought perhaps you'd like him. Young, not at his best even yet, but a better buck than his sire. Think Warren would want to use him?"

"Papa sure would admire to see him. Just whut he cravin' fer Lucy and Big Pearl. He splendiferous," answered Hammond.

Ganymede, aware of his own magnificence, made the most of it. He flexed his muscles, twisted his body from side to side, stooped and rose.

"Mede, squat down there and listen to me," said the master. "Mr Maxwell, here, is—or, rather, Mr Maxwell's father is an old friend of mine."

"Yes, suh," Mede said.

"He wants to keep the breed pure. Mr Maxwell wants to borrow you for stock, and I'd like to accommodate him. What do you say? Do you want to go with him? Nobody is going to make you."

"What you say, Masta. When do we start?"

"I'll tell you later. Mr Maxwell will stay here a few days. I'll tell you. Now, take your rags and go back to the quarters."

Mede threw his shirt and trousers over his arm and stooped to gather his shoes.

"Wait," Ham interposed, at last finding words for the exciting idea that had been growing in his mind since Mede appeared. "Mista Wilson, would you sell this buck?"

The old man hesitated. "You'd want him for yourself and not to sell again?" he asked.

Mede looked at Wilson, then at Hammond, and again at Wilson. He trusted his master, but was no indifferent spectator of his destiny.

"Wants him to keep," Hammond explained. "Fact is, I wants him fer a fighter. I ben lookin' around. Kin he fight, do you reckon?"

"Sure kin. Sure kin fight," Charles interposed. The very word thrilled him. "Buy him; why don't you?"

"I don't know," said Wilson. "He's strong enough. When old Xerxes was gored, the young one grabbed hold of that bull's horns and broke its neck. Can you fight, Mede?"

"Who you want me to whip? What for?" the Negro asked, with a show of interest, even of alacrity. "Yes, suh, I can fight. Yes, suh."

"I've heard something about this recent sport of fighting bucks, but I never saw a main of it. Something we didn't do in my days," said Wilson. "Must be exciting as a horse race, but dangerous. I'd hate to have Mede ruined in a fight."

"All the young gen'lemen has their fightin' boys," explained Hammond. "I ben a-cravin' one. Papa say I should buy me one, but buy a good one, one that kin whup."

"This here one is good. He kin win for us. Whyn't you buy him?"

"Don't know yet does Mista Wilson crave to sell him," Hammond answered.

"Yes, I'd sell him—to you," Wilson conceded. "That is, provided the boy wants to go. Think you want to, Mede? Want to be Mr Maxwell's fighting nigger?"

"And have those wenches all the time?" the Negro stipulated.

"Well, when we not readyin' fer a fight. Won't have you wearin' yourse'f out a-pesterin' wenches," Hammond made that clear.

"Wouldn't hurt him none," Charles interposed, and was ignored.

"Mr Maxwell will treat you well. Good food and plenty. Of course, things will not be the same as here. You would have to find Mr Maxwell's ways and follow them; obey him. What do you say? I can't live much longer, and it is better than being sold on the block to you don't know whom."

"It is better," Mede agreed.

"How much you want fer him, Mr Wilson, suh?" asked Hammond.

"I don't know. I just don't know. Mede is a sort of fancy nigger—something special that ought to bring a good figure. As I said, the Jew in Mobile lent me twelve or fifteen hundred on him—I don't remember the exact amount—and you know what that means he's worth," the owner speculated. "No telling what such a boy would bring in the market, but to you, to your father, to a good home where he won't be abused and overworked—is three thousand dollars out of the way? Is it too much?"

"I reckon he worth it. A right purty boy." Hammond hesitated. He reached out and pulled Mede toward him. "Kneel down," he commanded. He had forgotten to examine the teeth.

"Find anything wrong with him after you get him home, or if Warren doesn't like him, turn him loose and tell him to come back to The Coign. There'll be no hard feeling," Wilson specified.

"Papa will cotton on to him, all right," said Hammond, stroking the black shoulder.

"That's too much," Wilson decided. "Can't bleed the son of an old friend. I said three thousand; make it twenty-seven hundred and fifty. That's better. That's enough. That's all any nigger is worth."

"I'll come back next week and git him," Ham promised. "I ain't got that much—not with me. I'll come, sure. You won't sell this buck to somebody else, Mista Wilson, suh?"

"Don't talk nonsense. Take him along. Take him with you. You can send the money."

Mede rose to his feet, again picked up his clothes, then sank to his knees before the old man's chair, embracing Wilson with his arms and burying his face against his chest. He was convulsed with sobs.

"What's the matter, Mede? I asked you first, before I sold you. There, there, Mr Maxwell will release us from my bargain. You won't have to go. Get up."

Mede clung to Wilson the tighter. "It's best," he said. "I want to go. I want a wench. I want to fight. But I love The Coign. I love you, Masta. You're so good, Masta, suh, and so old. I love you."

Wilson ran his fragile fingers through the wool of the great black head and patted it gently. Then he loosened the boy's hold on him and pushed him away. Tears gathered in his eyes, but he did not wipe them away. He looked out of the window as Mede rose and gathered his clothes.

"That all, Masta?"

"That's all, Mede. You can go now. That is, unless your masta, your new masta, has orders for you."

"No, I reckon not," said Ham. "You kin go. Be ready in the mornin', early like."

The silence that ensued after the Negro had gone was broken by Charles. "He right powerful buck. We carry him to town and fight him next Sat'day? Eh, Cousin Hammond?"

"We trains him first. We got to learn him and toughen him."

Ben entered with an armload of wood for the fire, and discharged it. As he brushed the ashes that littered the hearth, nobody spoke. He rose to go.

"I sold Mede, Ben," his master announced.

"Sold Mede? I didn't think you'd do that, suh. Then The Coign is breaking up. We'll all go soon."

"Yes, we'll all go soon," echoed the master.

"Supper will be ready right away, suh. We're having a haunch of venison, that young doe that Old Frank shot up by the wood lot."

"Ought not to shoot does. Let 'em live and breed. Tell Frank not to shoot does," said Wilson, frowning. Frank had no sense of values.

The Colonel's punctilious observance of a host's duties was further demonstrated after the evening meal which Ben served with slow ceremony.

"We go to bed early at The Coign. Not much else to do. Reading by candlelight, hard on the eyes, although I want to go through Propertius once more, just once more, before I die," Wilson declared, pushing back his chair from the supper table and draining the port from his glass. "But you'll want wenches for the night, I suspect. I haven't fogotten when I was young."

"Not needful, suh. Really not needful. I plenty tired out from ridin' all the way from Crowfoot," Hammond made a polite protest.

"And you, suh?" The old man turned to Charles. "You're not too young to wrestle with a healthy wench? I have no desire to corrupt youth."

Charles looked at his plate with embarrassment. "I has a wench at home, suh. My papa given her to me."

"Well, well, I supposed so," said Wilson. "Ben, are those three girls ready? Bring 'em in and let the young gentlemen take their choice."

"That Lutitia can't come, suh. It's her time, her time of the month, suh," Ben explained.

"Well, bring the two," Wilson commanded. "I've been waiting for some personable young white men for these girls. Except for their brother, their half brother, I have no young buck for them and I do not feel like putting them to a wornout old man. They're too nice. Fact is, they're fancies."

Ellen and Edna had been waiting in the kitchen for this summons. They edged their way through the door in Ben's wake and took places in the shadows beside it. Edna smothered a giggle with her hand. Both were enveloped in starched frocks that reached the floor.

"Come here, my dears, and let the gentlemen look at you," commanded Wilson, extending his hand in invitation.

They came forward with a show of reluctance and stood beside

130

their master's chair. Both looked steadily at the floor. Wilson grasped Ellen's hand and patted it.

"You're virgin, aren't you, Ellen? That is, you are pure—you never had a man. Isn't that so?" the master inquired.

Ellen nodded.

"These gentlemen, Mr Maxwell and Mr Woodford, want you to sleep with them—in their beds. You know what that means, don't you?"

Ellen blushed and nodded again, and Edna suppressed another giggle.

"You want to do it? You're sure?"

"Whatever Masta says," assented Ellen. The assent of the other was silence.

"You gentlemen will have to decide between yourselves which is for which. There is little to choose, I judge. Come around and let the gentlemen look at you, Ellen."

Hammond's indifference was real. "Either," he said.

"I likes the little 'un, the light 'un. I'd sooner have her," Charles declared without reticence.

"These two and the other one are the only young wenches I have left. I had a young overseer at The Coign for a couple of seasons about sixteen or seventeen years ago—a good looking, well set up youth, named Hall, Willis Hall. White trash, I suppose, but he made good cotton crops. The wenches on the plantation were all crazy for him, and he just as crazy for them. I didn't have a good light stock buck at the time, and so I let this Hall have his way. I'd have him yet, I suppose, but he got religion, took to praying all over the plantation, finally wound up with a craving to preach. He had visions of some kind, said he heard the Lord calling him to gather sinners. One month he wouldn't touch a wench; the next month he was at them worse than ever. I think the call to preach was a mere satiety with yellow flesh and a craving for white women; niggers no longer good enough for him. He left, and I haven't had any luck with overseers since, nor a fair crop of cotton."

"Willis Hall? That was the preacher at Benson last year, till he got into some kind of a scrape," said Hammond.

"I hear of him around, now and again. Made quite a preacher," said Wilson. "Woman scrape, I guess?"

"No, somethin' about him and another feller from Natchez tryin' to steal a nigger. We'd a hung him if we had proof. Way it come out, they jest run him off."

131

"Well, Hall was the sire of these two. I think you may like them." Wilson got to his feet. "Ben will tell you where the gentlemen will sleep, young women; be sure you're clean."

"Your bedtime, Masta, suh," announced Ben. "Come along now, please, suh. Time to go up."

"Well, orders are orders, gentlemen," the old man sighed resignedly. "Ben will take care of you. I trust you enjoy those wenches, but no obligation. Goodnight. Ben will show you up when you're ready." As he spoke, the butler's hand under his arm helped him to rise.

Hammond rose and beckoned to Charles to do likewise. Wilson extended his hand to Charles first. As he clasped Hammond's hand, he said, "Bless you for coming, my boy. You're like your papa. You won't forget to give him my compliments."

Soon Ben came back. "Want for anything, gentlemen?"

"Only to go to bed," said Hammond. "Take us up, when you are ready."

"Then come with me, suh," said the old butler.

At the head of the stairs he threw open a door and bowed. "For the younger gentleman," he said. "I think you will find all you need, suh; but I shall return." Farther down the hall, he showed Hammond into a corner room, lighted by six candles in two candelabra.

Hammond looked around at the elegance, the didoed paper and the tester bed curtained with silk damask, before he saw Ellen, risen from her chair. No fire burned in the fireplace, which was small and looked as if it had never been used.

The butler apologized for the musty smell. "I had wished you to sleep in another room, freshly aired, but the Master designated this larger apartment too late, and I did not wish to admit the night air, suh," he said. "Here is a fresh nightcap, if you care for one, and there are additional covers on this chair if the weather turns cold. It feels like rain coming on."

Hammond sat upon the bed. "You'll got to he'p me off with my boot," he said to Ellen. "I'm cripped, you knows."

"Yes, suh; I know, Masta," Ellen said, advancing and kneeling before Hammond and reaching forward for his foot.

"Don't be afeared, Ellen. I ain't a-goin' to eat you up."

"I'm not afraid, Masta," but Ellen was afraid. She succeeded in drawing off his boots before she burst into tears.

"Everythin' all right, nigger. Don't cry. You not want a crip

132

to pester you, you don' have to. You kin go, time you gits my clothes off. I not very horny, noways."

"It's not that, Masta. I just don't know how. Don't know how you wants me, suh. I want to please you, suh."

"Of course you pleases me. You pleases me right good, firs' rate." Hammond rose to his stockinged feet and lifted and embraced the girl.

They were standing so when Ben returned with a pan of coals to warm the bed. "Wench won't strip, suh?" he asked, and before Hammond could reply he placed the warming pan on the hearth, yanked the buttons from the dress of the unresistant girl and her frock dropped to the floor. "Get them into the big house and they grow coy, act as if they thought a gentleman never saw a naked wench." Ben gave the girl's buttock a smart slap with his palm. "Fat," he said; "we'll have to work it off."

Ellen shrank from the old man, as she raised her dropped eyes in a hasty glance at Hammond's face.

"She just right. I likes 'em plump like." Hammond came to the girl's defence. "Nice limbs, too, not stringy like," he added, stooping to run his hand in appraisal over Ellen's calf. Ben's disparagement of the wench dissipated Hammond's indifference and aroused his interest.

"Perhaps you will find her comfortable, suh. May have to be firm. Use her like your own, suh." Ben had taken up the warming pan and was passing it slowly backward and forward between the sheets. He released the curtains and drew them along the sides of the bed, leaving a space between them through which to enter it. "If you need me," he added, "I sleep on the floor outside the Masta's chamber, which is next to this one."

"I ain't a-goin' to need you. The wench is all right."

"Shall I relieve you of your clothes?"

"Ellen will help me," replied Hammond, irritated by the preciseness of the slave's speech; it made him conscious of the shortcomings of his own. He was relieved when the butler said goodnight and left the room.

Hammond sat in a low chair and submitted to Ellen as she stripped his clothes from him, careful not to touch his flesh. Her head was down and Hammond was unaware that she was weeping until she stifled a sob.

"Whut the matter, Ellen?" he asked. "You ac' like a white lady, cryin' an' all. Don't you know you ain't nothin' but a nigger?

133

You don' like me, you doesn't have to stay." Hammond sought awkwardly to console the girl.

"I like you, Masta, I like you. Please let me stay, just tonight, just one night. I know I'm not pretty enough for your bed. I'm fat and I'm ugly, but I'll try."

Ellen's misgivings about her beauty were not justified. Her breasts were immature but firm. Her large brown eyes were shaded by long lashes and stood well apart in her oval face with its low cheekbones. There was a shallow cleft in her chin, and only the slight fullness of her lips hinted her Negro origin, for she was lighter than many white women, lighter, Ham reflected with growing interest, by two shades than his Cousin Beatrix.

Ellen was on her knees before him, and, chary as she had been of contact with his person while she removed his clothes, she lunged impetuously forward, embraced his body and planted her cheek firmly against his belly.

Her gesture aroused Hammond and he lifted her into his arms and kissed her with pity. Quickly pity turned to passion so that he was taken aback to realize what he had done. In his code, a wench was for fornication, not for dalliance. Only the previous night, he had been shocked at the display of Charles's affection for Katy. Perhaps his code needed revision. At the kiss, his blood quickened, his flesh tingled, and his indifference vanished.

He turned down the covers. "You crawl in," he said, "while I kneels down."

"But the candles?"

"Reckons I cain't snuff 'em?"

Next morning Hammond took his place at the table and helped himself to ham and eggs.

"Sleep well, Mr Maxwell? Your wench happy?" Wilson inquired perfunctorily.

The latter question opened a subject which Hammond was reluctant to broach. "That wench, Mista Wilson," he began. "Well, would you sell Ellen?"

"Sell Ellen?" the host chuckled. "I suppose then you were pleased with her. Remember, she'll never be the same again. Maidenheads don't grow back again."

"I never took Ellen's."

"No? She was difficult? You were strange to her. I regret——"

"Wasn't no fault of Ellen. She begged me, but I wants her mine—all of her—before I rapes her. Won't you sell her to me?"

"I suppose Ellen is as safe with you as with anybody, my boy,

134

safer. She's too pretty. It's her misfortune. She's a fancy girl, and will go to some sporting gentleman who will use her awhile and sell her again. I'd like you to have her. Did you consult Ellen?"

"She say she like me a kind a lot. She want to go with me. Will you sell her to me, suh? Ellen willin'."

"What will you give? What offer?"

"Whut you say, suh, Mista Wilson. However much you asts. But I wants to take her right along with me, if you please. I kin leave that Mandingo buck and come back fer him and bring you the money. But I wants to take Ellen. How much you wants?" Hammond in his urgency left himself vulnerable.

Ellen's owner was fortunately less interested in the price than in the buyer. He closed his eyes and the boy thought that he had dropped off to sleep. His lids fluttered and opened. "Um, fifteen hundred, I suppose. I know she would bring more after I'm gone, but fifteen hundred will do nicely."

"Thank you, suh. That ain't enough hardly."

"It's enough. If Warren doesn't like her, you can pass her on at a profit."

"Papa, he goin' t' like her. He got to like her. He got to," Hammond reiterated.

"If you don't take that cherry before you get Ellen home, Warren will. His rheumatism isn't that bad, I warrant."

"Then Ellen mine, and I kin take her along?"

"Yes, and I want to send her brother as a present to Warren."

"I'll buy him offen you, an' Ellen wants him," Hammond offered.

"No, I want to give him to Warren Maxwell, want to know that he will not be sold. Warren wouldn't sell a present."

"Mighty kin' of you, suh. But—niggers are worth money, suh. You could sell——"

"I know, but this young buck is different—sound and healthy, but frail, thin-skinned. Not built right for heavy work."

"But Papa don't——"

"I know it's an imposition, but Warren will take him to accommodate an old friend. Broken to the house, Jason will make Warren a good servant. No mortgage on him. The Jew wouldn't lend on him at the time. I can dispose of him as I please."

"Reckon it won't git you in no trouble with the Jew fer me to take along Ellen and the big buck without payin'?"

"No trouble at all. You can send me the money—enough to discharge the mortgages on them, that is. For the rest there's no hurry, no hurry at all. I'll live a few months yet, and if I don't——" Wilson raised his hands from the arms of his chair in completion of his sentence.

The entry of Charles diverted the host from his morbid speculation.

"You goin' to have to take a nigger on the crupper," Hammond explained to him.

"An' he cain't run, better you and me straddle your horse and let him have mine. That buck big as you and me together."

"Not him. Not the Mandingo. He kin keep up alongside. I—I bought me a wench and Mista Wilson here done give me a nice saplin' buck fer Papa."

"Cain't that saplin' run?" Charles asked. "You'll want the wench behind you I reckon. Whyn't the little buck ride the big one?"

"Better take along my old buckboard," Wilson suggested. "You can return it at your convenience."

"We make out all right, Mista Wilson, suh; Mede on foot, the young buck behin' Charles, Ellen behin' me. We go fine. Ellen ride astraddle, cain't she?"

"If you tell her to. It's the best way to ride double for a long distance."

Mede had the temerity to seat himself upon the portico, knowing that amid the adieux he would not be reprimanded. He held his shoes on his lap lest he should leave them behind, and pensively played with his bare toes.

Ellen's brother, Jason, slight and girlish-looking, rounded the house and joined Mede, but did not sit down. Ellen, when she came, was red-eyed from weeping, and she twice returned to the quarters but both times emerged again without carrying anything. She stood apart from the others.

Some twenty hands, old and of middle age, accumulated at the side of the mansion, but none ventured beyond its façade. Edna and Letitia ran furtively forward to give final kisses to Ellen, who clung to them, and to Jason, who assumed indifference. Mede watched them and knew that if those kisses had been for him he would have wept.

The occasion was a solemn one for the three, none of whom had ever passed the boundaries of The Coign. To go had been their own determination. Their old master would not have disposed of them without their assent.

The front door opened and Charles came out, followed by Wilson, guided by Ben. Hammond came last. The host shook the hands of his two guests, and amid expressions of mutual pleasure, Charles and Hammond mounted their horses. Charles was restive and annoyed at Wilson's prolonged farewell to the slaves. Hammond sat his horse patiently and waited.

Mede stood diffidently apart while the master kissed and blessed the boy and girl, adjured them to obedience. He went bashfully with hanging head when he was summoned, and when his master reached for his gross head a tear stood in his eye. Mede could not remember being kissed before and it suddenly came over him that he would never again see the man to whose kindness he had owed ample food, shelter, protection, the absence of positive abuse, what between master and slave is justice, mercy even.

The stallion, unused to being ridden double, shied and reared in protest when Ellen, with a boost from the groom, sought to mount behind Hammond. With the second try, she seated herself sidewise behind the saddle but her long skirt impeded her from getting her leg across the horse.

"Cain't ride that a-way," Hammond complained. "You'll slide off an' pull me with you. Have to straddle."

Ellen tucked her dress upwards until it reached her knees, slid backward over the horse's croup and manoeuvred her leg across in front of her. She then edged herself forward into as comfortable a seat as she could attain. She was uneasy about the display of her legs and tried to pull down her skirt.

"Nev' mind showin' your limbs. We ain't goin' to meet no ladies on the road nohow, day like this. Hold on to me tight till Eclipse here gits usen to you. Don' be afeared; I ain't pizen. Put your arms around my belly. That's right."

Jason, with the aid of the groom, swung himself handily behind Charles and encircled his body, the boy's legs dangling loosely over the gelding's loins.

"Ready, Mede? Then come along," said Hammond, putting his horse into motion and setting the pace at a slow walk as the riders rounded the lawn and turned into the avenue of walnuts. Mede followed the horses at a slow jog, carrying his shoes.

CHAPTER NINE

APPROACHING Falconhurst, Hammond's heart beat faster. He had been away less than a week, but homing aroused in him emotions which he did not understand. Here he belonged. From this soil he had been fashioned and he acknowledged his kinship with it. They reached the road that turned from the main highway toward the Widow Johnson's place, now probably Doc Redfield's. The way was straight ahead; Charles on his slower horse, which had gone lame a few miles back, would be unable to lose his way. Hammond loosed his reins and Eclipse, who knew as surely as his rider that he was nearing the end of his journey, broke first into a canter and then into a gallop. Ellen clung firmly to Hammond's body. Mede was unable to keep up with Eclipse, but lost ground gradually, and Charles made no effort to press his mount.

Before he reached the lane, Eclipse began to neigh at intervals and as he turned toward the house he nickered again and received a nicker in reply from the stables. Half down the lane Old Beller the hound came bounding and barking his greeting, not so much for Hammond as for Eclipse. Hammond had reached the house before the Mandingo had turned into the lane.

Three or four Negroes had appeared from behind the house to vie silently for the honour of taking charge of the horse, which Hammond, after Ellen had slid to the ground and he had dismounted, turned over to Napoleon.

"How you all are? How's everybody? Whure your masta?"

"We's well, thank'ee, suh, Masta. Right glad you back."

"Why? Anythin' wrong?"

"No, suh, we all jest glad. That all."

Meg was on the gallery, bouncing up and down in ecstasy, his face one broad smile. Unable to speak, he could only gurgle. Lucretia Borgia stormed out the door and gathered Hammond to her broad bosom.

"Whure Papa? Whure Papa?" Hammond demanded.

"He comin'," answered Lucretia Borgia.

And he came, half leaning on Mem's arm. The son kissed him, patted his shoulder, asked about his health.

"I right well: I better, sure better. Ol' rheumatiz most dreened

138

away," he assured Hammond. "That Alp gittin' it good, dreenin' right into him, but I'm a-doctorin' him pourin' toddy into him."

"I stirrred 'em, Masta, I stirred 'em, an' toted 'em, jest like how you say, Masta, suh. I took keer of 'em jest like you tol' me. I your nigger, Masta. Ain't I your nigger?" Meg pleaded for recognition.

"Sure is," with a clap on the shoulder, was all that Hammond had time to answer him.

"Whut this?" demanded the old man, turning to Ellen.

Before Hammond had time to answer him, the Mandingo, Jason atop his shoulders, loped down the lane. "A Mandingo, a young Mandingo! Whure you git him? Ol' Mista Wilson? A purty Mandingo! Jest whut I been a-cravin'."

"My fightin' nigger," Hammond explained.

"That a wench around his neck?" Maxwell indicated Jason, whose features seemed more feminine than ever by contrast with Mede.

"Not a wench. A buck, Mista Wilson sent him to you—a present."

"Whut Mista Wilson reckoned I wants with a wench-buck like that? Is it a cod? I reckon I got to keep it—a present you say? Cain't ever sell no present. Git down! Put down an' let me see!"

"Charles is comin'," Hammond declared. "His hoss is lame."

"Who Charles?"

"Charles Woodford, Cousin Charles, Cousin Blanche's brother."

"Cousin Blanche? Oh, yes. You sparkin' her? She purty? Whut Major Woodford say?" Maxwell piled question upon question.

"Cousin Blance an' me goin' to marry. That is, and you loan some money to Major Woodford." Ham qualified his assertion. "I promise him twenty-five hundred dollar."

"You ain't never goin' to git it back. You know that. That ol' leech, sellin' his own white daughter, an' her a Hammond."

"Shu-shu," Ham silenced his father. "Here comes Charles."

"We talk about it after."

Charles, when he had turned into the lane, had tried to put his horse to a gallop, which turned into only a rapid hop. The flourish of arrival he had planned failed to come off, but his welcome was none the less warm. Vulcan grabbed his horse and started to lead it away.

"Hold on, leave me see that laig. Wait," ordered the old man before he turned to his guest and grasped his hand. "Well, I declare, Major Woodford's boy, I declare. Come in, come in. A Hammond, too, every foot a Hammond, 'ceptin', of course, the eyes."

"My eyes—my eyes ain't straight," Charles shrugged apologetically.

"That ain't nuthin'," said Maxwell. "Worse than the eyes, you skinny—growed too rapid, I warrant, an' fornicated too much, knowin' the Major. Not enough corn whisky, knowin' Cousin Beatrix."

"Mamma temp'ance," explained the boy.

"We fix that at Falconhurst. Lucretia Borgia's side meat an' plenty of good corn, we send you home lookin' like they won't know you. Go in, go in the house. I want to look at this hoss's laig." Maxwell bent with effort to examine the horse.

"Be all right, an' he not used fer few days. Turn him out, pasture him day times. Hear, Vulc; bait him good an' turn him out."

As the three white men entered the sitting-room, Meg rushed from the dining-room with three steaming toddies on his tray.

When Mem appeared with the dinner bell, Meg sprang to the door of the dining-room and held it open. He was there to withdraw Hammond's chair, to open his napkin, to serve his food, to wave the peacock brush. Whatever he did for another, it was solely to please Hammond.

"I wonder did Lucretia Borgia feed them new niggers?" Maxwell bethought himself aloud. "Memnon, sen' Lucretia Borgia in here."

Meg was in the kitchen and back again, pushing his mother before him before Mem could finish pouring the coffee, set down the pot and reach the door.

"Here Mammy is. Here Lucretia Borgia," announced the boy as if the woman's huge bulk failed to dominate the room by its presence.

"Did you feed them niggers Masta Hammon' brung?" Maxwell demanded.

"They's et," she answered, " 'ceptin' I didn't give that big 'un all he crave. Cain't fill him."

"Give 'em all white vittles, all they kin eat. The big one, too. They's special. All you kin shovel in 'em. Hear?"

"I's listenin'."

"An' that Mandingo, make him swaller half a dozen raw eggs

140

—eight or ten; stir 'em up an' make him drink 'em down after he done et hisself full," Maxwell further instructed.

"I pour 'em eggs down or I choke him silly," Lucretia Borgia promised. "Whure them niggers come from? Whyn't they cain't talk good? Cain't know whut they sayin'.'"

"They learn. They learn," said Maxwell. "Treat 'em good. That Mandingo is fer Lucy an' Big Pearl. He goin' to be Masta Ham's fighter."

Lucretia Borgia expressed her approval. "I bin a-lookin' at him, myself. He sure a elegant buck."

"You don' need him now. Maybe next time."

Meg was back at the table, forcing food upon his master.

"Dinner bye," observed Maxwell, "an' I'll have to bring them niggers in an' look at 'em."

The new Negroes, except for their being fed, had been ignored, waiting in the dooryard. Mede lay asleep on his hands, half in the shade of the tupelo tree. Hammond went himself to summon the three, limped across the yard to waken the Mandingo, rocking him back and forth with his foot. "Better shuck down out here," he told them. "Don't want your dirty clo's in the house. New ones, anyways, after you-all washed."

Hammond led the way to the sitting-room. Maxwell's primary interest was the Mandingo, and he called him up first, leaving Ellen and Jason against the wall. Mede was restless with the tension of his examination, shifting rapidly from foot to foot, flailing his arms, tensing and relaxing his muscles, in his anxiety to display his symmetry and strength.

"I'm right plagued to show off these niggers like this. Craves you should see 'em rested an' well," Hammond made excuses. He was proud of his purchases, avid for his father's approval.

"You not showin' 'em off, Ham; you jest showin' 'em. I'm your papa, recollect; I not cravin' to buy your niggers." None the less, Maxwell pulled Mede towards him, inserted his finger into the boy's mouth and felt the teeth, after which, using both hands, he pulled the lips apart to note the occlusion.

"Reckon he be a right good fighter. Eh, Cousin Warren?" commented Charles.

Maxwell took a sip of toddy, smacked his lips as a preliminary to his opinion. "Twenty-seven hundred, you tell me? Whut the matter with that ol' man? That nigger, a Mandingo, is worth thirty-five hundred, mayhap four thousand any day in the New Orleans market. Never see a better buck."

Hammond sighed with relief. He knew the worth of his purchase, but had feared his father's verdict.

"Pure Mandingo? You sure?" demanded Maxwell. "Don't want no half."

"I tell you he Big Pearl's brother, by ol' Xerxes out'n Lucy."

Maxwell nodded. "Well, call Big Pearl. Might as well try 'em together, let 'em take up, an' git it over."

"Papa, that buck petered out. He no good today."

"I not tired," protested the Mandingo. "I am ready."

"I say you tired, you tired. Don't dispute," Hammond silenced Mede. He dismissed the Mandingo, and instructed the boy to get soap from Lucretia Borgia and go to the river to bathe.

Ellen and Jason came forward together, but Maxwell's survey of them appeared superficial and without enthusiasm. "Right smooth and righty purty," he appraised the girl. "Good milker, too, will be. Git good wench suckers out'n one like that; no good to breed bucks though—too thin skinned an' fine drawn, an' too much white. To bring good bucks, use a yaller wench ever' time, not less than quadroon. How much, you say?"

"Fifteen hunderd dollars. Don't care had she been five thousan', she mine an' I wants her."

"Whut you arguin' about, Son? You got her, ain't you? She's a fancy, all right. No denyin'. Easy worth the money—especially was she a virgin time you bought her."

"She still a virgin," Ham confessed, blushing.

"Whure you bin? Thought you got her fer your own self. Ain't no money in payin' fifteen hunderd fer a wench to sell agin. Too risky, might die or git raped takin' 'em to market."

"I got her fer my own self an' I goin' to keep her fer my own self—always. I tender of her. I guess, I guess I kind of loves her —as folks calls it. On'y wench I wants; on'y wench I ever will want; ain't you, Ellen?"

A blush suffused the girl's face. She smiled at her master. Indifferent as she had shown herself to the examination, to the estimate of her valuè, and the discussion of her virginity, her master's mention of love touched modesty and stirred her blood.

"How your wife, how Cousin Blanche goin' to like that?" asked the father. "Course, she 'spects you pester around, but she not like you lovin' one."

"Make no diff'ence whut Blanche like. She cry an' pout, anything you do. She pizen, I tellin' you." Charles' denunciation was as emphatic as it was vague.

142

niggers. Thought I wouldn't know him, called hisself Mason, but
t was Hall all right. Wanted to buy the twins, knows all about
em. Let it slip out that Brownlee told him."

"Brownlee?"

"Yes, Brownlee is in it. I wouldn't even show 'em. Told him
he two on 'em was down with the epizootic, nothwithstandin'
hat this 'un was layin' right here drunk asleep at my feet and
Hall a-lookin' right at him."

"Brownlee dead set on gittin' them twins, seem like."

"Got a buyer waitin' fer 'em in New Orleans, a rich Frenchie,
Hall say," the older man explained. "But I don't want no truck
with Brownlee, or Hall neither."

"Hall ain't too bad, I reckon," Hammond defended him.

"A nigger stealer," persisted Maxwell. "Right well set up
hough, an' handsome like. Talks good."

"You know who Hall is?" said Hammond. "He worked fer Ol'
Mista Wilson a long time ago—overseer at Coign Plantation until
religion struck him an' he felt the call to preach. Mista Wilson
like him—good driver."

"Ol' Wilson likes ever'body. Wonder Hall didn't steal all the
Coign niggers, 'ceptin' he hadn't started his preachin' then."

"Fac' is, Hall is Ellen's pappy, an' that Jason's." Hammond
felt some temerity in saying this.

"How?"

"Fact. Ol' Wilson said so."

"I swan. Mayhap he is after stealin' them. He kin have the
buck, fer all I care."

"You don't like Jason? He make a good little house nigger."

"I wouldn't a laid out no money fer him."

"I didn't."

"He right whure he fittin', a-flunkyin' that cross-eye of
Woodford's. But we cain't keep Cross Eye ferever jest for the
nigger to have somebody to flunky. So Hall is his pappy?
Reckoned they was something wrong with that buck."

"An' Ellen's pappy," added Hammond jealously.

"Don't hurt her none—not fer whut you wants her."

"I reckon, Papa, you right put out with me, spendin' so much
money fer Ellen. Seems like we didn't need her none. But
I wants her, Papa, I wants her." Hammond began to weep
in his effort to make his father comprehend his need for the
girl.

"There, there, Son. Don't you cry. The wench is all right,

"I cain't help. I never seen Ellen until after I'd asted Blanche,"
Hammond confessed. "Besides, Ellen a nigger. No white lady
goin' to care about no nigger."

"Mayhap not," Maxwell admitted with reservation. He turned
to Jason and shook his head. "Ol' Man Wilson jest gittin' shet
of this one. Know it ain't worth nothin'. Know I cain't sell a
present."

"Mista Wilson gittin' ol'. Fixin' to die. Right choice of this
young buck. Craves you should take keer on him."

"Whut the matter with Jason?" Charles wanted to know.
"Whut wrong with him?"

"Yes, whyn't you like him?" seconded Hammond. "He sound."

"Why, he slick an' thin-skinned as that wench. Half one thing
an' half t'other; that whut wrong. Fac' is, he look more wench
than buck."

"I couldn't refuse a present," Hammond protested.

"You could a run him home. Come in ridin' the Mandingo's
neck, tirin' him out."

Jason winced and hung his head at the old man's contemptuous
words.

"I likes him. A good nigger," Charles maintained.

"Keep it way from me, an' you kin have it. Reckon you kin
use it as a bed wench, too," the owner sneered.

Charles paled at the remark but ignored the implication.
Jason, feeling himself disposed of, retired to beside Charles's
chair and squatted by it, and Charles ran his hand through the
boy's hair.

Meg had loitered in the background during the latter part of
this colloquy, as if he had something to say. At length Hammond
turned to him.

"Please, suh, Masta, suh," Meg announced. "Tub ready when
you like it."

"Come along, Ellen," said Hammond, and then to Meg, "I
wants you should wash Ellen too after you washes me." He
started toward the stairs, Meg half running in front of him and
the girl following after.

The young slave undressed his master in silence, added hot
water to that in the round tub, and steadied Hammond skilfully
as he sat down in it. He lingered in his enjoyment of his washing
of the master's pink flesh. Then he aided Hammond to his feet
and towelled him briskly until he was completely dry.

Hammond was refreshed. His flesh tingled and the fresh linen felt good against his skin. He surrendered to the boy to put the remainder of his clothes on him, all except his coat. He seated himself on the bed beside Ellen, who had watched his bath with silent interest. "Now, you wash her," Hammond told the boy.

Meg did not relish the chore assigned him, but his master failed to see the condescension in the glance when Meg rolled his eyes towards Ellen.

Ellen rose from the bed, and Meg pushed her none too gently into the tub of water, spattering the carpet. To none of the three did it seem more incongruous that the young buck should bathe his master's wench than that he should be called upon to bathe his horse or his dog. Ellen's status as her master's concubine would stifle any desire she might arouse in a slave. Meg's passion, anyway, was not lust but jealousy. He set about scouring the girls' body with a determination to get the unpleasant job over as quickly as was compatible with getting her clean, and she did not resent the roughness with which he handled her.

When Meg had finished drying Ellen, Hammond instructed him to go to Lucretia Borgia and obtain a dress for her—a new dress, none of those patched-up rags such as the other wenches wore. "And then," he added, "you might as well wash yourself in that tub as is all ready, an' you wants to."

Meg's eyes rolled with scorn. "I don' craves to wash in her water, Masta, suh. I wants yourn."

Hammond grasped Meg, clothed as he was, and plunged him into the soiled water. "Nev' mind the water, nor whose; when I says wash, you wash. Hear me?"

"Yas, suh, Masta," Meg answered sullenly. "I never meant——"

"Never' mind. You a triflin' nigger, jest like your pappy. Now, go git that dress and come back here an' wash—good."

Meg departed, dripping.

Hammond's violent action had mollified him. He ran his hand over Ellen as she sat on the side of the bed. "This is whure we goin' sleep—ever' night. Come up here soon's you kin after supper. I's pettered from that ridin'. I'll need you early," he instructed her and went downstairs.

"Whut become of that Charles?" his father inquired as Hammond entered the room.

"Around, I reckon. Mayhap sleepin' or trainin' that buck. Glad to be shet of him an' we kin talk."

144

"His sister, Miz Blanche? You goin' to marry, are you set on it?"

"I reckon I am. You craves me, doesn't you? Cain't craw now, 'lessen you won't sen' that money to the major."

"I'll sen' it, an' you wants, but it looks like buyin' her. [C]kin tote it along home with him when he go. Had ought t[o] knowe[d] Woodford would scrudge money outn you some[...] like him. Cain't never collec' it back."

"I knows," admitted the son.

"Miz Blanche will make a good wife. Hammond bloo[d] nice? And purty?"

"Blanche all right—right light-haired an' fair-complecte[d] all. Course she all covered up all the time, an' right s[...] I hadn't seen this Ellen then, you knows."

"Ellen only a nigger," the elder man said casually and w[ith] contempt. "She right nice an' shapely, but she ain't [...] Couldn't marry her and have no son—leastwise not a white [...]"

"Course not. I'm goin' to marry all right. But I'm go[in'] keep me Ellen, Blanche or no Blanche," Hammond affirme[d] the father nodded his acquiesence.

"Whure that nigger of yourn? Minute you comes, he go [...] not stir me no toddy."

"He upstairs washing off. Not hot enough yet fer to was[h] in Ol' Tombigbee."

"Call that Mem, an' you kin find him. His ain't as good, [...] like, not as strong, like the ones your buck stirs, but cal[l] anyways."

Hammond called Mem loudly three times and at leng[th] came with feigned alacrity.

"I'd keep that Meg away from the Tombigbee, an' I was [...] This other'n right here with me all the time. Better keep y[...] up," the father counselled.

"Gaters? Early for 'em. An' no harm anyways."

"Worse. Nigger stealers. I'm not sure but seem like. N[...] stealers after them twins."

Unconvinced, but wary, Hammond asked, "Whut makir[...] think?"

"Well, mayhap not, but Willis Hall—you know that Pre[...] Hall they run away from Benson fer tryin' to steal niggers[...]"

"Never could prove nothin'," said Hammond.

"I know, I know. Well, this Hall come a-ridin' in here S[...] on a good sorrel, after you had went on Friday, wantin' t[...]

145

right fancy, an' right cheap at the price. Make a breeder outn her, once you gits tired of her an' 'Tense ripen up."

"Ain't a-goin' to git tired. I don' crave 'Tense or no other wench," declared Ham.

"The other'n is the one you payin' too much fer."

"The Mandingo? You said——"

"Not the Mandingo, but the other'n—the Woodford gal, Cross-Eye's sister."

"But, Papa. You want me to——"

"Marry a white lady. Sure do, but not buy her an' her whole family."

"You kin jest not send the money," Hammond suggested almost anxiously.

"We'll send the money. 'Tain't the money."

Charles entered the room and interrupted the colloquy. He threw himself in a chair, announcing, "I like it. Ain't no prayin' an' don'tin'. You an' Cousin Hammond treats me growed up. An' there ain't that Blanche a-cryin' an' a-wantin' an' carryin' on."

"You be goin' home agin purty soon. Don't git to likin' Falconhurst too good," warned Maxwell.

"I ain't never goin' home. I'm a-goin' to stay."

"I reckon not," Maxwell modified the finality of his statement.

"Not till I see Cousin Ham's fightin' nigger, no way."

"Got to train him first," said Ham. "Mayhap take weeks."

"Jason won't never make no fightin' nigger," Charles hazarded, hopeful for a contradiction. "Cries when you hurt him."

"No sense in hurtin' him," said Ham.

"I means trainin' him."

"Don't train him rough, or I'll snatch him away from you. I tol' you not to larrup that buck."

"Mayhap whut he needin'," said Maxwell. "Make a buck outn him."

"Charles an' me aims to go into Benson Satiday to watch the fightin', see who got fighters, an' whut kind of niggers they bettin'," Hammond told his father.

"An' carry Mede along—jest to show him," Charles added with enthusiasm.

"Mede stay home—hid," said Hammond.

"When you in Benson, better git a bottle of Dr Mulbach's Serpent Oil to rub on that Mandingo," Maxwell suggested. "It sovereign."

"Mede, he ain't sick, don't need no medicament."

"Better git it. Stink bad, but you need it a-trainin' him. Makes him limber and flexuous, rubbed on his jints. Circus folks all use Dr Mulbach's."

"Dr Mulbach's Serpent Oil, you say," Ham repeated to impress the name upon his memory.

"An' now we better dig up that pot, the one under the big tree, I reckon, and count out the money fer Wilson," the old man decided. "You-all kin tote it into Benson to Banker Meyer, an' git him to send it. No use procrastinatin' it."

"Reckon we kin trust Meyer to send it?"

"Cain't trus' no bank or banker long. But he'll send it. Meyer honestlike, as bankers goes. Safer havin' gold buried in a pot, but how else kin we send to Wilson?" Maxwell was not without misgivings.

"An' to Major Woodford?" Ham asked.

"Kin count that out an' keep it aside. Don't need no banker to send that. Charles here will be goin' first thing, an' he kin tote it. Cain't you, Charles?"

"Charmed to oblige you." Charles assumed formality.

"Oblige me? Oblige your papa." There was a hint of a sneer in Maxwell's voice as he got slowly to his feet.

Pole and another slave, named Pompey, were set to delve at the base of a large hickory tree for the pot of gold. Ham gave a glance at their work from time to time and told them to hasten.

"I knows I sunk it. Must be comin' to it purty quick now. Mayhap 'bout a foot or foot an' a half this way from whure they diggin'. They too close to that ol' hickory," Maxwell calculated.

"This it, Masta, suh?" asked Pole, as from his position at the bottom of the hole he handed up to Pompey a covered iron kettle encrusted with soil. "It right hefty, suh. Cain't hardly heft it."

"That it," said Hammond. "Brush off that dirt an' tote it in the house. Leave that hole open to put it back."

Halfway to the house with the heavy object, Pole's hands slipped on the slime and he dropped the pot. It landed almost upright but its lid fell off, splashing the water that had seeped into it and scattering half a dozen yellow coins. The accident earned Pole an oath and kick from Hammond, but no harm was done. The coins were recovered and the pot was tilted to drain off the remaining water, after which Mede, who had returned from washing in the river, encircled it with his arms and carried it handily into the sitting-room and placed it, as Ham directed him, in the centre of the floor.

148

"Kittle gittin' lighter," remarked Maxwell, shaking his head. "Was about nineteen thousand, an' I recollect aright, in this kittle. This will bring it down to," he hesitated, counting on his fingers, "to somers around twelve. We'll fill it up to a full twenty-five thousand with a little extrie fer good measure and bury it fer good next fall when you blocks that coffle in New Orleans—jest like them other three kittles we got buried around."

Lucretia Borgia had little concept of the value of money, and Meg and Mede none at all, but they came into the room to watch the ceremony of counting it. Maxwell sat in his chair and watched Hammond ease himself to the floor, one leg under him, the stiff one extended. He scooped the coins in his hands and let them trickle through his fingers back into the pot. Charles sat in a low chair apart and stared in wonder at the falling money, his imagination racing.

"There you are, Mede. That's you. That how much you cost," Hammond explained. "Reckon you worth it?"

The Mandingo replied with the anticipated embarrassed laugh. "No, suh, Masta, suh," he said. "Not that much." He had no idea how much it might be.

Ham stacked three piles of five hundred dollars each and pushed them aside. "That's Ellen," he said.

"Whur am me, Masta, suh?" asked Meg, stooping to gaze into the pot.

"You? You ain't nowhures. Ain't worth nothin'," Hammond replied with mock seriousness. "Folks don't buy niggers like you. They breeds 'em."

He reached again into the pot, scooping out coins which he added to the uncounted pile upon the floor. From the pile he drew five stacks of twenty-five coins each and set them aside. "That," he said, looking towards his father for approval, "is fer Major Woodford."

"That is Blanche," said the father dryly.

"She pizen," commented Charles.

CHAPTER TEN

TWO DAYS later the boys rode into Benson. Ham ordered a diamond ring for Blanche, much to Charles's disgust. Then they stopped at the tavern, where fights were held most

Saturdays. The tavern-keeper's name was Remmick, a big vehement man with a jovial aggressiveness of manner, heavy red jowls, big, blunt hands and closely cropped hair. He readily agreed to try to promote a match for Ham's Mandingo, being delighted both by the prospect of a good fight and at the chance of being able to oblige old Maxwell's son.

The boys were about to go when Doc Redfield sauntered in with unmistakable new aplomb. He greeted Ham cordially.

"Ain't seen you sence I done it. The Widder had me. Ain't goin' to congratulate me?"

" 'Course, 'course," said Hammond, at a loss for terms in which to congratulate a man whose marriage had been, by his own confession, made only for the purpose of acquiring the midwife's property and slaves.

They drank a good deal of corn to mark Redfield's married state, with the result that it was supper time when the horses turned in at Falconhurst. Meg stood on the gallery, and tried unsuccessfully to restrain himself from bounding up and down when he saw Hammond.

The boys dismounted and gave their horses to Vulcan to take to the stable.

Hammond found his father sitting before the fire, toddy in hand, bare feet resting upon the naked belly of Alph, supine in front of his chair.

"Son, my rheumatiz just been rackin' me again. I thought I'd dreen some of it out," the father explained as the son crossed the room. "Whut fer you so late? Supper gittin' col'."

"Had gotten to git this serpent oil," Ham offered as an explanation. "Two bottles; one seem not to hol' much. Sure is potent dose; tell all about on the outside."

"It good," the older man admitted. "Nigger, git my slippers."

"You've et?" Hammond stated rather than inquired.

"Hell, no; an I'm hongry. Ain't no comfort eatin' afore you gits here."

"Reckon you too painful to muss with Big Pearl an' Mede today?" Hammond hazarded.

"Not personal, no," replied his father. "But I tol' Lucretia Borgia. Reckon she coupled 'em. She didn't say."

"Want my mammy, Masta, suh? Want Lucretia Borgia?" Meg craved more details upon the subject, and Ham gave his assent.

The cook came, self-consciously, adjusting her dress, with Meg

150

at her heels all ears. "This nigger say you wants me," she declared and waited. She knew full well why she had been summoned.

"How you make out coverin' Big Pearl?" Hammond inquired. "She take him?"

Lucretia Borgia grinned widely and chuckled low in her throat. "He got that black wench good, yas, suh, Masta, suh."

"No trouble, then?"

"Naw, suh, no trouble afta' I show that big buck how."

"You still feedin' Mede up, Lucretia Borgia, ain't you? Raw eggs, an' all?" Hammond asked. "Meat a plenty?"

"Yas, suh, I'm feedin' him. Don't like eggs, but the more he don' like 'em, the more I pours 'em down."

"Fattin' up a nigger makes them lazy. Lean fighter best. Starve 'em down, an' rub 'em with whisky outside; that's what all the gen'lemen does around Centerville," declared Charles.

"Mine goin' to fight fat. That's all. An' serpent oil better than corn. Says right on the bottle."

Next afternoon Hammond took down from the mantelpiece one of the bottles of Dr Mulbach's Serpent Oil, shook it violently and held it to the light. He sat down and leaned over, propping his elbows on his knees, to spell out the statements on the label of the flat bottle.

Dr Mulbach's Serpent Oil (he read). The sovereign oleamen to promote the puissance of the musculature and the flexation of the articulative processes. Applied copiously to the masculine organs of generation, it assures supreme induration, facilitates penetration, and renders the act of kind more felicitous.

Dr Mulbach's Serpent Oil is an elixir rendered from the oleaginous portions of various ophidian genera, supplemented by the addition of costly gums and balsams from the uttermost parts of the known universe. Compounded from a secret formula handed down to Dr Mulbach from untold generations of his Aesculapian ancestors, it was appreciated by the victorious gymnasts of ancient Hellas and by the Roman gladiators, synthesized from the identical ingredients employed by its present manufacturers. Many kings and monarchs have been rendered potent by its use. Dr Mulbach's Serpent Oil is in daily use by the Sultan of Turkey and is recommended by him to all pashas with a numerous seraglio. No modern acrobats, contortionists, or pugilists would contemplate their spectacular feats without this marvellous adjuvant.

To obtain the superlative result of which Dr Mulbach's Serpent Oil is capable, it must be applied freely with maximum friction and manipulation of the joints. It should be patted into the muscles with great force and well kneaded.

Accept no substitute. Use only Dr Mulbach's Serpent Oil.

151

Fabricated and distributed only by
Dr Mulbach's Serpent Oil Company,
Rampart Street,
New Orleans, Louisiana, USA.

Hammond read aloud, so far as he was able to spell out the words; he made little effort to understand their meaning. He was none the less impressed by this verbiage. "Reckon Redfield would know whut signify all this doctor-talk. But stuff must be good."

"Good? It sovereign," declared the father.

"Thut whut the sticker say right here—sovereign o-l-e-a-m-e-n," confirmed Ham. "Boy, fetch me that stopper-twister from yo' mammy."

Meg brought the corkscrew and stood expectant while his master opened the magic flask. The cork came out more easily than was anticipated and a few drops of the contents splashed upon the carpet. Ham put the bottle to his nose, sniffed the contents, and wrinkled his face, after which he replaced the cork part way and held the bottle at arm's length. "It powerful vig'ous," he said, shaking his head.

"Scare up that Mede an' carry him out under the tupelo. Tell him I say," Hammond instructed Meg.

The boy started on his errand and glanced through the window. "He right there now under the old tupelo, sleepin'," Meg reported.

The boy started on his errand and glanced through the window.

"Wake him an' tell him we comin' an' wantin' him."

The father got to his feet and summoned Memnon, who was not to be found. Maxwell reviled him and fell back upon Lucretia Borgia, always available, to adjust the blue coverlet about his shoulders and to lead him across the open space to Lucy's cabin. Lucretia Borgia placed her muscular arm around his back, adjusted her step to his, and let him take his slow time.

Mede got to his feet and rubbed his eyes. "You want me, Masta, suh?" he asked.

"Step out'n them clo's. Shuck down an' leave 'em here under the tupelo. Goin' to snake oil you down and limber you up," Hammond explained.

"I rub on the stuff, after you snakes him, Masta, suh," said Meg, "like I done Mem?"

"You git snaked an' rubbed your own self you don't go on back in that house and dry up. Nobody brung you," Hammond chided

152

the boy who obeyed reluctantly and looked behind him as he went.

The party encountered Big Pearl as she emerged from the cabin, balancing a bucket on her head on her way to the well. "Put down that thing an' come along an' rub this buck of your'n —your'n and your mammy's, that is," commanded Hammond. "Whure Lucy?"

They found Lucy kneeling by a tub in which stood a crying Belshazzar, in process of being bathed none too gently.

"Here that new boy," said Hammond. "Papa say it all right fer you an' Big Pearl to have him, but don't wants the two of you wearin' him down."

"I knowed you would, Masta, suh; I jes' knowed it. I tol' Big Pearl this mawnin' suh. Thank'ee, thank'ee. Naw, suh, I won't wear him down," Lucy promised, and looked at Mede.

"Nor let Big Pearl," cautioned Hammond.

"Naw, suh, Masta," she said.

"He yourn," confirmed the old man. "But now you got to embrocate him, an' ever' day."

"Right here, front of ever'body? Shaz, you git yourself outn here. Which one of us?" asked Lucy, misinterpreting the meaning.

"Spread him out on the bed, belly up," Maxwell instructed. "You rub his torso, Big Pearl take care his legs. Masta Ham here pour on."

Mede understood what was expected. He reclined across the bed, arms raised and legs spread. Hammond upturned his bottle and released a trickle of serpent oil over the flesh beginning on the chest and moving the bottle downward over the belly and legs. "Come on, work it in," he directed.

The Mandingos began to smear the oil over the body. The more it spread, the greater the stench that arose from it. "That won't do. Got to work it in an' twist the jints," explained the old man.

The women renewed their efforts, but restrained their strength. To them Mede was, indeed, a great doll which they did not want to destroy. They did not shirk the effort, but their strokes were caresses rather than massage.

"Stan' back," said Maxwell, spitting his tobacco upon the floor. "You, Lucretia Borgia, show 'em how."

Lucretia Borgia advanced. "Gitn away from here," she said, sweeping the Mandingos aside. She raised her skirt to enable her to kneel upon the bed, bent over, and rubbed her hands over the

153

belly to absorb the oil. Not getting enough, she extended her palms to Hammond, who filled them from the bottle. She rubbed them together and went to work in earnest. She rubbed, she kneaded, she pummelled, without compunction or mercy. Mede's features writhed with pain, but no sound came from him.

Scorning to ask him to turn, she ran her arms under the boy's body and flopped him over as if turning a pancake, reached for the bottle, poured oil down the spine and over the buttocks, anointed her hands again, took a deep breath and fell to. Not an inch of the skin did she neglect.

"Set on his back an' hol' him down," Lucretia Borgia commanded Big Pearl. "I goin' to stretch his limbs."

The girl uncomprehendingly did as she was told.

"Hol' him down now; don' let him move," Lucretia Borgia warned as she raised the thigh toward the head. Mede emitted a grunt of pain. "Hollerin' won't git you nothin'," warned the woman; "jist make me bend you higher up." And she seized the other leg.

Meg appeared at the door and Hammond scolded him, "I tol' you to go to house an' keep outn this. Whut you want?"

"Please, suh, Masta, Doc Redfield come. Wantin' I should fetch him?"

· "Course, course, carry him here," said Hammond, going to the door and seeing Redfield, who had followed the young Negro. "Come in, come in," he welcomed the newcomer, extending his right hand.

"Whut that stench?" inquired the veterinary. "Kill a skunk?"

"Serpent oil," said Maxwell. "Embrocatin' Ham's new buck. Right gratified you come."

"Whut I wanted to see, that fighter Remmick tellin' about."

"There he lay!" proclaimed Hammond proudly.

"Down sick? Lucky I red by."

Hammond sniffed. "No. Jest a-oilin' him up. 'Nough fer now, Lucretia Borgia. Let him up."

Big Pearl dismounted from Mede's back, and he got to his feet.

"Best buck ever on Falconhurst," declared Maxwell with a show of modesty.

"Bes' I ever see—anywhures," Redfield expanded.

"But will he fight? Gentle as any kitten," speculated Ham. "Will he fight?"

"If you say fight, Masta, suh——" Mede intruded, causing Hammond to scowl. He refrained from reprimand, however.

154

Redfield and Maxwell had gone into the house and Charles had waited for Ham at the door. "We fights him the Satiday comin'?" he questioned eagerly.

"Mayhap, an' he ready, " Ham evaded.

"That Mandingo, as you calls him (I heard a heap about 'em but I ain't never see a sure-enough one before), he had ought to fetch prime suckers," Redfield speculated. "Got me a wench, one of the widder's, I'd like to mix up with him."

"Doc Redfield, you kin have the use of any buck we got, any time at all," Hammond emphasized his generosity, He was aware of the weight of Redfield's professional counsel at the tavern. "Course, I readyin' this Mede fer Satidays, but any time you wants him."

"Reckon fightin' peter out 'cos of preachers, like Mista Remmick say?" Charles demanded.

"Long as them sportin' gen'lemen in New Orleans goin' to fight their fancy niggers, young planters around Benson goin' to fight their field han's. Gits so that preachers an' them stop it in the tavern, gen'lmen carries bucks to the wood lots an' places preachers don' know; they still fights 'em," Redfield replied.

"Let gen'lemen stop goin' to Benson Satidays to spen' money, an' the preachers change they chune," said Maxwell. "Let yo' heart rest, Cousin Charles."

CHAPTER ELEVEN

FIGHTING OF Negroes interested Hammond as much as Charles, with the difference that one rationalized it as a business and to the other it was candidly a sport. Hammond was too serious in his dealing with his slaves to be wanton, and his seriousness never relaxed. He fed them, worked them, trained them, treated them, bred them, sold them, and fought them with a sole motive of profit, as his father had inculcated. Livestock kept happy and comfortable thrives best, and Hammond sought to keep his blacks contented. He relished his vocation and took pride in the discharge of the managerial duties which his father, perforce, trusted to him. He was a sovereign in his little realm with a sovereign's responsibilities and immunities. He felt himself obliged to be just, upon occasion to be cruel but always in the name of justice. He was even capable of tenderness, which he tried to curb.

155

Not that Hammond was insensible of any compassion for his Negroes, but he made no conscious efforts to be just. They were slaves, chattels, mere things, but he had a way with them that inspired their loyalty and even love, a care for their welfare begotten of a regard for their value.

Hammond initiated Mede's conditioning with much enthusiasm. He set Mede to moving wood from one side of the house to the opposite side, not that it made any difference where the wood was stacked, but it brought into play the Mandingo's muscles. Mede attacked this and similar tasks briskly. His muscles were already hard and his strength prodigious.

Even so, but for the urgency to send Charles back to Crowfoot with the ring for Blanche and the money for her father and the youth's disappointment if he should fail to see the Mandingo fight at least once before his departure. Hammond would have been tempted to keep Mede at home on Saturday and to give him at least one more week of training before he should fight him. Charles was quiet and agreeable, caused no trouble to the Maxwells, but it was imperative that he be sent home.

Would Mede fight at all? No trial had been made of his skill in combat or of his courage. Hammond blushed as he considered the possibility that Mede should retreat from a fight or worse still that he might accept defeat without fighting at all. However, there was no avoiding the issue.

On the day of the fight, the white men hitched their horses and the Negroes their mules in front of Remmick's tavern, while Hammond looked in the door to survey the gathering, which was already sizeable despite the early hour. The weather was clearing but clouds still hung in the sky and intermittently drifted across the face of the sun. To plough was not feasible and planters were free to come into Benson to buy, to visit, to drink, and to watch the fights.

Hammond had to go to the jeweller's to see about his ring and, afraid that some miscreant might tamper with his fighter, took his entourage along with him, leaving Mede and a boy named Atrides outside the shop while he and Charles entered. The bell on the door tinkled and the watchmaker laid aside his glass and rose from his bench.

The ring had arrived. It was a yellow, lustreless, rose-cut stone of some two carats in a severe solitaire setting. The watchmaker extracted it from its velvet-lined box and laid it on the top of his showcase with an exhibition of pride that concealed his inward misgiving. Hammond picked up the bauble, looked at it, and carried it to the glazed door for further inspection.

"Is that all?" he asked. What he had expected, he did not himself know, but at least something more gorgeous and spectacular then the ring proved to be.

"Right purty," advanced the salesman.

"Too purty fer her," said Charles impatiently. "Pay, an' let's go back to Remmick's. Them fights goin' to start."

"How much it cos'?" asked Hammond.

The jeweller replied, "Two hundred and thirty-five dollars, an' I'm not makin' much on it, I tells you, gittin' it here an' all."

"A heap of money," said Hammond, sighing and drawing forth a long leather pouch from which he slowly counted out gold coins. "You sure it solid, pure di'mon'?"

"I warrant you," affirmed the dealer.

"That whut she wantin'," said Ham with satisfaction. "Put that little box right in here among this money. Keep it safe."

"Let me know how the lady like that ring," said the jeweller as Hammond closed the door.

"Reckon you goin' home, come next week. Got to git this ring to Cousin Blanche an' that money to your papa," Hammond announced as they walked along the plank sidewalk toward Remmick's.

"Don' make me yet," Charles pleaded. "I likes Falconhurst better than Crowfoot. I likes you an' Cousin Warren better than Papa and Mamma, an' as fer Blanche——"

"Don' talk so. It ain't nice," said Hammond.

"It a fact."

"Hadn't ought to say it. You kin come again—later, after your papa have that money."

"Blanche be here then. She pizen."

Hammond made no reply.

"I gits home, Papa goin' to whup me," Charles thought aloud. "Me, I too big to whup, ain't I, Cousin Ham? Don' you think?"

"Whut fer your papa whup you?" Hammond asked absently, his mind on the tavern.

"Runnin' away," the boy confessed. "He didn't give me no leave to foller you. I asted an' he tol' me no."

"You fib to me. I know you lie when you said it," Hammond accused his cousin.

"Whut fer you fetch me along, then?"

"I reckon I lonesome-like an' want ridin' company."

"You bad as me then, carryin' me away an' knowin' Papa never said."

"You said he said, though. You swear."

"That the on'y way I gits to come."

"You goin' right home, leavin' Monday. Cain't stay an' me a-knowin'."

"I git whupped. I sure git whupped," the youth lamented.

They reached the tavern now full of milling men and boys, the Negroes ranged along the wall, the adult white men at the bar, behind which Remmick dispensed drinks expertly. Hammond stationed Mede and Atrides at the end of the line of slaves and told them to wait.

There were already seven fighting men, including Bill Kyle's one-eyed Sweetness, six stripling boys for betting and a single yellow girl of eleven or twelve years, not pretty but full-faced and plump. Hammond recognized Lew Casaway's Cudjo, a tall, well-made, dark mulatto with the top of one ear missing, with whom Mede was to be matched.

The other owners were negotiating their matches, examining their opponents' slaves and binding their bargains in corn whisky. The onlookers circulated and made small bets, the stakes for which they entrusted to Remmick, and bought each other drinks.

Three more gentlemen had arrived with their fighters and there were to be four bouts, leaving one owner disappointed at his failure to arrange a match for his boy. At last the bets were all placed and the gentlemen had drunk all the whisky they wanted. Remmick led the way to his backyard enclosures and called for the first fight, which was to be between Sweetness and a large, muscular, concave-faced black called Mose. Four or five men and two or three boys remained in the room while the owners stripped their fighters and gave them their instructions.

Remmick cleared an open space in the rough ground of the backyard as the two owners leading their naked slaves came out of the door, followed by the persons who had remained to see the boys stripped.

The impatient and anxious crowd stood two deep around the area that served as an ill-defined ring, upon opposite sides of which the fighters took their places, each escorted by his owner. The tavern keeper stood in the centre of the ring, his arm raised over his head.

"Now, ev'body stan' back, please, suh, an' keep the god-damn ring open to give the varmints room to FIGHT!" He dropped his arm dramatically at his final emphatic word and stepped to the sidelines. The owners gave their respective fighters a shove towards each other and retired.

The boys advanced cautiously. Each was patently afraid of the other, and alternately pursued one another around the ring without striking a blow. The bout promised to be tame and the crowd was displeased.

"I got a nigger kin whup 'em both together," said one man.

"Ifn he kin ketch 'em," added his neighbour.

"Better take 'em out an' snake the two of 'em, put some grit in 'em."

"They ain't gittin' hurt none, is they, Papa?" a boy asked solicitously, and everybody laughed.

The fighters continued to dance and threaten. After a while, Mose caught Sweetness fairly on the socket of his missing eye and rocked him on his heels. A fat-legged boy who sat tailor-fashion on the ground giggled in fear. Mose followed his blow with a lighter one to the ribs.

Sweetness was knocked a step backwards into the spectators, one of whom, angered by the indignity of being hit by the Negro, shoved him with considerable force back into the open ring and against Mose, who encircled Sweetness' neck, and the two fell together, Sweetness on his back. But not for long. Sweetness, without striking a blow, with a mighty lunge, exchanged positions and was on top. Here he was enabled to raise his arms and attain leverage for a blow to Mose's skull, upon which he unknowingly skinned his bare knuckles. Mose's arms were pinned between the two bodies; Sweetness' arms were free and he rained unimpeded blows on the other's jaws and face. Blood spurted from Mose's nose and the flesh beneath his right eye began to swell.

Mose extracted his arms and the two lay still, locked in an embrace. Mose strove to force Sweetness upon his back, or even on his side, but could do nothing. He succeeded in entwining his legs in the legs of his opponent.

Sweetness disengaged himself and rose to his knees, and Mose kicked him with his heel directly in the nose, at which the blood spurted, but the victim seemed insensitive. He was able to get to his feet and planted a double punch in Mose's lower abdomen, before the two united in another clinch and, after staggering to the other side of the ring, fell together to the ground and rolled over twice. A stone, dislodged from the ground, ripped Sweetness'

159

thigh, which bled unheeded, the blood mingling with the sweat that bathed him. The audience, which had been restless, grew intense in its interest. "Come on, Mose; kill the one-eye baboon," breathed Charles to himself.

"Hurry up an' burke him, Sweetness, an' you wants that corn," yelled Kyle, and his Negro appeared to hear, for his punches to Mose's belly seemed more brutal than the ones before. Mose flinched. The inconclusive combat went on with an intermittent exchange of blows of which those of Sweetness seemed the more telling.

The exhausted fighters by mutual consent paused and parted for a deep inhalation, and resumed their struggle. They went down and rolled over and over, but neither had a firm grip on the other. The fight had lasted a long thirty-five minutes, and nobody could see how nor why the fighters had manoeuvred themselves to lie end to end. Mose had Sweetness' big toe in his mouth and was biting it, while Sweetness tried unsuccessfully to kick himself loose. Sweetness gritted his teeth in his pain, but he succeeded in reaching between Mose's legs and twisted his scrotum. Mose's mouth opened and let go of the toe as he screamed in his agony, then fell silent. Sweetness did not relinquish his hold until the owners entered the ring and Gore conceded the victory to Kyle.

"Black ape," Charles muttered to Hammond. "I could whup that one-eye buck my own self."

The crowd was silent for a moment and then fell into a murmur of excited comment as all went toward the bar, where winning and losing owner each bought a round of drinks for everybody.

Mose staggered to his feet after everybody else had gone inside, and when he entered walking with legs spread and knees bent, his master reminded him, "You knows whut I goin' to do to you, losin' that Sam saplin' on you."

"Naw, suh, Masta, please. Don' do it, don' do that. Naw suh, Masta, suh," Mose begged.

"Dry up, an' begone over amongst the other niggers," his owner dismissed him.

The crowd returned to the backyard for the following bout, which was a tame but amusing event. At Remmick's behest to "Fight", one of the fighters, with a howl of horror, forced his way through the spectators, pursued by the second, and scaled the six-foot fence.

The owner, in his mortification, proposed to mount his horse and overtake the runaway, but Remmick declared it a contest and the bets upon the renegade forfeit. The loser disputed the decision without redress, and reluctantly bought a round of drinks and scribbled the bill of sale for his sapling. Doc Redfield assured him of the fairness of Remmick's verdict, and he felt better about his loss, but caught up the clothes the Negro had shed, set out to catch him and failed to return.

"The nex' set-to," announced Remmick, "goin' to be between Mista Gasaway and Mista Hammond Maxwell. Mista Ham got a new buck which none of us ain't see tussle, and this fight goin' to be right in'erestin'."

For the third time the crowd began moving out into the yard, but Remmick remained behind to pour out the cup of whisky with which owners were wont to fortify their fighters' courage.

Cudjo, out of his clothes first, took the cup from Lewis and downed it with two gulps, afterwards wiping his lips with the back of his hand.

"Whut species of nigger is that?" Lewis demanded. "His musk powerful pungent; smell like he rottin' to pieces. Whyn't you wash him?"

Hammond laughed as he reached for the cup that Lewis Gasaway had refilled. "That ain't the buck. That is serpent oil he rubbed with."

Mede sipped the whisky, which caused him to cough. "Do I have to drink this, Masta, suh?" he asked. "It will make me sick."

"Give here," said Hammond.

"Better pour it down him," cautioned Charles. "A nigger won't fight, lesten he drunken."

Hammond set the cup on the bar, but, lest the contents be wasted, Gasaway picked it up and gave Cudjo a second drink.

More to reassure Atrides that he was not being deserted than because of any concern for the garments, Hammond kicked Mede's discarded clothes towards the yellow boy and cautioned him, "Watch out fer these. Set still an' we come back."

Remmick leaned his elbows on the counter and surveyed Mede critically. "That nigger bigger withouten no clothes than in 'em. He bulge out all over."

"Wait till Cudjo waller with him," Lewis replied. "Cudjo wallop them bulges right offn him."

Remmick moved round the circle imploring the onlookers to stand back and make room for the fighters, which they did, then crowded forward again. Remmick stepped to the centre, raising his arm, and proclaimed, "We all knows this big varmint of Mista Gasaway's, name of Cudjo. The othern, Mista Maxwell's —whut you call him, Ham?"

"Gannymede," replied Hammond and, when everybody laughed, added, "Mede, fer shortenin'."

"The othern," Remmick repeated, "Mista Maxwell's Mede. Let 'em fight."

Hammond stepped back to join Charles on the edge of the crowd. Mede looked around as if bewildered, braced himself, but made no move. Cudjo, encouraged by Mede's uncertainty, advanced aggressively, one hand in front of him to protect himself, and the other drawn back with fist clenched. Mede waited. Cudjo's first blow was at Mede's belly and Mede accepted it; but before Cudjo could withdraw his arm, Mede had clamped him by the wrist. He spun the other boy around and grasped the other arm, bringing both behind Cudjo, who was impotent to strike. Cudjo sought to trip Mede with his foot, but Mede forced the other's arms at his back, throwing his body forward and compelling him to tiptoe to avoid the pain. Cudjo could neither escape nor resist. Nobody held a watch on the bout, but it seemed to the spectators that it had not lasted twenty seconds. Except Cudjo's tentative jab at Mede's middle, no blow had been struck and neither man was injured.

"What you want I should do with him, Masta, suh?" asked Mede, forcing Cudjo on his toes toward Hammond.

"Hol' on to him till Mista Gasaway give up," Hammond warily instructed his boy; and called across the ring, "Whut you wants, Lew?"

"On'y don't let your nigger kill him," returned Gasaway, laughing in embarrassment of defeat, and stepping forward to rescue his slave from Mede's grip.

"Hell of a fight," said one man to Charles, who slapped his leg and doubled up with glee. The others stood silent, awed by the Mandingo's strength.

"Ain't hardly fair, don' seem like," said Hammond magnanimously. "Put 'em back an' fight 'em agin, an' if you says."

Redfield wouldn't hear of it. "Fair fight, an' fair win," he declared. "Bes' buck beat."

Remmick, although the short fight would sell little whisky, was aware of the difficulty of settling the bets if it should be renewed to a reversal of the outcome. "No, no," he said, "Mista

Maxwell won clean." He also foresaw the rematch of the same bucks on another Saturday.

There was some dissent among the disappointed spectators, and a few men who had lost their bets were disgruntled, but the consensus was that Mede's victory was clean-cut and decisive. Gasaway, in his role as a sporting man, had no alternative but to accept it. He made a show of good nature as he bought his round of drinks for the crowd, and even condoned Cudjo's bad performance.

Cudjo wept as he pulled on his clothes and his master carried a cup of whisky to him, and reassured him, "It all right, never mind, you'll git 'nother go at him." Cudjo wiped his tears away with the tail of his shirt, and gradually recovered from his humiliation.

The last fight was a routine and unexciting fracas, an exchange of blows in which one of the fighters was knocked down, followed by a scramble on the ground. Major Watson's man bit off the lobe of his opponent's ear and knocked loose two of his teeth and, at the cost of a broken hand, was declared the winner after some thirteen rounds of combat.

After the fights, Hammond did not return to the bar but went to rouse his *ménage* for their departure.

As they rode back towards Falconhurst, Charles was jubilant in a review of the events of the afternoon. His winnings were small, but he congratulated himself that he had won at all. Mede's victory over Cudjo was in truth Hammond's over Lewis Gasaway, for whom he felt a strong rivalry.

They found the senior Maxwell nervous. He had tried to pace the floor but the pain in his joints forbade such activity, and he had had Memnon move his rocking-chair to the window that he might watch for his son's return. He sought to disguise his apprehension, and watched the boys and their Negroes dismount without moving from his chair. But when he saw the third Negro crawl from the mule, he knew that Mede had won his fight.

That night the two boys and Maxwell sat drinking and talking about Mede's victory until after midnight, and so cordial was the atmosphere that Charles began to hope he would be allowed to stay longer at Falconhurst.

Next morning, however, his hope was disappointed.

"Time Cousin Charles was gittin' started an' he goin' today," said Hammond on his return from his rounds. "His hoss waitin' an' saddled."

He got off his horse and went into the house, and when he returned Charles was with him.

"Has I got to go today?" Charles asked. "Don' know kin I fin' my way. Cain't I wait an' ride with Cousin Hammond? Ain't more than a month off."

"I wants your papa to git that money, an', don' let me fergit the ring fer Cousin Blanche," said Hammond. "Besides, your papa don' know whure you at. Git ready."

Argument was useless. Charles went into the house, and up to his room, but soon returned ready for his trip. A boy brought his horse and Maxwell arose and hobbled over to make sure its leg was completely healed. Charles shook the hands of his hosts in silence and, after he had got on his horse, Hammond handed up to him a cloth bag of gold coins.

"Take care of this," Hammond admonished. "It got that ring in it fer Blanche, right on top that money."

"I goin' to hug it right to me," Charles promised.

He rode away reluctantly, turning now and again to look back.

At midday, when father and son had settled themselves at table, Lucretia Borgia planted herself in the doorway to the kitchen. "Masta, suh, I wants to 'form you, that saplin' of Masta Charles never turn up to git his dinner."

"Jason?" asked Hammond.

"Yas, suh; that the one. Whut I do?"

"Don' do nuthin'," said Hammond. "He come up fer supper."

"Prob'ly off a-mopin' 'bout his masta," surmised the older man. "Loony-like about Charles, but never come to see him ride away."

"Mayhap watched from upstairs. Upstairs now, cryin', I venture."

"Charles treat it good, too. Like it, seem like."

"I minded him to treat him good and not to never lambaste him."

"He lambaste him nights," Meg interposed.

Hammond at first looked sternly at the young slave to reprimand the interruption; then asked, "How you know?"

Meg was confused by the tacit injuction to silence and the spoken question. "Jason say," he shrugged. "He like it."

"Nigger talk."

"You reckon Charles take that buck along?" Hammond asked his father. "He crazy enough."

"You see him ride off. Course not."

164

"He mayhap send Jason ahead an' pick him up. He untrusty."

"You trust him with twenty-five hunert dollars gold. Reckon you trus' him with a little yaller buck."

"That different. Charles crazy 'bout Jason."

"Wouldn't care, savin' the buck was a present," said the father. "Never grow into nothin' noway."

"Charles got him, I fetch him when I go to Crowfoot nex' month. Don' mean no harm."

"Had ought to ast, anyways."

"Course. Course. I'd a let him carry him along until I goes."

"Mayhap you right. That whure he go."

"Hope so, an' he don' come up," Hammond dismissed the subject. He was still too pleased by Mede's success in the fight to bother much about a runty little nigger like Jason.

But Ham's pride took a blow from, unexpectedly, Doc Redfield when the latter called at the big house the next evening.

"Why you so monstrous keen fer this Mandingo to fight?" queried the Doc, interrupting Ham in yet another description of the previous Saturday's victory.

"I craves my buck to win final—so as nobody goin' to misdoubt," taken aback, Hammond fumbled in search of his words.

"You-all got ever'thin' an' nothin' good enough," Redfield observed, accepting a toddy from Meg's tray. "Take me; I ain't never had nothin', an' marryin' a dozen or like ol' petered out niggers an' a quarter section plantation make me feel a gen'leman. Take you; got this place, always had it, an' the finest niggers around, and you frets a-cause your buck cain't strike the other man's buck dead jest a-lookin' at him. You real gen'lemen, gen'lemen born. Livin' up to it must be hell."

"It that Hammond blood," affirmed Maxwell. "Ol' Theophilus Hammond always had the best land, the best hosses, the best whisky, the best niggers, and the best women, an' none of 'em good enough to ease his mind."

"I don't reckon Maxwell blood count none," said Redfield, sipping at his drink.

The old man denied the implication. "I not prideful, never was prideful, nor my papa before me weren't. I knows my niggers likely an' prime. The kind I keeps because it the only kind worth pourin' vittles into, the kind that don't have to stan' a month in New Orleans jails waitin' for a body to buy."

The conversation turned to other themes, but Hammond did not forget the accusation of excessive pride. It came back to him

165

while Meg bathed him as he sat in the tub with his stiff leg extended. He wondered. Did a cripple, such as he, have a claim to pride? Was he seeking a vicarious soundness in his obsession with slaves without blemishes? As for gentility, a white cripple could still be a gentleman if he had, or ever had had, property. In addition, he himself had blood—three generations of planter forbears. Gentility was his birthright, which he could no more avoid than Redfield could acquire it. A gentleman must live up to his heritage, accept its perquisites and immunities, but the man proud of being a gentleman was something less than a gentleman, just as the man who aspired to be believed a gentleman, by so much, failed of his aspiration. Perhaps his own crippled leg, by curbing his pride, saved his gentility. Possibly that was its purpose, to chasten him. These unfamiliar reflections worried Ham.

Little could be expected from Ellen, but Hammond appealed to her that night. "Is I spreadin' my tail too much, lovie?" he asked her as she lay in his arms.

"How you mean, Masta, suh?"

"Doc Redfield say I gittin' too proud-like, buyin' a buck like Mede that whup all the otherns, an' a wench like you, lighter an' purtier than any other gen'lemen got. I don't crave to be 'sumptuous an' overbearin'. You don reckon I overbearin', not to white men?"

"Mista Doc doesn't know what a gentleman is like. I know he is white, but he ain't a gentleman, not like you're a gentleman, or old Masta Wilson's a gentleman."

"I ain't talk' 'bout Doc Redfield; I talkin' about me. Does havin' Falconhurst, an' good hosses, an' fine niggers make me too proudful?"

"I don't know how you treats white folks." Ellen was gradually assuming the vernacular of the plantation; "but you good to your niggers, sure good to them. Me, you——"

"How I treats you don't figure. You my bed-woman, and course I treats you choicelike."

"All of 'em—Meg and Memnon, Lucretia Borgia, an' Mede, an' Big Pearl, even the field niggers, all of 'em."

"I feed 'em good an' don' work them too hard. That all. With niggers nobody got to spread his tail; nobody. Niggers knows you better than they is. But when you better than another white man, you hadn't ought to let on you thinks it. He cain't he'p it 'cause he ain't got blood an' land an' niggers an' all."

166

"But you is better, Masta, suh," the girl emphasized.

"You reckon me marryin' that purty young white lady goin' to mek me more prideful? Make me so as no white man kin talk to me?"

Tears suffused Ellen's eyes and Hammond heard her sobbing in the darkness.

"Whut you cryin' 'bout? I didn't do nothin' to you," he said.

"I cain't help it. I cain't help it, Masta, please, suh. You goin' to marry an' I won't be nothing to you, nothin'." He felt her lift her hand and draw it across her eyes to brush away the tears.

"Doesn't you un'erstand?" Hammond demanded. "I got to— got to do it. I promised. Besides, it won't make no difference to you an' me. White ladies don't like no pesterin'; they not like wenches; they detests it; they jest submits to make a child. I still keeps you."

"But you goin' to love her—more than you love me. Masta, suh, oh, Masta."

"She goin' to be my wife, don' you un'erstan'?" the boy argued. "I got to love her like a white lady. I still goin' love you like a wench. Ain't nobody ever, white nor black, goin' to take your place. You always goin' to be mine."

"She goin' to be first."

"Course. She got to be. She white," he admitted. "Mustn't git to thinkin', 'cause I takes you into my bed, that you anythin' but a nigger. You purty and clean and sweetlike an' I loves you, but you ain't white, cain't have me a chil', not a white child."

Ellen knew that what he said was true and attempted no rebuttal.

"Not like me givin' you to no buck fer a breeder an' takin' me another wench. You my wench, rest easy; an' I don' want no other. Now, spread out an' let's go to sleep. I got plantin', come mornin'."

Meg's ear at the keyhole caught only random words of the conversation and failed to understand even what he heard. When he was sure the talking had stopped, he lay down outside his master's door and slept.

CHAPTER TWELVE

ON SUBSEQUENT Saturdays, Ham was unable to get fights for Mede in Benson, which augmented his belief that his boy was supreme, at least for the area around Benson. But even if

Mede should never fight again—and Hammond despaired of finding an opponent for him—he would remain, even to his decrepitude, a showpiece of whom no demonstration was required.

However, with the approach of May, Hammond had to set out to collect his bride, and fighting was relegated to the periphery of his interests.

His mother's room, closed since her death, was reopened and refurbished. The featherbed was tumbled, the former owner's apparel removed from the clothes press, the carpet taken up and dusted, and all made ready for Blanche's reception.

"Reckon we give Tense to Miz Blanche to be her nigger. She big enough, don' you reckon, an' clean an' a virgin?" Maxwell proposed. "That important. Don't want no impure wench a-servin' your wife."

"Needn't fret about that. Major Woodford goin' to give Blanche a little wench fer her weddin', I guess. Usual, ain't it?"

Maxwell snorted, "See that old man givin' nobody nothin'. Ain't got one to give."

"That money, Charles took along. Like he paid off on some of 'em. Wouldn't be genteel to not give her a wench that she used to."

"Better figger on Tense—'less, that is, you wants that one fer yourself. Cain't pester with your wife's wench."

"Not an' so long as I got Ellen, I doesn't crave no other," said the son.

"Dotin' more on that Ellen than right decent, seem like," cautioned the older man. "All well enough to pester with. Got to have you a wench, course. Remember, she jist a wench."

"I don' care. I don' want no other."

"No sense in you marryin', seem like."

"I hadn't bought Ellen when I promised Blanche. If I'd a went to Crowfoot by way of The Coign, I 'speck I wouldn't never a done it. Besides, you wants a gran'chile, doesn't you?"

Maxwell admitted as much.

"You mustn't neglec' to take Memnon down to the smith afore you go. Don't want no lusty, unringed buck in the house whure there is a white lady."

"Been puttin' it off. Mem scared of burnin'. Las' time the smith drop solder on him. Skeared yet."

"Fiddlesticks, smith not goin' to burn him, not to hurt much anyway. Don't got to punch through him this time; hole already in him."

168

"I take him, come mornin'," Hammond agreed.

"Another thing," bethought the old man. "Ain't decent all these saplin's runnin' around nekid—the bucks especial. They shock her an' she see 'em."

"They in the cabins an' the barn. They don't come around the house. Whut we goin' to do?"

"Better put shimmies on 'em. Tell Lucretia Borgia to git 'em made; she know which wenches kin ply a needle."

"Needn't come more than mid-leg."

"Long enough they cain't go aroun' kickin' up an' a-showin' theyself. An' these twins, got to learn 'em to keep buttoned up. They too little warrant ringin' for a year or two, but got to be decent an' talk decent. Hear?"

Both boys assented with a "Yas, suh, Masta, suh."

"Mine goin' to be all right in that riggin' I buy for him. Cain't fly open, an' I'll hang him up, I hears any dirty talk outn him. Alph too. Have to watch out your own self, I reckon."

"While you gittin', better git one of them brass-buttoned habits fer mine, too. Look real nice, the two of 'em alike, an' we kin use 'em on that Kit when the twins grows out of 'em."

"Don't reckon I better git new fer Mem? He's a-wearin' out."

"He do well enough. Make him brush his coat an' clean up."

It was plain to both the men that the presence of a white woman would necessitate some alteration in the plantation customs. Maxwell harked back to the time Hammond's mother had been alive and to the decorum that had reigned. In retrospect it did not seem to him onerous; Blanche could not be more exacting.

"Better fetch up them two mares from pasture an' have 'em clipped an' the harness greased," remarked Hammond.

"Goin' to take the surrey? Better drive them mares a little. Liable to be will', grassin' all winter."

"Thought the surrey. Cousin Blanche goin' to have a trunk, dresses an' all to fetch along. Goin' the north way, ferryin' good over all the branches. Won't have to swim the wagon."

"Good thing we got it. Hain't hardly been used sence your mamma—— Cain't abide wheels under me. Ruther straddle."

"But a lady—— Hard to ride side that fur."

"I knows. Ladies cain't straddle."

Hammond felt conspicuous and uneasy driving to Benson in a surrey to obtain the clothes he had ordered. A young man without a female companion seemed to him out of his realm in a vehicle. The mares, however, adjusted readily to harness; they

169

travelled in unison and without more skittishness than was expected from horses so long at pasture.

And the clothes he had had made were uncomfortable but would suffice for the purpose intended. The village cobbler had sought to make the boots as small as Ham could cramp his feet into and, however much pain resulted, they were neat, even dainty. His father was impressed with the dignity with which Ham strutted across the sitting-room floor, concealing his limp as best he could.

"Right well set up," was Maxwell's verdict. "Lady right lucky, I reckon."

"See that goods. Heavy. Wear like 'gater hide," said Hammond insistently, picking up the skirt of the coat and forcing it into the gnarled hands of his father. "Feel it."

"Right strong broadcloth, but ain't any too fine, not a bit. No better'n I wore the time I marry your mamma. Nothin' too stylish to marry in!"

In turn Meg was summoned to try on his new suit of which he had known nothing. "Better have him washed first," suggested Maxwell.

"Jest to try fer size, he won't dirty it none," Hammond declared. "Shuck down," he ordered the delighted boy.

Not bothering with stockings, which were a part of the outfit, he had the boy slip his naked legs into the breeches, adjusted the coat over his shirtless shoulders, and, seated on the floor, Meg pulled the shoes on his bare feet. They were his first shoes and he relished the enhanced status that would come from wearing them.

"You sure 'nough house nigger now," Hammond explained. "Got to ack like. No more rushin' around an' scufflin'. No more nekid skin. Go to keep these fixin's whole."

"I still goin' to be yo' nigger, yo' own?"

"I takin' you with me clear to Crowfoot, ain't I, whut more? Reckon you kin behave?"

"Yas, suh, Masta, yas suh, I behave; I behave good."

Two days later master and manikin set out on their journey. Pole had brought the surrey early in the morning and stood patiently at their heads holding the horses. Meg, magnificent in his brass-buttoned jacket, stockinged and shod, sat ramrod straight in the driver's seat an hour before Hammond was ready to depart.

There was much to be done. Putting on and adjusting the new clothes was itself a chore. A final trip to the Mandingo's cabin took up time.

Lucretia Borgia stood on the gallery beside Ellen, who had come out for the leave-taking. Hammond kissed them both. Tears came to Ellen's eyes but she did not sob. He kissed his father and hugged him to his body.

"You min' yo' manners, nigger, an' do what Masta say—ever'thin' jest like he say," his mother cautioned Meg. "An' take care them new clothes."

"I ain't takin' no blacksnake, but I kin sure tear him down with this buggy whip," said Hammond climbing into the surrey and shoving Meg toward the other seat.

"That's right, Masta," applauded Lucretia Borgia solemnly. "I hopes you goin' to smash him, Masta, suh. On'y way to tame a young nigger."

The world was green with May and the sunshine warmed it well. The rutted and washed roads slowed the surrey, which swayed on its springs, but there was no need for haste. The wedding was set for the eighth, and Hammond allowed four days for the journey.

Yet fine though the weather was, and despite Meg's excitement, Ham could not help brooding on the way. He dreaded what was ahead of him—his wedding, the prospect of which would have irked him less if the festivities connected with it could have been avoided. Crowfoot would overflow with guests strange to him, with whom he would be ill at ease. It was like Major Woodford to make the most of his daughter's marriage. The standing up to take those vows before all those people, the dinner afterwards, and the banter he would have to endure, the effort to behave like a gentleman when he wasn't quite sure of being one, all frightened Hammond. Taking refuge in vicarious good manners, he instructed Meg how to act; keep his coat straight and his pants buttoned, eat what was offered him and don't ask for anything else, don't pick his nose, don't break wind, and don't tell embarrassing lies.

Ham found no enjoyment in the lush green landscape, the planted acres, the brood of young bob-whites that scurried at his approach, the meadow lark's calls, the hawk, a speck in the turquoise dome, the snake that slithered across the road, causing his horses to shy. However, he looked forward to seeing Charles again, despite Charles' childish animosity for his sister, which was perhaps only jealousy.

It was not much short of noon on the fourth day when the carriage reached Crowfoot. "Set up straight now, we's gittin' there. I wants you to ac' good and right," he admonished Meg as he turned into the lane that led to the house.

"I is, Masta, suh," the small boy replied with resolution.

Hammond was relieved, and also amazed to see so little stir about the place. Possibly he thought, the Major had restrained himself from making a festival of his daughter's wedding. A ragged young slave scurried to take charge of the team, and before Hammond could reach the front door the old houseboy appeared from a side door to receive him.

"Whure at your masta? Whure Major Woodford?" Hammond demanded.

"He gone to church, Masta, suh. White folks all gone to meetin'," the slave replied. "I knows you though, suh. You that white gen'leman that come time back. I knows you. Come in, suh, if you please, suh." He threw open the front door.

"I'll wait here," said Hammond, sitting down on the edge of the gallery floor. "I reckon they not goin' to be long now, specially the weddin'——"

"They all goin' to Sterlin' Plantation to eat dinner—all 'ceptin' Masta Dick. He be comin' home, suh, this afternoon, he goin' to dip some niggers in the crick that ain't babtize yet. He comin'," the yellow Negro said, dragging out a large chair from inside the house.

"But the weddin'——" Hammond urged.

"Ain't knowin' nothin' about that, Masta," the Negro kept his counsel. "Masta never said nothin' 'bout that, suh."

Had he mistaken the appointed date, Hammond wondered. He got up and sat in the chair for a short while, Meg continuing to sit on the floor, but later Hammond arose and paced the driveway impatiently, glancing toward the entrance at every tenth step. He was aware of Negro eyes on him from the quarters, but ignored them.

"Kin I git you sompin', sompin' to eat, or sompin', Masta, suh, whiles you waitin'?" the house servant returned to ask.

Hammond wanted nothing except to be enlightened. "I'll jes' wait," he said.

"How Masta Charles come on, suh? You're the one, suh, he go away with, ain't you, suh?" the Negro asked.

"He back, Charles back, weeks ago," the white man affirmed. "Ain't he?" he then asked as an afterthought.

"Naw, suh, Masta, suh; naw, suh. Masta Charles ain't never come back."

So. That was the reason for the lack of preparation for the

172

wedding! No money, no bride! What had become of Charles? What had happened to him? And to Jason? Charles had absconded with the Maxwell money, the Maxwell ring, and the Maxwell slave. He was not only a thief, but worse, a niggerstealer. What a fool he had been to entrust Woodford's son with so much money! In his anger he had resolved to order his horses, when a horseman came down the lane.

Dick Woodford dismounted and threw his bridle to the Negro boy who had taken Hammond's team. Dressed all in black, he was a fine figure of a young man; save for the wild, ecstatic, irresponsible, drunken look in his faded blue eyes, he might have been handsome. But he was not drunk on alcohol. Hammond walked toward him.

"You! You that Maxwell!" Dick addressed Ham. "You the one that plight to marry my sister! Whut you do here? An' I weren't a preacher an' you a crip, I'd gouge your eyes out, both en 'em. Whut you do at Crowfoot?"

"Whut I do at Crowfoot?" Hammond restrained himself. "I come to marry Miz Blanche, like I said. This the day she set."

"After you conjure her brother away with you? An' never send no money like you was a-goin'? You think she marry no sich son-a-bitch like you?"

"I sent that money. Sent it by that damn nigger-stealin' brother of yourn!" Hammond's temper was rising.

"Don't cuss! Don't cuss! I'm a preacher, you know. Don't cuss," Dick retreated into his vocation.

"Then don't cuss your own sel'," Hammond admonished. "Nigger tellin' me Charles never come, never fetched Major Woodford that money?"

"An' you trust him with money? Trus' Charlie?" Dick was incredulous. "Cain't trus' that scoun'rel with four bits. I don't credit you send him."

"Five or six weeks back, he bin gone. Took one of my niggers along, my papa's, an' twenty-five hunderd dollars, gold."

"Gold! A nigger!" Dick sat down on the edge of the gallery and guffawed. "You cain't trust Charlie with a nigger more than with a dollar. Charlie out an' gone—maybe in the Texies by this time. Whurever Charlie be, the money sure spent an' that nigger sure sol'."

His laughter took the hysterical intensity from Dick's eyes. It was contagious and Hammond laughed with his cousin, but with less hilarity. It was a costly joke.

173

"But whut fer you take him along, first place?" asked Dick, drying his eyes with his hand. "It whut you gits, encitin' him along."

"Encitin'? Charles caught me up an' say his papa given his leave; he swear it," and Hammond retold the story of his being overtaken and joined by young Woodford.

"An' you believe him? Better turn it inside out, an' take it the other way, Charlie never say true in his life."

"At Falconhurst, he right good, right trusty."

"Gittin' ready fer devilment. But I believes you. Reckon you say true. 'Bout you an' Blanche, got to wait till Papa come." Dick rose to his feet. "Got to eat. Dinner ready. Likely ain't much an' folks away. But come along."

Meg was sent to the kitchen for his meal.

"Right likely little buck you got," Dick commented upon the obediently retreating child. "Breed him?"

"Him an' his twin, jest alike."

"Papa don' have no luck breedin', seems like wenches slips 'em or they dies or sumpin'. Ain' more than about a dozen young around."

"My papa don' have no trouble that a-way." Hammond took no credit for himself. "Coursen, we mostly buys, when we kin find 'em."

As the two went through the sitting-room and into the dining-room, Dick clapped his guest on the shoulder. "You all right an' right hones', seem like. Don't care an' you are cripped. You got money an' all them niggers. I goin' to like you, don't make no matter whut folks a-sayin'."

"My mamma was a Hammond," Ham explained proudly.

"So also is Charlie's mamma—and mine," Dick countered.

After dinner, Dick excused himself. "Papa havin' me practise preachin' on the people," he explained. "Ain't never baptized heretofore, but got to today—two or three wenches an' a buck ain't been saved. Papa puttin' it off. Don't crave wettin' his britches. Reckon you'd rather snooze or somethin'. I'll hurry. Won't be long." The fanatic gleam, trademark of his evangelism, reappeared in Dick's eyes as he stalked away.

To snooze was the last thing Hammond wanted to do. He paced the floor of the house, paced the gallery, paced the driveway. He wished that he had gone with Dick to the religious meeting for the Negroes and was moved to follow him, but thought better of the project. He had better wait. To be refused his bride he could endure, but he wanted to have the matter settled.

174

He thought of how much Blanche had cost him, twenty-five hundred dollars plus the ring and two journeys to Crowfoot, though of course the first trip had included his visit to The Coign and his purchases of Mede and Ellen, for neither of which he had any regrets. If only he had gone there first, before he had come to Crowfoot! But dear as Ellen was to him, she wasn't his wife. That was unthinkable. After all, he needed a wife to give him an heir.

At length Dick returned from his baptizing. "I ducked 'em, ducked 'em good," he called in triumph. "It was easy. I kin do it. On'y that lean wench slip away from me an' like to a-drowned, on'y she never."

"You all soaked. Look at your britches. Better put on dry," suggested Hammond.

"I took 'em off an' wrang 'em out," said Dick. "They goin' to dry. Whut I needs is a drink of corn. Medicine! I temp'ance of course. But carryin' things too fur to not use it fer medicine—keep from ketchin' somethin'. You not temp'ance, I reckon? Wantin' a drink?" He led the way to the spring-house where the Major kept his whisky.

Hammond was indeed wanting a drink and followed his host with a feeling that approached gratitude. One drink begot thirst for another, and the second for the third. The afternoon was growing late when the sound of horses' heels in the driveway broke the spell of their session. Hammond heard the orotund voice of the Major demanding, "Whose boy are you?" and heard Meg answer politely, "I's Masta Ham Maxwell's nigger, Masta, please, suh."

"You git out an' go up to your room, an' don' come down until I says," Ham heard the Major subdue his voice, which was still loud enough, and heard him boom a whisper into his wife's ear-trumpet, "Hammond Maxwell." When Beatrix failed to understand him, he repeated twice, slowly and syllabically as if to enable her to read his lips, "Ham-mond! Hammond Max-well!"

The woman replied with a startled intake of breath, "Oh!"

Dick and Hammond emerged from the spring-house in time to see Beatrix, all in brown, sedately, without a glance to right or left, enter the front door of the house. Blanche, in the selfsame challis dress in which Hammond had first seen her, followed her mother, but with a high-headed assumption of dignity and a tragic tread.

The Major maintained his ground in the driveway and waited

175

for the young man to approach. The carriage drove away toward the stables.

"Papa, this Mista Maxwell," Dick presented the guest as if he were unknown to his father.

"Reckon I don' know the skunk?" the Major demanded, drawing himself to his utmost height. "Had ought ter. Throwin' my poor girl into a decline! Whut he wantin' here now?"

"He sent it! He sent the money!" Dick hastened to appease his father.

"Then whyn't it come?" The Major did not credit his son's assurance.

"Sent it by Charlie! Sent it by Charlie!" Dick's feet stamped in rhythm with his laughter at the inconceivable stupidity of entrusting anything to his brother.

"That why he spirit Charles away, I reckon—so he kin tell he sent the money an' it didn't come. Right clever sharper. Ain't got the money an' never had it. Never meant to send."

Hammond had not spoken. Now he said simply and without show of rancour, "An' you doesn't believe me, doesn't believe I sent the money, doesn't believe I sent Miz Blanche no ring, doesn't believe your Charles stole no buck when he left, doesn't take my word as a gen'leman, all I kin do now is to ast you kindly, suh, fer my hosses. I come to wed Miz Blanche, like she say; this the eighth of May. You could save me the journey—the least you could do, suh, seem like. Will you be so good, suh, as to order my hosses?" He was proud of himself for the speech he had made.

"I never said it; never said I didn't believe your word. Wait a minute." The Major sheathed his horns. "Maybe we goin' to un'erstan' one another. Maybe we goin' to fix things up. I tells you: an' you sends that money, that is an' you promise to again, maybe you kin wed my daughter. Maybe you did send; I ain't sayin' you never. But you got to show faith, an' sen' agin."

"I craves my hosses, suh, if you please, suh. I ain't a-purchasin' your daughter—the second time. Ifn your son stolen your money an' my nigger, we pockets our losin's; but not another dollar does I beg from my papa fer you, not another two bits. Miz Blanche, she ain't to blame, an' I ain't to blame. I'll marry her, but I ain't a-goin' to buy her."

Major Woodford hesitated. Suitors for his daughter's hand were rare enough, and no other was affluent. This man in his family should stiffen his credit and later could hardly fail to help him out of his financial jam. Could he afford to wreck Blanche's prospects and possibly his own on the rock of pride? He decided that he could not. Moreover, he thought of Charles. Maxwell could not be expected to prosecute his brother-in-law for the theft of a Negro—the most heinous of crimes. If Charles should be caught, the theft would be ignored or passed off as a mere mistake. The Major would not desert his son.

All these things ran quickly through his mind.

"I willin' to make the sacrifice an' if Blanche's mamma is. She a Hammond, you know. She proud. But, other hand, I don't crave no case of green sickness, that it look like my daughter a-comin' to."

"Come in, come in," urged Dick. "It all right. Don't fret. Mamma do like Papa say. Always does." He ushered Hammond into the Empire drawing-room. Holding the door he asked, "Wants I should turn your nigger inside or sen' him to quarters?"

"He house tamed," answered Hammond, sitting gingerly upon the damask divan.

Meg came in and at his master's behest sat on the floor at Ham's feet.

The suitor heard the girl's father discussing the marriage with her deaf mother in the adjoining sitting-room. Dick was with them but had little to say. The Major sought to subdue his voice, but whispers loud enough to penetrate Beatrix's ear-trumpet were audible to Hammond in the drawing-room. Hammond made an effort not to hear, but if he failed to catch a sentence the first time it was spoken, he was unable to avoid it when it was repeated, as most speeches had to be. The Major's mind was made up, and his consultation with his wife a mere formula to enable him to excuse himself for his failure to impose, and to extract, harder terms, an effort in his capitulation to save honour.

He assured Beatrix that Hammond had denied abducting Charles, that Charles had claimed parental leave to go with him. He told of Charles's departure from Falconhurst with the Maxwell money and the ring for Blanche.

"That a fib," said Beatrix with indignation. "He ain't tellin' true. Charles would a brung it. My boy would a brung it right straight. He never sent it, I never raised Charles to be no thief."

"But he is one," countered the Major, "a nigger thief. He took away one of Warren's bucks." He had to repeat the statement three times before he could make the woman hear it; her difficulty was more a reluctance to credit the story than an inability to understand the words.

177

When the accusation penetrated to her consciousness, Beatrix gasped. Then she shrieked, after which she lay back in her chair. "He dead! Charles is dead," she uttered in her empty voice. "That's it. That nigger killed him an' stole that money. My boy! My pore boy! He's dead!"

"He ain't dead! You knows he ain't dead!" the Major laid his hands on his wife's arm for emphasis and consolation. "No sich thing. Charles is off, a-spendin' that money of mine. You'll see when he come ridin' up one of these days." He assumed as cheerful a tone as he was able and reinforced it with a grimace resembling a smile, although his assurance lacked confidence. He was, in fact, indifferent to the fate of his son, though not to the fate of the twenty-five hundred dollars.

"He dead. I say he dead. I knows it; I feels it," protested Beatrix, rolling her head back and forth on the back of her chair. "My boy dead." She broke into weeping.

Dick brushed his father aside to reach the trumpet. "An' he wasn't saved!" he screamed into her ear. "Charles never got right with Jesus! I knew it would happen. An' he dead, he burnin' in hell fire right now, burnin'!"

Major Woodford struggled with his son to pull him out of the range of the woman's earpiece. "Don't tell her that," he whispered. "Don't make her no worse."

"It so, an' you know it so," shouted the preacher. "Charlie wasn't saved, an' he a-burnin'. Mamma know he a-burnin'." Dick seemed to gloat over his contemplation.

"No! No! No!" cried his mother. "I pray for him; I been a-prayin' ever' day an' ever' night. Mayhap he saved. Mayhap, jest as that nigger come down on his head, he seen Jesus an' embraced Him." She toppled forward upon her knees and bowed her head in silent prayer.

The Major picked up her trumpet which had fallen to the floor and held it to Beatrix's ear. "Whut about that weddin'? Whut you craves to do about that?" he vociferated.

"Do whut you wants! Do whut you goin' to do anyways!" the bereft mother looked up in irritation at the interruption of her prayer. "You drive away Charles; now you a-drivin' Blanche. Sellin' her jest like she was a nigger. Go on an' sell her, an' that whut you bent on."

"I ain't neither a-sellin' her. He done send the money an' Charlie stolen it. He won't sen' no more." Woodford held the horn to his wife's ear and spoke loudly but not directly into the

178

horn. He did not know and cared little whether Beatrix heard him.

She refused to be diverted from her efforts to rescue her murdered son from the fires of hell and shifted the responsibility to the father for the disposal of her daughter. He laid the horn upon the chair and looked at Dick.

Dick nodded. "Go ahead," he said in a voice low enough not to interrupt the prayer further. "Might as well. He rich. An' besides, there ain't nobody else 'at a-wantin' her. First thing, she goin' be an' ol' maid, an' then whut?"

Major Woodford pulled himself together, hitched his neck, adjusted his coat, and assumed his most pompous mien. He strode into the adjoining room where Hammond waited.

"Blanche's mamma an' me, we talked it over," he announced. "We talked it all over an' we decided. We decided on lettin' love have its way. We cain't stan' up agin it. An' you wants my daughter an' Blanche a-wantin' you, that the way it goin' to be."

Hammond got to his feet. He had heard every word of the conversation. "I knowed you an' Cousin Beatrix weren't a-goin' to let me come all this way fer nothin'," he said, grasping the Major's extended hand.

"Better ride fer the preacher," the Major turned to Dick. "Ride fer Jones, an' bring him along quick as you kin."

"Afore supper?" Dick objected.

"Hell with supper. We got to git a preacher an' they goin' to sleep tonight. Tell Auntie Celia to keep somethin' hot, time you git back. But ride fer Jones. Whut's a-henderin' you?"

"Ain't no press," Ham suggested. "We kin wait fer mornin'."

"Put off a weddin' after it set?" The Major was horrified. "Bad luck; wouldn't have no case in it. Got to be today or not never. Set down awhile an' hold your peace, an' let me go up an' fetch her down."

The Major went upstairs and Dick disappeared by way of the sitting-room and kitchen. Later, Dick's horse passed the window at a trot, but its hoof-beats turned into the rhythm of a gallop before he had reached the road. Hammond waited. He grew ill at ease as the time elapsed and he speculated whether the girl had grown recalcitrant. The hauteur with which she had left the carriage and walked into the house might have been real.

Meg rolled solemn eyes toward his owner's face. He sensed a gravity in the situation which he did not understand. It was unthinkable to him that anybody, of whatever complexion, should seek to thwart his master's will, but he dared not speak or question.

The bloodlessness of Blanche's face was emphasized by a coat of rice powder as she came down the stairs, followed by her father. It was apparent to Hammond that she had sought to repair the ravages of tears, but he was left to wonder whether she had wept because of first being forbidden him or because she was now commanded to marry him. She continued to wear the challis dress which in the eyes of her lover enhanced such beauty as she possessed. She could not have chosen a costume better to enchant him. Hammond did not know it was the best in her limited wardrobe, and assumed it was the woman and not her dress that caused him to believe her beautiful.

She was trembling and austere when he rose to meet her. She paused at the foot of the stairs and he went to take her in his arms. She neither resisted nor returned the kiss he gave her, but looked into his face with a resigned, sad smile.

Conversation was strained. "I thought you wouldn't come," she forced herself to say.

"You knowed I'd come. I say I would when you set the time."

"You say you send me a ring," she accused.

"I did. I sent it. Charles tote it."

"Charles!" She spoke it in a tone of such contempt as to indict Hammond of stupidity in his trust of her brother.

"Mayhap he dead. Mayhap he kilt a-comin'," Hammond sought to justify his confidence in her brother. "Like your mamma a-sayin'."

"By rights ought to be, though he ain't," said Woodford.

Blanche sat down on the divan. "I ain't got no dress," she apologized, shooting a withering glance at her father. "Papa didn't think you comin' an' wouldn't buy me none."

"I was waitin' fer that money to come," harped the old man.

"I ain't a-weddin' no dress," declared Hammond, unaware how much he had been taken in by the challis. "We kin buy dresses, all you craves of 'em—all you needs." He modified his estimate.

The vision of unlimited dresses enchanted the girl. She smiled with a faraway look and pictured herself in silks and laces and jewels in a baronial hall surrounded by adoring gallants, who kissed her hand, no longer red and stubby with broken and bitten nails. Always she would remain true to her lover-husband, spurning the hearts that she would break. All the dresses she craved!

180

The sound of the supper bell summoned her back to Crowfoot and reality.

Meg was sent to the kitchen for food. The Major went in search of Beatrix, who had quietly vanished after her prayer. He returned discomfited and made his wife's excuses. In her apprehension of Charles' murder, she had retired with her grief and desired no supper.

The three went in. Hammond and Blanche sat on either side of the host, the empty chair across from him an accusation. The half-needed candles flickered in the dying daylight. There was a tentative tone to the talk, a constraint, an avoidance of the subjects closest to the speakers' thoughts. With pauses between subjects, which Blanche sought to hide with shy, flirtatious looks directed towards the boy across the table from her, the conversation ranged from the health of Hammond's father to the price of cotton, crop prospects, the weather, past, present and to come, the Negroes of Falconhurst and the rising market for them.

"Warren don't need no two hunderd head," opined Woodford. "Whyn't he sell off about half, the price they fetchin'?"

"We sells 'em when they grows. Took a coffle to the city las' autumn after pickin'; another ready to go, come fall. Most of ourn is saplin's, that is, an' suckers."

"I don' have no luck with suckers, seem like. Wenches won't bring 'em, an' when they does they punies an' dies or somethin'."

"Papa don' have no stew with 'em, not much. Coursen, he say, an' he could buy 'em half-raised, the kin' he wants 'em, sound and straight bucks, he'd sell off the wenches an' not breed no more, he say, but on'y jest buy."

"Warren jest talkin'," scoffed Woodford.

"Jes' talkin', I reckons," Hammond agreed. "He likes 'em little-like. Likes to raise 'em. But more money in buyin' saplin's than in raisin' suckers, an' don' take so long. But a body cain't find 'em —likely ones."

"Ain't hard. They plenty, plenty," said Woodford with an expansive sweep of his hand, "an' you ready to pay fer 'em."

For want of something else to do, they lingered at table after their hunger was satisfied. The night had grown dark and the moon had not risen. Shadows were cast against the wall by the saffron glow of the candles.

The party returned to the drawing-room and sat, stiff and self-conscious, awaiting Dick's return with the preacher. From time

181

to time, the Major, on the pretence of scanning the lane for riders, made his way to the spring-house for a swallow of corn. On each return, he went upstairs and the young people were able to overhear his part of an argument with his wife, who remained adamant in her belief that Charles was dead and in her refusal to bless her daughter's marriage. Her words were not audible, but from her husband's loud arguments it was possible to surmise what she was saying. She did not forbid the union, but refused any part in it, stubbornly placing the decision and any subsequent blame for it upon the tremulous shoulders of the Major.

The sound of the hooves of a single horse upon the drive interrupted the stalemated argument, and by the time Dick had called a boy and surrendered his horse, the Major was coming down the stairs.

"Whure Jones?" the Major demanded as Dick entered the door.

"Sime Maddox, he's a-dyin'," the messenger explained.

"Let him die, but whure Jones?"

"Out to Mista Maddox gittin' him ready, ready to meet his Maker," Dick elaborated.

"Well, I swan," swore the Major. "Why you calculate he wouldn't come? He won't git a cent out of Sime, not a cent, an' Hammon' here give him two, three, maybe five dollars. You fool, Dick, you god-damn fool. Now what we goin' to do?" He turned and went up the stairs again to report Dick's failure to Beatrix and to charge her with their son's stupidity.

"I ain't to blame I couldn't fetch him," Dick sought to absolve himself, dropping into a chair.

"Course," Hammond acknowledged.

Blanche dissolved in tears.

"Course he kin, good as any," the Major's voice from upstairs boomed with a new hope. "I fergot all about that. An' you'll come down, an' he do? An' give 'em your blessin'? Well, that whut we goin' to do."

Blanche wiped away her tears and raised her eyes toward her father as he came expansively down the stairs. She saw that he had a way out of the difficulty. Hammond was resigned to whatever might happen. Meg, once more on the floor at his master's feet, failed to fathom the impediment to the marriage, or to understand why his omnipotent master didn't surmount it, whatever it might be. Perhaps that was why the beautiful white lady in the flowered dress was weeping.

"Dick!" announced the Major, slapping his sitting son on the shoulder. "Dick! Dick a preacher. He kin do it, do it good as any. He sanctified; he a preacher! Whyn't we think? Why we send fer Jones?"

"Papa! No!" objected his son to his father's solution. "No, I cain't. I'm jest a-startin' out. I cain't wed no white folks—never did."

"You kin, you kin!" protested his father. "Ain't no different marryin' white folks than niggers, on'y no broom. You kin do it! Hammon' gives you the money, jest like he would Jones."

"Reckon it legal?" Hammond was sceptical.

"Legal as Jones," opined the Major. "Dick's a preacher, ain't he? No matter he ain't preached to white folks yet. He a-goin' to. He say the words an' I write it in the Bible, you married, married fast."

"I don' know the lines," Dick protested.

"Ain't no difference whut you sayin'. Jest home folks! Besides, your mamma wants you. An' you do it, your mamma comin' downstairs to listen. She given in to it, an' Dick doin' it. You don't got to string it out. All you do is jest ast 'em an' tell 'em. Good practice."

The brown figure of Beatrix descended the stairs. All the blood was drained from her solemn face, leaving her more sallow than before. She approached her husband without speaking, extending towards him her hearing device.

"Dick not a-wantin' to," called the Major into the horn. "Says he cain't."

"Course he kin. Dick jest backward," said his mother emptily. "Goin' to be a preacher, got to start in bein' one. Come along, Son."

Dick struggled bashfully to his feet.

"Stan' up, Ham; stan' up, Blanche. Stan' together here in front of this window," the Major arranged the party. "You, mamma, stan' right there by Blanche so as you kin hear good," he called into the horn.

Meg, ignored, arose also. He was unsure what was expected of him and half expected to be ordered back to the floor.

"I 'on't know. I reckon we got to kneel down first off," Dick improvised.

When all were firmly on their knees, Dick offered his prayer. "Dear God," he prayed, "we come together here before You to join together these white folks in wedlock, in holy matrimony," he repeated himself, uncertain how to proceed. "We begs You to bless their union with long life an' joys an' comfortin' one another in they ol' age. We prays You goin' to 'stow on 'em Your benediction an' goin' to bring 'em childern to raise up to praise Thee. We prays You goin' to bring 'em childern an' that them childern goin' to be boys, O God, 'cause Hammon' here, he wants a boy to help him manage that plantation of his paw's an' to take it offen his hands when he goin' to die, O God.

"My sister Blanche here, she stubborn, O God. Thou knowest she stubborn, O God. Take it out of her heart, God; take that stubborn streak she got right outn her heart. Make her give in to her husban', God, an' do whut he say an' obey his commands, O God, like she had ought to.

"Bless this service of marri'ge, O God, an' make it legal; make it legal an' bindin' on 'em both. An' bless Thy servant an' his ministry an' his preachin' and deliver me from temptations of the flesh, so as I kin serve Thee.

"An' bless my mamma an' my papa here. Shower down your blessin' on 'em an' on Charlie, if he alive. An' if he dead, save him from hellfire an' 'cept him into Your lovin' grace.

"An' bless this little nigger of Hammond's an' all his niggers, an' all my papa's niggers, O God. Increase 'em an' multiply 'em, an' make 'em obey they masters, O God, that they goin' to be released from they bondage when they die, O God, that they goin' to be free when they die.

"I reckon that all for now, O God. I don't bethink me of nothin' else. Jest do whut I'm askin', O God, in Jesus' name.

"Amen."

Dick spoke intimately to God and laid down his commands to Him, although he had no confidence tonight that they would be heeded. God seemed far away and concerned with His own affairs.

"Amen," Beatrix nodded her approval as she got to her feet. "I was knowin' you could. On'y thing, you fergot of Cousin Warren. Glad you blessed your brother, whurever he is."

The Major caught his wife's eye and placed his finger to his lips to silence her.

"Well, you ready?" Dick inquired. "Does you, Hammon', take this lady name of Blanche to be your lawful, wedded wife, fer better or fer worse, in sickness and health, through weal or woe, to love an' proteck till death or distance do you part?"

"Yas, suh," Hammond nodded in assent.

"An' you, on your part, Blanche, do you accep' this Hammon'

here to be your lawful wedded husban', fer better or fer worse, in sickness an' health, come weal, come woe, to love an' obey without no back-talk till death or distance goin' to part you?"

"I accep's him," promised Blanche firmly.

"Then that is all they is to it," affirmed Dick. "I goin' to announce you husban' an' his wife an' may God have mercy on your souls. Amen!"

Dick pumped the groom's arm and gingerly, reluctantly kissed the bride. The mother wept as she embraced the embarrassed couple and the father beamed his blessing.

"Ain't you goin' to kiss her?" Dick asked Hammond.

"He plagued, an' ever'body lookin'. Wait till they git alone," the Major condoned the omission. He grasped Hammond's arm with one hand and Dick's arm with the other, leading them out-of-doors and toward the spring-house.

Dick protested, " 'Tain't right. I'm a preacher. I'm temp'ance."

"Temp'ance this afternoon too, wasn't you?" asked the Major. "A cup of corn to celebrate your sister ain't a-goin' to sen' you to hell. Besides," he added, nudging his son-in-law in the ribs with his elbow, "Hammond goin' to need it."

Hammond did need it.

"Better leave 'em alone a spell together. Her mamma got to 'xplain to your wife whut marryin' goin' to mean—whut kin' of son-of-bitches men is." Without being subtle, neither was the prurient old man forthright in his allusions to the consummation of the marriage. Hammond was grateful for his father-in-law's restraint. He had feared a house full of guests and a ragging. Candour caused him no embarrassment, but to veiled allusions and euphemisms he found no words for reply.

Dick's libidinous imagination was swathed in a stern morality, which his calling imposed upon him.

"No white man goin' to touch a lady, 'ceptin' he wantin a' chil'," he declared.

"Whut he goin' to do? You an' your preachin'!" scoffed the father. "You reckon I a-wantin' you—or Charlie, or a gal? You talks like your mamma."

" 'Tain't right, makin' a lady submit to your lustin's. 'Twasn' whut ol' Saint Paul meant at all. That whut niggers is fer. You kin use a wench, cain't you?"

"Some men ain't got no wench, or they too black or somethin'. Whut do you say to that?"

"Mos' gen'lemen got 'em—one or two anyways," Hammond

185

declared himself mildly on the side of morality, which did not pertain to the unpropertied.

"Besides, it the law. The law givin' a man rights. Ain't nothin' fer a lady to say about," the Major chuckled as he clenched his argument. "They married, ain't they?"

"To increase an' multiply, they is. Yes, suh," Dick admitted. "But not fo' pleasurin'. That sin!"

"My only sin now'days is corn whisky," said the Major tossing off his fourth cup. "Help yourself. I reckon we better go in, afore my wife tellin' yourn to not let you in bed."

The men had tarried so long in the spring-house that the wives had gone upstairs. Meg had fallen asleep on the floor and Hammond had to shake him to wake him up. The Major escorted his new son-in-law to the door of Blanche's bedroom and went himself into the adjoining one where Beatrix could be heard still stirring restlessly.

Blanche was supine in her big bed, modestly swathed in a heavy nightdress buttoned at the neck. Hammond imagined the whiteness, the marble pinkness, of his wife's blonde body and the thought of contact with it revolted him. He was so used to the sight of darker skins that it made him queasy. He had married Blanche for her racial purity, of which her blondeness was the earnest, but he was grateful for the buttoned nightgown.

It was apparent that the girl had been weeping, which her husband ignored. The sleep-sodden Meg removed his master's boots and socks, and helped him off with his outer clothes. He failed to understand but did not question why the white man retained his undergarments.

"Ain't no quilt laid out fer you. Got to sleep in your clo's; but sleep straight an' don' muss 'em," Hammond cautioned the boy, putting him down outside the door. "An' I goin' to lambaste you, I catches you at that keyhole, goin' to hang you up."

Meg lay down too weary, too sleepy, for curiosity. Why, anyway, should he be curious?

Later Meg was awakened by his master's stumbling over his sleeping figure. Hammond emerged from the room, dressed in his coat, socks and boots in his hand, and directed the half sleeping boy to come along with him. They descended the stair and the master groped for a chair in which he sat while the slave dressed his feet. The master remained sitting, preoccupied and baffled. At last he rose, paced back and forth across the floor of the room, wandered to the door and paced the driveway. The

186

young Negro, without knowing why, was as much distressed as his master, whom he sensed to be sorely troubled.

Hammond started toward the stables, resolved to harness his own horses without disturbing the slaves and to take his departure, when the side door opened and Dick inquired whether it was he and what the matter could be.

"I cain't sleep, an' I got up," was all the explanation Hammond would offer. "I has a lot of trouble that a-way, not a-sleepin'."

"It's that Blanche!" Dick divined. "Go back an' tell her, tell her she married, she married an' it her duty. Want I should go up with you, or call Papa?"

"No, it not that. I jest cain't go to sleep. Cousin Blanche, she sleepin' soun'. Go back to bed," Hammond answered in a half voice. His resolution to escape was broken. He wandered the agonized night alone. Meg sat on the edge of the gallery and dozed.

Hammond was grateful to Mercury when the planet rose above the trees, an assurance that morning was not far off. He strolled unseeingly down the lane and into the silent road toward Briarfield. At the first light he turned and retraced his steps toward Crowfoot. He sat on the edge of the gallery floor beside his sleeping minion, for whom the owner felt a new and fierce affection. Upon Meg's loyalty he could count. For all his stupidity, ignorance, childish innocence, for all his mischievous lying and braggadocio to others, he was, as he proclaimed, Hammond's nigger, as steadfast as Lucretia Borgia herself.

Stirring began. Young Negroes crossed the area to the well. Blue smoke rose from cabin chimneys. Katy came from Dick's room and ambled towards the quarters. The plantation day had begun. Hammond dreaded the arrival of the Woodfords, with their unasked questions and ribald curiosity. He was grateful for Beatrix's deafness. Would Blanche demand why he had left her bed, or would she care?

Hammond looked up and saw the Major in the doorway, beaming and cheerful. The older man confined his comments to the fineness and largeness of the morning and to an insinuating inquiry about Ham's health and how he had slept. Hammond ignored the insinuation and admitted that he had not slept well and had risen early, but did not say how early.

"How Blanche?" hinted her father. "She comin' down—time for breakfast?"

"I reckon," said Hammond.

"I right plagued not to have a fancy weddin', but I wrote it in Beatrix's Bible. It will hold."

"I obliged you didn't go to nothin' fancy," declared Hammond.

"Couldn't. That money didn't come. I couldn't. And I cain't make you no present, Beatrix and me. Had ought to, I knows. Plagues Blanche's mamma."

" 'S all right. Nothin' I's a-wantin' savin' your gal, savin' Blanche."

"Had ought to give you a wench fer her—least I could do. Looks bad. Don't know whut Warren goin' to reckon."

"Him an' me already got one of ourn picked out fer her. He don't 'spect nothin'."

"You know how it is. Hands all mortgaged. Cain't part with 'em. Course, you wantin' to take up the mortgage an' pay it, help yourself. Take any of 'em, any I got," the Major made a show of generosity which he knew would be rejected.

Whatever aspect of cheerfulness, real or assumed, the others brought to the breakfast table, Beatrix's austerity of manner cancelled out. Her reluctance to part with her daughter was aggravated by her conviction that marriage at its best was for women a sorrow only less evil than spinsterhood. Her own had been. All night she had imagined Blanche's pure body at the mercy of male bestiality and had wept for her. Her horror of marriage as an institution embraced a resentment of the man to whom her daughter was married. She was at once impelled to implore him to restrain his appetite (which being male she knew to be gross) and restrained by a womanly decorum that forbade allusion to such a theme. Nor could she bring herself to suggest to Blanche that she demand forbearance from her husband.

Blanche's solemn visage was not, as her mother believed, inspired by Hammond's ardour, but rather by his lack of it, which had moved him to forsake her bed after scarcely an hour with her. Her dreams of married bliss had been quite different.

The team was waiting, harnessed to the surrey, by the time breakfast was finished, but the departure for which Hammond was impatient was delayed by Blanche's preparation, packing her limited wardrobe into a capacious carpet-bag. Blanche acknowledged her mother's admonitions with nods of her head and movements of her lips, some of which Beatrix was able to interpret. Seldom did the girl interrupt her work to go to the bed on which the elder woman sat to shout into her trumpet. Much as the mother regretted the parting, the daughter had no qualms at leaving home, which meant to her a pleasant adventure with a rich husband and a promise of luxury.

It was approaching ten o'clock before Blanche was fully ready to go. The men spent the intervening time in gossip and visits to the spring-house, although Dick, in an upsurge of virtue, refused to join his father and brother-in-law in their libations.

Blanche descended the stairs, again in the same challis dress, followed by the houseboy with the carpet-bag, which he stowed in the rear seat of the vehicle. Beatrix, in an effort further to delay the separation, proposed family prayers, for which Hammond declared himself to be unable to wait and to which Blanche was as loath to be subjected as was her husband.

"Git yourself up in that back seat an' watch that valise," his master admonished Meg. "Set up and don't scrunch down, 'cause you ridin' with your mist'ess."

"Ain't you fergittin'?" Dick demanded with a show of diffidence. At Hammond's questioning lift of the brows, Dick added, "Fer pronouncin' that weddin'. Ain't you goin' to pay? Course, you don' got to; I ain't a-astin' nothin'."

Hammond delved into his pocket for his poke. "I sure like to fergotten," he said, fingering the coins. "Glad you remembered me." Unable to find a five-dollar piece, which he deemed adequate payment for the ceremony, he forked over a ten-dollar piece.

"Too much, too much," protested the preacher, nevertheless quickly pocketing the money.

"Keep it, keep it all. Reckon we kin 'ford it. All in the family, anyways, now."

Hammond's statement gave the Major a hope of access to the Maxwell hoard. He contrived a beaming paternal smile.

Dick withdrew the coin from his pocket and, after polishing it on his trousers, extended it on his upright palm toward his mother. "The first preacherin' money!" he said with pride. "I goin' to keep it fer seed."

With mutual reluctance, Beatrix and Hammond exchanged a kiss. "God bless you!" she said. "Be good to her, Cousin Hammond, an' don' be too demandin'." She folded her daughter in her arms, kissing her again and again, while Hammond shook the hands of the Major and the preacher. Dick gave Blanche a dutiful peck upon the cheek and her father, after planting a kiss upon her brow, ostentatiously withdrew a soiled handkerchief and wiped his eyes, in which no tears were visible. There was no pretence about the paroxysm of dry sobs which beset Beatrix as

189

Hammond handed his wife into the surrey. The mother entertained no regrets for the match, but the separation from her youngest child moved her to an emotion which was either sadness or satisfaction.

Hammond climbed into the driver's seat and unwound the reins from around the whip. The Negro groom stepped away from the horses' heads and the mares swung into a trot. As they traversed the lane towards the road, Blanche did not look back.

The horses sensed that they were headed homeward and Hammond gave them their heads. The fine weather had dried the roads and reduced the ruts so much that the fast pace did not cause the carriage to bump and sway unduly.

"You ain't sayin' nothin'. Ain' you glad?" asked the girl.

"Glad?" questioned the preoccupied husband.

"Glad we married, glad we goin'?" she elucidated.

Hammond made no reply. When Blanche reached over and threw her arms about his neck, he shook her off and rolled his eyes in a glance into the rear seat to warn her of the presence of the slave who was apt to mark her indecorum.

"I your wife, ain't I?" Blanche defended her behaviour.

"I reckon you is," Hammond admitted, but was reluctant to speak further.

"Whut fer you gittin' up las' night? You didn't git no sleep," the girl pressed the theme.

"I's like that. I cain't sleep, seem like, when I thinkin'."

"You thinkin'? Whut you thinkin' about? You so funny."

"I thinkin', I wonderin' whut man had you afore me. You not believin' I doesn't know a virgin."

"I was too a virgin," the girl declared.

"Oncet," said her husband succinctly. "But not las' night."

Blanche began to weep, but her husband was indifferent to her tears. He turned and looked at the boy behind him, cautioning him to watch the carpet-bag. He was less concerned about the bag, in fact, than about Meg's comprehension of the conversation in the front seat. The boy had strained his ears to hear, knew there was dissension, but failed to understand what it was about. Meg sat back in the seat with an assumption of innocence. Whatever might be the cause of the strife, he knew that the right was on the side of his master.

"Hammon' Maxwell, you 'cusin' me of sompin' I never done. I never done it, I never done it, I never," reiterated Blanche.

"You ain't a-tellin' me." Hammond doubted the girl's denial.

190

"You don't reckon I ain't know a virgin when I see one—when I sleeps with one an' pleasures?"

"No! No! No!" she cried, and broke afresh into tears.

"Ain't no good of me sayin' and you sayin' not, but I knowin'. You cain't deny."

Blanche heaved a long sigh.

"Might jest as well tell me, tell me who it is. Mayhap I goin' to kill the son-a-bitch, shoot him down jest like he a skunk or somethin'. You might as well."

"I tellin' you there weren't nobody. I pure—till you."

"Me? I got the leave; I married to you. On'y had I have knew las' night, beforehan', I wouldn't of—wouldn't of married you."

"Hammon', Hammon', how you goin' to think sich a thing? How kin you?" She leaned toward him and embraced his neck, sought to find his mouth with hers, but he turned his face to avoid her kiss. She knew he was not convinced.

Once she was tempted to blurt out the truth but bit her tongue. If he knew, perhaps he might forgive, her veniality was so little and so long ago. That was why she hated Charles and Charles her, that was the tale she held over her brother's head. She had been thirteen and Charles scarcely two years older. They had been playing at keeping house, she the mother and he the father, her doll for a child. It had seemed at the time innocent enough although both knew that such an act was forbidden. Charles in his play had insisted upon his rights as her husband while she mimicked her mother's frigidity, although she could not disguise her enjoyment of her violation. It had occurred so long ago. How could her husband know and hold it against her? If Charles had been available, if anybody knew where he was, she might have told Hammond what she had withheld so long from her parents.

But she didn't tell and was adamant, categorical, wellnigh convincing in her denial. How did Hammond know that she had not been a virgin? What caused him to suspect? She did not consider his education with Sukey, Aphrodite, Big Pearl, Ellen and all the other women who had shared his bed at one time or another. She sat tremulous in the fear that her husband would reject her, return her to Crowfoot. That Hammond did not turn back convinced her of his doubt.

But Hammond had no doubt. He tortured his mind with his wife's debasement. The horses guided themselves, onward, homeward. Hammond did not turn them back toward Crowfoot. There was no turning back.

At length he spoke. "Well, we-all married—I reckon. Ain't nothin' we kin do—now. We married," he repeated. "We got to make the best of that."

Blanche felt the anomaly of her status, but was relieved that her husband accepted it. She sighed.

"But we mustn't tell my papa nothin' about it. He ain't never goin' to know you wasn' pure. Bust his heart, bus' it right open— thinkin' of Falconhurst goin' to the son of a——," he searched his mind for a word but found none he could apply. "Like you," he concluded his sentence.

Her half-forgotten childhood defection from virtue had seemed to Blanche a mere peccadillo, but she knew now that it was not. Her husband accepted her, but accepted her as something used, smirched, secondhand.

She had expected no continence in the man she should marry. The concept would have startled her. She knew her brothers' ways with the wenches and suspected her father's. The satisfactions of their lusts was a male prerogative to which no blame was to be attached. But why the restriction on females?

She foresaw herself as for ever suspect unable to offer objection to anything her husband chose to do. She had envisaged no such dénouement to the accident, the trivial accident, that had occurred years before, as she had conceived of no such cause for her husband's forsaking her bed and wandering the roads in the moonlight. But at least he had not rejected her, had not cast her off. He was driving forward, carrying her onward toward Falconhurst.

CHAPTER THIRTEEN

FEW TRAVELLERS were on the roads. The team overtook occasional pedestrians, mostly Negroes, who paused to wave and stare, and met infrequent white horsemen, sometimes two riding together, who saluted gravely and commented upon the weather. Once they came upon a caravan of gypsies, encamped by the roadside, two vans, a cart, three women in faded clothes that had once been gaudy, busily cooking over an open fire, a half-dozen idle men, and as many naked children, waving and shouting inarticulately and running after the surrey. Hammond whipped up his team in passing the encampment to protect Blanche from the sight of unashamed brats.

Hammond calculated on reaching home by nightfall on the second day and postponed stopping to eat, but by four o'clock Blanche was insisting that she was hungry. She objected, however, to stopping at any of the scattered cabins they passed, and Hammond refused to stop at either of the larger plantations where it might have been possible to obtain meals, but whose owners he did not know. He drew up before a little hut on the edge of a clearing, above the door of which was an askew sign with the single word 'Grocerys' in grey, which had perhaps once been black, upon an otherwise unpainted board.

Handing the reins to Blanche, Hammond got down from his seat and limped toward the entrance of the hut. He lifted the latch and went into the musty store. Boards between two hogsheads served for a counter, upon which rested slabs of fat pork and a quarter of a cheese. On a shelf were two bolts of calico, one blue, the other black. Barrels were scattered at random, and in the darkness of the room Hammond was able to see that everything was covered with a thin layer of dust.

He waited and, when nobody appeared to serve him, came out-of-doors, walked entirely around the building, which was the only one in sight. He hallooed to the forest, but when nobody answered he re-entered the store. He lifted the lids of the barrels and searched about. From a barrel partly filled with meal a mouse sprang out and startled him, and he saw that he had disturbed her nest of half-grown young. The only articles of food that required no cooking were the quarter cheese, and crackers, the last ten pounds at the bottom of a barrel. No knife was in sight, and so Hammond employed a mattock that leaned in one corner to hack off a piece of the cheese which was dried out and crumbled on the counter. Neither could he find bags or paper, in lieu of which he tore a piece from the bolt of black calico, laid it on top of a barrel and scooped the broken cheese upon it. To this he added crackers.

He estimated the value of the cheese, crackers and calico at thirty or forty cents, but to make sure of not cheating the merchant, whoever he might be, left a silver dollar on the board beside the cheese. He grasped the cloth by its four corners and carried it to the carriage. He closed the door as he went out and tried the latch to make sure it had caught.

"This all?" asked Blanche in her contempt of the meal.

"All I could find, 'ceptin' you wantin' some sow bacon an' no fire to cook it on. Wasn't nobody," her husband explained. "Keep

193

us till'n we git us home. Not fur, now." He reached into the cloth spread on Blanche's knees and grasped a handful of crackers which he turned and extended to the boy in the rear seat.

Blanche munched at the crumbs of cheese and bit into a cracker. "It old and soft, webs on it," she complained.

"Don' eat it, an' you don' want. You say you hongry," said Hammond reaching for a piece of the cheese. He had no feeling of hunger. He resumed the reins and the team trotted forward. Blanche continued to pick at the food, but ate little of it. At length she pulled the corners of the cloth together and, sliding it into the middle of the seat, brushed her skirt with her hands.

Hammond picked up the parcel and handed it back to Meg.

"Ain't much," he said, "but Lucretia Borgia goin' to fix us when we gits there."

As he ate the food, Meg sought to ingratiate himself with Blanche. She turned to look at him, and flinched, uneasy though she knew not why, under his eager gaze. He said: "Miz Lucretia Borgia my mammy. She the cook. She cook good. You goin' to see. Me, I Masta's, his nigger. I house tamed. I feeds him, an' dresses him, an' stirs his toddy."

They drove on, and only the horses' hoofs broke the monotonous silence.

Soon Hammond felt the pressure of Blanche's hand upon his thigh. He looked up from the road on which his eyes had focused in his reverie and heard his wife whisper, "That 'un, the little 'un, is a conjure. I knows it. He lookin' at me, at the back o' my neck. I feels it—like pins an' needles a-stickin' me all over. He conjure me. I skeared."

Hammond turned in the seat to look behind him. Meg was sprawled in the corner, head on side, fast asleep. "If Meg conjure you," the husband replied, "he doin' it in his sleep. Look back your own self."

"Then he playin' possum. I felt his conjure, felt it plain. He ain't asleep."

Hammond reached back and grasped Meg's knee, shaking him awake. "Wake up an' set up—straight. Don' you know you ridin' with your mist'ess?"

The urchin obeyed, mumbling "Yas, suh; suh, Masta, suh."

"Ain't no sich thing like conjure," Hammond told Blanche. "Jest nigger carryin'-on. They believes it."

194

"I believe it, too. Cain't tell me. That 'un, behind there, he a conjure. Doin' it in his sleep even. I knowed it when first I laid eyes on him. I wishin' you git ridden of him."

"I will—in two, three years, when he growed enough to git me a price."

"I reckon you don't believe ghostes neither?" When her husband failed to reply, she added, "Nor God, nor Jesus, or nothin'? I've seen em—ghostes, that is. An' Charles seen one oncet, a great big one."

Hammond did not interrupt her, and she added details of her apparitions and of her brother's.

The sun set clear, but there were clouds in the east that obscured the rising moon, but four days short of full. The horses recognized that they were approaching home and Hammond gave them their heads. It required a firm grip to restrain them as they turned into the lane that led to the house.

"Falconhurst," murmured Hammond reverently, as if he approached a shrine.

"This all?" demanded Blanche, as the surrey stopped and she looked at the house.

"This it!" declared Hammond.

A boy appeared from the shadows and a candle was lighted in the kitchen. A light also shone from Maxwell's bedroom.

"Git Vulcan to take care of these horses," Hammond told the boy. "They hongry."

Lucretia Borgia waddled onto the gallery. "Oh, suh, Masta, su'," she embraced Hammond with affection. "An' this the new miz? Ain't she purty?" and the other arm went about Blanche, who disengaged herself. "Ever sence your mamma die I been wantin' 'nother purty white mist'ess, an' now I got me one," continued Lucretia Borgia.

Meg scampered from the carriage and threw his arms about his mother's wide thighs, claiming her attention.

The elder Maxwell, attended by Memnon, the blue coverlet around his shoulders, appeared in the front door. "Ham," was all he said as his son went to kiss him. He brushed a tear from his eye.

"This Miz Blanche. This your daughter now, Papa. How you goin' to like her?" Hammond introduced his wife, a white figure in the dark.

The old man drew the girl toward him and kissed her forehead. "I goin' to like her an' you does, an' she like you. Welcome home, my dear, to Falconhurst. 'Tain't much, not fine-haired like Crowfoot, but it right comfortin'. We goin' to be content."

"Whure at you goin' to make the new house?" asked Blanche.

"Over on the knoll, I reckon," Hammond motioned, "—if we builds it."

"Come in, come in, an' be at home. I'd a stayed up an' I sure you comin' tonight," said the ole man.

"Go in with Papa," Hammond told his wife. "I'll wait fer Vulc to take the mares."

As soon as the door was closed, he turned to Lucretia Borgia. "How Ellen?" he asked. "Whure she?"

"Ellen, pore thing, jest a-cryin' an' cryin', ever sence you go, suh. She sleepin' with me in the kitchen, suh. She not wantin' to come out."

"You don' reckon it make no difference with Ellen, me a-gettin' married?"

"No, suh, I reckon not," agreed Lucretia Borgia doubtfully,

"Tell Ellen not cry. She my wench, an' goin' to be—always. You tell her. Tell her I see her, come mornin'. She knew I got to marry, Papa wantin' a chil'."

"I know, Masta, suh, I tell her whut you says. Won't do no good, but I tell her."

"Mede an' them all right? Niggers all well?" Hammond changed the subject.

"Reckon you goin' to barn Mede now. Big Pearl don' need him no more; Lucy neither."

"They's knocked?" asked Ham with satisfaction.

"Lucy say," Lucretia Borgia confirmed, but added, lest her own status be forgotten. "An' me, I feels like havin' me twins agin. Two of 'em. I feels jest like the other time."

"Cain't tell yet, I reckon," said Hammond and went into the house.

Hammond had hardly seated himself when Meg appeared with a tray of steaming toddies, three of them.

"Whut fer the other 'un?" the master demanded.

The boy looked up in his fear of having offended. "It fer Mist'ess, suh. That right?" he asked and sucked his lip.

"Ladies don' never drink corn. Don' you know that?"

"Corn? Inside the house?" demanded Blanche, amazed. "I'm temp'ance. Ain't goin' to be no corn whure I at."

"Medicine," explained the older man soothingly. "Jest medicine. My rheumatiz."

196

"In that case——" Blanche condoned.

"An' Hammond here, he tired. An' you are. Better swallow a toddy fer your headache, an' you got one. It vile, I knows; but it sovereign."

"I couldn't. It ain't right. Cain't stan' jest smellin' it," protested Blanche.

"Medicine," insisted Maxwell.

"My head does ache me awful, a-jouncin' in that surrey," said Blanche, reaching for the glass. She sniffed the drink, made a face, and tasted.

"Drink it down—hot as you kin stan'," the old man urged.

The girl took another sip. "I reckon it do ease my head," she conceded. "But it taste awful."

"Sure do," agreed the father, drinking.

Hammond described his trip to his father, also told of Charles's failure to return to his home, but said nothing of the Woodfords' absence on his own arrival nor of their threats not to permit the marriage. He was undecided whether his father should know of the unpleasantness, and postponed the narration of it at least until Blanche was absent.

Memnon rang the supper bell and went to help his master, who rejected his aid. Maxwell rose from his chair and, only partly in need of their support, encircled the waists of Ham and Blanche as he propelled them toward the dining-room. He took his place at the head of the table, but ate nothing, having eaten his supper before he went to bed.

Meg, in clean clothes that fitted him better than those he had worn on the journey, stood at his master's chair and heaped his plate with ham and fried eggs, begrudging Memnon the honour of pouring the coffee into which Meg hastened to pour molasses and cream. He concerned himself with Hammond only. Alph, even though there were no flies, stood on the other side of the table and waved the peacock brush.

Memnon served his mistress, who sought to impress her father-in-law with a display of her elegance. She toyed daintily with her napkin, extended her little finger, and was careful to rest her knife and fork, when not in use, on the bread beside her plate. Protesting that she was not hungry, she ate heartily.

Halfway through the meal, Hammond sent Meg to summon Lucretia Borgia, who came and planted herself confidently just inside the door from the kitchen passage.

"That Tense, you got her in an' ready?"

"Yas, suh, Masta, suh; Tense all washed, like you says, an' ready to wait on Miz Blanche."

The master suggested that the girl should come in and Lucretia Borgia went to get her.

"This the one I tellin' you Papa an' me pick out fer yourn, to wait on you an' do whut you wants her," Hammond explained to Blanche. "She goin' to be all yourn."

Lucretia Borgia returned, leading by her shoulder the light yellow girl, her head hanging in her diffidence. Her plain frock, reaching to her naked ankles, was clean and over it Lucretia Borgia had pinned a white fichu.

Hammond extended his hand toward the girl in invitation. "Come on over here, Tense. Nobody not goin' to do nothin' to you."

The girl, unafraid of the master, stepped forward.

"No, other side the table," he said. "This your new mist'ess, like I tol' you about. Curtsy to her, nice-like. You goin' to be hern, and do fer her, goin' to do whut she say, ever'thing she tell you. Un'erstan'?"

Hortense went to the other side of the table, as directed, and dropped what she was meant for a curtsy, but remained out of the range of her mistress's reach.

Hammond raised his eyes to his wife's face to see her pleasure in the present he had made her. "How you like her?" he asked.

"That?" demanded Blanche. "You 'speck me to put up with that? She your wench, that plain."

"Don't talk so. Not front of Papa." Hammond's face reddened as he spoke. "She ain't. I ain't touch her."

"Whut fer, then, she go to your side the table then. She ain't skeared of you, and' she is of me. Needn't tell me—I knows. A purty one like that, an' you ain't never touch her? I tell by the way she roll her eyes towards you."

Lucretia Borgia was unable to leave her master in the lurch. "No'm, Miz Blanche, ma'am," she protested. "Tense pure yet." She stooped to raise the girl's skirt. "You kin feel fer your own self."

"No! No! Lucretia Borgia!" cried Hammond. "Miz Blanche is a lady; don' know nothin' about them kind of things."

"Well, anyway, Tense a virgin. Masta ain't took her, ain't even look at her, yet," muttered the chastened Borgia. "Dido keepin' her pure fer him, time come he ready."

Hammond signalled with his head for Lucretia Borgia to

198

retire. Maxwell cleared his throat, and rubbed one hand with the other to ease the pain, which had suddenly grown worse. Blanche's flushed face flooded with tears; she regretted that she had raised such a subject. Hammond folded his arms and pushed his chair back from the table, waited for his wife's weeping to stop.

At length her tears were exhausted and he spoke. "You doesn't like this one, you kin have any of 'em. Go through the cabins an' take your pick." (He made unspoken reservations concerning Ellen and Dite.) "This Tense, though, is the best we got—soun' an' spry, an' well raised an' pure—ain't never been touched. Has she, Papa?"

"I ain't knowin'," the old man shook his head. "What difference? Ladies ain't in'erested."

"This one good as any," Blanche resigned herself; but could not refrain from adding spitefully, "I reckon you've had all of 'em."

"One more toddy, jest one, afore we go up," suggested Maxwell, embarrassed by the quarrel. "Do you both good. You petered out, a-marryin' an' a-ridin' an' all. Let your boy stir 'em, Ham. He like to, an' he stir better ones than Mem."

The quarrel subsided. Blanche wondered why she had raised it. There was only Hortense's delicacy and beauty to arouse her jealousy. She had no evidence for the charge she had made, but knew that such a wench could never have escaped Dick's, Charles', and probably even her father's, favours at Crowfoot.

She drained her glass. Her headache had vanished but she felt slightly dizzy as Hammond rose to escort her to the room that had been his mother's. He steadied her elbow as they climbed the stairs. Lucretia Borgia had taken Blanche's bag to her room, had lighted the candles, and given final cautions to Tense, who waited in trepidation to serve her new mistress.

"Git yourself ready an' in bed," Hammond said. "I'll come back."

"Whure you a-goin'?" his wife asked in surprise.

"Down an' talk some more to Papa. Let you git off your clo's. I comin' back right away. Let Tense here do fer you."

Reaching the foot of the stairs, Hammond detoured through the kitchen, where he knew he would find Ellen. He trembled in anticipation of seeing her. Meg was at the table eating the food that Hammond had left on his plate, and Ellen was drying dishes for Lucretia Borgia.

She looked up and saw her master in the doorway, spreading

his arms to her. The plate she was wiping dropped from her hands and shattered on the brick floor as she moved ecstatically toward him. Hammond embraced her and kissed her eager mouth.

Tears came into the girl's eyes, mingled fear and doubt and joy. She buried her face in his coat and shook with sobs. The boy held her close, saying nothing. At length he raised her head and kissed her tearful lids. A long while he held her in his arms, smiling down at her.

Meg went on intently eating his food, with an occasional furtive glance at the lovers. With this small servant or with his mother, the master had no reticence.

For minutes he stood, holding the girl without a word from either. At last he held her from him, looked into her eyes and said, "Tomorrow!" He surrendered her and was gone.

He felt himself refreshed, cleansed, triumphant as he returned to the sitting-room, where his father was drinking a final toddy. Hammond felt no need for one.

"That Miz Blanche, she techy like tonight. She tired. You not used to white ladies. Pay no 'tention when she key up," Maxwell advised his son, seeking to minimize the significance of Blanche's outbreak. "She a Hammond—high-strung. She make a good wife, an' she gits used to—things."

"Yes. She goin' to be all right, I reckon."

Ham rose to go to bed, and the old man signalled to Memnon to help him to his feet. At the top of the stairs Meg waited to aid his master with his boots. Hammond gave the father the anticipated kiss and went into Blanche's room.

"Whut you been doin'? Whut keepin' you?" she complained.

"Jest Papa an' me a-talkin'."

"He say about me?"

"He reckon you real nice. Papa ain't hard on nobody."

"Then he ain't mad, whut I say at supper?"

"He say you petered out." Meg was kneeling, removing his master's boots and stockings. Hammond took off his coat and shirt, and sat down for Meg to strip off his trousers. He stood up in his underwear.

"Whure this wench goin' to sleep?" Blanche demanded.

"Let her spread out on the floor," the husband suggested; "here at the foot."

"Not here. Not right in the room," Blanche protested. "Put her out the door in the hall."

200

"But Meg; he always sleep in the hall, out my door. Cain't have 'em together." Hammond hesitated; then he added, "At the foot is good enough. We isn't go to do nothin' this evenin'."

CHAPTER FOURTEEN

HAMMOND WAS out of his bed early. He had been five days at home. Here was his heart—in these cabins and warehouses and barns, in the cotton fields and wood lots and pastures. He drew back the curtain and looked at his precious own earth before he opened the door and with his bare foot nudged Meg awake to help him put on his clothes. In boots and underwear, followed by his valet, he went down the hall to his own room, where he had left the drab clothes that he wore on the plantation. He limped down the stairs and, without waiting to eat breakfast, went out of the door and toward the cotton field. In the distance was the gang of his slaves slowly wielding their chopping hoes. After breakfast, on Eclipse, he would go across to the gang to inspect its work. Early control of the weeds forestalled the need of chopping larger ones. The trouble was that the Negroes often chopped the cotton plants along with the weeds, caution them as he did. He did not credit them with the foresight that the more plants they destroyed the less cotton they would have to pick. The plants would require to be thinned in any event, but systematically and not by heedless chopping. He had made allowance this year for the seed that should rot and should fail to germinate, but it seemed all to have come up better than last year when it had been necessary to replant at intervals. Perhaps the white seeds of Petit Gulf variety that he had persuaded his father to substitute for the Tennessee cotton with its black seeds, previously grown on Falconhurst, would sprout with less loss.

Returning towards the house later, Hammond detoured among the cabins. He saw Tiger, his yellow first begotten son, now four years old, and stooped down, extending his arms to the petted little slave. Tiger, usually so eager for his sire's attention, turned and ran from him, and, running, tripped. Only his fall enabled Hammond to overtake him and gather him, screaming and kicking into his arms. Sukey, the child's mother, appeared from her cabin, a younger and darker child on her hip.

"Oh, it you, suh. You got him, suh," she faltered, seeing that the boy was safe.

Ham snuggled his face against the not-too-clean belly and kissed it before he placed the boy on the ground to scurry to his mother and hide behind her skirt.

"They says you gone off an' got ma'ied, Masta, suh—to a white lady?" Sukey phrased the statement as a question, and waited for a reply. "Um, um!" she mumbled. "I wishes you joy; sure does wish you joy." The woman sighed. She still enjoyed the status of having once born a child to her young master.

Hammond thanked her and passed on to Lucy's cabin to confirm what Lucretia Borgia had told him. Serpent oil assailed his nostrils before he reached the door. He found Mede luxuriating, naked on the bed, under Lucy's massage. Big Pearl stood behind her mother, holding the bottle of oil. As their owner opened the door he had heard Mede grumble, "Ain't you got no stren'th, woman? Now rub my shoulder hard. Hear? Hard. Twis' it." The tone was at once petulant and imperious.

"Lucy know how she goin' to rub you. Leave her do it," Hammond reprimanded the young Mandingo. "You ain't givin' orders. Git up."

"That Mede!" complained Big Pearl. "He always a-sayin! Do this, do that. Reckon he done it all; don' give nobody else no part."

"No part of whut?" Hammond questioned.

"No part of makin' that sucker I got in me; Mammy say I got."

"Big Pearl, shut your mouth. Masta wantin' to know, he ast," scolded Lucy, jealous that her daughter should blurt the proud tidings that it was her own prerogative to tell. "Big Pearl knocked, Masta, suh; she shore knocked, an' me too."

"You sure?"

"Shore! Cain't fool ol' Lucy."

"That mean a new dress," Hammond promised.

"Red?" asked Big Pearl.

"Red an' you wants it. Yourn red too, Lucy? We ain't got no red on hand, but I'll git it in Benson next time I goes. Dido will help you sew it. I right proud of them suckers you two got. Ol' Masta, he goin' to be proud too. Means a dollar, a whole silver dollar, each one, an' you has 'em alive."

"Masta didn't say about givin' me no present," said Mede enviously after Hammond had left the cabin. "Had ought to have new pants—sompin'."

"Nev' min'," Lucy sought to soothe the boy's feelings. "I give you half o' my dollar, Little Boy—when I gits it."

Hammond was late for breakfast. He found his father and his wife, toddies in hand, waiting in the sitting-room.

"Whut this?" he asked, looking at Blanche's drink. "I thought you temp'ance."

"I is; but my head ache me, and your papa reckon——"

"It all right. Right weak, an' her head hurtin'. Medicine." Maxwell tried to quiet his son's displeasure.

Hammond watched askance as his wife lifted the goblet to her mouth, sipped from it tentatively and lowered it. What kind of woman had he married?

"Ever'thin' all right, did you find it?" the father asked.

"I reckon," said Hammond without conviction. "The Mandingo kickin' up, talkin' back at Lucy, an' not a workin' hisself."

"Hide him. Touch him up," prescribed Maxwell.

Hammond withheld the pregnancies of the wenches as being too indelicate for his wife.

"Son, don't be makin' too much o' that young Mandingo buck. He big an' vig'ous, yes. But he ain't God. He yourn; you isn't hisn. He need a little snakin', pour it on. See whut that larrupin' done to Memnon; make him a new buck. You got to learn about niggers. They apes. On'y thing they feared of is the snake."

"Mede ain't a-needin' no dose of snake, Papa. Ruin his pride. Jes' about kill Mede."

"That buck your pet. That whut he is, your pet. Let him run over you an' you wants," said the old man, swallowing the last of his toddy and peering into the bottom of the goblet to see whether a trace might remain. He could well have drunk another, but refrained from ordering it, lest Blanche incur her husband's anger by taking another along with him.

"Mede!" Blanche pounced on the name, repeating it as if it would escape from her memory. "This here Mede, who he?"

"Why, it is Ham's fightin' buck, Mandingo," blurted Maxwell. "Ain't Ham tell you? He won't talk about nothin' else; an' he tote that black boy aroun', wrapped in waddin'." The older man was innocently unaware of saying aught amiss.

"Fightin' buck? I tol' you you couldn't have no fightin' buck. I tol' you I not wed you an' you got one!" Blanche flared.

Hammond's smile was half a sneer. "Whut you wants I should do with him? Boil him fer soap grease?"

"You kin sell him, I reckon."

203

"But I reckon I ain't a-goin'."

"I got sompin' to say!"

" 'Bout Tense, you has. 'Bout the rest, you ain't. I got to run this plantation. You'd be havin' me plantin' daisies, 'stead o' cotton."

"Ham jest a-keepin' him fer showin' off. Don' never fight him," concluded Maxwell.

"I goin' to. I goin' to, an' anybody got one to fight agin." Hammond rejected conciliation. He intended to brook no female interference with the plantation economy.

The girl was trapped. This serious, stern, satisfied, unromantic youth, whom she hardly knew, was her husband. He was an escape from spinsterhood, which even at sixteen had terrified her. The house was plain, drab, gloomy, not even as good as Crowfoot —not what she had pictured. No affluence was apparent to her. The older man she conceded to be kind, but a mere echo of the boy, She resolved to salvage what she should be able.

"Them dresses?" she proposed. "When we goin' to git 'em?"

"We git 'em," Hammond promised again. "Cain't go today. Maybe tomorrer, next day; Sat'day sure. Dressmaker in Benson, ain't they, Papa?"

"Dresses?" asked Maxwell.

"My papa never bought me none—that money not comin'," Blanche explained.

"Mind me to git some red goods fer Big Pearl and Lucy. I tol' 'em I would," said Ham.

"They——?" The old man checked his question, looked at his son, who nodded his head. "Mandingos," he said with satisfaction.

When they rose from the table, Maxwell stumbled and submitted to Mem's leading him back to the sitting-room. Blanche hesitated a moment and followed. Hammond tarried. Blanche saw him place his hand on Meg's shoulder.

"You tell Miz Ellen," Hammond in a low tone instructed the boy, "to wash good and wait upstairs. Tell her I come. Un'er-stan'?"

The boy nodded gravely.

Ham spent the afternoon around the plantation, but his mind more often than not was in an upstairs room back at the house. He returned earlier than he had intended and guided Eclipse toward the barn. Without unsaddling him, he turned the horse into his box stall. Then he limped toward the house, entered the kitchen, and made his way toward the stairs. Meg sat on the top step, elbows on his knees and cheeks in hands, waiting. Hammond's fingers on his lips enjoined the boy to silence.

From the sitting-room, Maxwell heard the halting step on the creaking stairs, made a surmise, but said nothing to his daughter-in-law who sat across the room from him. He harked in his thoughts back to the time when his own needs had been insatiable. When he came down some time later, Hammond stopped at the foot of the stairs to open and slam the front door before he entered the sitting-room. While he embraced his wife, his father disposed of his tobacco in anticipation of the casual kiss he knew his son would give him. Meg brought three toddies, and Blanche raised her eyes to her spouse for his disapproval before she lifted one of them from the tray. He offered no protest.

"They choppin' right good-like—slow, but ain't no hurry 'boutn them ol' weeds," Hammond told his father. "That Petit Gulf come thick; didn't rot none like that Tennessee."

"Littler boles," the old man objected.

"But more of 'em, and they busts wider."

"Mayhap," nodded Maxwell who had little interest in growing cotton.

"They don' need no watchin'," Ham reverted to the choppers.

"Then we kin go to Benson tomorrow an' git my dresses?" Blanche interposed.

"Might as well," her husband agreed. "Why not?" Just for a moment he was not reluctant to please her. He gave her a brief half smile of contentment, the reason for which she completely misunderstood.

CHAPTER FIFTEEN

BUT AS it turned out Blanche was joyfully forced to return again and again to Benson to buy linings and buttons, furbelows and trimmings for the dresses and to consult Miss Forsythe, the little dressmaker, and submit to her fittings. For Blanche it was a carnival of pleasant anxiety and anticipations. Twice a week, Hammond was forced to adjourn his work on the plantation and drive his wife to town, which he did without complaint. The leisurely hoeing of weeds in the cotton went on in his absence almost as well as when he was at home. In fact, when Lucretia

Borgia could steal the time from her other duties to go to the field for an hour or so, the choppers worked faster for the deputy than they ever did for the master.

On Saturday afternoons he left Blanche at Miss Forsythe's cottage while he went to Remmick's tavern to watch the fights and meet his friends. He had stopped taking Mede along, not because of Blanche's presence but because no other owners would match their boys against Mede.

However, everybody talked about Mede, inquired about his health and his training, suggested matches for him, but always with the slave of another owner. Hammond refrained from boasting about the boy, but the pride of ownership gave him constant pleasure.

"I'm a-breedin' him right now. Ain't fitten hardly to fight." Hammond would explain. "The dreen on him pullin' him down."

On the way home, Hammond listened inattentively to his wife's enthusiastic account of her visit to Miss Forsythe and her prognostications of how beautiful the frocks would be. They were her sole interest.

For between her excursions to the dressmaker's there was nothing for Blanche to do. Within the house, everything was done for her, and there was nothing out-of-doors to interest her. Besides, she feared the effects of the sun on her face, the whiteness of which she was at some pains to conserve. Afraid at first of the elder Maxwell, she grew to like him. He was generous, candid, and uncritical. She was a white woman, a Hammond, his son's wife. He asked no more. Her headaches grew more frequent and more severe. Her father-in-law was indifferent to the number of toddies she drank, even urged them upon her. Hammond did not disapprove the remedy, but neither did he know how much she consumed. He was out of the house much of the time, supervising the chopping of the cotton, seeing to the welfare of his livestock, giving orders and advice in the cabins, training his Mandingo.

His wife and his father exchanged gossip. She described her dresses to him again and again.

Maxwell talked of his wife, of her being a Hammond, recounted his son's childhood and the accident that had crippled him. After the fifth telling, Blanche ceased to attend to what he said, but for want of company she sat with him, wafted a worn palmetto fan, and sipped her toddy.

She had even less interest in the conversations between her husband and his father about the crops and the weeds and swine and slaves than in the older man's garrulity about the past. It seemed to her that Hammond was obsessed with the plantation. Every time he entered the house, it was to report the details of whatever project was in hand, the carelessness of some working man, the cold or cut hand or stubbed toe of some slave child. These minutiae of his stewardship interested his wife not at all, and, except as reflections of his son's activities, interested the father little more. He expressed his approval of all Hammond did. The concern of the older man was that his young Negroes should feed heartily and grow apace. Cotton was only to keep them moderately busy. He had never built a gin or a press of his own, but had hauled his crop to Benson for processing. It seemed to him that it might be better to devote the entire acreage to corn which the Negroes could eat, than to cotton for sale; he preferred to sell the produce of the plantation on the hoof. But if it amused Hammond to grow cotton, his father had no wish to interfere with the plan.

Blanche was bored and even nauseated by her father-in-law's eternal praise of his son, present or absent. If only Hammond would do something amiss, if only he would err, if his father would upbraid him or express in the son's absence some disapproval of his actions. The only fault the older man could find was that the son worked too hard, and in his voicing of it that fault became a virtue.

"An' you don' quit this a-strivin' and a-drivin' an' a-frettin', you goin' to bust down with rheumatiz afore that boy is big enough to take a hold," he warned.

"Whut boy?" demanded Ham.

"Why, your boy—the one Blanche is goin' to have you." Blanche blushed.

It was a reminder to Hammond. He had neglected his marital duties, which were not entirely pleasant, what with the pallor of the soft white flesh, which he was not forced to see but whose colour he imagined under the heavy nightgown.

Blanche had found out about Ellen. Hortense, with no evil motive, let the cat out of the bag and answered her mistress's further questions with an innocent candour that was not intended as a betrayal. Tense had grown up to believe that the slave was at the master's disposal, and was aware of nothing amiss in Hammond's relationship with Ellen except that it forestalled her own elevation to his favour, to which she had been taught to aspire. Hortense was able to tell little, from which the mistress surmised much. Blanche quizzed the elder Maxwell as subtly as she was able but his answers were evasive.

"Mayhap," he admitted, "I don' know," and he didn't. "Ham right considerin' that way, aimin' to spare a white lady."

Blanche had no desire to be spared, although she dared not say so.

"No 'um, Mist'ess, I ain't know nuffin', not nuffin'; no 'um," was all Blanche could draw out of Lucretia Borgia, who planted her feet wide apart in her determination not to betray her young master.

When Blanche turned to Meg, who had overheard his mother's denial of her knowledge, the boy only hung his head, rolled his eyes, and muttered it was hard to tell what. A lie to a white was an offence, but, in this, he recognized that the truth would be a greater one.

For once, Lucretia Borgia came to her son's aid, not for his sake but for her master's. "He 'on't know nuffin', Mist'ess, ma'am. How you 'speck he know nuffin'? That nigger don' even know whut you astin' him; 'on't know whut you talkin' about. Ain't no good pumpin' him."

Thus Blanche, for all her seeking, was unable to accumulate the evidence she wanted. She was baffled. Her husband's philandering with his wenches she would not have resented, but his dalliance with a single wench aroused her ire. She compared Ellen's beauty with her own, to the slave's disparagement; and what perversity of taste could prefer black to white? Nor could she credit that it was no preference, a mere concession to a white frigidity, which she could not admit she did not feel. Her mother, with the modesty befitting a daughter of a Hammond, had warned her with circumlocutions that a man's fidelity was not a lady's lot and that she should have to submit to a husband's attentions or neglect with such equanimity as she could muster. But that the neglect should come so soon!

Blanche could not, for several reasons, present her grievance forthrightly to her husband, charge him with dalliance with the wench. She had no direct evidence; the most she knew was what Tense had said innocently and inadvertently. He would admit a venial guilt, but pretend it was for her own protection. And how would she find words for the indictment, which was a subject too delicate for a lady's speech? A lady not only possessed no passions but took no cognizance of them in men and menials.

208

Moreover and worst of all, the charge would beget recriminations. Hammond, on their marriage night, had found her not a virgin, a matter which, although it was no longer discussed, she knew that her husband had not forgotten. To chide him would but arouse his memory of her own guilt.

While Hammond did not overtly flaunt his relations with Ellen, he was at little pains to conceal them. Sooner or later Blanche would know. Didn't every man, every planter, have a favourite wench or two?

So Blanche concentrated on the one consolation she had, her pretty dresses. About them, Hammond kept his word. And there would be more of them, a never-ending supply. When Hammond on a Saturday evening brought the three frocks home, Blanche could eat no supper nor permit Tense to eat. One after another, with Tense's help, she laced herself into them and swept down the stairs to show them off to the Maxwell men, whose satisfaction was not in the dresses themselves but in the pleasure the girl took in having them. They did not know how much of a factor in that pleasure was the allure the dresses were counted to have for the husband. She should be irresistible. She contrasted her finery with Ellen in her osnaburgs. She would show that black hussy who was the more beautiful. When, on going to bed that night, Hammond sent Tense to the kitchen to sleep that he might be alone with his wife, she knew that the clothes had triumphed.

Thereafter, Blanche wore her new dresses constantly, changed them three times a day merely to sit opposite her father-in-law and sip her toddies. Her joy in them soon subsided, however, especially as she went nowhere to show them off and nobody came to Falconhurst. Besides, they were tight. More and more she kept to her room, where she could relax her stays, dressing only to go downstairs to her meals.

But she missed her gossip with Maxwell, and her toddies. As the weather got warmer, the dresses became even more uncomfortable and Blanche had Dido make her some Mother Hubbards of blue calico, mere envelopes for her figure, like nightgowns. Hammond did not entirely approve of her wearing such a garb downstairs in his father's presence, but Blanche pointed out that she wore underclothes with these Mother Hubbards, and shoes and stockings. She was fully clothed and yet comfortable. There was nothing for him to cavil at. He still did not like them, didn't want his wife dressing like a wench. Somebody might come. In

209

such an event, Blanche said, she would go to her room and dress before the visitors should see her.

As the summer wore on, the girl dispensed with more and more of her undergarments, leaving off one thing one day, another the next. Despite the warmth of the days, she still drank her toddies, hot for her persistent headaches and relied upon the breeze of her palmetto fan to keep her cool. One day she appeared downstairs without her shoes, complained that the heat had caused her feet to swell. Hammond contemplated her unshod feet, but in view of the reason for them withheld his censure. The following day her feet were entirely bare. They were not beautiful.

Blanche, standing barefooted in a single garment, her stringy yellow hair uncombed, her cheeks blotched red with heat and eyes bleary from whisky, bore little resemblance to the girl girded in the challis dress whom Hammond had accompanied to church a few months before. But she was white; he had married her.

More and more frequently he used the summer heat as an excuse to absent himself from his wife's bedroom. In his own separate bed he was not constrained to wear his underclothes, and, alone, Blanche would be free to unbutton the neck of her nightgown.

On one such night late in June, Ellen lay in her master's bed. It was too hot for dalliance, too hot even for sleep, and they lay apart, the girl on her elbow waving a palmetto fan over his supine body.

"That enough," Hammond argued. "I right cool now. Lay out an' git some sleep. Don' need you should fan me like I goin' to melt. I ain't grease, or somethin'."

The girl merely stooped to kiss his naked shoulder and continued her fanning. "You hot, and you know I like to."

"Ain't no call to," he said, stretching luxuriously and raising his arms to cradle his head in his hands the better to take advantage of the breeze from the fan. "Mind me of the time I was a little saplin'; my mamma had Lucretia Borgia settin' by my bed a-fannin' me to sleep warmish evenin's, sometimes the whole night," he reminisced. "Lucretia Borgia let me sleep nekid, like I is now, though my mamma reckon I wear a shirt."

"You had Lucretia Borgia a long time?"

" 'Fore I was borned; 'fore my papa marry my mamma. Don't know whure Papa got her at; mayhap he bred her right here at Falconhurst. She gittin' ol', mayhap thirty-five. Still breed good though—she knocked again. Beginnin' to round out too, I noticin' this mornin'."

210

"She says I am," the girl announced.

"You is whut?"

"Knocked."

Hammond sat upright. "When? When Lucretia Borgia say?"

"Yesterday." Ellen was casual. "I don't know nothing about it. She says I missed my time of month."

"Don't mean nothin'. Nigger talk. Lay back," Hammond ordered, and he ran his hand appraisingly over the girl's abdomen. "Breasts hurtin' you? Notice anything?"

"They itch-like, an' ache a little, not much. They growin' some, I reckon."

"Mayhap Lucretia Borgia know. She right knowin' about such."

"You mad?" asked Ellen contritely.

"Mad?"

"Mad at me? I couldn't help it; you did it."

Hammond ran his arm beneath Ellen's body, drew her to him and kissed her mouth. "That how riled I is," he declared. "I a-wantin' it."

"But you won't be a-wantin' me," the girl began to weep. "Be givin' me to one of the hands—not a black one though, not to a black one!"

It was too dark in the room for Ellen to see the smile that spread over Ham's face. "Ellen, honey, I ain't givin' you away. You mine, mine. You an' me, we goin' to have a lot o' suckers, a whole gang of 'em, one mos' ever' year."

"Sukey an' the others?"

"They different. They jest handy-like. I ain't payin' Ol' Man Wilson no fifteen hundred dollars jest for three, four months of you. No, suh. I wouldn't take fifteen thousand fer you."

"You reckon I am——?"

"You missin' your time, and your breasts, Lucretia Borgia mayhap right. Leastwise, she goin' to be, an' she ain't. Us carryin' on like we is, not a-goin' to be long."

"You reckon it's a little buck?"

"I reckon. I gits bucks. All of mine been bucks so fur. Not a wench so fur, nor a crip."

"You reckon Miz Blanche's goin' to be a buck. I mean a boy child?"

"Ifn ever she have one. I ain't been doin' right by her—too hot in all that riggin'. I'm a-goin' to."

"Lucretia Borgia says Miz Blanche—she pukin' up every

211

mornin' and her feet swellin' up; Lucretia Borgia reckons that a sign."

"Lucretia Borgia reckons too much. She knowin' ever'thing afore it goin' to happen."

"I reckon you don't crave Miss Blanche have none?" Ellen's inflection turned her speculation into a question.

Hammond was quick to deny that such was the case. "Course I wantin' one, an' Papa do. Course I do." The weather had made the young man irascible. Ellen accepted his peevish mood. She fell silent, but continued to wield the fan above his naked body long after he had turned his back on her and fallen asleep. There was no moon and the room was so dark that she could distinguish only a vague outline of the man at whose body she gazed down in adoration.

For herself, Ellen hoped that Lucretia Borgia was not mistaken, since Hammond was not averse to her bearing a child. Would it arrive before the child carried by her mistress? It should, she calculated; her master had favoured her for months before he had married Miss Blanche. A surge of jealous hatred of Hammond's wife swept over her. She knew that she herself was the interloper. Did her master come to her from preference or merely to relieve his wife from the obligation to submit to him? Why should the white woman not relish the male embrace? Wherein was the difference between white and black? She thought of herself as black, and was glad of her skin; she would not exchange the ecstasy she obtained from her master's caresses for the chaste frigidity of white wifehood.

It would go hard, Ellen knew, but she believed that she would be willing to forgo Hammond's embraces if he were able to obtain as much satisfaction in Blanche's bed. The nights Hammond spent with Blanche, Ellen threshed in her bed and wept tears of agony, but she didn't question the wife's right to him. Jealousy she had admitted to herself, but never hatred. Now she hated. Now she willed Blanche injury, illness, abortion, death. Yet to murder her would alienate her white lover and defeat her purpose. If she could poison her secretly! There could be no rivalry—the other was white. Murder was the only solution.

Ellen was terrified that Hammond might surmise her fantasies. How soundly did he sleep? If he should wake now would he divine what she had been thinking? The more she tried to stifle her evil thoughts, the more they obtruded into her consciousness. She was unable to sleep, and when Hammond awoke in the faint

212

light of the false dawn, he felt the breeze even before he turned to see the girl, still reclining on her elbow and still patiently and monotonously swinging the fan to render his slumbers comfortable.

In the morning Ham rose at once to go downstairs to tell his father that both Blanche and Ellen were pregnant. He knew the delight the old man would take in the fact that the Hammond line was now certain to be continued. But he himself was scarcely less pleased about Ellen than Blanche.

CHAPTER SIXTEEN

THE FOLLOWING Saturday at the tavern Hammond saw the veterinarian, who obviously had something important to discuss. "Ain't talked to Remmick, have ye?" he asked, looking surreptitiously about him. He grasped Ham's elbow and led him out to the entrance porch beneath the wooden awning. "Don' say nothin', but Remmick got a letter. He goin' to show it you. Sportin' gen'lemen from the City comin', bringin' with 'em they big fightin' buck, want to pit it agin' yourn. You goin' to have a chance to pit your boy again' a regular New Orleans fighter," Redfield confided.

"How news about me a-havin' Mede git all the way to New Orleans?" Hammond pondered.

"Jest wanted you to know. Don' let on you anxious when Remmick tellin' you. Take it casual an' if you wantin' a good match."

Remmick did indeed hurry up as soon as he saw Ham, spread open before him without comment the letter of which Redfield had spoken. Redfield read it over Ham's shoulder.

"Friend Mr Remmick," the epistle ran; "it comes to me a rich gentleman Mr Maxwell has a fine fighter near to Benson. I got one to match against him. I take my fighter to Benson in a short time to match him. You tell the gentleman please have his Negro redy when I come. Mine is real large and strong like a bull. I go to Natchez. Then come to Benson. Your humble and obdt. servt. J. Neri." The letter was from New Orleans, undated. It was neatly written in an easily legible running hand, except for the signature, which was so formalized and embellished that it was impossible to be sure of more than the 'J' in it.

Hammond read the letter three times, turned it over and looked at the blank reverse. "Who this whutever his name be? This J. Neri?" he asked.

"Never seen the Frenchy, not as I know. Callin' me his goddamn friend. I don't know him," Remmick said, folding the letter and placing it in his pocket.

"Heared of me, about my Mede," speculated Hammond.

"From folks passin' through, likely. Lots of talk a-goin'," Remmick guessed. "Goin' to fight him? You bin a-cravin' a chance."

"'Pendin' on his buck and on whut he offerin' to bet," shrugged Hammond. "I ain't fightin' my buck fer no scrawny runt of a saplin'."

"Course I ain't knowin', but I reckons that Frenchy cravin' to fight fer money—not jest fer niggers. Likely, comin' all that way, ain't carryin' along no bettin' bucks." Remmick appeared to know more than he admitted about the business of the unknown letter-writer.

For all Hammond's assumed indifference, his eagerness to reach home to intensify the Mandingo's training detracted from his interest in the afternoon's entertainment. Before the final fight he departed, first having sought out Doc Redfield and asked him to come to Falconhurst. He wanted the veterinarian's appraisal of Mede's fitness to fight.

So anxious was he to step up Mede's conditioning, he galloped Eclipse all the way and went to the Mandingo cabin before reporting his arrival to his wife and father.

"I goin' to pit you," he told Mede excitedly. "Gen'leman from New Orleans bringin' one, big as a bull."

"I ready for him. I beat him for you, Masta," Mede declared complacently.

"You ain't either ready. You got to git trainin' good—runnin', liftin' that ol' log, Lucy oilin' an' workin' you."

Lucy acquiesced with a "Yas, suh, Masta. I rubs Mede ever' day, me an' Big Pearl."

"You still drinkin' down them eggs from Lucretia Borgia ever' day?" Ham demanded.

"She makin' me. I don' like 'em, Masta, suh."

"Nev' min'; you drink 'em down. Now git out there a-liftin' that log. Put it up an' down over your head till you petered out. Hear? Tomorrow we goin' to run you, young buck on your back; an' then we swims you in ol' Tombigbee."

214

Mede's training had been steady and consistent; Hammond had seen to it, even in those weeks when it seemed to him that he should be unable to find an opponent. Now, with the prospect of a fight impending, the owner was appalled at the thought that in any way he might have permitted Mede to loaf and stagnate into flabbiness. He resolved to make up in a week's intensity of effort all that the boy had lost, or had failed to gain, in the interval since he had fought.

Blanche, drinking a toddy, made a wry mouth of indifference to Ham's tale of the letter. Maxwell's chuckle assuaged his son's doubt. "You got him to fight with, didn't you? You got to crack eggs, an' you makin' a puddin'," he said. "Nev' mind a bust jaw or a gouged eye. You got him to fight, not to look at."

That then was one comfort. If Mede should lose, Hammond would suffer no recriminations at home.

Redfield lost no time in his visit to Falconhurst. As he approached the plantation astride his dun horse, he encountered Hammond on Eclipse following Mede, who trotted ploddingly, Belshazzar perched triumphantly on his shoulders. Although it was Sunday morning when no work was required of the Falconhurst slaves, the Mandingo had been lifting, jumping, stretching, contorting, and now running, under his master's relentless eye, for five hours. His scanty clothes were wet and his face shone with sweat, but fatigue, if he felt it, was not visible. It was Hammond's intention to tire his fighter to the point of exhaustion.

"Whut you meanin'?" asked the veterinarian jocosely. "Stinkin' up the country with nigger sweat?"

"I honin' him, honin' him right down."

When the white men had dismounted, Redfield glanced toward the Mandingo, and observed him as he came up the lane, watched him lift Belshazzar easily down from his shoulders. With a curiosity that appeared idle, he walked toward the big Negro, felt his biceps, his thighs, and his shoulders through the sweat-soaked garments, raised the boy's shirt to feel his abdominal muscles, making no comment.

"How he seem?" inquired Hammond anxiously. "I jest beginnin' workin' him; don' know kin I git him ready, come Sat'day. That Frenchy had ought to given me more time."

Redfield stooped to pick up a bit of soil with which to cleanse his hands of the Negro sweat. "Th' boy all right, I reckon; good. On'y I wouldn't work him no more, was I you. He hard now as

215

you kin make him an' he runs limber-like. You goin' to wear him down. Let him rest till you ready to fight him."

"He a lazy son-of-a-bitch," scoffed the owner, concealing his pride. "I 'on't want him goin' off on me."

"Might swim him some, an' keep him rubbed," prescribed the veterinarian. "Eats, I reckon."

"Eats good, white vittles an' eggs raw, 'bout a dozen ever' day."

Redfield nodded wisely in professional approval, and the gentlemen entered the house.

A half empty toddy glass stood on the table. Blanche, seeing the visitor through the window, had retired to dress in more fitting garments.

"Reckon my son tellin' you whut I want—'bout that Natchez ride," Maxwell opened a subject he had in mind, namely that Redfield should accompany Ham on the autumn slave-selling trip.

"Glad to, glad to 'commodate."

"Course, nothin' to do. Hammond here, he do ever'thing. He in charge," the father made clear, not to deprive the young man of his sense of responsibility.

"Better," Redfield agreed.

"I make it right with you; Hammond will, that is."

Redfield raised his hand in protest of payment. "Only neigh-bourly," he said. "Not a dollar, not a cent. You pay my keep on the road. A chancet to git out from under the Widder fer a spell."

"Course, course," Hammond promised, ignoring the aspersion on Redfield's wife. "But——"

"How many? How big the coffle?"

"Dozen or fourteen head, bucks that is; mayhap fifteen or sixteen. Ain't decided yet," Maxwell explained.

"Papa aimin' to send along three or four wenches too."

Redfield evinced surprise. "I reckon you wouldn't sell off wenches."

"Ol'," explained Maxwell. "Ridden of 'em afore they stops breedin'—that is if we kin git 'em showin' in foal in time."

"Bring more open," Redfield argued.

"Young yallers, mayhap, yes," Maxwell admitted. "These'n ol', thirty or sich, an' mos'ly right dark."

"Papa wantin' to," Hammond implied his reluctance to part with the women.

"Trouble about the Widder," Redfield complained. "Ain't sold

216

off. First thing you know, they stops breedin' on you an' ain't worth nothin'. May take along two or three my own self, the Widder willin'."

"You welcome, welcome!" declared Hammond. "Gotten anyways to take the surrey fer the wenches—'specially are they knocked. Room for two or three more."

"An' I a freeholder now—that farm of the Widder's. I kin sign your 'tificates you got to have in Louisianie and Mississippi that you ain't a-bringin' in runners or bad niggers."

"Banker Meyer always signs ourn," Hammond asserted.

"The Banker don't know nothin' about the niggers—never seen 'em. But he signs," the father chuckled. "He know Warren Maxwell ain't sluffin' off bad stock."

"Takes two, two property owners. 'James J. Redfield' will look nice right alongside of Banker Meyer on them papers. An' I know your hands. My name will mean somethin'."

Blanche had dressed carefully, Tense lacing her into her brown costume. Mincing and demure, she sidled into the room.

"You ain't a-knowin' Miz Maxwell yet, are you?" Hammond rose from his chair. "This her, this my wife. Doc Redfield, you hearin' about," he made the introduction.

Blanche simpered and curtsied, and the Doctor made an elaborate bow. "Hammond here, he bin a-tellin' me," the girl said.

"An' me, he tellin' me 'bout his beautiful wife," Redfield lied.

Blanche blushed at the flattery. "Right warm," she said, reaching for a palmetto.

"I knowed your mamma, she about your age. Hankered fer her, but course I didn't have nothin', that time. Your grandpa wouldn't hear of the likes of me, an I known better than ast. Miz Hammond her name was then, an' purty as ever you see, but dark; not fair like you—dark."

"Mamma gittin' deef now," Blanche sighed.

"So did your grandpa, ol' Orestes. You remember Orestes, Mista Maxwell."

"Like yest'day. Brother of Theophilus, but no sech a gen'leman."

"My ol' man worked there—Pleasant Hill, the plantation was called—overseer, when I was a boy. Mista Orestes was kind and generous, sober; mean when he drunk. I mind he made my pappy lick me oncet fer somethin' I never done, somethin' about a wench he keepin' fer one of his boys."

217

Maxwell saved his daughter-in-law's blushes. "I wasn't a-knowin' you worked fer the Hammonds."

"My pappy! They had hosses, good hosses, and niggers, and pigs an' things; that's whure I learned to doctor so good. The Hill onhealthy; somethin' always sick. Worst was the nine-days' sickness—carried new suckers right off, never saved a one, might as well knock 'em in the head oncet they gits it."

"I ain't never had it here," Maxwell vaunted.

"You right clean. Don't never let it start. Belly button swells up an' turns greenlike, ain't nothin' to do."

Meg appeared with four toddies on his tray, served his senior master first, as he had been taught, Blanche lifted her hand, but just in time caught Hammond's eye, saw the just perceptible shake of his head, and dropped her hand to her lap.

"I temp'ance. I never drinks corn," she denied.

" 'Ceptin' sometimes fer medicine, suffers awful when her head aches her," modified her father-in-law for the sake of truth.

"Course, course," assented the guest.

Blanche displayed her best manners, manners which her husband knew she possessed, having seen them at Crowfoot before he had married her. He was none the less proud that she had not forgotten them—the crooked small fingers, the dainty forkfuls, the abstemious appetite, which were reserved for the presence of guests. Hammond saw Redfield watching the girl with approval and admiration. She acquitted herself with elegance, and her husband was proud.

After dinner and another toddy, when Redfield was about to depart, Maxwell followed him to the sunny gallery. "You reckon she knocked up?" he asked the medical man, glancing behind him to indicate to whom the question pertained. "She puke mornin's. Lucretia Borgia reckon."

"Bin two months, 'most three, ain't it?" Redfield calculated. "Knowin' Hammond, she is, or she ain't a-goin' to never be. She is like to have a dozen, runnin', one a year. I reckon she be."

Hammond accepted the veterinarian's counsel to ease up on the Mandingo's training. He worked him only lightly, swam him daily in the river, saw to it that he was oiled and massaged, questioned him about his bowels. Mede had an easy week.

In view of Remmick's opinion that the New Orleans man might demand a money wager, Hammond dug up the pot of gold and extracted from it twenty-five double eagles, which was the maximum sum he was willing to hazard. He was concerned less about winning money than about winning the fight and proving his slave's prowess, but he felt that five hundred dollars was all that he could afford to lose. He preferred to bet Negroes, who, while they were saleable for money, were not gold itself.

When at last Saturday came, Maxwell's excitement over the contest was hardly less than his son's, and he could not be restrained from making one of his infrequent visits to Benson.

In their eagerness, father and son left Falconhurst earlier than need be, but despite their early arrival at the tavern it was apparent that things had already begun to stir. A half dozen horses were at the rack, and a murmur of talk came through the open door.

Hammond hitched his team in the shade of a large maple across the road from the tavern, helped his father to alight, and told the slaves to stay where they were. "Don' git down fer nobody, 'lessen I tells you—not even if a white man say. An' don't you eat nothin' nobody a-goin' to give you. Hear? Somebody tryin' to pizen you afore you fights."

"Eh," scoffed his father at his precautions.

The son led the father across the road, steadied him as he stepped upon the porch, and guided him into the tavern. Talk stopped in deference to so important a personage. Redfield was first to see and greet his friend.

"Couldn't trus' the boy, eh? Got to come?" Redfield suggested. "Boys, Ham's age, reckless, I reckon, bets too heavy. Got to hol' 'em down. How the rheumatics?"

"You know, Doc, Hammond trusty, I ain't no part of this fight. Jest felt like comin' along to watch—plumb outsider. Hammond kin bet ever' nigger an' every dollar on Falconhurst, he seein' that way." Maxwell underlined his disinterest so that his presence might not impair his son's prestige at the tavern.

"I jest a-coddin'," Redfield repaired his error. "Ham ain't a-needin' no didy changer."

When they arrived, Remmick hastened out from behind the bar to draw up a spindle-backed wicker-seated armchair for his honoured guest, and grasped his arm to lower him into it.

"Nev' mind, never min'," Maxwell at once repulsed and accepted the attention, pleased with his reception. "Corn fer everybody, mine with hot water an' a little sweetenin'. Son, you pay."

"Got to wait, suh, whiles I hotten some," Remmick apologized. "Ain't no call fer toddies. Won't take more than a minute."

"Don' stir yourself. I reckon I kin wait." Maxwell blinked in his effort to adjust his eyes to the interior darkness after the brightness of the sun. He squinted toward a figure against the bar and asked, "Ain't that Mista Brownlee?"

The other, unsure of his reception, came forward and extended his hand. "If it ain't Mista Maxwell, well! well! I'm often a-thinkin' about my visit to your place—whut do you call it, Falconhurst?—an' your good vittles an' fine stock, specially that twin pair o' saplin's. Sure like to buy 'em offn you. I knows jest whure I kin sell 'em, know jest the man to want 'em—fer pets, jest pets. I pay a good sum."

Maxwell shook his head and changed the subject. "How you make with them two you traded me out of?"

"Them two unsound bucks? I didn't lose nothin'," admitted Brownlee, by which he acknowledged that he had done well.

"How's niggers in gen'al?" Maxwell queried.

"They's high, still high. Cain't buy 'em."

"Thought maybe that new Louisianie law goin' to cheapen 'em."

Brownlee sniffed. "Nobody pay no attention to that fool law. Course, you cain't sell 'em at public cry in New Orleans, unless you makes out they bin a year in the state; but niggers ain't knowin' whure they comes from an nobody a-crin'."

"Mine all a-knowin' they Alabama."

"Learn 'em to say they Louisiana. Private treaty better anyways, if you got prime stock. They goin' to take that law back, come Assembly. Planters needs niggers—cain't breed 'em fast as they kills 'em in the cane."

Remmick brought Maxwell's toddy and waited for him to taste it. "Sweet enough, suh?" he asked, subdued and solicitous.

"Best I ever drunk," Maxwell savoured the drink.

The party crowded around the bar to obtain their drinks at the Maxwell expense.

"Reckon you mayhap owns that boy we come to fight, Mista Brownlee?" broached Hammond suspiciously.

"Wishin' I did," said the buyer, raising his drink to his host and downing it. "Whupped ever'thin' around about. Worth a fortune, jest about."

"Where is he?" Hammond appealed to Remmick. "Whure the owner?"

"He gittin' ready his boy, rubbin' him. He'll come." The less the haste, the more whisky would be consumed.

220

The room was filling when the side door, which led to the sleeping rooms of the tavern, opened and a swarthy, squat, muscular man appeared. Hammond knew who it was before Remmick announced, "Here Mista Neri now!"

"That Mista Maxwell?" demanded the Italian.

"This him," Remmick indicated.

Neri was direct. "Bring your boy?" he asked Hammond. "Want to fight him?"

"I ain't seen yourn," Ham refused to commit himself.

"Don't want to see yours. I'll fight him," said Neri aggressively. "I'll fetch out Topaz when comes the time. He's restin'."

"I seen him—not shucked down—but I seen him," the tavern keeper intruded into the negotiations, anxious that they should not fall through.

Hammond asked, "He big?"

"He high up. Ain't sayin' he little, but ain't no scuffler, as I kin see. Yourn kin whup, whup easy—that is I reckon, fur as I see."

"Gen'leman ain't seen Mede," called Maxwell impatiently from his chair. "You ain't a-choosin' a damn whore. Cain't tell, lookin' at him, kin he fight. Pit 'em, an' see who whups." The father did not want his son's caution to deprive him of the spectacle he had come so far to see.

"I got to see his bettin' nigger, howsumever," Hammond stipulated, and by these words conceded his willingness to make the match without an examination of the opposing fighter.

"Whut bettin' nigger? I don't fight my boy fer little niggers. I fight fer spondulix, nothing short," declared Neri with a show of scorn.

"I tellin' you, Mista Maxwell, Mista Neri not liable to match fer niggers," Remmick reminded Ham.

Hammond gave a sidelong glance at his father, who was unmoved, then asked. "How much?"

Neri drew from his pocket a sheaf of greenbacks and cast them loosely on the counter. "There five thousand—all I got. Any part of it. Mista Remmick, here, let him hold the stakes an' run the fight, judge it."

From the crowd of onlookers there was an audible stir, from one man a whistle of amazement.

The proposal bewildered Hammond. He produced his pouch and shook its gold upon the counter. "That five hundert. I ain't a-riskin' no more. It all I brung."

Neri reached for his roll of bills, folded it with a sneer, and returned it to his pocket. He started to walk away.

"Wait!" said Redfield, turning Neri back. "I might go two hundred on Ham's buck. I ain't got so much along, but Remmick here knows I good fer it."

Lewis Gasaway came forward and stacked fifty dollars beside Hammond's pile of gold. "I backin' Ham's nigger," he declared.

"I ain't risking my Topaz fer coppers. Not afeared that he won't win, but he may git hurt. Wouldn't have him battered fer seven-fifty. Twenty-five hundred, anyway; that's the lowest."

"Cover it! Cover it!" Maxwell urged Hammond.

"I never brung on'y five hunnert. I ain't a-betting more, 'ceptin' it be a nigger," Hammond's discretion overbore his humiliation.

"Go around to Banker Meyer. He let you have two thousand till Monday," urged Maxwell. "I'll sign. Won't take more than a minute—or half hour."

"When we got to borrow money to bet, I stops a-fightin'. We ain't debted and ain't a-goin' to debt," affirmed the son.

"Well!" The old man struggled to rise. "You ain't goin' to fight him, I reckon we take the Mandingo home an' put him over the fireplace to look at. Ever stuff a nigger, Doc Redfield? Reckon you kin make him look nat'chell? Hammond wantin' you to stuff his Mandingo. It hisn. I don't say nothin'."

"You still got them span o' twins, Mista Maxwell, suh?" asked Brownlee, detaching himself from the crowd. "They still sound and well, an' they not blistered?"

"You hear my son say we ain't debted."

"I will give Mista Neri two thousand fer the two of 'em, an' if he win 'em. Put 'em up with Hammond's five hundred against Neri's twenty-five hunderd," the dealer proposed. "You knows them two squirts ain't worth it, but I give it—two thousand. I got a fool in New Orleans a-wantin' fancies. Pets, jest pets. Needn't fret whure they goin'. They live—best in the lan'."

Maxwell resumed his chair, and ordered another round of drinks.

"You know, Papa, we promise Lucretia Borgia," Hammond interposed. "We cain't sell 'em withoutn her say."

"Not sell 'em, but we kin bet 'em," Maxwell rationalized a distinction.

"Promise to a nigger!" scoffed Brownlee. "Nobody goin' to hold you to it!"

The offer was enticing. A thousand dollars each for Alp and

222

Meg. They were more valuable as a matched brace than singly, it was true, and they were choice boys, delicately made, alert, and responsive. On the other hand, there was a remote chance that they would not grow up into big, muscular men. Maxwell remembered when, before the war with Britain, the La Fitte brothers had sold smuggled bozal Negroes in New Orleans by the pound. There was still value in weight, and the twins would never be big.

Maxwell sipped the toddy which Remmick had brought him. "Ham's say, I reckon. Them saplin's hisn, also. Be me, I'd take you up, Mista Brownlee. But it ain't me."

"Yourn a-goin' to win, anyways, Hammond," argued Remmick. "Ain't no risk."

"But they ain't here. I cain't bet 'em," Hammond hesitated.

"I drop out tomorrow an' pick 'em up, if Neri wins 'em. I trust you. I post my two thousand and your five hunderd agin' Mista Neri's twenty-five hunderd. Ifn he win, he take all the money an' I takes the span of twins."

Hammond reluctantly, against his judgment and with fear in his heart, agreed to the wager. Neri did not understand the arrangement, or pretended not to understand. It had to be explained to him twice.

"That's all right," he added, "jest so I git the money. Put up the real money with Mista Remmick. But I take no responsibility that these Maxwells will give you the niggers if they lose. I thought they was rich, or I wouldn't a-come. If you cain't afford it, there's still time."

Hammond again emptied his purse on the counter, Brownlee counted out the dollars, and Neri matched the joint sums. Remmick raked all together, wrapped the gold in the greenbacks and placed the whole sum in his pocket. Neri bought a round of drinks for the house, lifted his glass to Hammond, barely touched his lips to the whisky and pushed it from him.

"We savin' the big fight to the las'," Remmick announced. "Ain't any you other gen'lemen brung your varmints?"

"'Ceptin' Mista Gore, over there, ain't none brung none," Holden told the impresario. "Gore's nigger cain't fight hisself."

"I reckoned with Ham's buck matchin' the other one, wouldn't be no interest in no other fightin'," said Kyle apologetically. "I could brung one."

"Me, too," a dozen men muttered, one to another, some of whom owned no slaves at all.

"To tell truth, my ol' man a-watchin' I don't sneak none out. I tried," confessed Lewis Gasaway, laughing in his embarrassment. "Don't hold with me a-fightin'—'lessen I wins."

"Well, bring on you god-damn niggers," called Remmick, "an' let's see 'em." He had delayed the fight as long as possible, but now the crowd was milling with impatience and the less ardent were likely to leave. No drinks were being sold.

Redfield followed Hammond across the road to summon Mede, while Neri disappeared through the side door to bring his fighter. Maxwell remained seated. Gasaway, Gore, Kyle and a few others straggled out as far as the porch, but did not venture into the sun. The larger number remained at the bar to see the new fighter emerge. The division of the crowd was a rough indication of partisanship, although some men reserved their allegiance until they saw the fighters, and others, who had no intention of laying bets, were interested in the fight for its own sake and indifferent which side should win.

Mede was asleep in the back of the surrey, mouth agape, and Ham had to shake him awake.

"Come on! Git down. It goin' to start."

"Whut, Masta, suh?"

"That fightin'. You knows I goin' to fight you this evenin'; doesn't you?"

"Yas, suh; yas, suh," the big Negro drawled, half awake.

"All you ponders is sleepin'," Hammond censured. "Ain't aimin' to fight. Ain't thinkin' nothin'! I reckon we goin' to be whup. That othern is a gyascutus, ever'body sayin'!" As the time for the combat neared, Neri's fighter grew more formidable in Ham's imagining.

"I still a-bettin' my two hundert on yourn, if I kin find somebody." Redfield's confidence or loyalty was unshaken. "He goin' to be all right. Don' be so shaky."

The owner and the veterinarian flanked the big Negro to lead him across the road. The party on the porch parted to let the trio enter the room, and straggled after.

The crowd left an open space before Maxwell's chair, where Hammond paused. Men crowded to look over other's shoulders at the fighter, who, conscious of the scrutiny and now fully awake, began a nervous flexing of his muscles and shifting of stance.

"Quiet down. You ain't no stud horse," ordered the old man. "Shuck off his clo's, an' let folks see him."

Mede looked at Hammond for confirmation of the command, and at a nod began ripping himself out of his two garments, which he cast on the floor at Maxwell's feet. He towered naked before the crowd, unable to refrain from flexing his muscles.

A murmur of discussion ran through the onlookers.

Two or three adults reached out to stroke the Negro admiringly. Kyle commented somewhat idly to Hammond, "Gotten him a little fat, ain't you? Seem-like, jest a shade."

Redfield went quickly to his defence. "They ain't no lard on him, not a bit. He all sound meat. He jest big-made."

The side door opened and Neri appeared, followed by his gladiator, naked and glowering, and the crowd shifted its attention, leaving Mede alone in front of Maxwell's chair. Even Hammond, anxious for an appraisal of the challenger, moved with the others. Maxwell, who felt himself deserted, extended his arm towards Mede for help in rising from the chair, and the naked black boy sustained him as he made his way into the crowd that gathered about Neri and his man. Mede, noting that his old master was unable to see Topaz over the crowd in front of him, stooped and lifted him to his shoulder. Maxwell, resentful of the implication that he was not tall enough to see above the crowd, kicked the boy soundly with his booted heel, and demanded to be put down.

But he had had a good look at Topaz, a lanky mulatto, possibly a quadroon, whose height Maxwell overestimated at twenty hands. But he was obviously taller than Mede. Maxwell's entire impression of the Negro was one of length and leanness. The muscles were bunched and were individually visible as the joints articulated. The long, sloping shoulders seemed wider than they were by contrast with the body's taper to a small, lithe waist and rumpless hips. The rib formation was distinct, which led Maxwell to believe, at least to hope, that the man was underfed, despite his reasoning that no owner would risk his money on a starved fighter.

No mere youth, Topaz was fully thirty and possibly thirty-five years old, past his prime perhaps as a fighter, but seasoned and experienced in all the tricks of his enforced vocation. In contrast with Mede, a ridge of hair straggled down Topaz's sternum and spread above his nipples; it had been shortened to mere stubble. The hair on the chest covered but did not conceal a tattooed crucifix suspended by a tattooed chain about the neck. Not permitted by the conventions of fighting to wear a real crucifix or religious medal, Neri relied upon the tattoo as a protection. Yet the protection it offered was not only divine, for no antagonist would flout such a symbol. To strike the tattoo would court defeat not only at the hands of Topaz but at the hands of God.

Topaz's skull was long and lean, like the other parts of him. It rose to a pinnacle accentuated by his high, retreating forehead, a receding hair line, a sunken-cheeked lantern-jaw, small, amber, feral eyes, red and lashless, narrowly together under scant but meeting brows. It was easy to see that the two incisors on the right side of his upper jaw were broken off or missing, and his other visible teeth were pitted and stained. His most repellent aspect, however, was the absence of ears.

Neri's abrupt manner and laconic speech discouraged questions, but Holden ventured to ask him, "Whut 'come of his ears? Didn't he never have none?"

Neri seemed to feel himself on the defensive and replied, "He got one tore in a fracas, time back; and, cuttin' it off, I thought it well to slice off the other side. Didn't we, Topaz? Save it from tearin'."

Topaz cocked his head in order to hear his master. "Yes, suh; save tearin' it off," he concurred. "Ain't nothin' to tear," he added.

"Them burns, though, I didn't do them. He had 'em when I bought him," Neri absolved himself of wanton mutilation of his slave.

"Yes, suh," Topaz elucidated, feeling behind him, "Masta Henry burn my ass when I 'fuse to fight; it long while back, 'fore I didn't have no powder. I feared, that time. Ain't no more. Masta give me powder now."

It was a hint, a plea, upon which Neri acted. Drawing a phial from his pocket, he shook from it into Topaz's hand a small cone of white powder, which the Negro raised to his nose and inhaled at a single sniff. He wiped the residue upon his thigh, leaving a lighter spot upon the flesh.

"Whut that stuff you got smeared on it?" demanded Lewis Gasaway, noting the immediate moisture of the powder.

"It nothin', only lard," replied Neri, blandly. "Don't you all smear lard before fighting? Slicks, makes the strikes glance. Keeps the other one from gettin' aholt."

Hammond glanced at Mede, whose snake oil had ceased to serve such a purpose.

"Stand 'em together," suggested Remmick, "so that the gent'men kin see which one they goin' to bet."

Hammond limped forward, grasped Mede by the arm and led him to the centre of the crowd, that comparison might be possible. Topaz was at some aesthetic disadvantage beside the youthful black symmetry of Mede, although he towered above him in stature. The consensus was that the slaves were well matched.

"Time a'-runnin', gen'lemen," announced Remmick. "Ain't you goin' to bet?"

Redfield, Gasaway and a few others posted their bets upon the Mandingo, which Neri immediately covered and looked around for more victims.

A rumble of talk, claims and counter-claims, opinions and refutations, arguments and rebuttals, echoed about the building. Nobody attended much to what another said. All the whites, except Neri, had been drinking; some had drunk too much, but only one fight between spectators had threatened and Remmick, coming from behind his counter, easily quelled that. He maintained order in his tavern and all knew it. Moreover, none chose to risk exclusion from the fight.

Remmick delayed as long as he was able, but at last men had arranged their wagers; the sale of whisky had stopped; the circle around the fighters had broken; and the groups of threes and fours that gossiped and speculated were growing restless.

"We a-startin' up. All you—all gen'lemen repair to the backyard. We startin'," the tavern keeper proclaimed; and, as an afterthought, enjoined Holden, "Fetch along Mista Maxwell's chair, Sam, an' set him in the shade whure he kin see good."

The throng moved through the rear door, promptly but with order. Everybody wanted a place of vantage. Holden chose the most level place he could find for Maxwell's chair, with its back to the west that the sun might not be in its occupant's eyes. Lewis Gasaway courteously remained behind to lead and guide the invalid to the reserved seat of honour.

Brownlee, who had stayed discreetly away from Neri, none the less remained behind to offer him any aid he might need; and Redfield tarried to second Hammond. Their aid was not required. Holden filled the tin cup the bar reserved for Negroes and set it on the counter, but neither manager chose to use it. Topaz extended his arm towards Neri, opening and closing his fingers nervously. The owner, recognizing the meaning of the gesture, again withdrew the phial from his pocket and poured a cone of powder into the slave's open hand. Deftly and surely Topaz raised his hand and the powder disappeared at a single sniff.

"More in the bottle. It was half full. If we win——," the master promised.

"I a-goin' 'a," affirmed the Negro.

"Course you are," said Neri, reaching to pat the yellow shoulder with assurance and affection.

Redfield nudged Hammond. "I knows whut he givin' him," he confided knowingly. "Make him wil' while it last, but it won't las'. Countin' on winnin' quick. Tell your buck fight slow, wear him out."

"This nigger cain't whup, noways," Ham conceded. "Ain't train, cain't make him. I bein' a fool. That Topaz buck whetted sharp."

"We goin' to win," Redfield affirmed with a show of confidence he didn't feel. He turned to Holden, behind the counter. "Give Mista Maxwell a corn. He needin' it."

Sam set out glasses, filled them, and touched the cup as a reminder. The white man drank. Mede looked askance at his master, opened his mouth to speak, but was silent; he wanted to cheer Hammond, for whose faint heart he felt a kind of sorrow, but sensed that to voice his own confidence would only aggravate the owner's despair. Mede harboured neither fear nor doubt. He had a job to do, the job for which he had been purchased. His money was not at stake and he had no interest in the twins, no concern for his own body, for the pummelling he was about to receive, the pain he must undergo. His body was the property of another; the other accepted the risk. In the glory of victory, however, he should share, as he must partake, if it should come, in the shame of defeat. These were Mede's only stakes, victory or defeat.

Remmick appeared at the door, impatient of the delay. Neri and his fighter, he said, were waiting at the ringside, ready.

"Come 'long," Hammond said. He limped through the open door, followed by the towering Mandingo, with Redfield bringing up the rear. The crowd parted to give them a place at the ring, and Redfield continued around the space to Maxwell's chair, squatting beside it.

Remmick made his way to the centre of the area and raised his hand superfluously, for quiet had already settled on the sun-

228

drenched spectators. "Last, we ready. We goin' to start in. I don' know the why all this waitin'!" he deprecated the delay. "You-all knows about this event. You knows it between Mista Neri, come clean from New Orleans with his nigger, an' Mista Ham Maxwell of Falconhurst with his big varmint you-all seen fight here afore now. Mista Neri's boy name of Topaz, somethin' like that——"

"That right—Topaz," Neri nodded.

"An' Mista Hammond's name of Mede. They 'bout the biggest bucks, and' the fines' ever honour this here arena. Mista Neri an' Mista Hammon' both puttin' up big stakes—money an' niggers. Both these bucks been trainin' an' worked down right fine, seem like. We goin' to see somethin' choice, something like whut ain't never bin seen in Benson afore this, somethin' like whut they does in New Orleans." He ended, as he always did, with "Let 'em FIGHT," and he lowered his arm.

Neri cautioned Topaz not to forget to cross himself, and made the sign on his own front.

The owners simultaneously clapped their respective fighters on the shoulder and propelled them forward into the ring. Topaz danced out with a show of footwork in demonstration of his eagerness. If Mede was equally keen, it was not apparent. He strode stolidly to the centre of the ring, planted his feet on a broad base, and raised his arms for defence. But his defence was futile. Topaz danced around him, striking him with his long arms almost at will, and forcing him to shift his awkward stance. A dozen powerful blows found the exact marks toward which they were directed; a score of minor ones were deflected or glanced away. One mighty punch landed with a dull impact beneath Mede's eye, which began to swell, another cut his thick upper lip, which bled profusely, still another bruised the region just below the heart.

Topaz was a boxer, skilful and precise. He frisked in and away again before Mede was aware, each time planting his knuckles just where he chose. Mede warded the blows as best he could, but each time he intercepted a feint of Topaz's right hand, Topaz countered with his left, which found its mark. Mede seemed unable to counter, unable to block, and unable to strike. He was stolid in acceptance of his chastisement.

The spectators began to jeer. This was no fight, it was a mere flogging.

Topaz ceased to dance away. He was wasting his energy in

avoidance of an enemy who couldn't strike, wasting his skill upon an impotent adversary. Mede, however, absorbed the blows like a bag of sand. He just stood and took what came.

Topaz retreated for a deep breath. He was fatigued from victory. He returned with a fresh fury to the kill. Another blow and yet another. But he was making no impression upon this immovable object. He began to swear at Mede, to curse him, to vilify him with every punch. The words that squirted through Topaz's broken teeth spattered inane and uncomprehended upon their target. So they failed to anger him.

But he had taken enough blows. He moved forward, making no effort to ward himself. He poised himself, closed his fist and slung at his opponent, caught him on the upper sternum. Neri gasped at Mede's temerity; he expected the divine wrath. Topaz staggered two steps backward. Mede sent another blow to the same spot. Topaz staggered, slipped on a stone and went down on his back. Mede made a plunge for him and fell on top of him, pinning his shoulders. Topaz extricated his arms from between their bodies, circled Mede's waist and with the heavy nails of his long fingers clawed and ripped the skin of Mede's back. Eight streams of blood trickled through the sweat.

Mede sought to entwine his legs with those of his adversary, but Topaz was too agile. He succeeded with short punches to Topaz's face, but his arm lacked leverage. He made for Topaz's eye to gouge it from its socket, but the nimble yellow man writhed on the ground, tumbled Mede's body to one side, and sprang to his feet. His back was scraped by small stones, and his sweat was muddied with soil. When Mede sought to rise, a smart blow from Topaz knocked him back to a sitting position, whence by reaching out he grasped Topaz's knee and brought him down, his head in Mede's lap. Topaz bared his broken teeth to bite Mede, but by a turn Mede eluded him, extricated his legs from beneath Topaz's body, and sprang upright. The more agile Topaz was also again on his feet. He was again sparring, boxing, whipping sharp blows to Mede's head and face. Mede felt them, ducked to avoid them, but there was little force in their impact. They teased him and smarted, but they did not rock or stagger him. His face was bruised and swollen, his left eye all but closed, his brow cut and bleeding, but the right eye smiled with confidence and contempt. No longer did Topaz dance, the resilience had left his legs and feet. His fists still flew, but his arms were tired. He had lost his cockiness and his face was grim with a bloodlessness that beneath his yellow skin seemed like a pallor. His invective too had ceased.

Maxwell leaned back in his chair, chuckling at the spectacle. That his Negro was being whipped did not destroy his relish of the contest. He marvelled at Topaz's skill, the certainty and precision of his blows, the agility with which he ducked the occasional heavy fist Mede threw in his general direction. A country-trained Negro couldn't hope to compete with one trained in the city—a blundering bumpkin against the schooled expert. Maxwell admired a winner. He was not one to disparage superiority just because he did not own it.

"My two hundert ain't gone yet," Redfield whispered over Maxwell's shoulder. "I ain't a-givin' up."

"Might as well kiss good-bye that two hunerd," Maxwell looked up at his friend.

Mede found an opening and planted on Topaz's long jaw a blow that staggered him backward. Topaz's hand went to his face to feel the injury, to feel whether the jaw was broken. There was a long sigh from the spectators.

"He ain't done yet. I was thinkin' it about over."

"Jesus!"

"That varmint of Hammond Maxwell's is powerful powerful, when he kin get there."

"Trouble is that othern won't hol' still."

Kyle rubbed his own jaw, so vivid was the suggestion of Mede's blow.

Hammond Maxwell edged about the ring in the direction of Brownlee. He was aghast at the thought of defeat, the loss of the twins. "Mista Brownlee," he muttered. "I'm givin' you two thousand dollars fer them boys. Thay ain't worth it, but Papa, he ain't wantin' to part."

Brownlee shook his head.

"Twenty-five hunderd. That five hunderd profit fer you."

"They fancies. I gits me five thousand fer 'em, I gits 'em to New Orleans. A Frenchy waitin' fer 'em."

The fight was decided, but it continued. The spectators lost interest. Nobody was holding a watch upon the fight, which had now lasted the better part of an hour.

The fighters grappled, staggered, went down and wallowed in the dirt. Mede knelt on Topaz's groin, kneading it painfully with his knees. Again they were on their feet. Topaz sparring, Mede countering the light blows as best he was able. Mede toppled

Topaz again and fell on him, and was flung away. Still again they rose, and clinched and swayed, Mede's weight falling on the other's shoulders, while he pummelled his kidneys. The effects of Topaz's powder had worn away, and it was apparent that both were tiring. Again they were on the ground, struggled to their feet slowly, laboriously. Both heaved for breath, panted.

Mede came clumsily to his knees, and Topaz gained his feet but only momentarily for Mede hurtled forward and brought him down. They rolled again on the ground in the direction of Maxwell's chair, which he pushed back by a scant half foot to be out of their way. Topaz was on top, Mede supine. Too tired to struggle, they lay one on the other, Mede's arms clasped tightly around Topaz's waist. It was nearing the end.

No use to prolong this quietude. Topaz had won. It was undeniable. Remmick entered the ring to kick him off his opponent and award him the victory. As he made his way across the arena, there was a gurgling cry from one of the combatants, and a convulsion of Topaz's shoulders which ran down his back and body. His legs twitched and writhed. With a promise of further action, Remmick retreated from the ring and waited. The convulsion stopped and the negroes lay still in their embrace.

Seconds, a minute, sped by and still they lay. Remmick again started across the ring. Redfield looked at the ground and saw a pool of blood lying on the ground at Mede's shoulder. The pool grew and spread. The body of Topaz twitched again, his leg jerked crazily. Remmick reached down to dislodge Topaz from on top of his victim. Topaz was limp and inert. Remmick turned him over. Blood flowed from his neck upon his shoulders. Topaz was dead.

Relieved of his burden, Mede moved to rise, but sank back in the dust. He was able to draw up one knee and flex the leg. His mouth and teeth were stained with blood. He had gnawed his way into Topaz's neck and severed the jugular vein. He kicked Topaz aside and helped Mede to rise to sitting, but he fell backwards upon the ground.

Hammond rushed forward, amazed at his victory. Remmick raised his hand to announce his decision and to tell the crowd that there would be more fights the following Saturday, but nobody listened. Some men gathered about the corpse of Topaz. More sauntered toward the bar. The excitement was over. Holden brought a bucket of water and dashed it over Mede.

Neri came and bent over Topaz to see what had killed him.

Satisfied, he shrugged and spurned the wretched body with his boot.

Hammond and Redfield, one on either side of Mede, helped him to rise unsteadily to his feet. They led him into the tavern, where his clothes were. He sank to the floor where Hammond struggled with him to get his legs into his pantaloons, while Redfield went to the bar to requisition a cup of whisky.

Hammond took the cup and held it to Mede's mouth. "Drink it down," he commanded. "Whure you hurtin'?" he asked.

"I tired, I jest tired," said Mede, and tried to smile, but only succeeded in distorting his puffed face.

"We won. We won the fight. We killed that nigger," Hammond told him, not sure that Mede was aware of his victory.

"Yas, suh, Masta, suh," Mede acknowledged the information. "Take me home, please, suh. I wants old Luce."

Hammond helped him again to rise and, with the aid of Redfield, supported him slowly across the road to the surrey. The exhausted giant fell obliquely across the cushions of the seat and closed his eyes.

Stragglers were leaving the tavern. Returning across the road, Hammond met Alonzo Kyle and Asa Gore coming out. They stopped to slap Hammond's shoulder in congratulation of his triumph but refused to return with him for a drink in celebration. Gasaway had helped Maxwell back into the tavern and Holden had carried the chair in which Maxwell again sat downing a toddy. Remmick paid off the bets, and each of the winners bought a round of drinks for everybody. Hammond drew down his three thousand dollars, counted it carefully, folded the currency and stuffed it all, paper and gold together, into his pouch. Brownlee took back the two thousand dollars he had deposited for purchase of the twins, neither a winner nor a loser but disconsolate about his failure to obtain the twin mulattos. He left the room hurriedly. Neri had already gone.

The whole party escorted the Maxwells across the road. Mede lolled clear across the rear seat of the surrey.

"Swim that big lummox tomorrer," Redfield suggested. "Work out that stiffness."

"Salt him, salt him down in hot brine. Draw the fever an' take down the swellin'," Maxwell prescribed more drastically, climbing to his seat, Gasaway's hand steadying his arm.

Remmick pressed forward to shake Maxwell's hand and to thank him for coming. Maxwell was not a very old man but his

233

infirmity and solvency made him venerable. His presence had lent prestige to the tavern and to the sport it offered. "You all come back again; come often, suh."

Hammond said little as he bade goodbye around. It seemed to him he was as tired as Mede, as he mounted to the seat and took the reins. Even the mares were tired of standing in the heat and switching flies, but they turned with a will towards Falconhurst and supper.

They drove in silence most of the time, Maxwell massaging the swollen joints of one hand with the palm of the other. He, too, was tired and hungry and satisfied, pleased with the day.

Hammond had little to say about Mede's triumph. A queasiness caused a growing tremulousness of his hands upon the reins. Perhaps he had drunk too much whisky at the tavern. It would pass. He could compare his feeling only to that after the flogging of Memnom.

But it did not pass. It grew. He felt himself fainting, but he retained his consciousness. His hands shook.

He passed the right rein into his left hand and murmured, "You got to take 'em."

"Whut?" asked Maxwell.

"These lines. I cain't drive no more."

"Why, Son, you sick. You right white," declared Maxwell, frightened and horrified, as he grasped the reins, winding them for security about his crippled hands.

"I goin' to be all right. I'll take 'em back in a minute—soon as I kin. Don't hurt your hands. Reckon you got the stren'th?"

"They go. Don't need no drivin', jest hold the line," the older man assured the boy, between his gritted teeth. "We'll git home; ain't fur. Whut reckon ails you?"

"Don' know. Jest feel sinkin' like," breathed the young man weakly. "I be all right direc'ly." He braced his back against the back of the seat and inhaled deeply.

"Day too much fer you. You fretted 'bout the Mandingo. Ain't maimed much. He come all right in a day or two."

Hammond denied his anxiety about Mede. "I wishin' we never risked Meg and Alph, though," he added.

"Why? Good price fer 'em. A thousand apiece, fer jest saplin's. Ain't worth it. An' besides, we never lost 'em."

"But we promised Lucretia Borgia, an' then went an' chanced 'em."

"She ain't a-goin' to know. We never lost 'em," the father

reiterated. "It's your mamma in you—too tender-livered." His reproof was tempered with approbation.

" 'Sides I fancies 'em, them two, kind of. With them gone, it wouldn't be the same-like." The terror in his tone gainsaid the casualness of his words. Hammond valued the twins more than he had been aware.

"Ain't no danger now. It all over," Maxwell sought to soothe Hammond's anxiety.

A shiver descended Hammond's spine, but he sat forward. "I'll take the hosses now," he offered. "I reckon I kin drive."

"Nev' mind. I doin' all right, right well. My han's don't hurt me," Maxwell dissembled and fell silent. Ahead, he saw a woman in a Mother Hubbard dress disappear in the brush beside the road. The spot was far removed from any habitation and Maxwell wondered briefly what she might be doing. He did not mention her to Hammond, whose eyes were closed, although his father was sure he was not asleep.

He had forgotten the woman as he approached the spot where she had disappeared. Abruptly a Mother Hubbard sprang from the side of the road and grabbed the head of the horses, stopping them. The wearer was masked by a red handkerchief tied over the lower part of his face. Another masked man in a Mother Hubbard approached the carriage with a cocked gun.

"Raise you hands," commanded the second man. "Drop the hosses an' raise your hands. We want your money. Don't want to haf to shoot."

The man in front of the horses did not speak.

The Maxwells were unarmed and unable to resist. Bewildered by the suddenness of the unanticipated danger, the older man unwound the reins from his hands and raised his arms. "Don't fight 'em. Do like he say," he adjured his son. "On'y wantin' jest money."

There was no alternative for Hammond, with the point of the highwayman's gun in his ribs. Half comprehending, he too slowly raised his hands.

Mede roused himself and made as if to rise at which his older master turned his head and ordered, "Don't do nothin'. Set you still."

"Whure is your poke?" demanded the robber. Hammond lowered his right hand to withdraw it, and the robber cautioned him, "Keep 'em high. Tell me. I'll git it."

"In my pocket," murmured Hammond reluctantly and weakly.

235

The robber felt him over, located the purse and withdrew it. Holding it before him, he backed toward the overgrown forest at the roadside. "Drop the hosses and leave 'em go," he called to his companion.

"Ought to cut his harness, loose the hosses, and let 'em walk," replied the other.

"Let 'em ride. One is old," said the man with the gun. "Come on." He disappeared into the brush. His partner relinquished the horses and followed.

The robbery had been almost casual, entirely lacking in melodrama. The highwaymen had appeared, made their demands, garnered the money, and departed as suddenly as they had come. It would be as futile to pursue them as to resist.

"Turn 'round. Go back. Go back fer help," Hammond urged.

"You think they goin' to the tavern to spen' that money?" Maxwell asked calmly. "They half toward New Orleans already."

"Neri?" suggested Hammond.

Maxwell nodded, as he readjusted the reins about his hands. "An' the other one, the other at the hosses, Brownlee, or I miss. 'Bout his size. They in cahoots all along." He clucked to his mares.

"They could taken the niggers an' the hosses. We couldn't a-done nothin'."

"Didn't want 'em on they hands. That's hangin'." The older man paused and then chuckled. "Look comical in them dresses an' them kerchiefs over they heads. Reckon they reckoned we ain't a-goin' to know 'em."

"We don'—not fer sure."

"We knows, but cain't swear, cain't take oath."

"All that money," lamented Hammond.

"Five hunert dollars, ain't it?"

"Three thousand."

"But on'y five hunert out. The other we won from 'em. They jest a-takin' it back. Jest one half grown nigger worse off than when we started—'bout that. It ain't bad."

" 'Tain't fair," said Hammond.

"Nigger fightin'. Got to expect it—anything." Maxwell did not condemn the sport. He merely noted its hazards. "Don't tell nobody how we was bilked—'ceptin', maybe, Doc Redfield. Nobody needin' to know. Neri an' Brownlee ain't a-tellin'. We eatin', jest the same."

"An' we got the twins," Hammond groped for consolation.

236

The encounter had rallied his strength. The weakness he had forgotten now returned. A clammy sweat drenched his body and chills followed one after another down his backbone.

Maxwell gave the mares their heads, and they required little guidance or urging, but the strain upon his flaccid arms was racking. He sought to conceal his discomfort from Hammond and succeeded. They rolled through the waning daylight in silence.

"I gotten us here," observed Maxwell as the team turned from the road into the lane at Falconhurst.

Napoleon ambled forth to grasp the horses. Lucretia Borgia appeared on the gallery.

"Whure Memnon?" the owner demanded.

"He comin', Masta, suh."

"Tell him hurry. Hammond here sick."

Lucretia Borgia rushed impetuously forward in her solicitude. Memnon came up to help his master down from the surrey and was cursed for his pains. "Git aroun' to other side. God-damn slothin' fool. Lift down your young masta. Lift him careful. He sick."

Before Memnon could pass around the vehicle, however, Lucretia Borgia had grasped Hammond and had lifted him from his seat, stood him upright, supported him with her vast arm around his waist, and was leading him toward the house.

Memnon recircled the surrey, but again before he could reach the other side, his master had crawled down under his own power and was stretching his muscles and flexing his hands. He was fatigued; but the realization that he was still good for something caused him to forget his pain.

"Git him abed," he instructed nobody in particular. "Heat him up a sad-iron fer his feet. Cain't you see he sick?"

Lucretia Borgia required no instructions. She was taking Hammond into the house as fast as he was able to walk. Again he was a frail and petulant little boy, whom she could at once master and serve, command while she pampered.

"Whure Meg? An' Alph?" Hammond demanded.

"They eatin', Masta, suh. Feedin' 'em 'thout waitin' fer you all—gittin' so late."

"Call 'em here. I craves seein' 'em, jest seein' 'em," murmured Hammond weakly, pausing at the edge of the gallery.

Lucretia Borgia bellowed their names. "Come here to yo' masta," she roared sternly, as if to indict the twins of some negligence. "Why you wantin' them, Masta? They done some-thin'?" she asked.

"They all right? I near to sold 'em, both of 'em," he confessed. "I don' want to sell 'em. They mine."

The twins appeared and asked in unison, "Yas, suh, Masta?"

Hammond gestured the boys nearer. He placed his hands on their shoulders and drew them toward him. It was enough. He had confirmed with his senses that the slaves had not vanished.

Meg, without prompting, fell in on one side of his master to lead him. Only after Hammond had satisfied himself of the presence of the twins did he bethink him of Mede. He turned and called to him. "Git down outn that seat," he commanded. "Have Lucy wash you down and rub you good. You all right, come mornin'."

The Mandingo roused himself and tried to obey, but in dis-mounting from the carriage sank to his knees between the wheels.

"Run fer Lucy," Hammond told Alph. "Hurry!"

"Nev' mind," said the father. "You go on. Git you abed. I'll see Lucy puts him away."

But Hammond tarried, supported by Meg and Lucretia Borgia, until Lucy arrived, terrified and convulsed with anxiety, followed placidly by Big Pearl.

"Ain't it a pity, ain't it a pity?" repeated Lucy over and over as she helped Mede to rise to his feet. "Whut they do to you? Whut happen?" she demanded.

"We won. I kilt him," Mede murmured the only explanation he could give.

"Wash him down good an' rub him in bed," Hammond pres-cribed. "I'll send some sleepin' medicine fer him."

"You looks so funny. Sho' do look funny," commented Big Pearl as she and her mother, one on each side, dragged the Mandingo to his feet and supported him toward their cabin.

Hammond watched them go and reluctantly turned to be led himself into the house and up the stairs to his bedroom. He sank back upon the bed and submitted to being divested of his clothes. Maxwell and Memnon followed, and Ellen came, panicking in apprehension.

Nurses more devoted could not have been found although there was nothing for them to do. Hammond turned and snuggled himself in his bed. He reached his hand from beneath the covers and drew Meg to the side of the bed, permitting his hand to rest on the boy's thigh. Sure of his possession, he closed his eyes.

238

Meg could not escape, might not even fidget, lest he wake or disturb his master. He was elated at the distinction of his master's
touch, and grinned in his triumph over Ellen in being chosen.

All night the household was astir, although, once abed and
quieted with laudanum, Hammond required no attention. With
morning he opened his eyes drowsily and tasted the soup that
Lucretia Borgia had kept steaming through the night. He felt no
hunger and was unable to drink three spoonfuls, but Lucretia
Borgia was repaid for making it. His fever had subsided but had
not entirely disappeared. He thrust his legs from the covers and
sat on the side of the bed, fell backwards across it, enjoyed the
play of the air on his feverish flesh. At length he summoned the
resolution to rise and, over Ellen's demur, bade Meg to dress
him.

"You ought not, Masta. You sick. I goin' to call Old Masta,"
Ellen threatened.

"Keep on your britches. Ain't any damn wench drivin' me. I
got to 'tend to that boy; like is, he hurtin'."

"Mede? He kin come up here," the girl argued.

"Stinkin' up! That oil an' all!" He dismissed the idea.

Still weak, once on his feet he felt better than he had anticipated. He surmounted the dizziness that overtook him at the
head of the stairs and resolutely hitched his way down them, one
step at a time, Meg on his left side to help and balance him. At
the foot of the stairs he braced himself, opened the front door and
strode into the open. As he moved from the cool shade into the
sunshine, which was already growing hot, he shivered again.

"Go on back," he turned sharply on the young slave at his side.
"God damn! Has you got to try an' tail after me, ever' step I
takin'? You'd reckon I 'longed to you, ruther as you 'longin' to
me. You don't leave me be, I goin' to trounce you, trounce you
good. Now, go long." This tirade was an effort to negate the thing
that had sickened him, about which he felt some shame. He
refused to credit that his fear of losing the Borgia's twins could
have brought on his fever and laid him low.

Hammond limped across the area and entered the Mandingo's
cabin. Mede lay in the bed, Lucy feeding him his breakfast
morsel by morsel with her fingers. His eyes were mere slits
between bulging blue-green lids. His cheeks were knobs, his thick
lips were everted with swelling, and his nose spread amorphously
over his face. Unable to chew without pain, he swallowed the
bites of fat pork whole as Lucy stuffed them slowly into his mouth.

"He funny," giggled Big Pearl. "That nigger shore look funny."

"Hush up, you big black mouth," Lucy admonished her. "You don't, I makes you look funnier than he do. Cain't you see he painin'? Ain't got no gumption?" In the mother's indignation she turned also on Belshazzar, who was munching his breakfast, and ordered him, "Take that bone you suckin' an' git outn hyar! Cain't you see Masta come? You jist in his way. Be polite, cain't you? Git out."

Hammond ignored the household strife. He walked to the bed and asked, "How is you, boy? Is you hurtin' bad?"

"Naw, suh, Masta, suh. I all right—goin' to be. I right tol'able, suh, please suh," the slave replied thickly and painfully, with a grimace intended to be a smile.

"He near kilt," Lucy put in. "He don' got to fight no more, Masta, do he? Mede near ruint."

"Whut you reckon I got him fer, jest to pleasure you an' Big Pearl? Other bucks good enough fer that. When he well agin, I'm going to fight him when I tell him. Mede craves to fight, don' you?"

The slits of eyes turned upwards at the outer corners in an implied smile, as the boy bobbed his jaw in an effort to nod his head.

"He kill that othern. He tell you?" Hammond praised Mede, who grinned broadly despite the pain.

Lucy answered with an "Umm! Umm!"

Hammond bent over the bed and touched the tender flesh of the eyelids with his forefinger, pinched the bulged cheeks, felt the lips, opened the mouth to examine the teeth. None was missing or broken.

When Hammond cast back the covers to examine Mede's body, the stench of serpent oil suffused the room. The torso was swollen in spots, and Mede flinched at Hammond's prodding of them. But worst of all was the knee when Hammond tried to flex it.

"Please, suh, Masta, suh," Mede begged while his master manipulated the joint.

"I better sen' fer Redfield," Hammond opined aloud. "He goin' to fire that knee an' make it bend."

"No, no, please, suh, Masta, not that white man. He goin' to hurt, hurt bad. It git well, Masta. I kin ben' it now, almos'. You do sompin', anything, but not him."

"Don' want a stiff knee, do you, like I got?" It was the worst

240

fate that Hammond could suggest. "That red poker jist take a jiffy; Doc Redfield kin fix it."

Mede sat up in bed, weeping. "Naw, naw, no," he cried. "Please Masta, suh, don't let him burn me." He grasped Hammond about the shoulders, and buried his face in his coat, tears of terror streaming from his face.

The white youth hugged the Negro to him and let him cry. "Doc ain't a-goin' to hurt you none more than he got to. Won't take more than a minute. I wish they done it to me," Ham tried to appease his black child.

Mede clung but the tighter to Hammond's body, racked with convulsive sobs. Fearful not at all of the worst such an opponent as he had fought yesterday was able to do to him, he quailed at the concept of a hot poker in the hands of the veterinary.

CHAPTER SEVENTEEN

B Y WEDNESDAY the swellings on Mede's face had subsided and his features were recognizable. He had quite recovered his spirits. Best of all, his knee had so mended that he was able to walk without a limp, if not without pain. Hammond instructed Lucy to continue the embrocations and the manipulations.

Mede was too precious to risk in productive work, and, aside from the occasional use of him as a stallion, he was wholly unprofitable. This the Negro was not long in surmising and set himself up as a spoiled darling. Disdainful of the lesser slaves, he was as arrogant as he was exigent with Lucy and Big Pearl. His favours were a condescension and the women to whom they were delegated were expected to be, and were, grateful. He was as abject toward his white owners as he demanded his fellow-slaves to be to him, and he submitted willingly to the most rigorous regimen of exercise and diet that Hammond's ingenuity could devise.

That bugbear of the cotton planter, a wet picking season, beset Alabama. Wind and rain assailed the opening bolls, which wilted and rotted before they could be gathered. The Maxwells threw their whole force, adults and children, into the 'patch' on those rare days dry enough to warrant working, but the pickers were so indiscriminate that much of the sound fibre was mildewed by contact with the soggy bolls included in the bags. Hammond cautioned the hands each morning not to pick wet cotton, but it filled the picking bags as well as the dry. He had the women go through the wagons to sort out and discard as much wet fleece as they were able before the crop was hauled to Benson for ginning. It was futile, since all was dank, if not before it was picked, dampened by the dragging of the jute bags through the mud and puddles of the field.

Would the rain ever stop? The crop had grown and matured well, better than Hammond anticipated when he had planted it, and he gave the credit to the Petit Gulf variety which was new at Falconhurst. But for Petit Gulf there was a long picking season; the bolls on a plant kept bursting for weeks, a few at a time. And the afternoon downpour or the all-night drizzle blasted them as they burst.

If Ham was disappointed in the failure of his crop, Lucretia Borgia was desolated. She stood in the gallery, watching the rain descend and shaking her head while she supported her distended abdomen with her hands intertwined beneath it. For all the eupepsia with which pregnancy endowed the woman, she could not abide with complacency misfortunes which beset the family. Her moods mirrored those of her younger master.

The elder Maxwell, on the contrary, took a perverse satisfaction in his son's discomfiture, the satisfaction he had taken when Ham's castle of blocks had toppled and the boy had to learn by trial and error to build securely. To Maxwell, the failure of a crop was but a lesson in the futility of planting. "He goin' to learn," he told Blanche over their toddies, "whut I been tellin'. Cain't make cotton on wash-away lan'. Jest some'in to keep the niggers from settin' an' rottin'. The harves' in niggers—growin' niggers, regular nigger farm. Cain't learn him, seem like, Falconhurst ain't a cotton plantation at all. Course, I know," he conceded, nodding, "cotton genteel. Goin' to be a gen'leman, you got to grow a little patch of cotton. The Hammonds all growed it—an' all busted." Neither rancour nor irony was in his tone.

Lucretia Borgia's child refused to wait for the end of cotton picking. As the Maxwells sat down to breakfast one morning, Meg came galloping impetuously from the kitchen, peacock brush in hand, and announced, "Masta, please suh, my mammy fetch you a sucker. Come see, please suh, come see." He even laid his hand on his master's arm and sought to draw back his chair.

'Nev' min'," said Hammond. "We seein' it after we eats. She doin' all right? Whut kin' she fetch? On'y one?"

242

Memnon came with a platter of ham and eggs. "I bringin' you nice sucker, Masta," he claimed credit. "Me and Lucretia Borgia."

"How know it yourn? She pleasurin' with that Pole, wasn't she? Mayhap hisn!" Maxwell said between bites. "Been two of 'em, I'd reckon it yourn."

"It mine! You see an' it not," Memnon was confident.

"Then you weakin' down some. Why ain't it twins?"

Memnon shrugged.

"Whut kind is it?" Hammond wanted to know.

"It little an' light, light red," explained Meg.

"They all comes light. They blackens," Hammond deigned to explain. "But whut kin'?"

"Jes' a wench, Masta, suh," admitted Mem with reluctance.

"Well, anyways, better look at it, Ham, an' give the wench a dollar, you gits time, after breakfas'."

"Whyn't you? Sun's out and dry. I got to watch after them pickin' hands."

"You know she ruther you, Son; your dollar shines brighter. 'Sides in my time I've looked at so many they all lookin' like squirmin' water-dogs. See that it whole, arms an' legs an' all; an' tell Lucretia Borgia somethin' nice. Ain't no rush 'bout her cookin', tell her. Let her lay two, three days an' she a-wantin'."

The weather had taken a turn. Day followed day of fine sunshine obscured only by the blue October haze. Retarded bolls came to maturity and burst wide on the browning plants until the field from a short distance seemed covered with snow. Not only was the harvest copious, but it was easier to gather since each plant carried many ripe bolls. What is more, the cotton was dry. The crop was not a failure after all.

Hammond gave much time now to the autumn expedition to Natchez and New Orleans, for the purpose of selling a coffle of slaves, on which it was agreed he should be accompanied by Doc Redfield. The slaves selected for sale were put on increased rations and strenuous labours. Hammond added raw eggs to the boys' diets, and set bottles of serpent oil about the dusty window ledges of the meeting house with instructions that each should anoint another and be anointed in turn every night before they should lie down to sleep. The stench of the nostrum was so vile that nobody could doubt its efficacy.

The boys imagined themselves going up and down the crowded streets of the city in search of masters that suited their taste.

With no ideas of what a city might be or what a street was like, each pictured a concourse of men competing to buy him.

They were sobered by Napoleon's warning, "You-all ain't a-goin' to do nothin', savin' Masta say. He goin' to sell you to who he reckon, an' you-all ain't goin' to have nothin' to do with it. Leastwise, me. I doin' whut Masta tells me."

All knew that Napoleon spoke the truth, but it did not forestall their dreams of felicity. All looked ahead to the excursion into the greater world. They considered themselves the aristocrats of the plantation; they had been chosen.

Hammond looked with satisfaction upon the strong and strengthening bodies and fed them tales of New Orleans that intensified their desires. He half believed his inventions. In his own interest, he imagined easy sales at high prices, and intended to dispose of these boys to none but gentlemen, masters who would treat them well. They were a fine assortment, just on the brink of maximum development, the edge of youth still on their features, the lustihood of maturity in their thews. His father had taught him to choose the exact time when a slave was likely to bring the largest price.

Only by comparison with Mede did the members of the salesdraft seem jejune. Watching him exercise, bending, squatting, jumping, lifting, Hammond felt that he was sacrificing nothing in disposing of the other boys. The Mandingo alone could replenish the plantation.

Some two weeks after the birth of Lucretia Borgia's baby, Dite was beset with labour. She was promptly put to bed and Ellen hovered over her. The child was Hammond's own and no chances were to be taken with amateur obstetrics. Vulcan, who knew the countryside, was put on a mule and sent to fetch the Widow Johnson. (Redfield continued to refer to his wife as 'the Widder', and as the Widow Johnson she remained in the minds of the Maxwells.)

That lady arrived driving the same big, heavy-footed grey mare hitched to the same vehicle in which she had driven on her professional errands since long before she was married to her former husband, a kind of rattletrap calash with the hood thrown back (nobody had ever seen it up), lop-sided from her heavy occupancy of the left seat. The front wheels, with only a few scabs of paint remaining on the spokes, converged at the tops; the rear wheels diverged. She got down with a bustling alacrity that reflected the urgency of her task, smoothed her voluminous bombazine skirt of the exact shade of dark bottle green as the

244

remaining pile on the plush of the gig's upholstery, grasped three soiled muslin bags that contained her herbs, and went toward the house, the warts of her face emphasizing the tic with which her features at ten seconds intervals registered her determination and haste to respond to the call of professional duty.

Mede, although not a stable hand, saw the rig unattended and deigned to come for the mare and lead her to the barn. He also saw Redfield approaching and called Big Pearl to care for the second horse.

The doctor dismounted and handed the bridle to the girl, who took it gingerly. Mede, seeing her fear, exchanged horses with her. "Here," he suggested, "you take this 'un. He gen'ler. Won't rare up."

Unable to refrain from professional observation, Redfield greeted the girl approvingly. "The way you bellyin' out at this stage, you goin' to have a purentee gyascutus."

Big Pearl was flattered by the compliment, showing her teeth in a giggle.

Memnon opened the door and Redfield knew that he would find Maxwell in the sitting-room. Blanche, barefooted, her pregnancy obvious, was with her father-in-law, but she hastily left by way of the dining-room with her toddy goblet in hand as the guest came down the hall.

"Whure the Widder?" Redfield asked.

"I don' know. I reckon, an' she come, she went right away up. It's Dite, Ham's own wench; that is she was before," Maxwell explained.

"An' he wantin' the best for her. The Widder, she right good."

Hammond came in and sat down, brushing Meg away with the drink he brought for him. Plainly anxious, his ears were cocked more for sounds from upstairs than for the conversation of the older men.

"They sayin' the vomit ragin' in New Orleans," Redfield made talk. "A gen'leman at the tavern, come right from there, sayin'."

Maxwell refused to take alarm. "Ever' summer," he nodded, "Ever' summer the same. The cause I not cravin' Hammond go there in summer—the vomit an' waitin' until after cotton when ever'body got they money."

"Had ought to be gittin' better this time of year," Hammond ventured. "Ain't no danger now, October."

"Won't be danger, time you-all ready. Cool weather cleans it right up."

A creaking of the stairs followed by the swish of bombazine brought Ham to his feet. He opened the door as the midwife came down the hall hugging in her arms a baby wrapped in a shawl.

"No trouble, no trouble at all," she declared. "I wasn't needed. Anybody could do it."

"Whut kind?" Hammond plucked at the shawl.

"I ain't rightly had no time to look. Buck; I think so, anyways," said the woman, opening the parcel.

"An' it yourn, it a buck," said the proud grandfather. "You don' fetch nothin' else. Reckon you ain't got no wenches in you."

The shawl laid back, Hammond was aghast. The red baby, kicking and crying, was covered with a golden fuzz.

"Mustee," breathed Ham.

"Mustee?" repeated his father, rising to look at the child. "Troublous, all on 'em. They comes white, they makes trouble. Reckon though you cravin' to keep it." The old man proposed no alternative.

The baby ceased to cry and directed its unfocused gaze at Redfield, who remarked, "Maxwell eyes, regular Warren Maxwell eyes, blue as lobelia flowers."

"I better claim it mine, mayhap. Save trouble around." Warren Maxwell all but tittered as he gestured vaguely to indicate the part of the house where Blanche might be.

"She ain't carin', not about this one," Hammond sighed, reluctant to be relieved of the credit for paternity. " 'Sides, it was afore she come, afore we got marr'ed."

"It mine," the old man insisted. "Remember it mine—the las', I reckon, I ever go' to sire. An' we'll name him 'Doc', after Doc Redfield here."

He called Meg to stir fresh toddies for a christening toast to Doc, but the Widow, avowing her temperance, rewrapped the blond baby in its shawl and took it upstairs to its mother's breast.

But while Lucretia Borgia was up, cooking meals and bossing the plantation, two days after the delivery of her child, Dite remained ten days abed, cared for solicitously, even lovingly, by her successor in her master's bed. Ellen was not unmindful of how soon she herself might require such attention. Dite was indifferent to the baby, except that she valued the status it gave her to bear her master's child, but Ellen loved it for its own sake; it was a baby, a blue-eyed, white baby, and it was Hammond's.

246

Some days afterwards, on a hot and still afternoon, Maxwell sat in a big chair in the shade of the gallery, asleep, with Alph asleep in the sun at his feet. Both had been drinking toddies from a single goblet. It amused the white man to make the small Negro tipsy by giving him frequent swallows from his own glass. The goblet had toppled and spilled on the floor beside the chair and the spot was speckled with flies drawn by the sugar. Hammond was in the field, supervising the gleaning of cotton, perhaps the final picking. Maxwell's head tottered to his right shoulder and fell forward, and his face contorted in his dream. Alph, supine, snored lightly.

The clatter of a gallop was subdued by the rustle of drying leaves on the lane. A gallop betokened haste at Falconhurst. It brought Lucretia Borgia from the kitchen to see what could be so urgent.

"It cholrie, it cholrie," shouted Redfield, springing from his horse.

Maxwell raised his head and opened his eyes, blinded by sunlight. Seeing who it was, he muttered hospitably enough but without enthusiasm, "Come in! Come in!" And then he called, "Mem, another chair! Meg, stir us some toddies! Somebody take Doc Redfield's horse! Whure at are all them niggers? Under foot when nobody wantin' 'em."

He kicked Alph awake with his boot, and the boy took the horse. Lucretia Borgia brought another chair.

All the while Redfield, staring with wild eyes, reiterated, "It's cholrie! it's cholrie, I'm a-tellin' you! Ain't the vomit, no sich thing, it's cholrie!"

"Whut you talkin' 'bout, Doc Redfield? Who got it? I ain't hearin' of any aroun'." Maxwell wanted meaning from the incoherence.

"The tavern! I jest rid from the tavern, hard as ol' Skelter could fetch me."

"Who down with it? Remmick down?"

"No! Ain't nobody down aroun' here—yet! Cain't you un'er-stand? In New Orleans, got cholrie in New Orleans! Two men passin' through, runnin' from it."

"Oh, that all? Reckon that place ain't never clean shet of cholrie, or somethin'. Drink your toddy."

"But it ragin', sweepin' the whole place. Ever'body either dyin' or gittin' out, goin' to their plantations or upriver or whurever. One day you're hearty, next day you dead."

247

"Ain't that a fac'? Anywhure?" Maxwell refused to show alarm. "The *Advertiser* ain't said nothin'."

"The *Advertiser* won't, but it true. You ain't leavin' Ham go there? I ain't a-goin', not a step. Got to leave me out."

"Neither ain't Hammond, an' it bad as you sayin'. You know danged good an' well, I ain't sendin' no thousand-dollars-a-head niggers, leavin' Hammond alone, into no pest hole."

"I reckoned," Redfield breathed easier. "I hatin' to quit that trip, but——"

Hammond rounded the corner of the house, greeted the visitor, and his father broke the doctor's news.

"'Tain't nothin'. I ain't bein' balked," he affirmed. "Cotton all picked, niggers primed an' ready. I goin'!"

"Not an' cholrie ragin'," his father argued in a wheedling tone as if to a small child. "Not a-sayin' yet awhile it be, but ifn——"

"I not askeared," said Hammond unconvincingly.

"Well, I am," Redfield confessed. "You goin', you goin' alone."

"You not skeared, no," conceded Maxwell. "But them niggers! Barracoons ain't clean. An' besides, ever'body away, there ain't no sale fer 'em. Won't bring nothin'."

"Might risk Natchez," suggested Redfield. "It ain't got upriver."

"Might," Maxwell assented. "Might, New Orleans. 'Pends on whut the *Advertiser* say. Natchez a good market—'Forks-of-the-Road'."

Nothing was settled. Hammond's disappointment disturbed his father. Cholera in New Orleans was perhaps not so general as the rumour at the tavern had led the doctor to believe.

But the next issue of the weekly *Advertiser* confirmed the panic; the epidemic could no longer be ignored. Persons who had a place to go were getting out. Business was stagnant. The facts which had earlier been concealed were now enlarged fivefold and flaunted. If the newspaper was unable to repress a panic, it was profitable to produce a sensational one. It proclaimed unctuously that the *Advertiser* staff would remain to serve, perhaps to sicken, if not to die.

That Hammond should go to New Orleans at such a time was unthinkable. It would be not only hazardous but futile.

Redfield came again, gloating that the truth had borne out his rumour. After a canvass of their respective advantages as a place for selling slaves, Natchez was chosen over Mobile. Buyers from

248

Louisiana and emigrants to the Texas country were more likely to be found at Natchez, where the market was always brisk, even when New Orleans flourished. Cane was more profitable than cotton had ever been, even before the Alabama soil was sapped. Buyers would be flusher on the river than on the gulf. Cholera there, by some reasoning, seemed less likely. Natchez it should be, and the start should be made a week from Monday, at sun-up. That would be, Hammond consulted the almanac, the fifteenth of November, mid-month, early enough before Christmas and late enough that crops would be sold and the money yet unspent.

"I doubt me that you gits as much as you reckons, but take it. Git whut you kin, but take whut offers, Son, an' don' repine. Don' bring none of 'em back with you. Takin' 'em along to sell, sell 'em. May have to hold a public cry of 'em, but private treaty better. That a-way you knows who is a-gittin' 'em, how they goin' to be dealt with," Maxwell counselled his son.

"Armfield and Franklin got a jail at the Forks, right neat an' shipshape. Best place, an' you kin git 'em in; ever'body know whure it at, an' ever'body wantin' hands goes there first or last," he continued his advice, Hammond giving it close heed. "Course, ifn A. and F. full—new-come coffle or niggers not sellin' or sumpin'—you got to look aroun'.

"Doc, he purty guiley. You mire down, he he'p you out. On'y use your own noggin, not hisn. Comes a wrangle between your way and hisn, do yours; I wants you should learn. But when you dubious, ast Doc."

Hammond drank in the instructions and resolved to remember them. They left him a free hand.

"Not many boys, nineteen, goin' about carryin' a coffle to market."

"An' I not take 'em, I cain't reckon how they git there," Hammond rebutted, stung by the emphasis upon his youth.

"You right," acknowledged the old man, "and I'm proud that you kin, proud I got you. I don' know whut I'd do."

In the days pending Hammond's departure, he had to listen over and over again to his father's charges and advice. He did not resent the necessity, since he had confidence in the paternal sagacity and, besides, the instructions were so vague as to leave him free to do as he believed best.

"You ain't carryin' me along?" Blanche attacked the subject one night after supper when Maxwell had left the dining-room.

"You say you take me along to New Orleans, come fall and cotton pickin' over."

"I ain't goin' to New Orleans. Cholrie. You knows it. I ain't goin' there. Besides, look down at yourself. You in no shape to go, no shape at all. No white lady hanker to be seen the way you are. You got to stay close to home until that boy come." To mitigate the girl's disappointment, Hammond added, "You stay close an' ack nice, I bring you sumpin' when I come, a fine cloak or sumpin'."

"I don' never go nowhures. I cain't wear it," she retorted.

"Well, sumpin', sumpin' nice an' sumpin' fer the boy when he goin' to come."

"I reckon you goin' to carry along that Ellen nigger? That the cause you ain't carryin' me."

Hammond sniffed in feigned amusement. "Ellen's belly stickin' out much as yourn, almos'. Ellen knowin' she cain't go. Ain't neither one of you no good to me, the way you are."

"Then you fixin' to pleasure with all them white ladies ever'- body sayin' Natchez full of, them white whores. That whut you goin' fer?"

"I goin' to sell niggers, business, an' you knowin' it," Hammond gave way to his indignation. "Besides, I don' crave to pleasure with no white ladies."

At this Blanche began to cry, for although she knew that her husband was repelled by the whiteness of a woman's skin he had never told her so before. He believed it to be skin colour and the odour of white bodies that he did not like, whereas in fact it was a need to possess to command his sexual object, in a manner he was unable to do with a woman free and white. He feared a rebuff. His choice was not between white and black (or yellow), but between free and chattel.

Compassion prompted Hammond to suggest toddies for Blanche and himself as they entered the sitting-room, where the elder Maxwell was already drinking. He knew that nothing was more likely to assuage his wife's resentment of his preference for dark skins.

The same night, Meg, struggling to remove his master's boot, broached, "Whenabouts, Masta, suh, we goin'?"

"When we goin' whure?"

"When we goin' that place, you know, suh, to sell them niggers?" Meg shrugged in acknowledgment of his ignorance. "I 'on' know whure."

250

"You reckons you goin' along?" asked the master with a low chuckle. "Well, you ain't."

"I yo' nigger," Meg pouted.

"I know you my nigger. An' I takes you along, you goin' to be somebody's else nigger; I'll sell you along the others in Natchez."

The boy recognized that the white man was joking, but his lacklustre smile of response was tinged with fear. He was not for sale, he knew; but his master's whims were unpredictable. "Who goin' to jack yo' boots off fer you, suh?"

"I got sixteen other niggers to jack my boots. Don' need you. You stay home here an' stir toddies fer your ol' masta. That whut. Ever'body wantin' to ride along." To prove that there was no malice in his refusal, Hammond pinched the muscle of the boy's thigh until he grunted with pain.

The Sunday before the departure was given over to visiting and to farewells among the slaves. These were not painful. At Falconhurst family loyalties were not encouraged and hardly existed. Slaves born on the plantation knew their mothers, but for the most part were separated from them before puberty. Most of them had never known their fathers, who, in any event, had been disposed of and forgotten before their young were old enough to be concerned about them. Among slaves family pride, unless they knew they were bastards of white fathers, was unknown. The Maxwells, with awareness of these phenomena, deliberately loosened and severed blood ties.

The sales-draft had been fed and worked and massaged and primed not only to bring them into a physical condition to command a high price on the market but also, however incidentally, to enable them to face their fortunes with enthusiasm. They were leaving Falconhurst with no regrets. It was not that they had been mistreated or even thought that they had; they knew of no other kind of treatment than the kind that had been meted them and had nothing with which to make a comparison. They had been adequately fed, sheltered under a leakproof roof, worked lightly, and, except switchings for childish peccadilloes, never flogged. What better could a slave ask?

To the Maxwells they were cattle, valuable cattle reared and conditioned for sale. It was as unprofitable to abuse Negroes as hogs or horses. The owners took pride in the husbandry, care and comfort of their servants. It was no desire to escape from Falconhurst or their masters that motivated the slaves' ardour for leaving; rather it was a knowledge, if vague, that there was another world with other people, faces, scenes, activities, away from the plantation, and with this went youth's desire for experience, adventure.

On the day of their departure the morning star had hardly risen, when Hammond, hearing a clatter of horse's hoofs, sent Meg to open the door for Redfield, to care for his horse, and to mix a toddy for him. Ellen helped Hammond to dress in his plum coat for his journey and to pull on his boots. Lucretia Borgia was up, preparing breakfast, and his father met Hammond in the hall at the head of the stairs. Blanche remained abed and her husband did not disturb her. She heard but was indifferent to the bustle in the house.

The Negroes who were to be sold had risen and were gathering in front of the house, along with some others who had got up to see the spectacle of departure. The carriage pole had been removed from the surrey, and shafts substituted, between which there was now hitched a decrepit black mule with a white blaze down its forehead. Florida and Sheba were already in the back seat, calling for Fanny and Twinkle to hasten, else they would be left behind. Hammond had appointed Twinkle to drive the mule. Lucretia Borgia had prepared large parcels of pone for the journey and had packed them into the surrey at the feet of the women.

Hammond consumed a hearty breakfast, Redfield a lighter one, his second, and Maxwell was unable to eat at all. He continued to spout counsel and warnings, all of which he had spoken a dozen times before.

Vulcan had the gentlemen's horses, and the three Mandingos watched from a corner near their cabin. Doc Redfield shook his friend's hand and vaulted to Skelter's back.

On the gallery, Hammond kissed Lucretia Borgia, turned to kiss Ellen, lastly embraced and kissed his father, seeing the tears in his eyes. He mounted his horse and rode around the crowd of Negroes, giving orders and trying to separate those who were going from those remaining behind. He lined up the slaves in a column of twos, Pole and Vulcan at the head. The surrey would follow the men. Pole fell out of ranks to buss Lucretia Borgia, much to the visible displeasure of Memnon.

"You ain't a-goin' to have no more of that, boy, is you?" Doc laughed rhetorically.

"I gits me a kin' masta whut got plenty wenches, Masta, suh," Pole answered, undaunted as he resumed his place.

"We goin' now," called Hammond, and the column moved,

roughly and out-of-step down the lane, Maxwell and the house slaves waving from the gallery, the Mandingos from their cabin, the stay-at-home slaves chattering and cheering, Redfield cracking his whip at the heels of the moving men.

The pace was slow, the male slaves plodding along on foot, the women following in the surrey with the decrepit mule. Hammond permitted the boys to stop and rest when they were tired, since he did not want them jaded when they should reach Natchez. Redfield was impatient of such delays. After the Widow Johnson, the white whores of Natchez seemed to him a prospect of paradise.

CHAPTER EIGHTEEN

BACK AT Falconhurst, the owner, after his son's departure, engaged in an hour's orgy of orders, but succumbed to his toddies soon and left the management of the plantation to Lucretia Borgia. There was little to be done except to see that the Negroes were fed, which was Lucretia Borgia's task even when Hammond was at home. Cotton was picked and there was little at the season for the slaves to do.

Blanche came downstairs and sat with her father-in-law. He did not restrict her toddies. Besides that, she was happier with her husband away, since she knew that he was not in dalliance with Ellen. She was less jealous of the other slave girls and not at all of Tense now. She resented the distortion of her figure by pregnancy, knew that Ellen was just as big, but did not credit that pregnancy had deterred Hammond from his attentions to the Negro woman.

There was little for Maxwell and Blanche to talk about that they had not discussed a hundred times. Maxwell recounted again the virtues of his dead wife and of the son she had left him, subjects unpleasant to Blanche, since he seemed to imply her shortcomings by his praise of the others. He had no such intentions. She liked better his dissertations about plantation economy and slave husbandry, about which she cared nothing but in which she recognized no criticism of herself. She could lie back in her chair and let her thoughts rove until Maxwell had talked himself out and fallen asleep. Meg was always at hand with another toddy when her glass was emptied.

Tuesday Blanche woke early, and was unable to go back to sleep. She lay thinking of Hammond's trip and of how she would

253

have liked to be taken with him. She arose, put on her Mother Hubbard, and joined her father-in-law. The day was warmer than any for a long while; otherwise, the same as yesterday, the same talk, the same toddies, the same growing burden in her body, the same dinner, the same ennui. After dinner there were more toddies, until Maxwell resolved to sit on the gallery with his feet in the sunshine, leaving her in the house.

She was aware that she was a little drunk. Her feet were unsteady when she crossed the sitting-room and went down the hall toward the stairs. She threw herself upon her bed.

Suddenly Blanche rose, stood swaying on her feet. "Carry here that yaller slut, that Ellen sow," she told Tense. "Carry her up here. I knows whut I goin' to do to her. Git her."

Tense hesitated.

"You fetch her. I goin' to whup her, whup that pup of Hammond's right out o' her. Fetch her."

Tense had no alternative but to obey her mistress, and went down the hall and down the stairs. Blanche rummaged in a drawer of her dresser and brought forth a long whip, stood beside the window trying to snap it. She was so much engrossed by her efforts to manipulate it that the time did not seen long to her before Tense returned with Ellen, unalarmed and curious.

"Peel down, you slut," Blanche greeted the girl. "Tear off her osnaburg, Tense, all 'em. I goin to lambaste that big belly o' yourn, goin' to cut you up so bad with this snake that no white man ever goin' to look at you, lettin' alone pleasure you."

Ellen stood big-eyed and terrified before her, making no move to comply with the command but not resisting Tense's efforts to remove her clothes. Blanche waved the whip aloft and brought it down on Tense, struggling with Ellen, who entirely escaped the futile blow. Ellen made no move to escape. To resist her owner's wife did not occur to her; she belonged to Hammond, and Blanche had the right to use her as she should see fit.

Blanche uttered a low stream of invective as she swung the whip. She was livid with rage. Ellen did not understand Blanche's words, but sensed the insults to which she was unable to reply. At length she could endure no more. She screamed, and at length sank to the floor, weeping.

Lucretia Borgia heard the screams, located them as coming from Blanche's room, and burst through the door.

Blanche, surprised, dropped her whip and retreated to the bed, where she lay face down and kicked her heels in the air.

Lucretia Borgia stood just inside the door, arms akimbo. She dared not reveal the indignation she felt.

"Go an' call Ol' Masta," she commanded Tense. "Tell him to come. Help him climb them stairs. Fetch him."

"No, no, no," Blanche called from the bed. "Not him, not him. Cain't you see, she nekid. Ain't nice he should come."

Lucretia Borgia stood silent. "Go," she told Tense again. "Bring him quick as you kin."

In the interminable time before Maxwell arrived, nobody moved except that Lucretia Borgia stooped and flung toward Ellen her dress.

Maxwell surveyed the room, saw the whip, cast carelessly to the floor, the weeping girl on the floor, Blanche on the bed. "Carry her out and down," he ordered Lucretia Borgia, gesturing toward Ellen.

When they were gone, he walked toward the bed and leaned over it. "Whut this mean?" he demanded of Blanche. When she made no answer except a sob, he repeated his question and added reprovingly, as to a child, "It ain't nice, ain't ladylike. Now git you up an' we go down an' drink a toddy." It was the only recrimination that he could offer a white woman. He knew that he could add nothing to the shame the girl felt.

Hiding her face in the pillow, Blanche implored, "Go 'way go 'way, go 'way." She was sober now.

Maxwell knew that the incident would not be repeated. He made his way downstairs and ordered a toddy. Rocking in his chair, he was beset by doubts of what Hammond would say about what had occurred. Perhaps, if Ellen could be silenced, he need never know about it.

He drank his toddy and waited for another. His back was turned to the door of the dining-room, and when he heard it open he assumed it was Meg. It was Lucretia Borgia.

"Masta, suh," she said, her lips dry with terror. "Masta, suh," she repeated but could not go on.

"Whut ailin', now, Lucretia Borgia?" he asked, irritably.

"She slip it, suh, Masta, suh. She slip it."

"Who slip whut? Whure that saplin' with my toddy?"

"Ellen, suh, done slip that sucker she carry."

"Whut you mean?" he asked, unbelieving.

Lucretia Borgia repeated the tidings, and asked, "Whut I goin' to do?"

Maxwell got to his feet, while the impact of the information

255

penetrated his consciousness. "I don' know. Put her in Ham's bed. Is she bad? The sucker alive?" he asked; and answered his own question. "Course not."

Maxwell followed the cook back to her kitchen, where Ellen lay on Lucretia Borgia's pallet, exhausted. There was nothing he could do now. He went to the medicine shelf, poured a dose of laudanum, carried it back to the girl, stooped and with his own hand held the glass to her mouth. "Tote her up to his bed," he again admonished Lucretia Borgia.

Meg followed him back into the sitting-room with his toddy on a tray. It would now be impossible to conceal the afternoon's occurrence from Hammond. How to mitigate his wrath? He blamed himself for permitting Blanche to drink so many toddies.

"Tell that Lucretia Borgia, come here," he instructed the boy.

"She up, suh, Masta—with Miz Ellen," answered the boy, aware that something, he knew not what, was amiss.

"When she come down, tell her. Don' fergit."

It was half hour before the woman presented herself.

"Miz Blanche," Maxwell began directly, "did she hurt that Ellen, cut her with that snake?"

"No 'um, suh. Never touch her at all, hardly." Lucretia Borgia knew the white man wanted her denial. "Miz Blanche ain't know how to han'le that whup."

"Then it wasn't no snake that move Ellen to slip that chil'?" he asked hopefully.

Lucretia Borgia saw her cue. "Oh, naw, suh. Naw, suh, Masta. Ellen about to slip it anyways. Wasn't no snake."

The man ruminated his tobacco while the woman waited. "We ain't goin' to tell Masta Hammond when he come home nothin' about it," he concluded.

"No, suh, Masta," the woman acceded. "On'y he goin' to see first thing that Ellen ain't totin' no chil'."

"Course, he goin' to see that. Cain't hide that she slip it. Only ain't saying' why, ain't sayin' Miz Blanche——"

"Miz Blanche never do nothin', never do nothin'." Lucretia Borgia repeated to impress the idea upon herself.

"You tell that Ellen. Tell her not to say to her masta when he goin' to come—nothin', nothin'. I talks myself to Miz Blanche. Ellen not goin' to say nothin' at all."

"Yas, suh, Masta, an' if you says," Lucretia Borgia agreed.

"I says," the master ordained with finality.

CHAPTER NINETEEN

THE COFFLE reached Natchez by easy stages Friday afternoon, entering by the east road, moving through the wide, dusty streets, busy with traffic, to the Forks-of-the-Road north of the city. Hammond was disturbed by a sense of unhappy augury when the disappearance was discovered one morning of Ace, a mustee slave bought from Briarfield. But he decided to go on to Natchez rather than waste time hunting Ace now. "He mos' likely run back to Briarfield," Ham told Redfield. "I go get him later."

The Negroes arrived fatigued and dust-covered from their long journey, but their interest in what appeared to them to be a great city buoyed them. They had never seen so many people.

Hammond had his choice among the half dozen barracoons, all of which were well-nigh empty. Because his father had recommended it and because it appeared cleanest and most spacious, he chose the slave jail of Armfield and Franklin, a mere stockade, enclosing an open space surrounded by sheds and cabins. A battered sign, 'Armfield and Franklin, Negroes and Mules,' sagged wearily from a post before the gate.

A middle-aged Negro woman sat on a broken chair, smoking a pipe, before one of the cabins, and two half grown children, boy and girl, played in the dust not far removed from her. A crippled male slave, a rail on his shoulder, hobbled across the far end of the area.

Two mulatto men, stalwart but bored, slouched out to meet the Maxwell coffle, and one returned to the best of the houses, immediately inside the gate, to summon the white man in charge, who came rubbing the sleep from his eyes, but, once fully awake, brisk and alert enough.

"Nice coffle," he affirmed, eyeing the Negroes. "All healthy, I reckon. Yes, plenty of room fer 'em now, but Mista Franklin shippin' this week or next from up Washington. These not sold, time hisn come, got to ast you should move."

"How is niggers?" Hammond asked.

"High, high," the white man said. "Cain't git 'em, an' cain't keep 'em. That ol' wench a-settin' an' them saplin's, they an' one ol' man, him cripp'd, all we got fer sale—an' others ain't got hardly no more."

"These of mine had ought to sell?" Hammond said hopefully. "I was thinkin' mayhap that cholrie in New Orleans——"

"Helps sales," the man completed the sentence. "Ever'body come here instead. Town full. Of course, I not knowin' how much you hopin' of this coffle; but, looks of 'em, they had ought to sell right peart. Nobody got none fer sale."

Hammond dismounted and handed Eclipse to Phrensy.

"Got to charge you, though, charge you good. Town's full from New Orleans. Ever'thin' up. Four bits a head ever' day, an' two bits fer the mule." The caretaker by his tone admitted the outrage of his tariff, but went on. "We got ever'thin' though, washin' places an' all, chains an' you need 'em, a good post fer floggin', an' we feeds good, all they wants."

Hammond didn't haggle about the price, although it seemed to him high. He began showing his slaves to their quarters, instructing them to wash and rest, warning them not to venture beyond the gates of the stockade. The brisk white man and the moping mulattoes helped him in settling the Negroes, who were well contented with what they found.

The Natchez House and the Planters Hotel were both full. Their lobbies were alive with people, the streets under the awnings seething with activity. The packet from New Orleans was due with another consignment of refugees. The desk clerk at the Planters suggested that Hammond and Redfield might by chance find quarters at Squires and directed them there, a block down the main street and another block to the right. Redfield was reluctant to leave the turmoil of the larger hotels, but there was no choice.

Squires was not a hotel at all, only a large boarding-house, functioning as a hotel. The big-busted, florid woman who rocked on the verandah looked the men over as they came up the wooden sidewalk, bordered by weedy grass.

"Jist one left," she announced, "one room. An' it ain't big. One bed fer two of you, and maybe a pallet on the floor fer somebody wantin' it. Rates up, besides. A dollar and a half a day now, each one of ye. Take it or leave it, I ain't carin'. Be somebody, an' you don' want it. We feeds good. Ever'body satisfied."

The men had not spoken. The woman adjusted her hair behind her ears and resumed her rocking, her eyes focused upon a house across the street to emphasize her indifference. There could be but one decision; there was nowhere else to go.

"I reckon, an' you got a place fer our hosses," Hammond ventured.

"Four bits, four bits a day extry," the woman declared.

Hammond accepted her terms and the woman began to call loudly for Royal. Nothing could more belie Royal's name than his looks when he arrived. Knock-kneed and rachitic, a sunken-cheeked black man with greying hair appeared from the interior of the house.

"Royal, you need tearin' down," the woman began. "Whyn't you come when I call? Don' say you cain't hear me. You hear, you comes."

"Yas, ma'am, suh," said Royal unperturbed, and waited to learn what his mistress wanted.

"I go to have Herman tear you down, you hear, you damn black nigger. Royal, you hear me, you. Reckon I kin spare you tomorrer to Herman. He sen' you back spry or dead, one of the two. Cost me money, havin' you whup, cos' me money. But I'm a-goin' to, so help me."

The Negro responded without sign of fear, "Yes, 'um."

"These gen'lemen goin' into number seven. You take 'em. Take 'em up an' show 'em. Both in the bed," she instructed.

"Dinin'-room open at five. Better come early, wantin' the best," she called to her guests as they moved away following the slave.

Hammond, after inspecting the sparse comforts of the room, felt tired. He remounted Eclipse, none the less, and rode back to make sure his Negroes were at ease and fed.

When he arrived, he found the two mulattoes handing about among the slaves great pans of beef stew. The women had beds to sleep on, the men large heaps of long straw. All were comfortable.

A single horse was tied to the hitching rack, and a man was surveying his slaves.

"That the owner. Got to talk to him," the white caretaker explained to the buyer. "I ain't got nothin' to do with 'em. They hisn."

The man, florid-faced, round-bellied, short of leg, and noticeably bald when he removed his hat to wipe his head, came forward. "That one, he look right good. How much is he?" He pointed towards Phrensy.

"He fifteen hundert," Hammond improvised a price, not knowing what he should ask. "A right peart one, prime an' soun'."

The man grunted and turned to Lute, felt him through his clothes. "An' that varmint? How much?"

259

"He cheaper. He only twelve hundert. Jest as good, though not as high up an' reachy-like."

The man grunted again. "Right reasonable," he nodded knowingly. "Sold fer no fault?"

"They warranteed, all on 'em," Hammond said.

"Might want one or two of 'em myself, an' I got friends cravin' some. Any wenches?"

Hammond interrupted the women's supper to show them off.

"Breeders yet," the buyer commented. "Not many breeders offered. Three on 'em knocked an' showin'."

"They all knocked," Hammond assured him, "though Twinkle here ain't showin' much yet."

"I wants one or two, shore do wants one or two," the man said, feeling the women's arms and lifting their skirts to look at their legs. He returned to the boys, felt them over and threw stones for them to retrieve.

"Wants I should strip any of 'em down fer you to see?" Hammind inquired.

"No; reckon not. Not this evening'. Come mornin'——" he made tentative plans.

He turned to Phrensy, asked the slave how he would like him for a master. "I treats 'em good, treats 'em all good. Good Christian home. One of my family," he promised.

At length, he took his departure, mounted his horse and rode away, his gross, red face turned over his shoulder, still considering the slaves.

"That ol' Major Wilkins," the caretaker explained after the man had gone. "Ain't got no hands, an' never had none; no money. A little tetched, I reckon. Always lookin' aroun' fer niggers. Coffle comin' in, he al'ays first to look 'em over."

"I reckoned he goin' to buy two or three. Kind of wasted my wind on him, seem like," said Hammond in disappointment.

"No, Major won't buy; cain't. But he spreads things. He talks," the caretaker reasoned. "Ever'body, ever'body in Natchez goin' to know you here with servants fer sale, soun' an cheap. You ain't waste no words. The Major good to have."

Doc Redfield had saved a seat for Hammond next to his own at the long supper table at Squires Boarding House. Mrs Kennedy, the woman with whom arrangements had been made on the porch, sat at the end of the table nearest the kitchen, while her wizened old husband presided at its head. The supper party was for seventeen, all men except Mrs Kennedy.

"Just met ol' Major Wilkins, tellin' that they's a new coffle at Armfield's at the Forks," one small man essayed conversation with nobody in particular in the midst of buttering a biscuit.

"Ol' Wilkins!" one laughed.

"Like, all sick. All goin' to die, come from the South. I'd be afeared o' 'em," a man sitting beyond Hammond expressed a guess.

"No, these from Alabamie or somewhures east, the Major said. Right healthy an' soun'," the small man corrected.

"Any fancies? I'll have to ride out," declared Mr Kennedy. "Bin a-cravin' me another 'un."

"No fancies! I won't have a fancy aroun', an' you knows it, Ben Kennedy. 'Nough trouble with Dipsy here," Mrs Kennedy pointing at the mulatto girl circling the table with a dish, "without no fancies. You men won't leave be poor Dipsy, though, Law knows, she ain't no fancy."

"Servants is up, seem like," commented the little man, with another biscuit.

"They ain't none offered, savin' a few, an' they triflin' an' puny."

"Folks afeared of New Orleans. All the buyers from Louisianie comin' here, an' nobody bringin' 'em in."

"I'd sell Royal, here, an' anybody wantin' him," said Mrs Kennedy, and then qualified her statement, "—an' if I could do withoutn him."

A man to whom Royal was offering a biscuit pushed back his chair and grasped the black boy's leg, felt it evaluatingly, pulled him forward and ran his finger into his mouth. "Won't bring much. Teeth gone, an' legs crooked. Won't las' a month in the cane," he expressed his opinion.

Hammond said nothing about his ownership of the coffle. The boarders at Squires were not slave-buyers, despite their talk.

Supper over, and travel-fatigued as they were, Redfield wanted to go to the bars and gambling houses. It was for these he had come to Natchez. Hammond joined him, straggling after, limping. The bars were ablaze with lights and mirrors, far different from the tavern at Benson. Nudes adorned the walls. Drinkers were numerous, all kinds of men, men gaudily dressed in top hats with golden seals on heavy chains across their waistcoats, roughly dressed labourers, sportsmen and speculators, all with a hectic, heedless desperation to escape from something that threatened them. Many of them had recently come from New

261

Orleans, refugees from the city's epidemic. Another packet was expected the same evening, and many expected friends among the passengers.

As Redfield and Hammond trudged from bar to bar, absorbing the sights and the excitement, they saw the same faces in the mirrors behind the counters. Redfield felt inclined to sit in a game of brag, and Hammond looked on until his partner had lost some twenty dollars and rose to relinquish his chair to a man waiting behind him. While twenty dollars seemed to Redfield a considerable loss, to the milling crowd money had no value. Tomorrow, they thought, they might die. At least they had escaped from the City, and they were concerned with little else. What was money for, if they had it?

A pallid tout showed Hammond and Redfield the way to Maggie's, and then disappeared. Maggie was herself buxom and had been handsome when she was half her present age, and the women in her brothel were comely enough. There must have been a dozen of them, but they were too busy to waste time talking to the clients, of which there was an increasing stream. Men were everywhere, upon the lounges, standing in doorways, sitting on floors. Maggie's was reputed to be the best place in the town.

The women all were white. Hammond was squeamish about white flesh, and indifferent to the delay. The women had no allure for him. They were not his property; rather, they belonged for some fifteen minutes to whoever would pay for them. Hammond bought a bottle of wine, but the women were all too busy to drink with him and he was forced to share it with Redfield and with a strange man who stood near the table where the wine was served by a sluttish mulatto girl.

Redfield, however, had dreamed all summer of the debauch he would have in New Orleans. This was only Natchez, of course, but he was not to be cheated of his orgy. At Hammond's suggestion that they wait no longer for women, Redfield demurred.

"I been sleepin' with that warty widder. Now, I goin' to spen' my money an' buy me a purty, smooth, young 'un, whilst I kin," he argued. "Course, you got a young piece; I ain't wonderin' you don't hanker after these."

A chubby little blonde touched Hammond on the shoulder. "Come on, Honey," she said, "you mine. I bin a-servin' an' a-pleasurin' ol' men all evenin'. Now, doggone, I got aroun'. I bin a watchin' your baby face ever sence you come in, plannin' how I goin' to git to you."

Hammond shrugged. "I reckon not," he declined her offer. "I ain't a-feelin' good."

"You bus'? That whut the matter with you?" the girl asked compassionately. "Won't cos' you nothin', a purty boy like you."

"I ain't bust," Hammond denied, drawing out his purse. "I jest ain't a-feelin'."

The woman admitted her defeat. "Well, I cain't make you. Come back when you feel like; ast fer Zelda. Won't cos' you nothin', un'erstan'? Who a-waitin'?"

Redfield pressed forward. "I goin' with you," he volunteered.

The girl looked at the man, then looked toward Hammond and made a sneering face. "Well, come on," she resigned herself.

"You goin' to wait?" Redfield asked and received an assent from his companion. He walked rapidly away with the woman, leaving Hammond yawning, alone.

Maggie circulated apologetically. "I have a lady fer you right away," she told Hammond. "I'll have more girls tonight on the packet, plenty of 'em comin' from New Orleans."

"I 'on't want none," Hammond told her. "I jes' a-waitin'."

"You jes' plagued," Maggie assured him, encircling his shoulder with her arm. "Needn't be plagued. None of these ladies goin' to hurt you. You ain't used to comin' to places like this; is you? You young, an' sweet. I knows."

Hammond blushed. He did not know how to deny the innocence with which the woman charged him. Perhaps in part the charge was true, but he felt no embarrassment.

He heard a familiar voice and looked up to see the protuberant figure and florid face of Major Wilkins, who held a man's elbow in his grip. He heard the Major say, "These, these different. These young an' prime. An' cheap, too. Fine lot as ever I see. I goin' to buy two or three of 'em my own self. They ain't a-goin' to las', I tells you, when folks knows about 'em. Better ride out first thing in the mornin', you wantin' to pick 'em over. At the Forks-of-the Road, Armfield's."

Hammond failed to hear the other man's reply, but he knew that Wilkins was talking of his slaves, a walking advertisement. He saw Redfield approaching, walking briskly until stopped by Major Wilkins, who grabbed him and led him aside. The Major described the slaves awaiting sale at Armfield's and again declared his intention to purchase some of them, this time three or four, for his own use.

"I knows," Redfield told him. "I'm with 'em, don't own 'em, not exactly, but I'm along with 'em; I'm a sellin' 'em."

"Well, I congratulate you. A fine lot, fine as ever was. I comin' out tomorrer to look 'em over an' buy me a few, quite a few," the Major declared before Redfield could escape from him.

To how many persons Wilkins had told his story Hammond didn't know, but it would do his sale no harm.

Redfield was satisfied and ready to return to Squires, unable to understand how Hammond could resist the allure of Maggie's wantons. "See that big red-headed one?" he asked enthusiastically as the two made their way along the lightless street. "I'm goin' to try her nex' time."

"I won'er what that fat Major mean, tellin' ever'body 'bout our coffle," Hammond changed the subject. "Reckon, come mornin', I got to put a notice in the paper."

When they entered their room in the dark, Redfield stumbled over an unoccupied pallet on the floor at the foot of their bed. "Reckon we goin' to have company," he remarked.

Hammond removed his clothes in the dark, requesting Redfield to help him off with one boot. He withdrew his poke from his pocket and placed his money under his pillow. He went immediately to sleep, but was vaguely disturbed later by somebody coming into the room and going to bed on the pallet. The new guest whispered curses at a servant who was helping him to undress and who subsequently disappeared.

Hammond heard, but didn't open his eyes. After his long ride, although the mattress was of lumpy moss, the bed was pleasant and he slept well. The sunshine lay in a long patch on the floor when he awoke. Whether it was the light that roused him or the figure moving about in the room he did not know.

It was a grotesque figure, very black and very fat, bare of leg and foot beneath soiled, brilliant red Zouave trousers. Hammond turned on his side to watch the fat boy, as he fumbled with the brushing of his master's garments. His motions were slow, mere gestures towards his task, with which he seemed little concerned. The morning was cool and the Negro was not exerting himself, but sweat rolled from his brow down his obese cheeks.

Hammond lay there watching and listening when, from the pallet, which Hammond was unable to see, came the question, "You don' let me sleep, you know whut I goin' to do to you? Larrup you, that whut!"

"I ain't makin' no noise, suh."

Hammond recognized the voice from the pallet and sprang from his bed. "Charles! Charles Woodford!" he exclaimed. "Ever'body thinkin' you dead!"

The man on the pallet opened his eyes and fixed one of them upon the naked man limping toward him. "Cousin Hammon'," he said. "How you come here?"

"Nev' mind, nev' mind how I come. I found you now. Whure my money? Whure my nigger you stole?"

Charles looked at him blandly. "I never stole your nigger or your money neither. What you talks about, Cousin Hammon'?"

"You know whut I talks about—that nigger, that money, that ring."

"Not that Jason whut Cousin Warren give me? Not him, Cousin Ham?"

"Yes, him. Why you go an' stole him?"

"I never. You knowin' I never. You heard Cousin Warren tellin' me he mine an' do with him how I wants. You right there; you hearin' Cousin Warren, your own self." Charles rose on his elbow.

"Papa never meant that, no sich thing, an' you knowin' he never. Whure at your paper fer him?"

"Comin' from a gen'leman, I reckoned I didn't need no paper. Cousin Warren never give me none."

"You knowin' Papa mean Jason yourn while you at Falconhurst. He not yourn to sneak away with."

"He ought to have said. I thinkin' all time he mine—like he say. Too late now," shrugged Charles with the shoulder raised in the air. "I done sol' Jason. I never knowed he weren't mine."

Hammond remembered his father's telling Charles that he might have Jason, presumably for the duration of his visit. He was unable to credit that the boy accepted the Negro as a permanent gift, and yet there was no way to gainsay Charles's contention.

"Well, an' that money?" Hammond went on to the next subject. "Whut money?"

"That, whut I sent with you to your papa. You never took it."

"Oh, that. I borrowed that offn Papa. It hisn, Papa's; it not yourn. I borrowed that. I'm goin' to pay him back one day—when I kin, handy."

"That my money, an' I wantin' it," declared Hammond impotently.

Charles merely laughed. "It wasn' yourn. You givin' it to me to take to my papa. I jest take it, a borry, offn him, not offn you,

265

an' come to New Orleans. Always did want to go to New Orleans. You don't reckon Papa goin' to do anythin' about it?"

"He goin' to whup you, whup you jest like you was a nigger," threatened Hammond.

"Let him jes' try. I through whuppin'. Through! Hear me? Through!" Charles rose to sitting position in his earnestness, and then reclined, laughing. "He got to kotch me firs', anyways."

Whether Charles had stolen the twenty-five hundred dollars from the Maxwells or from his father was a question open to dispute. It was more of the nature of a breach of trust than a theft, in any event. Even if Hammond has chosen to press the charge, Charles explanation had taken the wind from his sails. Whose was the money, once it was in Charles's hands, the Maxwells' or Woodford's?

"An' that ring?" Hammond pursued. "Whut 'came of that? I reckon I givin' you that?"

"Hell, no! I got that, got it right here on my finger, an' if I kin git it off. It's growed right tight." Charles struggled with the ring, sucked his finger and twisted the ring loose. He threw it at Hammond's feet. "I was goin' to give that to Blanche whenever I goin' to see her. Reckon you goin' to see her firs'. You take it to her."

Hammond stooped to pick up the ring, satisfied with his recovery of it.

"How she? I reckon you married with her? No way to keep you from," Charles went on. "Reckon you foun' I say true when I tell you she pizen?"

"Yes, we marry. Fergit you not a-knowin'. Blanche, she real well, 'ceptin' she knocked. She goin' to have a chil'."

"No? Blanche? That real interes'in'!" Charles' surprise was not feigned. "I hope it not come gotch-eyed, like me."

Why should the boy consider such a possibility? Hammond disguised his concern at the comment.

"How my mamma? Seein' her?" Charles inquired. "Still a-readin' in the Bible, I reckon."

"She well. Leastwise she was, time of the weddin'. Ain't seen her sence that. Dick's took up preachin', let go the law."

"Preacherin' better fer him. Don' have to know nothin' jes' to preach." Charles was little concerned. "Whut fer you come to Natchez? A new wench?"

"I brought a coffle across, me an' Doc Redfield there in bed. They out to the Forks."

"Sellin' good? Niggers up."

"Jes come yestiday. Ain't had time yet."

"They goin' to sell, all right. Ain't no buyers goin' to New Orleans at all. All comin' here. Your Niggers ain't even been near New Orleans? They sell. Right comic, how we met right here in the same room."

"Whut you doin' here?"

"Refugeein' from New Orleans. Come up on the packet las' night. Ain't hardly nobody left there, all either dead or gone away."

Charles crawled from his bed and submitted to being dressed by the fat Negro boy, whose name was Shote. "Fat as I kin make him," he said, "an' still he don' sell. Money in monsters, if you kin get 'em, but too many jest fat ones. Nobody think fat ones funny no more."

Hammond noted the change that his brother-in-law had undergone. His face had cleared of its pimples and he had put on weight. His flesh was soft, his contours had rounded. Except for his eyes, one would have called him handsome.

"I bought me a little humpback with skinny legs, funny-lookin' imp," Charles continued. "Didn't have to give fer him hardly nothin', hundert an' fifty; sold him to a gam'ler very next day fer five hundert dollar. He usin' him for luck. Then I got a zany half-wit young wench. Didn' know nothin'. Couldn' talk none. Follow me aroun' like a puppy, but couldn't keep no clothes on her. Tear 'em off fast as I could put 'em on. Fellow give her to me. Hadn't had her a week when a man at the Exchange thought she was funny an' offered me three hundert fer her. Wanted her a pet fer his boy. I see they is money in freaks an' monsters, if you kin git 'em. Bethought me of this Shote an' rode across an' bought him. Had to pay too much—three and a quarter fer him. He too old. They wants funny ones young. Oh, I kin git four fifty, five hundert fer him any time, but I wants seven hundert. Ain't he the fattest you ever seen? I laughs jest to look at him." Charles patted Shote's fat rump with pride and a trace of affection. "Three years younger an' he'd fetch a thousand. Somebody goin' to want him. Better to bring him along then leave him at New Orleans to ketch it an' die."

Hammond got into his clothes and struggled with his boot. "Kin your Shote help me? I gits worse ruther than better, seems like," he said.

"Course, course. He'p Mista Hammond, boy. Do whut he

267

tell you." Charles was his old accommodating self. He was glad to make his peace.

Hammond would not have chosen to encounter Charles, would have chosen to forget him, to charge him off as a cheat and a thief. But the boy's explanation of his behaviour was pat enough to raise doubts in Hammond's mind—it was not exactly theft, nor theft from the Maxwells. He had returned the ring at least, at the first opportunity.

Charles, having no purpose in Natchez except to escape from New Orleans and its cholera, would have attached himself to Hammond and resumed their relations as if nothing untoward had occurred between them. He waited for Redfield to get into his clothes and accompanied him and Hammond to the dining-room for breakfast. Hammond's treatment of the boy was tepid, but he eventually got rid of him only because Charles had no horse upon which to ride to the Forks-of-the-Road.

Redfield went there directly, while Hammond remained in the city to place in the newspapers an announcement of his arrival with a consignment of Negroes for sale and to buy new clothes for the slaves, in which he believed they would appear better to possible buyers. He made haste with his errands and reached Armfield's before ten o'clock. Redfield had ascertained that the slaves had been fed to repletion. They sat on benches before the doors of the sheds with nothing to do but wait for somebody to come and buy them.

Hammond's arrival animated them and the distribution and fitting of garments caused great excitement.

"Shore you clean?" Hammond demanded as he handed out trousers and shirts and dresses. "Don' want you should put new trogs on dirty!"

"Wash yestiday, Masta, suh," declared Vulcan, "soon as we come."

The novelty of new clothes delighted the Negroes, who ran from one to another showing them off and exchanging garments in the hope of a better fit. Some of the boys cut capers that aroused a laugh from the others. A few of them who had expected to be permitted to amble about the streets in search of buyers for themselves were disappointed at their confinement in a mere barracoon, but they were none the less comfortable and well fed.

Curious neighbourhood youths and a few men straggled into

make casual inspection of the merchandise, but none had money to buy.

The newspapers with Hammond's advertisements would not appear before morning, but the owner was already disappointed that the public interest in his slaves was not greater. It was two o'clock before a prospective buyer came.

He was a roughly dressed, stooped young man with a black beard, riding an unkempt, long-haired horse. "Hearin' you got niggers?" he said to the white caretaker as he dismounted awkwardly, although the slaves were in his view.

"They hisn," the caretaker replied, waving the customer in the direction of Hammond. The slaves rose and lined up for inspection as Hammond had taught them.

The man walked down the line, eyeing the lot individually, stopped occasionally to feel a boy's muscles. "Right likely," he commented of none in particular. "Right likely. 'Ginia or Kaintucky?"

"Alabama," Hammond answered him.

"Right likely," the man repeated, "—comin' from there. Whut's that one? How much?" He pointed toward Vulcan.

"Him?" Hammond hesitated before naming a price. "He eighteen hundert."

"Yes," said Redfield coming up, "an' worth twenty-five of anybody's money.

The man whistled in his alarm at the price.

"Others less. He the mos' costive. You shore kin pick a good nigger," said Hammond. "First thing, fallin' on the bes'."

The man examined the other boys and asked their prices, but returned again and again to Vulc. Lute, the cheapest of the adult males, was only a thousand dollars. The man asked Vulcan, Pole and two others to remove their shirts, and Hammond told them to strip down naked. They were prime with nothing to conceal, and he was proud of them.

"Purty bucks, an' not a mark on 'em," said the man admiringly, running his hand down the back of one. "But eighteen hunert? Too much. Give you twelve fifty. Whut say?"

Hammond shook his head dubiously and looked at Redfield for counsel.

"That a breedin' buck," said Redfield. "Some of them others jest as good, you goin' to work 'em."

"I only jest got me three wenches, an' they all got bucks.

269

Ain't a-needin' no breeder, but I likes the looks o' that one," hesitated the man, looking again at Vulcan.

"I reckon your bucks ain't as good as this one. Give your sluts to him, an' he bring you twins—likely. He that strong," suggested Redfield.

The man sighed, convinced but reluctant. "Six months?" he asked.

"Cash," clicked Hammond, positively.

"Well, I ain't got it. Jist ain't got it."

The vendor made no reply.

"Got to go to the bank, I reckon. Bank will 'commodate me. Al'ays have. Keep that 'un fer me; I'm comin' agin. Name of Bryce." He walked towards his horse, mounted it, and rode away.

Hammond was not pleased with making no other sale. Of course, he had Bryce's word that he wanted Vulcan, but no money had changed hands and the sale was not made. Hammond and Redfield sat around the lot for the rest of the afternoon but there were no more serious customers. Men came, four of them altogether, and looked at the slaves, handled them, but only one asked their prices and he only idly.

"Wait fer them newspapers to git to workin'," urged Redfield, who was in no hurry to have the sale over with and return to Benson. "Nobody a-knowin' we here yet awhile."

"Mayhap we better arrange a public cry," Hammond pondered. "They got auctioneers, good ones, in Natchez, like as not."

"They charges," Redfield objected.

"Either that, or take down our prices some."

"Prices all right. Jest that nobody know," Redfield soothed.

The slaves had their meal of the day, and the white men mounted their horses to return to Natchez. Hammond was dejected. They were late for supper at Squires, and men were leaving the dining-room as they entered it. They passed Charles, who had already eaten.

After supper, Hammond, in no mood for fleshpots, went early to bed, whereas Redfield set out again for the saloons, gambling halls and brothels, which had been augmented by the influx of refugees from New Orleans. Hammond felt for his purse, which he had placed beneath his pillow, when he later heard Charles bedding himself down upon his pallet; not that he feared that Charles might try to rob him. Charles was mildly repugnant to him, and he would have preferred him elsewhere, but there was no way to rid himself of the boy.

270

Next morning, however, Charles was gleeful and talkative. "I bought me a special nigger last night. Ain't never seen one like him."

"With my own money, you bought him. With money you stole from me. Good as," Hammond modified his indictment.

"Hell no! That money gone long ago! Reckon I ain't got me no money? I been tradin' niggers an' bettin' fights, me an' Mista Brownlee, ever sence I come to New Orleans. I right well fix'."

"Brownlee! You mix up with that snake, Brownlee? Brownlee, the trader?"

"Mista Brownlee right nice gen'leman, you gits to know him. Right shrewd, too. He was, that is."

"Was?" Hammond asked for clarification.

"He dead, you knowin'. The plague got him. Come down one day, dead the next. It like that, the cholrie."

"Mayhap you knowin' Neri, too?"

"Neri, Brownlee's pardner? Course I know him. Gone west, Texas, I reckon, afore Brownlee die. Some trouble or other, over stealin' a nigger. 'Bout bust, I hearin'."

This news, welcome as it was to Hammond, did not console him for Charles's purchases and profits.

After breakfast, Ham and Redfield rode to the sales lot and waited. In the late morning, men began to arrive and to look over the stock. None found what he was looking for at a price he could afford. All conceded that the Negroes were a prime and likely lot and that the prices were not too high, but they were prepared to buy adult bucks at only five to seven hundred dollars. They knew slave prices had risen, but they were seeking for bargains and were not too particular about health and stamina.

Hammond and Redfield had gone to Natchez for their dinners and had returned to the Forks when, nearing two o'clock, two men, apparently brothers and enough alike to be twins, dismounted from sleek thoroughbreds, which they turned to a mounted yellow groom to hold for them. About forty-five, they were expensively but conservatively dressed in black with highly varnished boots. Well made and agile, they swung across the yard and approached Redfield.

"The servants yours, suh?" the slightly taller demanded politely.

"To say true, they hisn. I'm with 'em though," replied Redfield, reluctant to deny ownership.

271

The man turned to Hammond and said, "They tell me you have some right likely boys for sale, suh, if we aren't too late."

"I reckon they's likely, suh. I ain't seen better, suh. Like to 'spect 'em, suh?" asked Ham, inclining himself in a bow as nearly like the man's as he could manage with his stiff leg. This was a gentleman, Hammond could see, and he did not like to concede that he was not. He clapped his hands and called sharply, "Luke! Pole! Lute! Phrensy!"

These boys appeared from the cabins and joined the other slaves in the line-up. "Shuck down all of ye. Give the gen'leman a look at you," commanded the master.

The Negroes had begun removing their clothes when the stranger intervened with, "Never mind stripping them, suh. I'll ask to see any that interests me, suh."

The master did not countermand his command and the slaves continued to remove their clothes until all stood naked. The buyer walked down the line, glancing at the boys, and grunted his satisfaction with them. "A good lot, the kind I've been looking for," he turned to his brother, and then he addressed the owner, "Yes, suh; a likely lot, suh."

Hammond was pleased with the praise. It was easy to perceive that the man was a connoisseur. "They right good, I reckon. Good as we could raise 'em, my papa an' me. An' biddable. Not a whale on a back in the lot of 'em."

"No difference, that, suh," said the man walking again slowly down the line. "They will do what they're told, never doubt, suh. And clean backs won't last with my drivers. Cain't keep them from using the whip, suh; sometimes too hard. Since I never sell one, a few scars don't hurt. I grow sugar," he explained. He stopped before Lute, reached down and felt of his thigh, pulled him forward out of the line. "That's one," he said. Next he chose Vulcan; when Hammond told him that Vulcan was spoken for, although no deposit had been made on him, the man returned him to the line. Hammond would have sold the boy, if the man had insisted.

"No difference, suh. One about as good as another. All sound and likely," said the man, choosing another. "Two is all I aimed to buy, all I need; but these are so good," he mused, pulling forward two more of the Negroes.

Having tentatively selected four, he went over them carefully looking for possible ruptures, broken or crooked fingers and toes,

272

missing teeth. He could find nothing wrong. He ran the boys and told them to jump. He was satisfied.

"Why so many?" asked the brother. "You need only two?"

"Right now, yes!" said the buyer. "But next year, who knows? Don't find this kind every day. All young and sound."

"Cane uses 'em up," admitted the brother.

"Yes, and most growers figure seven years for a nigger. Mine last me about eleven or twelve. I've got one that's been working fifteen year. But he was sound and young to begin. If Papa failed to teach us aught else, he did say, and proved, that it pays to get stout niggers and work 'em hard. Cheap niggers are cheap niggers."

The fraternal colloquy delayed the transaction until the buyer turned to Hammond with, "This four, how much do you want for them?"

Hammond hesitated, adding on his fingers, "I reckon 'em at fifty-four fifty fer the lot," he hazarded at last.

The buyer puffed out his cheeks dubiously. "Niggers are up, I know, suh. Good demand, suh. I suppose your price is all right, figured by the head, and you can get it. But——" he hesitated. "I considered that if I take four they would come a little less—less by the head, that is." There was no disparagement of the stock.

"They worth it, ever' dollar," Redfield interposed and would have said more but for Hammond's interruption.

"I don' know," pondered the owner. "I might, jest might, make it fifty-two fifty fer the lot."

"How about five thousand; twelve fifty a head? I'll give that much, suh." He implied, but did not assert, that he would not give more.

Hammond had made no sale all day and was over-anxious. He paced the lot slowly, head down, considering. He looked up and demanded, "Cash?"

"On the barrel head!" said the man. "I'll give you my cheque on the Natchez bank and leave the bucks until you cash it. Have to ask you to feed them a few days anyway, until I start home. I live over beyond Baton Rouge and am staying here with my brother."

It was agreed and the principals retired to the little office to exchange the cheque and the bill of sale.

"Put on your trogs an' git you inside," Hammond said sharply to the remaining slaves. "You," he turned to Lute, "you an' you otherns sol'. Anybody come, you stay in there. Don' crave you aroun' bein' looked at, spilin' a sale. Your new masta come fer you two or three days."

The afternoon was waning, and Redfield was impatient to eat his supper that he might go to the Globe and the Woodbine, later to Maggie's. No more buyers could be expected and, having made sure that his Negroes would be adequately fed, Hammond was ready to return to Squires boarding-house. He and Redfield had started across the lot toward the horserack, when the little bearded man arrived to complete his purchase of Vulcan. Hammond had abandoned his belief that the boy had been sold. It was necessary to return to the office, receive the man's money and give him a bill of sale.

When called out for transfer, the big Negro dropped to his knees and grasped Hammond about the legs, weeping. "I knowin' I got to go like Masta say," he blubbered, "on'y Masta so good an' Ol' Masta so good. Won' never have good masta like that agin."

"This gen'leman, your new masta, goin' to be good to you an' you mindin' whut he goin' to say. You do ever'thin' jest like he tellin' you. He feed you good, 'n ever'thin'."

"Yas, suh, Masta, suh," Vulcan agreed.

"Mayhap, you behave, he got a wench or two fer you to take up." Hammond concealed the tears in his own eyes in a show of jocularity as he grasped Vulcan's arm, raised him to his feet and clasped his shoulder in farewell. He watched as the Negro followed his buyer across the lot without a backward glance. The bearded man mounted his small horse, which walked out of the gate, Vulcan trotting easily by its side.

"Well, that all of Vulc," Hammond sighed. "Reckon that man treat him good. Cain't never tell."

"Come on, an' you ready," Redfield suggested. "You got yo' money, ain't you? Whut you carin' whut he do with him?"

The sales for the day had been satisfactory. After supper Hammond went with Redfield down town, swallowed two or three drinks in a crowded bar, but when Redfield decided to sit down to a game of brag, the younger man, unused to late hours, went to the boarding house and to bed.

It was past midnight when Redfield came in, undressed quietly, and got into bed at Hammond's side. He lay a full minute and nudged Ham into partial consciousness. "Whyn't we stay—jest a

274

spell, jest a few days longer?" he demanded plaintively, "I jest now gittin' acquainted."

Hammond grunted a reply.

"I had that sorrel at Maggie's tonight," the older man continued. "After her, kind of hard pilin' in bed with the Widder."

Hammond feigned sleep and did not talk to him. A little later he heard Charles stirring for bed and getting into his pallet. He finally dropped to sleep. Later he awakened with a pain in his abdomen, which was intermittent, but grew worse.

It was toward morning and light was breaking, when he could endure the pain no longer. He nudged Redfield and told him, "I'm sick, Doc Redfield, suh. Cain't you do nothin'?"

"Where you hurt?" asked the doctor.

"My belly. It achin' me turrible."

"Cain't git no doctor, no real, human doctor this time of night, an' stores ain't open. I didn't bring nothin', no medicine, along. Jest got to stan' it till mornin' breaks, an' I'll git you somethin'."

The boy resigned himself to suffer. Intense pains, each of which he hoped would be the last, swept over his lower abdomen, and he was alternately icy cold and burning with fever. Redfield, on his back, snored complacently beside him. Hammond half dozed between his spasms of pain.

Through the window, he saw Mercury rise and swing slowly upward and at length the east grew red. He again nudged his bed-fellow and pleaded, "Doc Redfield, suh, cain't you do nothin'?"

Redfield roused himself and placed his hand on the boy's brow, which he found intensely hot. "Hurtin' yet?" he asked fatuously. "Somethin' you et, pro'ably; that catfish, I reckon. Had ought to be good, this time of year."

Hammond denied having eaten his supper.

"That it; all that corn on your empty guts," diagnosed the doctor.

"Cain't you do somethin'? You could to a nigger. I knows you could."

The doctor piled from his bed reluctantly, and slipped into his clothes. "That store had ought to open up purty quick. I'll git you somepin', some laudanum, I reckon, and castor oil."

"Hurry up, please, suh," urged the sick boy.

Redfield walked around the bed. The light was enough for him to see the glazed glare of the fever-burned eyes. He felt the irregularly rapid pulse and asked Hammond to show his tongue.

He threw back the covers and pressed the boy's abdomen and got only grunts. He knew not what he was seeking, but nodded gravely as if he had found it. "Laudanum and castor oil," he muttered under his breath, and aloud sought to encourage the youth. "You jist stopped up. You goin' to git well," he said. "I fetch some medicine, soon as I kin git in to git it."

When he was gone, Charles, who was disturbed by the doctor's rising, got up from his pallet and came to the bed. "Whut wrong, Cousin Hammon'? You ain't sick?" He had but to look at the unblinking eyes.

"Wait," he said, "while I puts on some clothes. It right col', nekid, these mornin's."

"I'm burnin'," Hammond rebutted.

"Keep them quilts up tight. Mustn't kotch col'," Charles warned.

He dressed quickly and came again to the bedside. "You got it, you reckon?"

"Whut? I don' know. Whut?" Hammond spoke weakly and without inflection, without interest.

"It! The plague! Cholerie! Sure as you're born! Comes this way' jest like you doin'. Dead afore tomorrow night. Most of 'em dies evenin's late."

Hammond was indifferent.

"Like me an' ol' Redfield will git it too, sleepin' right with you, same room."

"Doc Redfield say it jest belly ache," breathed Hammond. "But it bad, sure bad."

"He only a hog doctor an' a nigger doctor. He don't know cholerie, how it come on, well one day, dead the nex'. You gotten it, cholerie."

A knock at the door was Royal, the boarding-house slave, who had brought two bottles which Redfield had entrusted to him.

"Please, suh, gen'man say tell sick gen'man to swallow these, please, suh. Gen'man say tell he goin' to the Forks; he goin' to slop some niggers he got there," the Negro explained.

Charles turned to Hammond. "See?" he declared. "He know. Redfield know whut ail you. He not comin' back. This medicine ain't goin' to do no good; nothin' won't."

"Mayhap, it ease me some," said Hammond, extending his arm for the bottles. "Got to die, might as well die without this hurtin' I got."

Charles poured out the laudanum, which the sick man swal-

276

lowed, and followed with castor oil. Charles was visibly frightened, picturing himself ill and dying within the week. He, none the less, went to breakfast, and Hammond felt very lonely, deserted. If only he had brought Ellen, or even Meg! Neither would have left him to die alone. Then he felt guilty in his need for them. Why should they die of cholera because he had to?

Redfield's failure to bring the medicine himself betrayed his belief. He would not come back. What, Hammond wondered, would become of his Negroes—and his money? Would Redfield take the money to Hammond's father? It bothered him even more than the thought of death.

Charles, of course, would not return. One could not expect it of him, after the quarrel they had had. He had escaped from New Orleans only to run into the thing he had fled. Hammond was amazed that the boy had tarried to give him the medicine. One thing about cholera; it was short. He would die and be out of his pain tomorrow.

He burned with fever, but the pain was abating. The last two spasms had not been so severe. The laudanum had done it. It was the precious syrup, but it was across the room and he wanted another dose. Had he the strength to get out of bed to get it? It would expose his fever to the chill air. He must keep well covered.

He had resigned himself to isolation, when Charles unexpectedly returned. He had with him a slave bearing a large japanned tray, but would not permit the servant to come into the room. Instead, he took the tray at the door, and carried to to the bed.

"Got to scruge up, if you go to eat this. Cain't swallow it layin' down," Charles said cheerily.

The sick man looked at the heavy meal on the tray—fried ham, eggs, corn-bread and butter, grits, and coffee. The sight of it turned his stomach. "Set it down," he said. "Rest it. I cain't eat it now, hurtin' too bad. But ifn you jest fetch me more of that medicine—the first kind—mayhap I goin' to eat later on, mayhap."

Charles poured an ample dose from the laudanum bottle and Ham drank it. "On'y thing 'at seemin' to help," he said. "Leave it here by me. I goin' to crave more of it a'ter you goes."

"I goes? Goes whure? I ain't goin' nowhure. I goin' to set by you an' tend after you. Nobody else ain't goin' to—seem like."

" 'Tain't no use. You cain't do nothin'. I goin' to die," breathed the sick man resignedly.

"I 'spec' you is," the other answered.

277

"Ain't no use of you a-gittin' it, you an' Redfield. Jest leave me that laudanum here, right by the bed."

"If I goin' to git it, I done got it. So has Mista Doc Redfield; he sleepin' right with you. Me? I ain't goin'. I goin' to stay an' make you easy. You my cousin, even an' you doesn't like me no more."

Charles paused and Hammond made no comment.

"You ain't wantin' no breakfast, then turn over an' see kin you go to sleep," said Charles, approaching the bed and helping Hammond turn upon his side. "I goin' to hang up my quilt at the window an' keep the light offn you. Don' fret. I be here, right here, an' you goin' to wake up."

The pain had subsided and Hammond was able to fall into a fitful sleep, in which he muttered and mumbled, wept and cried out. Charles, more than ever, was sure that it was cholera. All the symptoms were as he had heard they were. He speculated about how long his brother-in-law might live and about his chances of occupying the bed when he was dead. He doubted whether Redfield would consent to occupy it with him. Perhaps he would have it alone for a week until he too died. He sat still by the bedside and pulled the quilts back around the patient's neck when he sought to throw them off. At noon he slipped quietly from the room and went to dinner, but revealed to nobody that there was a case of cholera in the house. Eating lightly and without appetite, he returned to his bedside vigil. The room with its closed windows smelled of fever.

Early in the afternoon, the patient woke.

"I reckon you wantin' a reverend, ain't you? Somebody to pray with?" Charles asked. "Well, one of 'em wouldn't come, an' if he knew whut ail you. I ain't much good at it—prayin'; but I try an' you wants."

"Too late fer prayin', now," replied the sick man turning on his side and drawing the quilts about his neck. "Don' reckon I needin' it, anyways. I ain't never done nothin' whut wasn't right, nothin' that God kin hol' agin me."

His denial of his own sinfulness relieved Ham. He felt himself better, asked for a piece of meat, at which he nibbled and gnawed. His fever had subsided. He was free from pain. He knew he was doomed to die, but he felt better. He sprawled on his back and stretched his legs.

"I wonder is Doc Redfield takin' care o' my niggers," he began to worry.

278

"That whut the nigger say whut brung your medicine," answered Charles. "Nev' min', they all right. An' whut difference, anyways? You never a-goin' to know an' after you dead."

"I ain't a-goin' to die. I feelin' me better. Not strong, but better," the patient announced. "Don' they ever git up from that cholerie?"

"Not many of 'em. Few."

"Then I ain't got it at all. Ain't never had it. I gittin' me up, come mornin'."

"Hopin' you right," sighed Charles. "You ain't got it, I ain't a-go' to ketch it."

After an interval of silence, Hammond said, "Right kin', you settin' by me an' lookin' out fer me, 'specially you thinkin' it cholerie. Right kin', after ever'thin', an' all."

"Nothin' else to do, with you my cousin. Couldn' leave you all alone to die," Charles belittled his charity.

"Cain't blame Redfield, not comin' back, thinkin' I got it. Cain't blame him, not bein' no a-kin." In Hammond's very denial there was a show of resentment, but his animosity to Charles was at an end. Charles had more than made up for his theft—if theft it was—of Jason and of the money entrusted to him. Perhaps, Hammond reasoned, the boy really had believed the Negro a gift and had intended to return the money to his father.

Hammond did not feel up to supper, but Charles brought him a bowl of soup. Redfield, Charles learned, had not returned to the boarding-house for either of his meals. The boys settled to sleep, and when Charles got up to serve his cousin shortly after midnight, Hammond suggested that he join him in the bed.

"He ain't comin'," he argued, laughingly. "Might as well. I ain't got nothin' ketchin' an' it better'n that hard pallet."

Charles acceded to the suggestion, not so much because the bed was softer than the pallet but because the invitation was an earnest of forgiveness. The previous night it would have been unthinkable.

The following morning, Hammond put on his clothes with Charles's assistance.

Hammond had been burned out with fever and was still weak. He insisted, however, upon mounting his horse to go to the Forks to see after his slaves. Charles, more because he wished not to disrupt the renewed friendship than because of Hammond's need for him, rented a horse from the livery stable and went along.

Six of the slaves, four men and two women, were missing.

279

Hammond could not believe that they had run. He went to the office to consult the caretaker.

Hopkins told him, "He, that gen'leman, sold off some of 'em yestiday. I ain't knowin' how many of 'em. It all right, hain't it, me lettin' 'em go? Mista Redfield got your leave to sell 'em?"

Hammond reassured Hopkins. Confident of Redfield's honesty, at least in his relations with him and his father, he was nevertheless relieved to see the veterinary ride into the lot. Redfield came forward, embarrassed, amazed to see Hammond.

"I reckoned I better take care o' the varmints," he opined, "seein' you sick. I knowin' you wasn't bad."

"Wasn' nothin'," Hammond minimized his illness. "Cousin Charles here, he set with me."

Redfield detected recrimination in the statement, and turned the subject. "We had a good day. I ridded us of six of 'em—two of 'em wenches."

"I see they gone," nodded Ham. "I believin' nobody goin' to want them females. Git good prices?"

"Thousan' apiece fer the wenches. I ain't changin' the prices you set. Could o' sol' two otherns, ifn I could o' lowered 'em some." He deliberately saved the best to the last. "You know that 'Poleon? I done right well with that one. Eighteen hundert."

"How come? On'y askin' fifteen. How come?"

"Well, this little ol' man wantin' a good breeder. Said so right straight out. Sol' off all his common bucks; wantin' a good one."

"Not Pole. He ain't no good. You knowin' he ain't got a sucker in him. That the why Papa sellin' him. You know that good an' well. That ain't hones'."

Redfield chuckled at his deception. "That man ain't goin' to know short o' six months. I tol' him Pole had knock all them wenches. He believe it."

Hammond was vexed. "Who is he? Whure at he live at? We find him an' take Pole back agin. We kin tell him you didn't know Pole barren."

"How I know whure he live? Name of Miller; that how the bill of sale made out."

"Miller? They is lots o'Millers."

"You cain't fin' him. Let him go. Take you money," Charles counselled.

"Ain't no other course," sighed Hammond. "Fifteen hundert of it. Pole worth that, but not no more. Doc Redfield here got to keep the rest of it. I ain't havin' it." Thus he salved his conscience.

Redfield demurred, but at Ham's insistence finally accepted. He relished that three hundred dollars, but knew it was a reprimand.

"Ain't nothin' but bad luck, this whole trip," Hammond lamented. "First, that mustee runnin'. After that I taken down sick. An' now I cheatin' a white man on a barren buck."

"Leastwise, you ain't gotten the cholerie," said Charles cheerfully. "An' we cousins again," he added.

Next morning it was raining when Hammond awoke. He lay awhile listening to the patter on the shingles, speculated about the wisdom of setting out in the wet day, itemized, thumb against successive finger ends, the details to which he must attend before the journey could get under way.

He spent four vacuous days in getting rid of the last two wenches, whom he finally exchanged for four young boys. The delay irritated him for he would rather have been scouring the country for that escaped mustee. When he reached Falconhurst, it would mean that he must set out again to search, probably in vain, for the lost boy.

But the responsibility was now at an end. He had discharged it to what was sure to be his father's satisfaction. True, he would have to endure his father's censure, expressed in cackling laughter, of the mishaps like the running of the mustee, the sale of the sterile Napoleon as a stallion. However, the old man would take no glee at his son's illness. Possibly that might curb his amusement at the boy's blunders.

Over against the bad judgment with which Hammond charged himself, he set the heavy bag of gold—almost twenty-three thousand dollars; he was not sure just how much—he would lay at his father's feet. On the whole, he had done well.

He put on his clothes, and Charles got up and helped him with his boot.

He had promised Blanche to bring her something from the city. What? Garments she could not wear in her pregnancy. After breakfast, he set out in the rain to buy some gimcrack—anything. He was not interested. A ring? He had for her the ring with diamond that Charles had returned to him.

At the most lavish jewellery shop, Wineberg's, he found pendant earrings, round disks gaudily encrusted with garnets. That would please a woman. He bought them, and thought how pretty they would look against Ellen's duskiness, how barbaric. Jewels on a Negro, he knew, were wasted, but how pleased Ellen would

281

be! She demanded nothing, expected nothing, but earrings would set her apart. On a whim, he bought a second pair exactly like the first.

Not as a present, rather as a utility, he acquired for his father an open litter, such as the one in which he had seen an invalid going about the streets, carried on the shoulders of two Negroes. It would enable the rheumatic to traverse the plantation and take a more active part in its management. The stores where Hammond inquired for the article he was unable to name understood his description well enough but had no such thing in stock and shunted the purchaser from place to place. At length he learned of a man, now dead, who had ridden in a litter, no longer in use, and it's owner's heir was happy to give it to anybody who could find a use for it. Stored in a stable, the bed was faded and covered with dust and chaff, and the frame was somewhat sprung, but the pieces fitted together well enough and it was usable if not beautiful. Hammond would much have preferred to pay for the contraption and was embarrassed by the donor's generosity. The transaction ended with Hammond's fulsome declaration of his undying gratitude and his invitation that the generous man should come to Falconhurst and see his gift in use.

The rain had abated to a drizzle. Hammond, against Doc Redfield's counsel and Charles's wish, decided to make for home. They ate their final dinner at Squires, relinquished their room to Charles, and paid their score.

Redfield proposed one more drink, which Hammond refused. "We losin' time," he said.

Charles walked to the door and out on to the uneven brick sidewalk to watch them mount. He shook Redfield's hand and held Hammond's a full minute, patting his shoulder.

"Whyn't you carry that big buck of yourn acrost? Course, after cholerie is out of the city. I knows four or five fightin' gen'lemen down the river whut got niggers, good niggers. I makin' a match fer yourn any time, any time at all."

"You meanin' my Mandingo?" asked Hammond.

"Yeh, that Mandingo, or whut you call him," Charles specified.

Hammond made no reply. He motioned the boys with the empty litter into action. Redfield led the mule for a hundred yards and when he dropped the bridle the mule trudged after him.

It was plain that the progress could be no faster than the boys could trot with the litter on their shoulders, and Hammond resigned himself to it, for he would not leave the hammock behind. Redfield was in no haste, and the pace suited the old mule well. The slogging over the rough roads and the necessity to keep in step bored the boys more than it tired them physically. Each few miles, Hammond permitted them to sit by the roadside and rest.

Nothing untoward occurred on the journey. Hammond had counted upon making sixty or seventy miles a day without difficulty, whereas, with the boys carrying the litter, thirty miles was a good day's journey, thirty-five was the maximum, and one day they covered but little more than twenty.

The journey, Natchez to Falconhurst, used up seven days and on the final night there was no pause to sleep. The closer Hammond approached his destination the more impatient to reach it he became. Two hours before daybreak he abandoned the party to Redfield's care, gave Eclipse his head, and, breaking into a gallop, reached Benson before anybody was stirring and by eight o'clock turned into the lane at Falconhurst.

Lucretia Borgia and Meg seemed to sense the arrival; on hearing the hoofbeats they came pell-mell to the gallery, where they waited for their master to alight. Lucretia Borgia gathered him in her arms and Meg stroked his long coat.

"Whure Papa an' them?" the master demanded. "Ever'thin' all right?"

The latter question Lucretia Borgia refrained from answering. "Ol' Masta, he good; he well, Masta, suh. I reckon he never hear," she said. "Git him, Meg. Tell him Masta done come."

But it was unnecessary. The older man appeared, radiant in his delight. He hugged and kissed his son until the youth led him into the house.

"Whure—whure Blanche an' all of 'em?"

"Blanche ain't a-feelin' real good. She ain't come down," the father explained.

"Drunk?"

"Well, no," the old man hedged. "That is, she ain't drunk much. No more than she needin', in her shape."

Hammond shook his head in doubt as he took a toddy from a tray with which Meg appeared. "An' how Ellen? Whure she? Whyn't she come?" he asked.

"Why, Ellen, I tell you," the old man hesitated. "She gone an' slip that chil' she totin'." There was a long silence as the father noted his son's consternation.

"Ellen right 'shamed. She a-skeared o' seein' you, Masta,

suh," Lucretia Borgia interpolated. "I tellin' her you not be mad."

"Slip it? How come?"

Luctetia Borgia left the explanation to the master, and he only shrugged his pretended ignorance.

"Whure she? I got to see her, got to know," said the distraught youth. "I got her somethin'. I brung her a presen'."

"She in the kitchen, a-waitin'," Lucretia Borgia told him, and he set down his toddy without tasting it and went to find her.

Ellen was tremulous in anticipation of seeing her lover. As he entered, she faced him, but backed away as if to avoid his blows, which she would have withstood better than the anger she expected. "I never meant to. Masta, I never meant to," she pleaded, bursting into weeping.

Hammond encircled her in his arms. "It all right; it all right," he assured her. "You well? Ellen, Honey, you gittin' better, we make you another one. Cain't you un'erstan', Honey, it all right. I isn't mad."

Ellen could only bury her face in his coat, sobbing her relief that she was not blamed.

"Look, Ellen," said Hammond, forcing her to arm's length. "Look. I done fetched you somethin' from the city, somethin' goin' to make you purty. Not that you a-needin' purtifyin'." He drew from his pocket the small packet and unwrapped the earrings from the tissue paper around them. "There. Don' that happify you?"

Ellen took them, moved. "They fer me? They fer me? They purty enough fer a white lady," she beamed her thanks, and fell again to weeping.

"I fetch some jest like 'em, same thing, fer Miz Blanche," said Hammond.

"Miz Blanche, she already got holes; she kin wear hern. I got to have my ears punched."

Hammond had forgotten the need to pierce the ears. "Won't hurt much. We tend to it first thing."

"They purty. They awful purty, Masta, suh." In her enthusiasm Ellen had forgotten her miscarriage. "You hadn't ought. They cost."

"Nev' mind, an' they did," Hammond scoffed.

Ellen held the jewels to her ears. "Ain't no other nigger never had aught so purty."

"They markin' you mine, my own, jest like my letters burned

into your hide. You well enough fer tonight? See that you clean. Have Lucretia Borgia wash you all over." Hammond did not press for a cause of the accident. He returned to give his father an account of his trip.

"Whure Doc Redfield?" the father asked on the son's return to the sitting-room. "He go on home? Whyn't he stop by? Better have that boy heat up your toddy."

"Doc Redfield, he a-comin' with the niggers. I rode ahead."

"Oh," the father was mollified. "Niggers goin' down, I reckon? Ourn didn' hardly fetch nothin', the cholerie an' all?"

"Niggers up, goin' up all the time. Natchez full of folks, runnin' from cholerie. We done right good. Course, one run, that mustee," Ham admitted.

"Git him?"

"No. Still a-runnin'. I reckon he go home to Briarfiel' where we bought him. I'm goin' there fer him tomorrer."

The father was complacent, but chuckled his disparagement of the boy's carelessness. "Won't do no good," he shook his head. "That boy near white. He strikin' North. I reckoned Redfield more watchful."

"He wanted I should chain 'em," Hammond absolved the doctor. "Here they are, a-comin'."

They went together out upon the gallery to receive Redfield, herding his charges down the lane. The doctor dismounted, exhausted, and shook the elder man's hand.

"Whut kin of gyascutus is that them bucks a-totin'?" the old man asked.

"It a carryin' bed fer you to ride in aroun' the plantation. You kin go anywhures now—down by the Tombigbee, up to the buryin' grounds, out to the cotton, anywhures you craves," Hammond expanded with pride.

"Huh!" sniffed the rheumatic. "You expectin' me to ride in that contraption, you wrong. Ain't goin', not a step. I got my own legs yet. Not strong, but I got 'em. Afore I ridin' aroun' nigger-back, I stay in an' rest me."

"Ever'body in Natchez usin' these carryin' beds," Hammond exaggerated. "Ever'body who cain't git aroun'."

"Cain't he'p. I won'. May be all right in Natchez, an' down in Brazil, an' in all them fine-haired cities, but me out here in the country—no. It ain't no Alabama dingus at all. Mayhap, all right to pleasure in, right sof', an' you ain't got no feather bed, but fer a growed up man to go bouncin' about on niggers' shoul'-ers—why, even field niggers would lose their respeck."

Hammond knew that the rejection was final. He had wasted at least four days in bringing the litter, all to no purpose. Pride. He told the bearers to cast it on the gallery floor against the wall of the house.

Instructing Lucretia Borgia to feed the four children well and afterwards to bed them down on long straw, Hammond drew Redfield into the house for breakfast. In the course of it, the doctor, fortified by two preliminary toddies, recounted with embellishments their experiences in the city. Redfield omitted to discuss the sale of the sterile Pole, since he had himself made it; nor did he mention Hammond's illness and the meeting with Charles. This was a convenient negligence. He had heard Hammond's promise to Charles not to tell Blanche about seeing him and he hoped that the secrecy from the wife would extend to the father. He had compunctions about neglect of his companion, although Hammond had never mentioned it.

After breakfast, the older man suggested, "Bring your bag of gol', Ham, an' pay off Doc Redfield. Might as well, right now. How much we owin' you, Doc?"

"Nothin', nothin' at all. Won't take nothin', not a cent," affirmed Redfield.

"Why?" Maxwell demanded. "Hammond here has had a right fruitful trip. We countin' on payin'. Only right!"

"Beginnin' with, Hammond pay ever'thin', all I spent. Besides that, I sell one of them bucks fer three hun'ert dollars more than he a-wantin' and he said I should keep the money. I didn't crave——"

"That case——" Maxwell conceded. "But we willin' to pay. I right obliged you goin' along. If Ham got sick or a-needin' somebody——"

The allusion caused Redfield to wonder whether Hammond had told of his illness before his arrival. Maxwell was capable of such an oblique accusation. Redfield saw fit to take his departure. He could detect no lack of cordiality in the leave-taking.

Hammond even accompanied the guest to his horse, after which he went to the cabin to examine the Mandingos. He found Mede reclining on the bed. Lucy standing above him feeding him bite by bite.

"Whut ails him? Ain't he got stren'th to eat his vittles?" Hammond demanded with irritation.

286

"Yas, suh, Masta, suh. Mede stronglike," replied Lucy. "On'y he likes I should feed him, layin' down. An' I likes to. He so purty." To the woman, Mede was like a great doll, a helpless baby to humour.

"I'll purty him," Hammond threatened.

The boy arose to permit his master to inspect him. Hammond detected a softening of the belly muscles that he did not like. He accused the slave of neglecting his training. "Cain't git no work out of you up here. I reckon you better be barned agin. Room a plenty down there now. This takin' up——"

"No, no, Masta, suh. He workin' all the time. All the time, Mede here runnin', jumpin', a-liftin'. All the time. All the time." There was anxiety in Lucy's voice.

Mede was indifferent to the threat. He accepted whatever happened.

"Well, keep him workin' hisself. I be home to stay in three, four, five days, an' then I takin' him in han'. I learn him whut workin' is."

After riding all night, Hammond was fatigued and he returned to the house. Blanche, big-bellied and blowzy, had come downstairs.

She rocked her chair gently and greeted her husband with, "Whut you fetch me? You gone a long while, an' me here a-waitin' fer it!"

He drew the trinkets from his pocket and gave them to her. They pleased her beyond his expectations. She could only gasp and gasp again in her excitement.

"They di'mon's?" she inquired.

"Not di'monds," Hammond opined. "Di'monds white. These somethin' else."

"They costs, I reckon."

Hammond admitted that they had some value. "Put 'em on," he suggested.

Blanche struggled to insert the clasps into the small holes in her ears, which had shrunk from disuse. She ignored the pain.

"Now I cain't see 'em no more. Are they purty?"

"Your hair brushed, an' they goin' to be. Cain't see 'em now, your hair so snarly-like an' hangin'." There was no note of censure in the statement.

"Now, folks goin' to know who your wife, who you buyin' jewellery." Blanche turned her florid, bloated face from side to side the better to display the gift. Garnets accentuated the girl's blondeness.

The indiscretion of bringing identical presents to his wife and his concubine struck Hammond for the first time. Why had he not foreseen Blanche's resentment, which was sure to follow? There was no occasion for a gift to Ellen, who had expected none —except that he loved her. The gift had been made and could not be withdrawn. He kept silent about it.

"These ain't nothin'. They don' mark you my wife. But I got somethin' that do. I got me that di'mond ring at las'." He got out the soiled ring Charles had thrown at him and placed it on her finger. "Now, that there is a di'mond," he said.

Blanche examined it proudly and kissed it on her finger. "How it sparkle!" she wondered, holding her soiled hand in the air and twisting her gross wrist. "Now I kin have my chil'. I married right. Plumb married."

"We married all right, even before. Your papa written it right in his Bible," Hammond asserted without satisfaction. "It hold. That chil' of yourn legal."

"I knowin', but now I got me the di'mon' ring."

Hammond was cheered by the simple girl's pleasure with her bauble.

"She ain't got none," Blanche gloated.

"Who ain't?"

"That Ellen."

"Course not. She jest a nigger," Hammond scoffed.

"She slip her chil' while you away," Blanche introduced the subject tentatively and cautiously. She wanted to make sure that he did not know the cause.

"That whut Papa say. Don' know whut make her. I wantin' you should be careful."

"I is. I ain't slippin' nothin'. I's glad, glad she slip it. I didn't do it, but I's glad."

"How come? Whut fer you glad? That sucker worth a hunderd, two hunderd dollars the day she drop it," Hammond attributed his interest in the accident to the monetary value of the child.

"Oh, she thinkin' she so purty an' all, rollin' her eyes. Jes' another nigger!"

"Ellen don' mean no harm. She right nice, an' smooth," Hammond defended his property.

"You a-thinkin' that chil' yourn?"

"Whut chil'?"

"That Ellen's," Blanche said spitefully.

Hammond shrugged an assumed ignorance. He had never

288

denied to his wife his relationship with Ellen or any other wench.

"One of the bucks, likely; liable all of 'em. She pleasurin' with 'em all, 'specially that Mede," the wife asserted without denial from her spouse. "Leastwise, it come black," she went on, "or real dark, ever'body sayin'."

"Who sayin'? Who?"

"Folks, niggers, ever'body who seen it. Real dark."

Hammond did not dispute the assertion. If the belief gave his wife any satisfaction, she was welcome. He was tired of the night's ride, and tired of the conversation.

"I reckon I better lay me down awhile," said Hammond. "I got to go agin, come mornin'."

When he awoke, Blanche was with his father, and he found no opportunity to tell of his meeting with Charles; nor could he tell of his illness without dragging Charles into the story. But such considerations paled before his joy at being home. Falconhurst, for Ham, was the centre of the world.

CHAPTER TWENTY

BUT THERE was the unfinished business of Ace's escape, and the following day Hammond set out on his ride to Briarfield. Meg arose to dress him and Lucretia Borgia to prepare his breakfast. He was irked by the necessity to make the journey, irresolute in his determination to flog the truant slave when—and if—he should find him.

He rode rapidly. His horse had not been taxed on the trip from Natchez and had rested in his spacious stall the whole of the previous day. The morning was crisp with just a hint of frost, and activity warmed both horse and rider.

Riding hard, he reached Fairfax in time for supper and Briarfield the following morning in time for dinner. But at Briarfield there was no news of Ace. The slave had not returned to his erstwhile home.

Hammond was resigned; he had only half expected to find the boy, in any event, and he did not know where else to seek for him. Then a signpost reminded him how near he was to Crowfoot, and his wife's parents. He had no will to go, but felt an obligation, since he was so near.

"The ol' Major goin' loony, folks says," the innkeeper at Briarfield told Hammond. "Don't know, my own self. Ain't seed him fer a long time back."

"I ain't heard nothin', an' Miz Maxwell ain't," Hammond expressed his doubt.

"It's that boy that done it, that Charlie runnin' away. Jest drove his pappy crazy."

Then Hammond knew he must go and see.

When he rode into Crowfoot, he noticed that the plantation was in a better state than when he had last seen it. Fences had been repaired, gates were upright, weeds had been mowed, cabins whitewashed. The house was tightly shut up, although smoke came from the chimney and he knew somebody was at home. At length a Negro woman came from somewhere to take his horse and it was necessary for him to knock upon the door for admission.

The Negro man, who after a while answered the knock, said, "Masta Dick out, suh, Masta. I ain't know wha' at are he. Come right in an' set down, suh. You Miz Blanche's man. I knows you."

"But whure Major Woodford? Whure your masta?" Hammond inquired.

"Set down, Masta, suh," suggested the servant, leading the way to the parlour. "I tell Mist'ess you come."

Hammond heard him in the sitting-room, trying to make Beatrix understand his presence, and heard her hollow "Oh!"

When she entered to greet him, she appeared browner than ever, more sallow and bloodless, her teeth more discoloured, in the same brown dress. And she was older, many years older. She walked with her horn to her ear.

"Oh, Cousin Hammond!" she greeted him, falling into his arms. "I been a-thinkin', thinkin' and a-prayin', wishin' you'd come. How Blanche? How she? How my little girl?"

Hammond screamed his reassurance into the horn, but was by no means sure she understood. "Whure the Major, Major Woodford?" he asked. "I reckon he out?"

"How?" She wrinkled her face and extended the horn.

Hammond repeated his question.

"Papa?" she asked. "He is porely. He jest set an' don' say nothin'. Come an' see him."

Hammond followed Beatrix into the sitting-room, where the Major sprawled in a large rocking-chair, slowly and aimlessly moving to and fro. He looked at Hammond without recognition.

Beatrix took him by the shoulder and shook him. "It's Hammon', Cousin Hammon' Maxwell, Papa. Don' you know him?"

Hammond would hardly have recognized his father-in-law, he was so changed. He was fat, and his face was so bloated that no wrinkles showed. It was utterly without expression. He paid no attention to Hammond, seemed not to see him. Hammond picked up the Major's hand from his lap, shook it, and replaced it. It returned no pressure.

"Papa, he's porely," Beatrix explained again.

"Who runnin' Crowfoot?" Hammond asked and repeated. "It lookin' real nice, better, that is."

When Beatrix finally understood the question, she answered, "Why, Dick, he runnin' it, best he kin. Oh, he ain't give up preacherin'. I couldn't stan' that. He still a-servin' God, but he had to take a holt. Wasn' nobody else, an' Charles gone, dead I reckon. We ain't heard nothin'. I keep a-prayin' an' a-prayin', askin' God to fin' him, us a-needin' him like we do."

Hammond made an effort to reply but was unable to make himself understood. Beatrix rambled on, and the guest merely nodded and shook his head, grimacing to acknowledge what she said. Major Woodford spoke not a word and appeared to hear none.

Beatrix looked out of the window and said, "I wonder whyn't Dick come. It time fer him. He kin talk; I cain't hardly 'cause my hearin' gittin' bad. You notice?" Hammond nodded and the woman fell silent.

It was half an hour before Dick's footsteps were heard on the gallery, during which time Beatrix and Hammond sat looking at each other and the speechless Major at neither of them.

"Consarn, consarn!" Dick greeted his brother-in-law. "Consarn! I knowed you was come. Saw your hoss in the stable. Right glad to see you, right glad! Ain't nobody to talk, Papa losin' his min' an Mamma gone deef, savin' the niggers."

"Wasn't knowin' about your Papa. Whut ail him?" Hammond asked.

Dick shook his head. "Ain't no knowin'. Jest sets and don' talk none. Min' clean gone. Ain't led the right life, I reckon; drinkin' and carryin' on. Ain't right with Jesus."

"Blanche will be right sorry to hear," said Hammond.

"Blanche?" Dick asked, as if he had just thought of his sister. "Blanche? How she come on?"

"She well," her husband assured. "That is, as well as kin be, allowin' the shape she in."

"Whut shape she in?"

"Why, she knocked. She in a family way. She goin' to have a chil'." Hammond did not know how to put the fact with more delicacy.

"Consarn! She is? You sure? When it comin'?"

"Don' exactly know. Couple of months. She bulgin' big," Hammond said proudly.

"Then the marriage took that I said over you. You din't lose no time gittin' her knocked! Consarn!" Dick turned from Hammond to his mother and asked, "Hear that, Mamma, whut Ham a-sayin'?"

Beatrix adjusted her horn and Dick re-asked his question. She shook her head and leaned forward to hear.

"Hammon say Blanche, she goin' to have a baby." Dick repeated the statement three times.

When she finally understood, Beatrix was shocked, alarmed. "Oh, oh, you horrible man, doin' that to my little girl. No! No! She too young!" the mother cried, dropping her horn and wringing her hands.

Dick retrieved the trumpet. "Whut you reckon? They married, isn't they? Whut fer you reckon they git married?" he screamed at the woman, who failed—or refused—to hear him.

Major Woodford took no cognizance of what was said, but stared vacantly into a far corner of the room and continued to rock.

Hammond was too embarrassed to reply to his mother-in-law. He wished he had not come.

"I'll pray, I pray. Jest somethin' else to pray about," the woman wept. "First, Charles, then Papa, now pore little Blanche. An' it seem like Jesus jest don' pay no attention. He knowin' bes'. Mayhap. He goin' to hear me now."

"Too late," laughed Dick, clapping Hammond warmly on the shoulder. "Consarn, whut else they fer—women? Course they goin' to have babies. Won't hurt her none. Blanche, she right buxom."

Beatrix wiped the tears from her eyes, and asked, "When it due to come? How long?"

"Month or two, I reckon. Blanche, she right big," Hammond faltered.

"An' I cain't go, cain't be with my pore little girl an' do fer

292

her." Beatrix shook her head and burst into fresh tears. "Papa done gone crazylike, an' I cain't leave him alone—jest alone with Dick. He'd do somethin' to Dick. Oh, oh, oh! Seem like you the cause of all my trouble. I wisht I never seen you, wisht Cousin Sophy hadn't never had you!" She arose and fled from the room.

"Consarn! Which is the looniest, her or Papa, I ain't a-knowin'!" said Dick, shaking his head. "Charlie an' Blanche is lucky or smart or somethin', gittin' away an' shet of 'em—leavin' me to fret an' manage."

"Plantation lookin' better—right smart better," Hammond congratulated his cousin.

"Yas, I went an' sol' off a couple of ol' niggers. Had to; don' care an' they was mortgage, I jest made 'em over same as they was mine. I had to git me some money to plant with. An' I put the otherns workin'. Papa never made 'em do nothin'. Got three or four of the wenches bringin' suckers, an' sows all in farrow. Go to plant me a cotton crop an' a corn crop, too. Do jest like it was mine, my own. I reckon, with Charlie dead, I'll be heirin' it anyhow, purty soon. The ol' folks cain't live long."

Major Woodford stopped his rocking. "They tryin' to kill me, Dick an' Beatrix," he said in a loud whisper. "Tryin' to pizen me, all the time, tryin' to pizen me. Cain't you do somethin' about it, Hammon'?" These were the first words he had spoken to Hammond, the first intimation that he had recognized his presence.

"I reckon they ain't, suh. They don't want you should die," Hammond sought to placate the old man.

"He always a-thinkin' that. Cain't pay no 'tention to his loony talkin'," Dick interposed.

"They gits shet of me, an' Dick goin' to kill his mamma, an' he thinkin' he have Crowfoot all hisself," persisted the father. "He fergittin' Blanche an' you—an' Charlie, if he alive yet."

"Blanche ain't a-needin' her part. Don't fret none about Blanche an' me," Hammond soothed.

"You right sure you never killed Charles? He went runnin' off with you an' he never come back. I reckon you done kill him. Good riddance. Wasn't no good, no way. I ain't a-blamin' you, ain't a-blamin' you at all," the Major condoned.

"Charles yet a-livin'. That is, I reckon," Hammond was tempted to tell of his seeing Charles at Natchez. He wondered whether

293

in the circumstances it would violate his promise, but he decided to keep silent.

"I ain't a-blamin' you fer killin' him," persisted the insane man. "Whut you do it with, shootin' or pizen? Whure you bury him?"

The accusation, even while he recognized its irresponsibility, made Hammond uneasy.

"You got him talkin', leastwise," said Dick. "He ain't talked none, ain't opened his mouth, fer a month. Papa," he turned to his father, "Hammon' never kilt Charlie. You makin' things up, jest like you makin' out Mamma an' me tryin' to pizen you."

Major Woodford put out his tongue at his son, withdrew it and set his lips in a hard line. He resumed his rocking and said no more.

"Mustn't never min' him. He loony—kind of," Dick said. He accepted his father's infirmity factually a thing to be faced and acknowledged, and had no reticence in discussing it in his presence.

"Supper done ready, Masta Dick, suh," old Washington, whom Hammond had last seen as a coachman, appeared to announce. He helped Major Woodford to his feet and shepherded him toward the dining-room. The younger men followed.

Beatrix was already seated at the table and Wash drew the chair opposite her for her husband. Dick and Hammond sat between them, facing each other. Dick said a prolonged and passionate grace in a loud voice directed into Beatrix's trumpet, but she was unable to hear the words.

Woodford ignored the prayer and as soon as he was seated began reaching for the food, to all of which he helped himself in huge portions.

"Seem you could wait fer the blessin'," Beatrix protested, "'specially when they's company." To Hammond she added, "Got to overlook Papa. Don' know whut he doin'. Cain't git him to wait an' be nice."

The old man ignored her, pretended not to hear. Before the prayer was finished, he had heaped his plate with victuals, and, grasping it with both hands, he lifted it towards Wash and said, "Taste."

The Negro took the plate, and, using his fingers instead of a fork, lifted some of each of its contents to his mouth. Of the chicken, he had no alternative but to bite it from its bone.

"Papa reckons we tryin' to pizen him an' he tryin' the vittles on the nigger," Beatrix explained the strange rite. "It don't kill the nigger, he guesses it all right fer him."

Woodford's eyes were focused upon the features of his slave. When Wash survived the ordeal and handed the plate back to him, he accepted it with a show of disappointment that the Negro had not died. But Major Woodford took this as evidence that the food was safe and began a furious stirring and mixing together of the various articles on his plate, after which he bolted the conglomeration like a cormorant, wiping the plate clean with bread. He then calmly pushed back his chair, rose, and left the room. The others had hardly begun to eat.

"Papa ain't hisself," Beatrix sighed, "actin' that a-way. He plague us right smart, Dick and me."

"He ain't bad, on'y he don' do nothin' an' don' say nothin'. He'll git over it, I reckon, when he takes a notion," commented Dick.

"How?" demanded his mother, leaning towards him with her trumpet. "Whut you say?"

The young man shook his head to indicate to her that his speech had been unimportant. Excluded from the conversation, she abandoned the effort to follow it and set to eating her meal. She could see the movement of the lips of the young men, knew when one was speaking and the other replying, and was curious about the drift of their conversation. Her loss was not great however, since all that Dick told Hammond she already knew, and since Hammond's tale of his trip to Natchez was so filled with reservations about his seeing Charles and about the money derived from the sale of the slaves, it was deprived of all reality. He did declare his errand to Briarfield and urged the necessity to pursue Ace further as an excuse to escape from the stifling hospitality of Crowfoot, with its deaf, religion-bound woman and its crazy man. Dick alone he could have endured.

Supper over, Hammond asked for his horse. Beatrix, who had heard nothing about the runaway slave, was shocked and injured by his show of haste.

"You doesn't like us at Crowfoot, seem like," she complained. "Won't never settle down an' stay awhile."

"Cousin Hammon' got to kotch him a runnin' nigger," Dick bellowed into her horn. "Consarn, cain't you un'erstan'?"

Beatrix looked blankly from one face to the other in her failure of comprehension. "Seem like he could stay one night here as

295

good as at Briarfield. There ain't no moon an' he cain't go on no ways."

"He after a nigger," Dick bellowed again; and then in a normal voice added, "She gittin' worse, seem like. She cain't hear, 'specially when she ain't a-wantin' to."

"You tell Blanche that I cain't come, but I kin pray, I kin pray," said Beatrix, beginning to weep. "When she git shet of this one, don' make her have no more, Cousin Hammon'. Havin' a chil' ain't nothin' to a man, but it a turrible trial fer a lady. I've had four of 'em, countin' the one that died. Papa jest that heartless. Don't you be heartless. Tell her I goin' to pray."

Hammond made no promise. When he bade farewell to Major Woodford, the host permitted him to shake his hand, but said not a word and did not cease his rocking in his chair. The perfunctory kiss Hammond planted on the cheek of his mother-in-law was an obligation.

"Consarn, but I'd like to ride with you, a-lookin' fer that buck, but I cain't. Bound down. That whut I am, bound down," Dick bewailed his fate.

Hammond had no intention of pursuing Ace further, since he had no clue as to where to look. Baffled, he was bound merely for home.

So he came thankfully back again to Falconhurst. He had had some misgivings lest the plantation should have suffered from lack of his management during his long absence at Natchez, which his single day at home had not resolved, and was mildly disappointed to find how little he had been needed. Lucretia Borgia, in addition to her duties as cook, had taken to herself the function of supervision, from which nothing and nobody escaped. She had seen to it that the slaves were fed and cared for, also that they were kept busy enough not to deteriorate or grow slack and lazy. When tasks were not apparent, she made them—mending of clothes, cleaning of cabins and barns, chopping of unneeded wood, spading of garden patches. She even assigned chores to the children, the pulling of weeds, the sweeping of areaways between the cabins, the gathering of faggots. Hammond was pleased with the order that he found.

The gold he had brought from Natchez was still in the house, and he had his boys unbury the kettle from under the tree, added the Natchez money to the hoard, and reburied the treasure. For lack of anything to be done, he lightened the slaves' work and allowed them more leisure and ease. All except Mede, whom he

296

believed to have shirked his training and whom he put to arduous toil, chopping down trees and splitting the wood for fences, and after a day at that, forced him to run behind Eclipse for half an hour, to carry weights, jump for him, both high and long, to bend and twist and turn, anything to bring the slave's muscles into play, to flex and harden them. Mede's strength was prodigious, but he was lazy and saw no reason to exert it, and his master never surfeited watching his activity. Lucy, anointing and massaging his exhausted body with serpent oil at night, harped on his lethargy and exhorted him to greater effort to satisfy his master. The more she grumbled, the harder she rubbed. Mede listened but little to the sermon she preached, but he relished the friction and pummelling she gave him, and when she was finished and drew the quilt over his nakedness, he sprawled in relaxation and went to sleep. He accepted it as his prerogative that he should luxuriate upon the bed alone, spreading his legs and threshing his arms, while the women slept together and with Bel upon the puncheoned floor, nor did they dispute it. When from time to time, he permitted Big Pearl to join him, for which the girl was always avid, he ousted her after his appetite was satisfied and thrust himself out to cover the whole mattress and to sleep alone.

Mede not only hardened but grew, increased in stature and in girth. His legs were like hickories, his arms like pylons, his belly like an anvil. He ate hugely and slept at every respite. His owner had no anticipation of finding an opponent with whom to fight him, but kept him in training as a showpiece and ready if a worthy adversary should appear. Disregarding Wilson's warning that the Mandingo hybrids tended to treachery, Hammond bred Mede to several of his wenches and already three or four, in addition to Lucy and Big Pearl, were pregnant by him. Lucy was complacent about such use of the boy, but Big Pearl was fiery though impotent in her jealousy, placing the blame on Mede rather than upon her master where it belonged. The youth was always acquiescent in such an assignment but never eager, although the women considered themselves favoured and boasted to their neighbours of the alliance. Mede knew himself to be his master's property, to be used as the master saw fit to use him; if as a stallion, Mede was grateful not only for the mate allotted to him but for the short respite from training that he knew would follow. Hammond begrudged him those intervals as much as the loss of his strength, which he sought to restore by forcing

297

upon the exhausted youth an additional pitcher of milk and eggs.

Hammond had no such concern for his own virility, for every night he shared his bed with Ellen, who treasured his caresses as if every one might be the last. She had no awareness of his obligations to his wife, and Hammond believed that by preferring her he was relieving Blanche of her distasteful duty to him. To Ellen, the master was the master, whom she would have obeyed even if she had not loved him so entirely. She could not credit her good fortune in being chosen for his mistress and dreaded the day, which she anticipated, of being displaced and relegated to another.

Lucretia Borgia, as pleased as Ellen with the earrings, had pierced the girl's lobes with a darning needle to accommodate the jewels, and when Hammond returned from Briarfield he found Ellen with short straws through her ears to prevent the punctured lobes from closing as they healed. Three days later, unable to wait longer, Ellen withdrew the straws and inserted the earrings, which enhanced her dark beauty. The gift was an assurance of her owner's affections, and she brushed her hair back and swung her head for all to see.

The other slaves admired Ellen's jewels without envy of them; after all, she was the master's own wench and entitled to an ornament to mark her status.

Blanche, one day in the kitchen, where she had gone to mix a toddy for herself, unknown to Maxwell, glimpsed Ellen's earrings and knew they were duplicates of her own. Her temptation was to tear them from the girl's ears, but Hammond was at home and she knew the wrath it would kindle. She forbore. Instead, she went upstairs and unscrewed her own trinkets from her ears, but could not bear to throw the pretty, gleaming things out of the window, as she had intended. She put them in a corner of a drawer of her commode.

The light was failing when Hammond came in from work, but when he entered the sitting-room he perceived that the earrings had disappeared from his wife's ears. "Drops git to painin' you?" he asked, fingering the lobe of his own ear.

"No!" Blanche bit the word.

"Why ain't you wearin' 'em then?" he inquired naïvely.

"That slut, that dirty nigger slut of yourn. You brung her earrings jest like mine. Think I'd wear 'em? No!" Blanche began to weep in her anger.

298

Hammond now saw how grave was the offence of making identical presents to his wife and to his concubine.

"Now, now," he said. "It ain't nothin'."

"Her time gittin' near," consoled his father. "She right squeamish. All white ladies is, about this time." He abhorred dissension and sought to quell it.

"Might as well burn your letters right on her face—an' mine. Bran' 'em right in, so all the world goin' to know who we-uns belongs to. Nobody cain't touch a woman with no red earrings. She Hammon' Maxwell's woman, white or black," Blanche screamed. "I ain't your whore to be marked off." She rose, waving her arms, and made towards the hall.

Hammond caught her by the shoulder and placed her again in her chair. "That di'mon' ring, I goin' to take that too, an' you doesn't behave. Then whut you goin' to do? That boy you totin' in your belly goin' to be a bastard an I does. Want he should be a bastard an' ever'body sayin'?"

"No! No! No!" Blanche cried.

"You know our weddin' don' hold. Dick, he ain't no reverend, ain't no purentee reverend, jest a reverend fer niggers. Ain't got no right to marry whites. It all I got to do," Hammond threatened, "jest to say we ain't married an' sen' you home to your crazy papa and have your bastard."

The girl knew no better than to believe what Hammond himself half credited. She had no answer, but shrieked hysterically.

"Now, Son, it all right," Maxwell tried to calm the storm. "You wedded; you know you wedded fast to Blanche here. Hadn't ought to skear her this time. She slip that chil', liable to, right here an' you go to skear her."

"I don' care. Ellen mine an' I goin' to have her, whutever you says," Hammond declared petulantly.

"Have her! Have the slut! I ain't carin' an' you has her, on'y don' try to mark us off with your ol' red earrings. You cain't marry her. She ain't white. She jest your bed slut. I your wife, I your wife," Blanche shrilled, rising again and making toward the door.

Hammond let her go and could hear her climbing the stairs.

The father was more distressed by the scene than the son or his wife. It always distressed him to know Hammond in the wrong and he could not deny now that he was behaving brutally. "Go foller her an' love her up, Son," he urged. "Tell her it ain't so. Tell her you married fast. Tell her you sorry."

"She kin go to hell, all I care," sulked Hammond. "Ellen, she mine, she mine, an' I keepin' her. Keepin' her, do you hear, keepin' her?"

"Course. Course you keepin' Ellen. I ain't findin' no fault with Ellen," Maxwell pacified his child. "Only Blanche, she white. She your wife. Hadn't ought to rile her, 'specially now—how she is. Nobody ain't stoppin' you keepin' your wench."

"I reckon I hadn't ought to brung her them earrings like Blanche's, only they so purty on her ears, an' I never thought," Ham conceded.

Blanche did not come down for supper, and neither of the Maxwells had any appetite for food. The elder drank toddies, hot and strong, when the meal was over. The younger man abstained and sat in silent contemplation in the flickering candlelight until it was time for bed.

By next morning the tempest had subsided. Blanche appeared for her breakfast as if nothing had occurred and was as affable as usual. Hammond offered no objection to her after-breakfast toddy, and after he had gone she drank another and another, which Maxwell made no move to curb. She had rather pointedly, however, failed to resume her earrings, which Hammond noted without comment. He also noted and admired Ellen's, gleaming in her ears.

CHAPTER TWENTY-ONE

CHRISTMAS WAS not ignored on Falconhurst. The three days of idleness granted to the slaves—except the house slaves—were reckoned as a right and not as a mere absence of tasks. The livestock were fed and cared for, but otherwise nobody worked—not even in the patches allotted for gardens. Even Mede was permitted to break his training, which caused his master some misgivings lest he grow flaccid. The house Negroes were relieved of none of their duties, which in any event were not onerous—except Lucretia Borgia's and she would have been desolated to be deprived of her bossy overseeing of everything and everybody, including her masters. Held to their usual tasks, discipline within the house was relaxed and licence was given for acts and speech that would not have been tolerated at other times. Maxwell shared toddies with Meg until the boy stumbled with tipsiness.

Presents were few. Clothes and blankets, such as would otherwise have been needed anyway, were issued to the slaves, many of them merely mended and washed, handed down to smaller adolescents from youths who had outgrown them. Each child was given a stick of candy. Some ate it at once and afterwards regretted that it was gone. Others, more prudent, sucked on it charily and required days for its final consumption. A few put it away without tasting to cherish for its beauty. Blanche gave Tense some crumpled ribbons to prink her hair, and Tense was delighted.

All the boys too old for candy were assembled before the house and each was allotted a hot toddy. Maxwell went out on to the gallery to drink with them. A few relished and savoured the potion, and the others pretended to, for the conceit it gave them to drink with the master.

"Um, um, ain't it jest good?" one yellow boy, seeking to deny his distaste for the concoction, asked a somewhat darker one who stood beside him.

"That ain't nothin'," Alph, with no glass in his hand, boasted. "I has it anytime I wants, right out of Masta's glass, ever' day I has it, right outn his glass."

The half-truth begot the wonderment, if not the envy, it sought. "Does you now?" the yellow boy raised his eyes.

"For my rheumatiz, jes' like ol' Masta's. He dreen it into me," the urchin bragged.

The greeting of 'Chris'mas gif', Chris'mas gif'' was exchanged whenever two Negroes met, all over the plantation throughout the three days. It was all they had to exchange, and none knew quite what it meant. It implied goodwill. Despite its meagreness, the season was jocund and lighthearted. All were happy.

"The way it had always ought to be," Maxwell declared. "Them young saplin's got more growin' into 'em in three days than they gits in three weeks of work time. You kin jes' see 'em laugh an' grow."

"They grows, I reckon it," conceded Hammond. "Only that sugar-candy rot their teeth an' not a-workin' is makin' 'em triflin'."

"Whut they got to work fer? Whut it bring 'em? Whut it bring you or anybody? Let 'em grow." The old man was no disciple of industry. Let who would labour; the increment upon which he depended was unearned. The hours Hammond devoted to the training of Mede his father did not begrudge, for that was sport, but he deplored the other work, the daily round of the plantation management to which his son devoted so much time which, in the father's opinion, would be better devoted to sitting swizzling toddies. His concept of Negro husbandry was to feed the stock and to encourage it to reproduce and to grow. He loved his slaves collectively, as if they had been puppies, and valued their homage, and faith, and dependence. His constant anxiety was lest his vassals be underfed or overworked.

One night late in January Big Pearl had her baby.

When Lucretia Borgia arose, she found Belshazzar at the door, sent by Lucy with the news.

"Whut you wants me to do?" Lucretia Borgia assumed indifference. "Is Big Pearl bad sick, or somethin'? Sucker livin'?"

"Yas, 'um. It livin'. Big Pearl done had it; she ain't sick no more," Shaz explained. "Mammy Lucy say tell you to tell Masta, ma'am."

"Whut reckon I goin' to pester Masta ev' time a wench farrow young?" Lucretia Borgia sniffed. "Go on along from here."

Shaz, baffled, retreated. He had executed his errand.

While the masters were at breakfast, Lucretia Borgia, with a casual air, her own infant in her arms, entered the dining-room, ostensibly to ask whether the coffee was hot. "Mem so triflin', cain't trus' him to have it hot," she said at first. As an afterthought she relayed Belshazzar's tidings.

"Whyn't you say?" asked Hammond, startled in his satisfaction, pushing back his chair. "Whut kind?"

"I sayin' suh, right now. I never axed whether it wench or buck," Lucretia Borgia shrugged.

"Eat your breakfast," said the father. "One would think it was yourn, your own."

Hammond ignored the counsel, hurried from the house, and limped toward the cabins.

"It done come. Big Pearl done had it, suh, Masta," Lucy greeted him at the door.

Big Pearl, still on the floor, rose to sitting, the naked baby in her arms, tugging at her enormous breast. "You goin' to give me somethin', Masta, suh, ain't you, Masta, suh?" she asked.

"I reckon it worth a dollar an' a new dress an' it sound. Is it soun'? Ain't anythin' missin' 'bout it?" Hammond had his misgivings of the brother-and-sister relationship.

He squatted by the pallet, and took the baby in his arms. He

302

felt it over. There was nothing abnormal about the child except its size and vigour. With its bowed legs it lunged and kicked as if trying to escape, and then it broke into a lusty, raucous, tearless cry.

Hammond placed his palm on Big Pearl's forehead, but could detect no fever. He patted her shoulder and offered praise for her and her child.

When he returned to the house for his breakfast, his father had finished eating and was in the sitting-room. Meg had brought him a toddy.

"It fine—a buck," he told the old man. "Ain't no more the matter than if Big Pearl never seen that Mede, than if they wasn't no kin at all. Reckon you got stren'th to walk out to look it over?"

"I've seen 'em, seen hunderds," Maxwell waved his hand in distinterest. "Ain't no more than worms at first."

"This 'un a baboon, big enough to be, 'most. Look jes' like Mede, jest like him."

"Well, whut did you reckon? Mede got him, didn't he? That Mede, about the bes' boar nigger we ever had. Reckon we goin' to use him on all the wenches hereinafter."

"You knowin' whut Mr Wilson told—not to cross up Mandingo with other niggers. Makes 'em bad."

"No!" said Maxwell. "Any nigger is bad an' if he not watched. I wants 'em vig'ous. We sells 'em afore they comes scurvy an' hard to han'le."

"Whut we goin' to call it?" asked Hammond, reverting to the child.

"Time 'nough, time 'nough," said his father. "How is Ol' Mista Wilson?" he pondered.

"How he?" Hammond failed to understand. "I reckon he dead, this time."

"I meanin' callin' the sucker that—Ol' Mista Wilson? Good as anythin'. That whure we got him—leastwise whure we got his pappy an' mammy. He'd like it, even an' if he dead, Ol' Mista Wilson would."

"I reckon it good as any, an' you thinks," Hammond conceded. "We ain't a-sellin' it anyways."

"Sellin'?" the older man bristled. "No, suh, we ain't. It goin' to live an' die with us right here on Falconhurst. They doesn't come like that once in a coon's age."

Lucy's baby followed her daughter's earlier than was anticipated. There was some anxiety on the part of the masters lest it might be premature, although the girl baby appeared fully developed. Indeed, except for the comparison with Old Mister Wilson, it was tremendous, approximately twelve pounds, sinewy and viable. Lucy had wanted her baby to be a boy, not for her own sake, not that she would treasure a girl the less, but that she knew a boy's greater value, especially if it were black. A black wench was of little worth, and Lucy feared her master's censure for having one.

Her foreboding, however, was wasted; for the young master welcomed Lucy's daughter with admiration and praise for its mother.

"That a godsend, a windfall," declared Maxwell when his son told him of the child's sex. "Hence, we don' got to fret us about our Mandingos runnin' out. We goin' to raise this one an' put it to Big Pearl's buck, soon as they growed enough. It will keep the breed alive."

Hammond shook his head in misgiving of his father's long-range project.

"Heed you do it, if I ain'tn here to carry it through," cautioned the old man, and Hammond, who had never before considered seriously that his father might die, promised.

Blanche, who had contemplated with an indifference that amounted to disdain the birth of Negro infants, was terrified at the prospect of her own confinement, which she knew was near. She knew that it was a painful process for a white woman, and she remembered a Mrs Jackson, a friend of her mother's, who had died in childbirth. She wept in self-pity as she sat opposite Maxwell with a toddy in her hand.

"Reckon mayhap I goin' to die?" she asked him. "I not wantin' to die yet, not yet awhile. I'm afeared."

Maxwell reassured the girl as best he could. "You ain't a-goin' to die," he said. "Like, won't have no trouble at all. Course," he hedged, "some does."

"I dies, an' Hammon' going to be sorry, sorry he treat me so," the girl wept. "He goin' to be sorry."

"Hammon' right good to you. He good to ever'body," the father defended his son. "Course, he right busy, out an' about, drivin' an' overseein'."

"He find time fer that Ellen. Don' slight her none." Blanche brushed the tears from her red eyes with the back of her hand.

"You don' un'erstan'," argued Maxwell. "Hammon' doesn'
304

care nothin' 'bout Ellen. She jes' a nigger. He a-savin' you. You know that. His mamma, Sophy, Miz Maxwell, was always right thankful when I pestered with the wenches an' left her be."

"Yes. Only Hammon', he don' pester none only Ellen. Ifn he pleasured with the otherns, Lucy an' Lucretia Borgia, an' all of 'em, I wouldn't care none." Blanche had difficulty with the idea. "On'y he don't. It's Ellen, all the time Ellen, ever' night Ellen. Don' even look at the others, no more than at me. He sweet on Ellen. Thut whut he is."

"Ellen, she young an' handy, an' he know she goin' to be clean. It goin' to be different after you have your boy."

"I don' care an' if I dies. I don' care. It serve him right," Blanche pouted.

The baby clothes left over from Hammond's infancy were brought down for the use of his child. Lucretia Borgia knew just where they had been laid away on an upper shelf in a wardrobe in a spare room. She found them—somewhat coarse linen, yellowed by the years, dusty, some of them unaccountably stained. They were all together, the long dresses and underskirts, twice the length of the child, the short ones for later use, and even blue calicoes, picked out with white stars, that Hammond had worn until he was four. Pinning blankets, bellybands, and soft diapers, all that might be needed were included. Lucretia Borgia put the women to the task of washing the baby clothes and drying them on the weeds in the sunshine to eliminate as much of the yellowing of age as was possible. She herself ironed the dresses that were decked out with pleated yokes and ruffles of hand embroidery. How many times before she had smoothed those self-same garments. She chuckled to remember that this dress he had worn when Hammond took his first step, that one when he had come down with a fit of coughing until they had despaired of his living, the other when he had first garbled her name in speech. What a tyrant he had been, but how sweet the tyranny!

When all were clean, Lucretia Borgia carried the garments into the sitting-room and stacked them beside Blanche's chair. Blanche sorted them out, the long from the short. They would suffice for her child, although she had expected to have new ones.

Maxwell watched her in silence. He revered these garments for the sake of him who had worn them. They were irreplaceable, beyond duplication. He could but wonder that Blanche should prefer new ones. Once, while she sorted them, he reached

305

out and took a well-remembered little dress into his own hands and, gazing on it, he saw again Sophia Hammond and her infant son. Before he handed it back to his daughter-in-law, he had spilled his toddy on it and had wiped his tear-filled eyes upon its hem. He said nothing. Blanche would not understand. He was glad that Hammond was not there to see his weakness.

The following Thursday Blanche had her child. She arose and came down to breakfast, eating heartily but unaccountably failing to drink the toddy that Meg mixed for her. To her husband's inquiry she replied that she was tolerably well.

"Tol'able, jes' tol'able," she said, "mindin' how I am." She had no intimation that her time had come.

Hammond went out to his work as usual. He was clearing some unused acres in preparation for planting them to corn, not because he needed the land, but to give his Negroes a task that would keep them employed.

At ten o'clock by the erratic clock on the mantel the pains first assailed Blanche. At first they were only a vague discomfort which caused her to leave the sitting-room and to go to her bed. Maxwell sipped his hot drink, undisturbed, and had Meg stir up another. The day was cloudy, threatening rain. His first intimation that Blanche was in labour was a cry, a loud shriek, more of terror than of pain, followed a moment later by another louder one. He heared Lucretia running through the hall, flat of foot, and up the stairs. He roused Alph, dozing on the floor beside his chair, and sent him to seek his young master.

"Tell him come, come quick, drop ever'thin'. Tell him Miz Blanche is sheddin' her chil'," he instructed the boy.

The boy left the room at a trot and Maxwell heard him slam a door as he left the house. He also heard rapid footsteps on the floor above him, and another shriek. He got to his feet and wandered down the hall, uncertain whether to climb the stairs, when he met Lucretia Borgia hastening toward the kitchen.

"She havin' it. Miz Blanche havin' it. She hurtin' powerful bad," she informed her master without stopping.

"I reckoned," he said to her disappearing back. There was another scream of anguish, more audible here than in the sitting-room.

Lucretia Borgia returned from the kitchen carrying a large bucket of steaming water in one hand and a sheaf of clothes piled on the other arm. "Take here, suh," she ordered her master.

"Stan' outn my way." As she hastened up the steps, she called over the banister, "That Tense wench, she ain't no help, no help at all."

Maxwell realized that he could be of no help either and retraced his steps to the sitting-room, where he did not sit down, but toddled back and forth across the floor to relieve his anxiety. Scream followed scream, but they seemed to grow weaker. Meg appeared with an unordered toddy on a salver, which his master accepted. The boy was wide-eyed with interest in the proceedings upstairs.

"Miz Blanche droppin' her sucker, suh, Masta?" he asked with enthusiastic innocence.

Maxwell's open palm crashed against the impertinent child's cheek, hurting the arthritic hand more than the cheek. The boy did not know for what he was punished, since he had intended his question to be courteous. But white men were strange. One never knew how they would respond. He retreated to the kitchen.

Alph returned out of breath. He had hurried to find his master, as he was instructed, and had run all the way back.

"He comin', Masta, suh. He comin'. Masta, comin' fas' as he kin," he reported between gasps.

"Come here an' take a swig of toddy. You petered out runnin'," said the master, who, repenting of his temper to Meg, made amends with indulgence to his brother.

The screams issuing from the house told Hammond why he had been sent for even before he entered. "How long she been carrying' on?" he asked his father and without waiting for a reply proposed, "I goin' to sen' fer Murrey, put a nigger on a mule an' send."

"Lucretia Borgia's up with her. She goin' to be all right. Hurtin' though, seem like. Better git Murrey though, I reckon. Ain't much of a doctor. I don' trus' him but he the bes' they is," concurred Maxwell.

"I'll sen' Mem, I reckon. Otherns too young an' don' know the way," suggested Ham tentatively, and the absence of reply implied his father's consent. He went to the kitchen to find Agamemnon and to give him his instructions.

He returned to the sitting-room with the assurance that Mem was on his way to summon the physician. He seated himself in a chair, but could not stay quiet, and rose and limped back and forth across the room. He shuddered at the screams that came

307

from above. "Reckon I better go up? Reckon I kin help do somethin'?" he asked his father.

"Jest be in Lucretia Borgia's road," replied the father. "She on her high hoss, mindin' me to stan' one side. She goin' to slap you down, you git in her way. You'd think I her servant, 'stead of her mine."

"Tense helpin' her, I reckon."

"She sayin' Tense ain't no account," said Maxwell.

Conversation languished. Father and son had nothing to say to each other, and yet they were as one, listening for the cries that came from above. Both suffered with the girl who was struggling to produce an heir for them. The shrieks subsided into groans, which grew less frequent. The older man believed that this betokened a growing weakness, an exhaustion of the woman in labour, but he did not say so to his son lest he aggravate the apprehension he knew was in the young man's heart.

The clock ticked away on the mantelpiece. Maxwell was so used to its click-clack that he had ceased to notice it, but now it impinged on his consciousness and he marked each passing minute. Before Memnon had had time to reach Benson, Maxwell was rising periodically to patter to the window to scan the driveway for his return with Doctor Murrey.

Hammond climbed the stairs. Walking down the hall, he rapped with his knuckles on the bedroom door before he opened it. Lucretia Borgia was bent above the bed.

"I takin' care Miz Blanche. It mos' here. It comin'. You go on downstairs an' set down, Masta, suh, an' don' hender me," Lucretia Borgia looked up to command. "Ain't goin' to be no dinner fer you an' yo' papa, nor fer none of us, savin' whut Dite an' Elien kin set," she added.

The tone of the woman's words braced Hammond's spirit.

Memnon returned. He had found the doctor, who had said that he would come. Hammond settled down to wait for his arrival, confident that when he came he would deliver the baby quickly. Toward two o'clock the screams ceased; the silence was oppressive, more painful to the husband than the wails had been. He wondered whether his wife's strength might be completely spent, even whether she might have died.

A heavy step upon the stair! Lucretia Borgia was coming down. Hammond was exhausted, expecting the worst. Lucretia Borgia came into the room, cradling in her arms a swathe of white clothes. Protruding from the clothes was the head of a child, red and amorphous. Lucretia Borgia was all a-grin with satisfaction. She went first to her young master and bowed to display her precious burden, and then to Maxwell.

"How Miz Blanche come on?" Hammond demanded.

"She sleepun' now, I reckon," the woman said. "She jest 'bout petered a-havin' it."

Hammond breathed easier.

"He ain't very big," Maxwell looked at the child critically. "Like, he'll grow."

Lucretia Borgia hugged the baby to her chest. "He? It ain't no he," she announced.

Maxwell's heart sank. He had wanted a boy. But he made no comment.

Hammond looked again at his child's face. "It's gotch-eyed, like Charles," he declared.

And it was. The eyes were distinctly crossed, not with the normal strabismus of the newly born, but with a divergence which would prove permanent. Charles in Natchez had expressed the hope that the child would not be cross-eyed. Had his kinship with his sister had anything to do with the phenomenon, Hammond asked himself.

The least he could do was to go up to see the mother, but when he came, she was sleeping. Tense crept softly across the room to let him in, her finger to her lips. He stood by the bedside and looked down on the exhausted girl, sleeping on her back, her hair drawn back in a long braid. What if the child was a girl? What if its eyes were crossed and it was small and wanting in vigour? She had done her best, he reasoned compassionately. Perhaps her next child would be a sturdy boy.

When he went downstairs again, Lucretia Borgia still held the baby in her arms, jostling it up and down to quiet it and looking devotedly into the tiny, wrinkled face.

"Who you plannin' to suck it?" queried Maxwell.

"Its mamma ifn she kin, if her milk come good," Hammond answered casually.

Lucretia Borgia turned away in repugnance at the proposal, but interposed no word.

"No white lady goin' to suck her chil'. Poor trash mayhap sometimes when they ain't got no wench come fresh. Spoils 'em," explained Maxwell.

"We ain't got no right fresh wench, our own self," Hammond objected.

"Let me, Masta, suh," proposed Lucretia Borgia. "My sucker most weaned, an' I got milk yet. Plenty milk."

"Your milk too ol', an' you too ol'," Maxwell shook his head. "You always wantin' to git into things, always wantin' to be It."

"Lucy the freshest we got," suggested Hammond.

"She too ol', too," said the older man. "Milk from a young wench always better, sweeter like."

"Then Big Pearl is all we got," sighed the boy.

"That black gyascutus in the house!" scoffed Maxwell. "She cain't walk, she got to gallop, knockin' things aroun'. Besides, she got Wilson. Ol' Mista Wilson, growin' like he is, take a lot of milk."

"See how Big Pearl treat that young 'un!" said Lucretia Borgia. "Throwin' him aroun', jest like he a bag of oats, jest like he a iron baby."

"Course, Lucy kin help out with Wilson, need come, an' leave Big Pearl's milk fer Sophy," Maxwell reasoned.

"Sophy?"

"Sophy," Maxwell repeated. "Goin' to name her Sophy, I reckoned, after her grandma."

The son nodded his head in acquiescence. "Lay her down," he told Lucretia Borgia, "an' fetch Big Pearl."

"You going to give suck to your new mist'ess, Miz Sophy," Hammond said when the black girl came in. She had never before been admitted to the house.

Lucretia Borgia lifted the baby gently and placed her in Big Pearl's arms. Big Pearl gave a scream of delight and smothered the child with kisses. "Ain't it sweet, so white an' red!" she cried.

"Ol' Mista Wilson's nose will be out of joint," Maxwell laughed.

"I reckon she milkin' enough fer two," commented Hammond.

For a while now, time ceased to have meaning. No longer did the ticking of the clock impinge upon Maxwell's awareness. That Doctor Murrey did not arrive was now of no importance. Memnon reavowed that he had seen the doctor at his home in Benson and that he had promised to come, but Mem was hardly to be trusted. He believed that he was telling the truth, but there was no knowing to whom he had talked or what had been said. Mem feared doctors, believed that they carved people alive, especially black men, and his traffic with Murrey, if at all, had been as brief as possible. If the birth of the child had been prolonged or if it had gone amiss, the blame would have fallen upon Memnon, but, since all was well, he escaped with small censure.

CHAPTER TWENTY-TWO

LATER THAT afternoon the weather turned warmer after it began to rain, first in a steady drizzle, and then with pelting showers. It was a dreary afternoon—good for toddies before a slow-burning fire. All had gone well, except the sex of the child, but the acceptance of the name he had so casually and cannily bestowed upon it mollified Maxwell's displeasure. He revised his vision of a handsome, alert, and precocious grandson, one who should be to Hammond what Hammond had been to him, into a vision of a granddaughter as beautiful, charming, gracious, and complacent as that Sophia who had given him Hammond. With Hammond blood from both sides of her house, he foresaw a paragon of womanhood.

Even though the services of Doctor Murrey had not been required, Maxwell was disappointed that he had not come. He had little confidence in the man's skill, but, such as it was, it was not fitting that a planter's child should be born without its benefit. Besides, Doctor Murrey enjoyed corn whisky, and Maxwell had foreseen a pleasant interval, after the doctor's task was accomplished, of toddies before the fire and an interchange of gossip.

The erratic clock had just struck five when Maxwell heard in the lane the approach of horses, which took him to the window, where he recognized the doctor's vehicle, a kind of hooded calash, drawn by a team of weary bays. He was glad that the doctor had come; now they could have their seance, and it was so late that perhaps the doctor could be persuaded to remain for supper, possibly to spend the night.

He called for Memnon to open the door, but heard the patter of Meg's bare feet running to forestall Mem's welcome. He watched a white youth wind the reins around the whip on the dashboard and alight from the rig awkwardly. He was enormously tall, emaciated, cadaverous. He made his way round the vehicle to its other side, and, reaching in, appeared to have much difficulty in helping out of the seat a man whom Maxwell recognized

311

to be the doctor, dressed in a long coat and beaver hat. A Negro boy took the horses, while the doctor clung clumsily to the youth who tried to support him. The doctor took three steps and stopped. He stood unsteadily, supported by the youth. The doctor was drunk, dead drunk.

Maxwell made his way to the front door, of which Memnon had taken charge and driven Meg away.

"Not much use us comin'. He's drunk," called the youth. "Got to git him to bed, if one is ready. How the wench come along? Had it yet?"

"It ain't no wench. It Miz Maxwell," Maxwell explained.

"A white lady? Then I cain't do nothin'. Doctor don' hold with me doctorin' whites—jest yet awhile. I could have done it, an' if it been a nigger," the boy said.

"The chil' done come. It a girl chil'," Maxwell explained.

"Then we git him in bed. He be all right later on. He gits this way," the tall youth explained.

Hammond, hobbling down the stairs, overheard and called to Memnon, "Git out there an' he'p, he'p the white gen'leman, cain't you? Cain't you see? Gittin' slothy agin? Wantin' I should touch you up?"

Memnon wanted no touching up. He rolled his eyes toward his master and leaped forward to support the doctor on the other side from the youth.

"Carry him upstairs an' put him into bed—that room agin mine, not down next your mist'ess. Mus'n't rile her now, the way she is," Hammond commanded the slave.

The pot-bellied, florid little doctor staggered unsteadily through the door, securely embraced by Memnon. He remembered to remove his high hat in a gentleman's home, but otherwise surrendered to the slave's ministrations. Memnon led him gently up the stairs, the youth, embarrassed, falling behind. Maxwell, disappointed of the chitchat he had anticipated, retired to the sitting-room again. Hammond followed the guests up the stairs, waited in the hall while the youth and Memnon removed the drunken doctor's clothes and thrust him into bed, and then escorted the young man down the stairs.

As they entered the sitting-room, Maxwell settled himself more firmly in his chair, not after all to be bilked of his conversation. "Readin'?" he asked.

"Yes, suh. Much as I kin, suh, the doctor this way," replied the tall youth still standing, diffidently.

"Set down, set down," invited the old man. "Meg," he called, "stir us a toddy."

The youth chose a chair and seated himself. "No, thanks, Mista Maxwell, suh," the boy slowly shook his head. "No toddy fer me."

Maxwell looked at him with a kind of alarm. "You're ol' enough," he opined. "Temp'ance?"

"Jest fer me," the boy said, "not fer you or nobody else. If I am goin' to make a doctor, I ain't wantin' to be like him." A feeling of disloyalty in what he had said caused him to add, "Doc, he's right good. He knows, when he ain't drinkin', only he drinks and cain't stop, seems like. Worser all the time." His curved lips grew straight with his determination, a serious glance fell from his blue eyes, he brushed his bush of black hair from his forehead with long fingers, and he sought to restrain a blush from his fuzz-covered cheek.

"In that case," conceded the old man, unable to find an argument to alter the boy's conviction. "Live in Benson?" he asked, accepting a toddy from Meg's tray.

"Yes, suh, now, that is, readin' with Doc Murrey an' stayin' with him," the young man made clear. "I belong out at Bankside. You knowin' me, Mista Maxwell, suh; leastwise I knowin' you. I'm Willis Smith, son of Willis Smith of Bankside Plantation," he proclaimed proudly.

"Laws! Willis Smith's boy. Course I know you, know your papa that is. Good blood!" Maxwell nodded, impressed.

"I remember back, you come to our house, buyin,' saplin's, stayed fer dinner," Willis recalled. "I didn't like you that time, 'cause you wantin' my playboy off of me, only my papa wouldn't sell him."

"I recolec', I recolec'; you cried to keep him," said Maxwell. "Wouldn't eat no dinner, so afeared your papa goin' to sell him. A right likely Jew-faced yaller boy."

"That right. Out of Old Cinthy, she say by a Jew peddler. His name is Job, 'cause papa say he have so much patience with whut I do to him," Willis explained. "I gotten him yet."

"In Benson?"

"No; Job at the plantation still, suh. He married up, an' I don' want he should have to divide from his wench an' her baby. He still body-servants me when I go to Bankside."

"Willis Smith? Willis got plenty, used to have. Whut fer he makin' a doctor outn you? You the oldest, ain't you?"

"Yes, suh, I Papa's oldest boy, oldest livin', that is. Papa, he ain't rightly makin' me no doctor. I makin' me one. It my own doings. Yes, suh."

"Whut the world comin' to?" Maxwell speculated. "Fathers ain't got no say, seem like. Willis knowin' you had ought to stay on the plantation an' make a planter. He needin' you."

"The world needin' me. People, people needin' me," Willis' eyes shone with fervour. "My little sister, you remember her, Nellie, she die. Purtiest little, yellow-haired chil' ever live, an' the sweetest, sweet as clover honey. Puttered sore throat, folks said; they wouldn't let I should kiss her. I knowin' right then, when we layin' Nellie away, I goin' to make me a doctor. Wasn't no call she should die. The doctor drunken, Murrey drunken. I ain't a-go' to be drunken—an' I go' to study hard an' learn. I goin' to save folks from dyin'."

Hammond, who had taken no part in the colloquy, interposed, "That case, one would think Doc Murrey——"

"Ain't nobody else," the boy interrupted him. "Only doctor in Benson. Besides, he good when he ain't drunken. He kin learn me, an' he got books, doctor books, big ones, that I kin read."

"All them big words," Hammond shook his head in doubtful wonder.

"I cain't say 'em, cain't soun' 'em out," Willis admitted. "But they ain't no call to. I kin spell 'em out, an' know whut they mean, most of 'em. An' Doc Murrey tells me, drivin' along when he ain't drunken, an' shows me on sick folks how to do. He knowin' he got to give up purty quick, an' then I got to take a-holt an' do the bes' I kin."

The youth's assurance was balanced with modesty, but sustained by a will to learn, a curiosity, and a determination to succeed in his vocation.

The supper bell rang. Willis felt called upon to look at Doctor Murrey before he should eat, but suggested that the Maxwells should not delay their meal. They waited for him. He found the doctor asleep on his back, snoring lightly, and adjusted the quilts that had slipped from his neck.

"He goin' to be all right. No cause to fret," the young man announced on his return. "But we got to stay the night out. Ain't no other way. Reckon you kin sleep us?"

"Course, course," Maxwell said hospitably. "Ain't no other way. Wouldn't hear of you goin' out in this dark, rainy night."

"Then the doctor kin look at Miz Maxwell, come mornin'," said Willis by way of excusing the need to remain.

"The chil' done come," said Hammond. "Ain't needin' him now."

"I could of kotched the baby jest as good as Murrey; I helpin' him with so many, I know jest how on'y he won't have it yet awhile. Afeared, I reckon, afeared I goin' to crowd him out."

"I ain't a-blamin' you none," Hammond allayed the apprentice's uneasiness. "Blamin' anybody, I blamin' him."

Willis watched with anguish as Memnon helped the old man to rise from his chair, heard him protest profanely at the move to lead him to the supper room, glanced askance at the difficulty he had cutting his ham, but kept silent. Lucretia Borgia, with the supper, made up for what she deemed the scantiness of the dinner prepared by Dite and Ellen. The talk was as usual about the price of cotton and the price of slaves.

In the return to the sitting-room, Willis was forced to curb his impulse to offer support to Maxwell, whom he had heard upbraid the Negro for seeking to help him on the way toward the dining-room. The old man's frailty excited the boy's sympathy and his desire to exercise his healing arts, but he respected the older man's reticence about his malady.

"I knowed it was comin', this rain, knowed it in my han's an' knees," said Maxwell, rubbing with his right hand the knuckles of his left, as he sank into his chair. "Rain a-comin', my rheumatiz backs up on me, ever' time."

"You right bad," said Willis.

"Yes. That the cause of me takin' all them toddies. Helps me, seem like," sighed Maxwell, accepting a glass which Meg had brought him.

"Corn licker for rheumatiz better outside than in," Willis suggested. "Better rubbed on than drunken," Maxwell's observation had given him the cue he had sought. He sidled his chair toward the patient, placed his hand upon his brow, felt the pulse, asked to see his tongue, all without concept of what he wanted, to learn—mere gestures of diagnosis.

Maxwell relished rather than resented the attention. "I'm betterin', betterin' right along—on'y tonight, this rainin'." He shook his head. "I dreenin' it, dreenin' it through my feet, into this buck here." He reached his glass down to Alph, sprawled on the floor beside his chair and said, "Better take a swallow, boy; you be needin' it afore mornin'."

Willis looked doubtful. "It may be he goin' to git it, git it bad. Only that ain't a-goin' to git you shet of it. It jest dreen into him, not out of you," he explained authoritatively. He reached down and felt the young Negro's brow solicitously.

"You reckon he gittin' it? Feel anythin'?" Maxwell asked anxiously.

"Not yet; an' even if he had, it don' mean you sheddin' it."

"Might as well die, I reckon," Maxwell added.

"Now, Papa," Hammond interposed. "You all riled about it comin' a girl. Whenever Papa git riled, his achin' gits worser."

"Whut that got to do with it? My achin' is not in my head," Maxwell bristled. "It in my han's, an' feet, an' all over me."

"Rheumatism?" Willis pushed his chair back from the patient in resignation. "I don' know. I ain't come to the part in the books yet. That is away over under 'R'. But I'll git there. Jest wait. An' when I do——" His promise was only implied, but it gave the invalid some hope.

"You think rubbin' with corn——?" asked Maxwell tentatively.

Willis shrugged his uncertainty.

"Serpent oil? That would be better," Hammond expressed his opinion.

"That stink so bad. I'd sooner ache," Maxwell breathed.

"Serpent oil! Serpent oil! Doctor Mulbach's, or whoever's? That ain't jest only goose grease—of course, flavoured up to make it smell an' coloured green. It ain't never been near no snake. It the rubbin' whut does it, whut make it work," declared Willis with some indignation.

"It say on the bottle, right on the bottle——" Hammond defended the remedy.

"Whut an' if it does say?" Willis scoffed. "Kin make up anythin' and print it on the bottle. Ask Doc Murrey if it ain't goose grease."

Hammond preferred to believe the maker of the nostrum rather than this callow tyro. All doctors, he told himself, disparaged remedies that could be obtained without their sanction.

"I ain't usin' it, even an' if——" Maxwell affirmed with finality. "One more toddy an' I reckon I better go up. Jest one won't drunken you, Doctor Willis, an' it will warm you, retirin'."

To be called 'Doctor' flattered Willis and he was tempted to acquiesce, but thought of Murrey and shook his head. "Thank you, suh, I don' aim to be like him that a-way," he said.

"I reckon how you don' crave no wench to pleasure with, neither," said Hammond. "I was jes' a-thinkin' which one."

Willis felt his white face burn with blushes to the roots of his hair. He had heard of the custom of many plantations of providing guests with a woman for the night, but he had not previously encountered it. At Bankside his mother's scruples forbade such dalliance within the house. Of course, what occurred furtively in the cabins, she did not know about and did not care.

"I reckoned I sleepin' with Doc Murrey," he evaded a direct answer. "Ain't hardly room an' he drunk an' spread out."

"We got another bed. Ain't no call to double," said Hammond.

"Well, in that case, an' if you got a clean young yaller," Willis faltered.

"I was thinkin' of Dite," Hammond said to his father.

"An' if you not wantin' her your own self no more," Maxwell nodded.

"I got me Ellen," said Ham. "Dite, she young, she light, an' she not musky."

"When I say 'clean', I meanin' the clap. She ain't got the clap?" specified Willis.

Hammond laughed. "None of our niggers got it, an' none ever had it," he boasted.

"It goin' aroun'," asserted Willis, and his blush subsided as he saw that it was unobserved in the candlelight.

"It always goin' aroun'," said Maxwell, rising, and rousing Alph. He called loudly for Memnon, who came to help him to bed.

Hammond settled Willis in the bedroom at the end of the hall, next to his own, and returned to the kitchen to summon Dite.

The girl giggled. "You reckon he goin' to have me? Whut I goin' to do with my sucker?"

"I keep him good," Lucretia Borgia volunteered. "He wantin' suck, I give it to him. Now, go'long, like Masta say. The young white gen'man right nice. I noticin' him durin' supper. Course, he young." Willis's youth justified the falling of the mantle upon Aphrodite instead of upon herself.

The following morning Doctor Murrey arose, fully sobered after his debauch. He accepted heartily Maxwell's invitation to drink before breakfast and downed his whisky undiluted. He insisted upon seeing the child he had come to deliver and praised its beauty, although no parts of it were visible except the tiny wrinkled, red face and the dainty hands. The eyes were closed in sleep and he did not see the strabismus. The naked and sturdy Old Mister Wilson was also asleep, in Big Pearl's other arm, and, although the Doctor did his full duty in his admiration of the white baby, his professional interest centred in the Mandingo.

"Heft it oncet, jest heft it," Maxwell urged.

"No good wakin' it," said the doctor, feeling the child's thigh.

"No harm. Jest heft it," insisted Maxwell, grasping the baby's ankle and drawing it from the mother's arm. The doctor laughed to hear the wrathful squall of the startled young thing and took the leg from the owner's hand, holding the boy from him to avoid being soiled. He jostled the baby to estimate its weight, which was greater than he had deemed possible.

"Fifteen—sixteen pounds," he estimated.

"More, more; bigger than that," Maxwell urged.

"Of course, the dam here is a burly varmint," observed the doctor, handing the baby back to Big Pearl and stooping to raise her skirt to admire the bulk of her leg.

"Had ought to see the stud buck. Purentee Mandingos, both on 'em," Maxwell boasted. "Both."

"I never studied up on the tribes," shrugged the doctor, "A nigger is a nigger, I always reckoned."

"All, only a Mandingo," pursued Maxwell. "They half rhinoceros, I guess; they that stout. But they gentle and biddable as a goslin'. Never git out of hand."

As Willis entered the room he was unable to curb his blush, but his bearing was manly to the point of truculence. He wondered whether Maxwell had told the doctor about Dite, not that he feared his anger but rather his raillery. The doctor was hardly in a position for indignation.

"Did he talk your leg off?" asked the doctor, slapping the boy on the shoulders. "Does usually. Knows all there is to know about ever'thin', thinks he does."

"I kin reckon. He right in'erestin'. Knowin' a lot, so young," Maxwell assented.

"I goin' to learn him to doctor, if he don't try to learn me," laughed Murrey. "Reads books; thinks he kin learn doctorin' out of books, tells me whut's in 'em. Got to learn it from sick folks, I always tellin' him. Ain't I, Willis?"

"He sayin' how he Willis Smith's boy. I know his papa," said

Maxwell. "Looks like him too, in daylight, same lengthy build, but better lookin', better put together."

"Yas, he is well set up—goin' to be when he stoutens out," the doctor nodded approvingly. "Mista Smith give him to me and said make him a doctor—the boy is set that a-way. And, by God, I will, if he don' try to go too fast."

After breakfast, the doctor sought to justify his futile visit by looking at the patient. Hammond led him and Willis to Blanche's room, where he found the girl sitting up in bed with a large breakfast before her. She shrank from the doctor, refusing to permit him to touch her, even to feel her brow for fever; anyway, it was apparent that she had none.

"Cain't I have a toddy, Doctor? Jest one," she begged. "Hammond, he won't give me none, and won't have the niggers stir me one."

"Best thing, best thing in the world," said the doctor. "All you wantin' of 'em."

"She havin' 'em all the time beforehan'," said her husband, "I reckon it time to stop. I not wantin' she should be——" Hammond checked himself out of consideration for the doctor's weakness.

"Havin' 'em before, she got to have 'em now. Cain't quit right off. Got to taper—taper slow. Liable to have fits otherwise. You don' want fits."

Hammond gravely acknowledged that he did not.

"That, toddies, hot as Miz Maxwell kin take 'em, an' her in bed, not gittin' out too soon is all, all she need," the doctor declared. "Good as new, ten days or two weeks."

Willis stood in the background, listening, learning, saying no word. Blanche's eyes lingered on him in admiration. She would not have shrunk from his touch. Lucretia Borgia had already told her that Dite had been Willis's bedmate and she was jealous of Dite's fortune.

The men went downstairs, but after a short while there was a knock on the bedroom door. Tense opened it to Willis, a steaming goblet in his hand. He had mixed and brought the toddy which Murrey had prescribed. Not trusting Tense to serve it, he carried it himself to the bedside, and with his left arm supported Blanche's waist as she drank from the glass in his right hand. Willis was unsure whether it was admiration for the girl's blondeness or his vocation as a healer that had prompted him to detach himself from the gentlemen and return to the room.

319

Blanche drained the glass slowly to prolong the apprentice physician's embrace of her body. Her breasts were filling up and beginning to itch. She was tempted to tell the young doctor about them and show them to him, but out of modesty refrained. Instead, grasping his hand in both of hers, she raised it to her brow and let it rest there. He asked to see her tongue, and then felt of her pulse, which beat rapidly. Later he laid his ear against her breast to listen to her heart. He was not sure of the symptoms he sought; he was merely playing at being a physician.

"You right good an' powerful kind," said Blanche. "I not afeared of you at all. I afeared o' the othern."

"There ain't no call to be afeared. I craves that you git well and up. That is all," the boy responded. "That toddy goin' to help you right smart."

"You reckon? I feels better a'ready," the girl declared. "I goin' to have 'em—all I craves of 'em. That whut that doctor done say. Wasn't it?"

Willis said that it was.

"Won' have you to hol' me up while I drink 'em though," said Blanche, surveying the standing boy.

"I comin' back, in passin' by, to see how you comin' on," the youth promised.

"Come soon, come often," Blanche urged.

Willis glanced at Tense before he stooped and kissed his patient.

As Tense showed him out the door, he seized her arm and guided her into the hall where, through her dress, he felt her immature breasts and patted her buttock.

"You good an' not tell nothin', whut I did, I goin' to ast your masta kin I have you next time I come. We have good time, pesterin'," he told the innocent girl.

Tense answered him, "Yas, suh, Masta, suh." There was no other reply to a white man.

Tense was not sure what she was not to reveal. She had seen the young man kiss her mistress, but did not know it was not a convention among the whites, whose nature and customs were inexplicable. Nor did she resent the young man's boldness to herself, which was a white prerogative, and besides she found it pleasurable, though vaguely disturbing.

In eight days Blanche was able to come down the stairs with Lucretia Borgia's aid. In the interval, she had quieted her impatience with toddies, which, in view of Doctor Murrey's advice, Hammond no longer denied her. He made it a practice to go to her room mornings and evenings, and, when he had time, at midday, but did not relish the chore, since the girl was always tipsy or peevish or both. He was, however, glad to find her sitting opposite his father in the sitting-room when he returned for dinner, even if she was sipping a toddy.

To her husband's inquiry, Blanche replied, "I reckon I strengthin' some. I reckon I is. I allow as these toddies, the doctor say about, helpin' me strengthen." The doctor's advice justified her drinking as much as she chose to drink.

Toward her child Blanche was, and remained, as indifferent as though she had not borne it. She ignored Big Pearl except to tell her to take one of the babies from her presence when it cried. This was usually Sophia, who failed to thrive. Old Mista Wilson, on the other hand, a glutton at the breast, grew and prospered and seldom cried. Once, when the boy's impatience of Big Pearl's breast excited him into a bit of crying, Blanche ordered the black mother to take him to the kitchen and spank him until he should give them some peace. Big Pearl was by no means reluctant, but her blows only aggravated the noise which endured until the baby fell asleep from exhaustion.

The favouritism the nurse showed for her master's child was not wholly sycophancy, but a true preference for the small, doll-like, white Sophia over the big, robust and self-willed, dusky Wilson. Big Pearl truckled to Blanche and cowered before her, but she loved Blanche's baby better than her own. She was unable to keep her thick lips from Sophia's face and body. She lifted her tenderly and cuddled her against her sturdy bosom to still her fretfulness, whereas to Wilson's occasional tantrums she was indifferent, lifted him as often by a single arm or leg as by his body, and cuffed him soundly whenever he annoyed her.

While Maxwell and Blanche sipped their toddies, Ham paid little heed to her frequent eulogies of Willis Smith and her speculation about why the boy had not kept his promise to come again.

"Not that I a-carin' an' if he don' never come, only he hadn't ought to say like that," she always wound up.

"They's lots of sickness aroun', an' with Murrey drunk, I reckon the boy is powerful busy," Maxwell replied. "I'd as soon have him as Murrey anyways, even an' if he ain't full-fledged."

"Ruther, ruther have him," sighed Blanche.

Blanche had been up two weeks when Lucretia Borgia one day accosted Hammond as he passed through the kitchen.

"I reckon you had better do somethin' about Dite, suh, Masta," she suggested. "She got somethin', sure has. Kotched it from that young white boy whut come a-doctorin'."

Hammond questioned Aphrodite. There was no doubt about her malady and only one person from whom she could have contracted it.

"The damn son-of-a-bitch," he ranted to his father. "Spreadin' the clap aroun', 'stead of curin' folks. Spreadin' it, jest a-spreadin' it. I feel like takin' my gun to Benson an' shootin' him dead."

"That Doctor Smith never do it. I know he never, Hammond," Blanche protested. "Ain't only a nigger, no way."

"Nigger or not a nigger, it could be all on 'em, ever' one we got," Hammond said, sinking to a chair, his face in his hands. "An' we keepin' our stock so clean. Never had nothin', nothin' before."

"Nev' mind, Ham," Maxwell sought to appease his son. "Take Dite's sucker offn her?"

"I shore did. I done that quick. I don' reckon he got it yet awhile."

"An' we sen' fer Redfield. He do somethin', dry it up, or somethin'," the father continued. "It ain't bad anyways. Half the niggers on half the plantations in Alabama git it one time an' another—not to say the white owners."

"That the reason he, that Smith, talk so much about the clap an' how he cure it—knowin' he got it his own self." Hammond rose and walked the floor to refrain from weeping.

"You'll be seein' Redfield, come Sat'day in Benson. Ast him. Tell him to stop by, passin' along."

"I was aimin' to put Dite and Mede together first thing, seein' the kind of suckers he bringin'," Hammond said. "Now we cain't."

Redfield lost little time. He came on Sunday morning, and after a toddy with the Maxwells, father and son, examined Dite. To the veterinarian it was something of a joke that the Maxwell slaves should have a venereal infection.

"Long time, long time you ain't had nothin', Mista Warren. I recollec' me back ten or twelve year ago you had a buck——" he harked back.

"Bought him, bought him my own self, had it a'ready," Maxwell nodded. "But I sol' him agin, 'fore he done nothin', 'fore he spread it aroun'. Only Ham don't crave to sell this one.

322

Aimin' to keep her, her the mother of his chil' an' all. Don't want he should sell his own flesh."

"Well, it soon wear out," Redfield predicted. "Ain't much to do with it, save not to spread it." He drew a packet of cloth from his pocket and added, "I brung along some dried weed the Widder gathered an' say it right good. She say it sovereign, in fac'. Me? I ain't sayin'. Might try it. Make a tea. It bitterer than gall."

"That Smith!" Hammond spat. "Him goin' to make him a doctor!"

"Might be anybody," argued Redfield. "You never had it. I have, many's the time; I reckon your papa—when he was young."

The gentlemen had returned to the sitting-room. Blanche's step was heard on the stairs, and it was necessary to change the subject. Meg brought more toddies, including one for Blanche who noted a momentary silence and wondered what the talk had been about.

Redfield did not tarry long, but at his departure Hammond insisted upon his looking at Mede, who was in excellent fettle, and at Mede's progeny, which won his enthusiastic approval.

Blanche did not have to wonder long what the talk had been about, since she learned the gist of it from the servants. Even then, however, she failed to understand the situation, since Dite was not confined to her bed. Blanche wished that the victim had been Ellen.

CHAPTER TWENTY-THREE

IT WAS a wet and windy spring. Many of the cotton seeds rotted and failed to germinate; large areas in the lowest ground had to be replanted. The plants that broke through the soil were yellow and unthrifty, but the weather did not deter the weeds and the ground was too wet to hoe. Hammond was displeased with the prospects for his cotton crop.

"Cotton? Whut's cotton?" chuckled the elder Maxwell to relieve his son's anxiety. "It's the nigger crop whut pays."

On days when it was impossible to hoe the fields, the slaves were permitted to idle, to work if they could in their own patches

323

of garden, or just to sit and doze or converse and laugh at each others' antics or sallies of such wit as they had—all but Mede. When there was no work for Mede, he was exercised. Hammond forced him to run in a large circle with a younger slave astride his shoulders, to jump and leap, to lift logs, to flex and twist his body, to wrestle with two less powerful slaves at the same time. The owner found relief from anxiety about cotton in watching the Mandingo labour and the slave never appeared to tire. Mede, magnificent though he had been when his master acquired him, had matured, broadened, and filled out during his year at Falconhurst, until he was now more handsome and formidable than ever. Hammond desired as many progeny from the boy as he could obtain, and from time to time delegated women to be his mates. The matings were supervised like those of other animals, as if the Mandingo had been a stallion or a bull. The girls sometimes made a giggling or pouting remonstrance to their master's presence, but Hammond was stern and Mede was unabashed. The docile slave thought of this surveillance as a master's right, if not duty, to control his every act.

Many of the cotton seeds that were believed to have perished finally came up and the resown areas had to be thinned. The yellow leaves of the cotton turned green under the sunshine, although the sickly plants never turned vigorous. Hammond's discouragement abated in the belief that his efforts had not all been wasted, that the crop would warrant chopping, though he knew he could not ask the exhausted soil of Falconhurst for a bountiful yield.

Hammond timed his trips to Benson to enable him to look in on the fights at Remmick's although his interest was desultory when he had no participant in the contests. He drank with the sporting men and laid small bets upon the fights without much caring whether he should win or lose. His prime purpose in attending was to remind the others of Mede's prowess, which he did with understatement and mild disparagement, lest it seem that he was boasting.

Hammond's habit was to go every week to the Post Office, a cubby hole partitioned from the back part of the grocery store, to obtain the *New Orleans Advertiser,* to which his father was a subscriber. There was seldom any other mail for him. However, early in June he found a letter addressed to himself. *H. Maxwell eskuir.* Hastily he tore it from its wrapper. It turned out to be a broadside, an advertisement of an auction. AUCTION, AUCTION,

it read in bold type. NEGROES, MULES, HORSES, PLOUGHS, WAGGONS
SATURDAY, JULY 7 AT THE COURTHOUSE BLOCK AT WAYNESBORO

Vended at public outcry to the highest bidder, without any
reserve, for cash, will be 32 NEGROES, 32, all sound and likely, men
women, boys, girls, 11 young mules, yearlings and older, 3 mares,
all good breeders, assortment of ploughs, wagons, buggies, etc., etc.,
from the estate of the late deceased EDWARD ALLEN. The heirs must
have money to settle debts, etc. This is a public opportunity to
secure prime stock at your own price. Never anything like it.
Come one, come all. (Signed) A. C. Murry, Auctioneer.

Hammond had no idea where Waynesboro might be, but he
was the only H. Maxwell in or around Benson and he knew it
was intended for him. He folded the broadside carefully, returned it to its wrapper and placed it in his pocket to show to his
father. The receipt of mail other than the newspaper was so
uncommon that any piece of it was always considered and
digested.

Maxwell read the advertisement carefully. "You goin'?" he
asked.

"No! Away out there, Waynesboro or whurever?" scoffed
Hammond.

"I don' know. I don' know," pondered the father.

"They short of money, seem like. Sellin' off."

"Seem like," Maxwell agreed. "Mebbe it useful you go see."

So in the end it was settled that Hammond should go to
Tennessee for the Allen auction. Blanche was elated when [she
heard of the plan.

"I got to have me new trogs," she announced enthusiastically.
"Miz Forsythe kin make 'em. I got to purty me up, goin' a-
visitin'."

"I don't know. We see," Hammond put his wife off. "That
kerriage, I don' know will it stan' another long trip. I'll see.
I kin go quicker alone, straddlin'. Besides, this is business. You
better stay home with Papa. That better."

Blanche wept. "I don' never git to do nothin' or go nowhure,"
she lamented. "You always gallivantin'. Won't never take me
along." She rose, sobbing, from the supper table and stalked
out of the room. In a few minutes her footsteps on the stair were
heard. That she should go to bed without her after-supper toddy
was unthinkable.

Father and son sat in silence a long while, then at length the older man brought himself to speak what had been on his mind for some time.

"You ain't doin' your duty, Son."

"Ain't? How ain't I doin' everythin'?"

"Blanche, I meanin'."

"I ain't done nothin' wrong."

"You ain't done nothin' right either," accused the father. "You wantin' a son. How you reckon you goin' to have one. Skylarkin' and pleasurin' with your nigger ever' night, an' lettin' your wife res' alone?"

"You say, your own se'f, a white don' relish pesterin'. Ellen jest a-savin' Blanche. You say it all right, em a-havin' Ellen. I don' care an' if it ain't."

"It all right a-havin' her, yes. On'y it not all right to be loony over her."

They said no more, but that night Hammond was last to bed and went to his wife's room. When he failed to come to his own bed, Ellen, feeling herself displaced and abandoned, as she had long believed was inevitable, cried herself to sleep.

Early next morning, however, Hammond invaded Lucretia Borgia's kitchen and found Ellen drying dishes. He walked to the table where she stood and encircled the girl with his arm. "That las' night is jest sometimes. You mine tonight, and hereon," he told her. "Don' you fret, don't you ever fret, Ellen. You mind, you mine."

Later Blanche came down to breakfast more affably than was her wont, and said nothing further about the projected trip. Her husband's word was final and she knew it. She drank more toddies than usual, and Maxwell didn't interfere. Hammond was out of the house, training Mede.

Blanche drowned her disappointment in hot toddies but kept silent about it. Maxwell, who enjoyed the girl's tippling companionship, backed her up. "She delicate, kind of like. She needin' it to give her stren'th," he said, and the husband said no more.

Wednesday was the fourth of July, and Hammond on Eclipse set out for Waynesboro. He carried in his saddlebags a bag of gold coins to purchase any slaves that should suit his fancy.

"The 'portant thing is young niggers," his father had told him, "We're short on 'em, needin' 'em."

"I ain't a-bringin' back no trash to feed. You always says your

326

own self you cain't make no money pourin' good vittles into puny stock."

The older man was pleased that his tutelage had borne fruit.

That Ellen, dressed as a boy, should depart an hour before her master and wait for him upon the highway was the father's plan. He saw no reason why Hammond should not take his slave with him if he wished, but he sought to protect Blanche from the rancour she would feel at the awareness that her husband preferred Ellen's company to her own. Blanche had not risen to see Hammond take his leave, and the ruse was wasted. She appeared to be resigned to his absence, since it left her free to drink as many toddies as she might want.

Just when her plan of revenge took shape she herself was never quite sure. Perhaps it began to seethe in her befuddled mind the night Hammond had decreed that she should remain at home and it may have been assuming a more definite form from that time forth.

The afternoon of Ham's departure, Maxwell fell into a doze and Blanche went to the kitchen to obtain a toddy about which he should not know. She felt that he was more censorious of her drinking than he professed and believed that she was justified in swigging one toddy about which he would never know. She found the kitchen filled with negroes—Lucretia Borgia, her brood, Memnon, Dite, Big Pearl and the babies, her own Tense —but she missed Ellen, of whose presence or absence her jealousy always made her aware.

"Whure at that Ellen?" the mistress demanded, addressing her question to anyone who might answer it. Since it was directed to no particular person, nobody replied, but rather an ominous hush fell over the Negroes. Blanche repeated the question, "Whure at, I say, is that Ellen?"

Lucretia Borgia waited for another to speak, but everybody left the answer to her. She hesitated and mumbled, "Ummm, I don't know, Miz Blanche, ma'am. I don' know whure she gone. She right here, time back." Lucretia Borgia had no will to betray her master.

Meg giggled and stifled his mixture of amusement and embarrassment with his hand over his mouth, whereat his mother slapped both his cheeks with the full leverage of her strong arm. The child was as loyal to Hammond as the woman, and if she had ignored his laughter, the woman, half drunk, would not have

327

seen it. Even half drunk as she was, she surmised what had occurred.

"Time back?" she asked, closing her eyes in her befuddlement. "How much time back? How long ago? Whure at she now? Whure she go to? Don' lie to me."

Memnon and Dite left the room, but Big Pearl sat stolidly, nursing her babies. The twins could not control their curiosity.

Lucretia Borgia's lower lip dropped into a pout, as she hummed rather than spoke the answer, "I don' know ma'am. I don' know, I tellin' you. I don' know."

"Well, I knowin'. She done gone with her masta. That whure she at. I know. You cain't tell me. I know," Blanche screamed, swallowing her hot toddy between breaths and pouring out another. "Ain't nothin' 'ceptin' a whore nigger, that whut she is, just a whore, with her red earrings. She don' care no more about Hammon' than about the blackes' buck on the plantation, 'ceptin' he kin fetch her red earrings to mark her hisn. Hisn! Now I know why he won't never take me along nowhures. You 'on't got to tell me. I know." Her voice rose in a maudlin crescendo until she shouted the final sentences as she left the kitchen, supporting herself by whatever furniture she could reach.

"Better go after her," Lucretia Borgia said to Tense. "Git her in bed."

The following day Blanche kept to her room, Although there was nothing to be said that they had not hashed over a hundred times before, Maxwell was disappointed that the girl did not come down to sit with him and drink her toddies. Once when he called for Meg to bring him a drink, Memnon brought it instead with the excuse that Meg had gone to carry one to his mistress. Maxwell surmised that Blanche's indisposition, whatever it might be, would not deprive her of her drinks. The July day was humid and through the distorted panes, he could see the heat waves rising from the ground in the butter-coloured sunshine. He was half stupefied with whisky and he intended to remain so until his son's return; it was the only anodyne for the emptiness of his heart, drained by Hammond's absence.

Blanche lay on her bed. She turned on her side and said to Tense, "Fetch me up here the bigges', blackes' nigger buck we's got on the place. That Mede nigger. He the one. Go, fetch him along here."

"Whut, ma'am, you wantin' him fer?" Tense had the temerity to ask.

"Nev' mind. Nev' mind. I say fetch him. I knowin' whut I goin' to do; I goin' to pay him back. That's whut."

"Masta not goin' to like. He not leavin' no fiel' nigger come right in the house," Tense demurred.

"I say fetch him, didn' I, nigger?" the mistress demanded. "When I says do somethin', you do it. Hear me? You listen to me!"

"Yessum, mist'ess." Tense started to go.

"Fetch him through the kitchen and up the steps quiet like. Quiet, you hear? Ifn that ol' man a-snoozin' down there in that settin' room hear you comin', I goin' to tear you down. Tear you down, you hear?"

"Yessum, mist'ess. I be still as I kin," promised the slave girl.

"You make noise or leave that Mede make noise, I goin' to shuck you down an' lash you within an inch of your life. You hearin'? You listenin'? Now go and fetch him. Tell him I said."

Tense went. She found Mede stretched naked on his bed, half asleep, with Lucy, her baby in one arm, standing over him, fanning his hot body with a frayed palmleaf fan which had been discarded by the masters. Tense delivered her summons.

"What she want of me? What mistress want?" Mede was incredulous, for he had sensed his mistress's hatred of him. "I'm afeared," he admitted. "I ain't got no leave to go in that big house."

"Mist'ess say. I tellin' you come along. White folks say," said Tense impatiently. "Mist'ess drunken, an' I reckon she cravin' somebody to pleasure her."

"No!" Mede exclaimed with horror and fear. "I ain't goin'. My masta be mad. He shoot me dead, Masta Hammon'. An' mist'ess don' like me no how."

"She say——" argued Tense.

"You got to do whut you told," declared Lucy.

Mede trembled as he got to his feet and pulled on his pants and shirt.

"Masta goin' to slice me an' feed me to the buzzards," he said, knowing it to be literally true.

"Like, it ain't whut mist'ess wantin' at all," Lucy opined. "She white, mist'ess is. She ain't a-cravin' no big, black lummox like you."

"That whut she want an' you doesn't do it, she goin' to tell

329

Masta you tried to rape her. I knows," said Tense, shaking her head. "I knows. Ain't nothin' mist'ess won't do. She lie about you soon as look at you. Come along."

"I won't do it. I ain't a-goin' to," Mede protested as he followed Tense between the cabins and across the entryway and into the house.

The Negroes in the kitchen were amazed to see the giant Mandingo following the yellow girl, whom they knew to be executing her mistress's command. Meg followed the pair and saw them ascend the stairs. Dite looked in quandary at Lucretia Borgia, who only raised her brows. Big Pearl laughed aloud and opened her dress for Old Masta Wilson to nurse.

On the stairs, Tense cautioned Mede to be quiet, but he was unable to avoid the creak of the steps under his heavy tread. In the upper hall he stepped aside for the girl to lead the way to their mistress's room.

"Now, git outn here, nigger, and wait," said Blanche to her maid. "Wait till I calls you. An' don't you be snoopin' and a-listenin'. Hear?"

Tense admitted that she heard. She went out, closed the door, and sat down on the top step of the stairs, her face in her hands. Of the details of what occurred in the room, Tense was never sure, but she formulated imaginings which she assumed to be fact and which were as vivid to her as if she had been present and had seen and heard all that took place. She was terrified, for she knew that, however innocent she might be in the execution of her mistress's commands, her master's wrath would explode against the innocent as well as the guilty if he should ever learn or even suspect Blanche's philandering with the Mandingo. Tense did not love Blanche and it was not Blanche's fate that caused her to tremble, but rather her own and that of all the Negroes on the plantation. They would be the victims of the master's terrible vengeance.

There remained the task of getting Mede silently down the stairs and back to his cabin without the cognizance of the elder Maxwell. Time passed, Tense knew not how much.

At length Blanche's door opened and Mede emerged, walking stealthily. He passed her silently, making his way alone down the stairs without speaking. She looked at him and saw red jewels in his ears, the earrings her master had brought her mistress from Natchez. As he passed her at the head of the stairs, a drop of blood fell from his ear upon the carpet. Blanche had pierced his ears and inserted the earrings without waiting for the apertures to heal.

Might the gift of the earrings have been the purpose of the summons of the Mandingo into the house? Tense believed that it was not. How often in Blanche's absence had she taken those earrings from the drawer in which they lay and turned them in the light to watch them glitter! How she had coveted them for herself. She believed that with them in her ears she would be as beautiful as Ellen and perhaps might become her rival for her master's affection.

With a cloth Tense wiped the drop of blood from the carpet and, going toward Blanche's room, she felt others under her bare feet and cleaned them up. She entered the room; it stank of the serpent oil with which Mede was anointed, but the windows stood open and Tense did not know how to cleanse the stench from the room.

Blanche appeared elated, triumphant. She ordered Tense to have Meg fetch her a toddy, and when he came with two drinks instead of one, she was, despite the warmth of the day, lacing herself into her heavy brown dress.

"Mede done gone?" Meg asked knowingly. "I stirred one fer him too."

"Mede? What you knowin' 'bout Mede, nigger boy? Mede ain't bin here. I ain't seen him," Blanche protested. Suddenly in her guilt, all her old distrust and fear of Meg returned, she caught in his eye the half sinister look that Hammond never saw. She remembered how she had accused the boy of being a conjure on that first ride to Falconhurst after her wedding.

The boy laughed aloud and, impudently lifting the second drink from the tray, sat down on the bed to drink it. "Whut Masta goin' to say when he find out? Whut Masta say?" he taunted. Blanche felt sick with apprehension.

"Your masta ain't needin' to know nothin'. Ain't his business nohow. Nigger, don' you tell him. Don' you tell him. Don' you go stickin' your nose in." Blanche made a show of confidence but failed to conceal her fright from the boy. "Nigger, I's tellin' you, an' you go an' blabber anything about me an' Mede, I's tellin' you, I goin' to have you skinned clean down with the snake."

Meg snickered at the threat. "Who goin' to skin me, Mist'ess? Who goin' to skin me?" he taunted. "I reckon you goin' to be good to me now, so I ain't a-goin' to tell. You do whut I say. You gives me anythin' I wants, Mist'ess."

The mistress capitulated. "Whut you wants, chil'? Whut you wants I should do?" Hard as she tried to appear calm, the tone of the questions betrayed Blanche's anxiety.

The boy lay back on the bed and laughed. "I tellin' you," he said, "you goin' to do whut I says."

"You ain't a-goin' to tell?" Blanche half stated, half questioned. She reached down and, drawing the youth to her, embraced him.

"I ain't an' you does to me whut you doin' with Mede—any time, whenever I says," Meg exulted. "Tonight, after they all in bed, I come an' we pleasure?"

"Tonight," Blanche conceded. "But come quiet like an' don' tell nobody."

She finished dressing and went downstairs to join her father-in-law.

He roused from his nap at her entrance and thought of toddies. Meg brought them with his wonted deference but, unseen by his master, challenged his mistress with a single look directly into her eyes.

Maxwell sniffed as he accepted his goblet. "Whut that stink?" he demanded. "You stenchy, boy?" He grasped Meg and, pulling him toward him, smelled him over and found him clean. "Somethin' stink," he repeated. "Smell like that Doctor Mulbach's Serpent Oil. Send here your mammy, boy."

When Lucretia Borgia entered the room panic seized Blanche, who, aware that the cook knew what had occurred, shrank back into her chair and averted her glance. Lucretia Borgia stood awaiting the question.

"Somethin' stinkin'," declared her master. "That Doctor Mulbach's, smell like."

Lucretia Borgia sniffed audibly three times. "I cain't smell nothin', suh, Masta. I reckon I stopped up or somethin'," she excused her failure.

"You ain't had that Mandingo in the house?" Maxwell demanded sternly.

"No, suh, Masta, suh, No, suh, I ain't had him." Lucretia Borgia looked fixedly at Blanche as she shook her head.

Blanche was grateful for the generous denial from the woman, for whom she had never concealed her dislike. But it was not she whom Lucretia Borgia was shielding; rather it was Mede and all the Negroes of the plantation.

"Sure smell like that Doctor Mulbach's," reasserted Maxwell.

"The wind, it a-comin' from that a-way," Lucretia Borgia nodded toward the cabins. Despite the absence of wind from any direction, Maxwell accepted the explanation and dismissed the cook.

Blanche was reassured; she was safe. After Mede, she did not fear or dread her night with Meg, who, only two or three years younger than herself, she still considered as an infant. He was at least clean and emitted only his racial odour. She put from her mind the thought that henceforth she would be at his mercy, in constant terror of his tongue.

The allure of the white woman for Meg was that she was white and forbidden, the fascination of breaking a taboo. The plantation abounded with black and yellow girls, whose seduction would, if discovered by his master, have provoked a scolding, or even a possible switching, nothing more, and they would have assuaged his ripening lubricity. But he was his mother's son. The passion for dominance which she assuaged by efficient service to her white masters and ruthless mastery of the other slaves he indulged by blackmail of his mistress. He knew the hazard—death.

Two days later, the day of the auction, Blanche sent again for Mede, this time with less temerity. She abominated him no less than ever, but the compulsion to embrace him stemmed in vengeance for her husband's dalliance with Ellen. Hammond would never know, but the revenge was none the less sweet. Blanche resolved that Mede should be at her disposal, that she would enjoy him (or pretend to enjoy him) when she would. With rings in his ears, she had marked him for her own.

Mede felt no sense of triumph. He was in terror lest his master should learn of his dalliance with Blanche, which he had not solicited and did not want, but white commands he had to obey. He knew the risk as well as Meg; but his mistress's procedure was so peremptory that there seemed less peril in complying with her desires than in denying them. Even in the most intimate of their embraces, he sensed her scorn for his blackness, her contempt for his race, her loathing for his person, but, as well, her satisfaction with his maleness.

Hammond returned from Wayneboro in a bad temper because he had not found there any suitable young slaves to buy. The change in his wife's temper did not strike him immediately upon his return from his journey, but he soon began to notice that she was more genial and generous, amiable and kind than he had come to expect of her. She was up of a morning, and complained not at all of her physical ills nor of the treatment he accorded her. Except for two or three, sometimes four innocuous toddies a day, she had ceased her tippling and she seemed to desire no more whisky than she took. She was considerate of and gracious to the servants, who responded to her reformation with efforts and desires to please her greater than obligation had ever begotten.

Even in her rare contacts with Ellen there was no show of irascibility. She called Big Pearl into the sitting-room and played with Sophy, in whom formerly she had shown no interest. Hammond was, of course, pleased, but could only speculate what had occurred to work such an alteration in the girl's nature in his ten days' absence. Whatever it might have been, it engendered his affection, and he found himself dividing his nights between his wife and Ellen, who, however sorrowful when her lover failed to appear, felt herself secure in his love and took no umbrage. Aware as she was of his marital obligations and his desire for a legitimate son, she adored him the more that he should do at least part of his duty to his wife.

When Hammond saw the red earrings in Mede's ears, his first emotion was anger, which was soon replaced by amusement. He knew at once that it was Blanche's move of retaliation for his gift to Ellen, but it was so jejune, so futile, that it caused him to smile.

"Whure you git them bangles, boy?" he asked, knowing the answer.

Mede was terrified to tell, but dared not refuse. "Mist'ess, suh, Masta, please suh," he mumbled, hanging his head.

"Whut she say when she give 'em to you? Who stuck the holes in your ears? Who put 'em on you?"

"She say wear 'em, not take 'em off, suh."

"Well, we goin' to take 'em off. Whut fer, you reckon, a fightin' nigger wear bangles in his ears? Jist somethin' to grab aholt of an' tear your ears off. Lean down here," Hammond ordered, and began to unscrew the nut that held the jewel in the left lobe. "Who punch that big hole, and whut he do it with? Wasn't no call to make it so big."

"Mist'ess, suh. She do it with eatin' fork," the Negro explained, flinching.

When the master turned to the other ear, he found it inflamed, swollen, and festered. "This one sore, like," he said. "Jes' about rotted off. Whyn't you do somethin', take it out or somethin'?"

"Mist'ess say wear 'em, suh, Masta, please. I asted her please take 'em out, but she wouldn't. She say wear 'em."

"I hopin' that ear ain't a-goin' to rot. Jes' about spoil you. Bad enough havin' them big holes," said the master, and pressed the pus from it, at which the slave grunted in his pain. "Don' you ever let nobody do nothin' like that to you agin. A fightin' nigger!"

The jewels were now useless. Having been in a Negro's ears, no white woman could ever be asked to wear them. Hammond looked at them as they lay in his hand, speckled with dried blood, and then he cast them into the weeds at the side of the cabin. Lucy saw where they fell, and later retrieved them. She secretly placed them among her trinkets, the silver dollars she had received at the births of her children, a crinkled small sheet of foil, and a brass breast-pin, but she never wore them.

"Mus' have stopped trainin', the minute I turn my back on you," the master said suspiciously, feeling the slave's thighs and abdomen, "All soft and out of kilter."

"No, suh, Masta, suh," Lucy defended Mede. "He work. He work good, all a time you gone, savin' when that ear make him sick. I make him work."

Lucy, Hammond knew, was truthful. "Well," he said, "we got to do somethin' 'bout them legs an' that sof' belly. Lift Shaz here up on your back an' start a-runnin' with him right now."

Mede was relieved to get away. He knew that his master's mere suspicion would be dire. But Hammond did not suspect. Of course, he knew, even without Mede's confession, that the earrings had come from Blanche, a foolish, simple girl's essay at vengeance, but that there was more to the story never entered his imagination. That his wife, a white woman, should have willing carnal commerce with a Negro, any Negro not to consider the brutish, burly Mandingo, was literally unthinkable.

That night at supper he let her know that he was aware of her prank when he told her, "You most ruint my bes' buck, punchin' his ears. One of 'em mayhap rot off yet. It do, an' it goin' to lessen his price five hunderd dollars. I don' want no one-eared nigger aroun' to look at."

Blanche was duly alarmed. "I never meant nothin'. I never thought it would rot him."

"I knowin' you never," Hammond forgave her. "On'y don' do it no more. A white lady fingerin' a nigger buck ain't nice."

335

The injury to Mede's ear healed, and the boy was unblemished except for the large punctures. The Mandingo's value was not diminished; in fact it grew with the boy's maturity, the increase of his strength, and the intensity of his training, to say nothing of the trend of slave prices in general.

CHAPTER TWENTY-FOUR

THE SUMMER days grew hotter and the humid nights provided little respite from the torture of the days. There was scant rain that year, and the sunshine which followed an infrequent shower seemed even more intolerable than that which preceded it. The Tombigbee ran low in its channel and an odour of decay emanated from its banks. The cotton, slow in its beginning growth, was further stunted by the heat and drought, which only stimulated the purslane and other weeds which luxuriated between its rows and which the field slaves sweated to keep under control. Seldom sanguine, Hammond was now despondent as he rode between the rows of cotton to assess the prospect of their yield and to search the brazen sky for the hint of a cloud. Now and again he checked his horse to give a half-hearted admonition to some hoe-hand about the weeding, but the cotton was scarcely worth the chopping. Moreover, Hammond was concerned about the draft of slaves for market the ensuing fall. There would be three or four men ready for sale, possibly five or six, but, for the rest, they lacked maturity and it seemed desirable to hold them over for another year.

This, indeed, was the real purpose of Doctor Redfield's visit to Falconhurst early in August, purportedly a casual call to inquire about Maxwell's health. The veterinarian had relished so heartily his expedition to Natchez the previous fall that he wanted to make sure of his inclusion in the party for the forthcoming trip—this time probably to New Orleans, since the fears of cholera had abated. It was his plan to introduce the subject casually since he did not wish to betray his concern, he had hardly finished drinking his first toddy with his host when they were interrupted by an unwonted clatter and bustle in the driveway. Redfield hastened to the open window.

There was no such equipage anywhere in the countryside, and Redfield knew them all, as the four-in-hand coach which met his vision. It was of another era and, from the dust with which it was covered, appeared to have come from afar. Dark red in colour, ornamented in gold leaf, with silver handles on the door, it was drawn by four stout horses, three chestnuts and one grey, with a spare chestnut ridden by an outrider.

"Who this?" he asked his host, assuming that the visitor had been expected and fearing that his own visit might be inopportune. "Ain't nobody I knows of got anythin' like it. Must have come a ways."

Maxwell got to his rheumatic legs as rapidly as he was able and joined Redfield at the window. "Mus' be a mistake," he said. "Ain't no fine-haired folks like that a-comin' here," he said and called to Memnon.

The outrider, a stalwart yellow boy, sat his mount, uncertain whether to get down; another yellow boy crawled from the box beside the black, middle-aged driver and went toward the door. All were attired in sand-coloured liveries, faced with blue, and silver buttoned. All wore tight breeches, white silk stockings, and silver buckled shoes. Except for the grey dust on their cocked hats and the shoulders of their coats, they were neat as they were impressive. Memnon reached the front door and held it open and Maxwell hurried into the hall in time to see the boy from the box twist the handle of the coach door and an octoroon boy emerge, smart in a suit of light grey silk, ruffled shirt, and silk stockings, who waited beside the door to hand out another person. There was a pause while the man inside the coach seemed to be putting on his coat.

First an arm and hand appeared which the Negro in grey grasped deferentially to help its owner to alight in safety. Next came a leg in light blue trousers strapped under varnished boots, and at last the whole man, clad in a long grey coat, which he was at pains to adjust and from which the Negro flecked a spot of dust and smoothed a wrinkle while the white man rubbed the fatigue of sitting from his knees.

He was a little man, daintily made, whose hunched back Maxwell thought must be due to long sitting in the coach until the man began to walk and he saw that it was a permanent hump. This lack of lateral symmetry, along with a rapid mincing, gave to his gait an aspect of trying to fly with one wing broken. So at least, it struck Maxwell. It was not as if he were unable to walk without assistance, but his Negro grasped his elbow lightly to guide his locomotion. His straight, long hair, what was left of it

337

for he was balding, hung about his ears and over his collar. Small, sharp, black eyes flashed from his swarthy face, which was so marked with sharply defined carmine spots on the cheekbones that Maxwell suspected they were painted there.

"I seek Mister Maxwell," he said, precisely, accenting the last syllable and toying with a soft, small moustache with a heavily jewelled hand that was fragile in its length and slenderness. Maxwell was unsure whether the gesture was diffidence or a display of his diamonds.

"I'm Maxwell, at your service, suh. Walk in, please, suh, and set," Maxwell put on his politest manner. "Have Meg stir us a toddy, all 'round," he told Memnon and led the way toward the sitting-room, followed by the stranger, who was escorted by his slave. "Who have I got the honour, suh?" he asked before sitting down.

"It is that I am Mister Roche, R-O-C-H-E," the stranger spelled the word out. "Roche, the name of my mother, from New Orleans and La Allouette Plantation, below the city. Jules Adrian Marie Roche, in fact the natural son, so I am told, of the late Governor El Baron de Carondelet, who made provision for my rearing and for my fortune. I am then in part Spanish; my mother, she was French." He spoke slowly, separating his words and speaking them distinctly as if in fear that he would not be understood. He appeared to formulate his sentences in another language and to translate them hesitatingly into English, which was indeed the fact. His only error was in the stresses which he transferred to final syllables of his words.

Maxwell was taken somewhat aback by the man's candid confession of his bastardy, in which he seemed to take pride. The host took little cognizance of the name, and did not speak it when he introduced Doctor Redfield and waved the gentlemen to seats.

The grey-clad lackey took up a rigid position behind his master's chair.

The man came directly to the point. "You possess twins boys, is it not so?"

It sounded like an accusation to Maxwell, who was quick to deny it. "I only got one son, name of Hammon'. His mother was a Hammond, gal of old Theophilus, an' he never had no twin. You comin' to the wrong place, wrong man."

Roche smiled and stroked his moustache again. "I do not make myself understood well. My English, it is not good. I am not

338

meaning your son, but I have been told you had twin servants, very beautiful twin boys."

"Oh, them. Yes, I reckon we got a span of saplin' bucks, likely yallers, but not nothin' beautiful, like you sayin' about 'em. Likely an' soun', but not beautiful. They bucks, an' it ain't fitten bucks be beautiful."

"Then I have been misinformed. But is it perhaps that I may behold them?" The man leaned forward in his chair as he spoke.

"I reckon you kin," said the owner. "One a-comin' now with toddies. Othern around somers. Jist alike. You seen one, you seen the othern."

"Like as buckshot," Redfield interposed. "I bin comin' to see Mista Maxwell sence before they born, bein' his vetenary, an' I ain't tell 'em one from other."

"They ain't fer sale though." Maxwell set his mouth determinedly. "Look at 'em all you wantin'."

Meg served his master first, then Redfield, lastly the elegant stranger who accepted the drink and set it aside, then grasped the boy and pulled him toward him. Meg looked at his master for permission to resist.

"Oh, but it is you who are mistaken; he is beautiful, beautiful, beautiful," the man in his enthusiasm emphasized; and then modified his evaluation, "barring spots or scars on his body under his raiment."

"Not a pimple, not a pimple," Maxwell asserted pridefully. "Meg," he commanded, "kick off them trogs an' let the gen'leman look at you. Course, I sayin', they ain't fer sale."

"I thought you raised for the market. I was informed," said the Frenchman.

"We do. You was told correct. But not this span. They worth more later, growed. It hard a-buyin' saplin's to raise in this market. Niggers so high."

The sleek adolescent stood naked for his examination, unembarrassed by his nudity, enjoying the attention he was receiving. He raised his hands over his head to permit the stranger to view his body, and capered to show his agility.

Roche was ecstatic: "He is perfect, perfect. I must have him. I will pay. I will pay much."

"No, I reckon not," Maxwell shook his head. "Hammond, that my son, is right fond of this one, and anyways I wouldn't bust up the span. I reckon we wouldn't take five thousand fer 'em, the pair of 'em."

339

"An' worth it, every cent and dollar of it," Redfield put in, sensing a sale.

"And I pay it. I make you a tender, an offer, gold, cash—if the other is as good and beautiful like this one."

The price was preposterous for two fourteen-year-old boys, but Maxwell assumed an air of disinterest in the belief that he could obtain a larger one, if only this fatuous Frenchman had the money which his garb, his jewels, his slaves, and horses, and coach betokened. "I sayin' I wouldn't take five thousan', not that I would. They ain't fer sale," declared the owner.

"How much? How much do you entreat?" insisted Roche, his hand on Meg, to whom he turned. "How should you love it, to be my minion?"

"A house nigger?" asked the boy, shrugging in an effort to disengage himself. "I ain't no fiel' nigger."

"Of course you are not," said Roche.

"An' you feeds your niggers good?"

"All you want to eat."

"I likes to stay Masta Ham's nigger."

"Nev' mind," the owner curbed the slave, whose fate was not for him to choose or even to speculate.

"Is it that I may see the other, the twin for this?" Roche urged undiscouraged.

"Meg, you find Alph, whure he at, an' you fetch him here," Maxwell commanded. "You hear me?"

Meg was glad to get away and bounded out of the room.

"There remains the price," said the stranger, beckoning to his slave for help in rising to his feet and resuming his chair. "Six thousand, say; would that interest you?"

Maxwell shook his head, stubbornly. "I reckon we goin' to keep 'em, suh," he said, knowing that he would accept the price, but determined to get all that the buyer would give.

"Mista Maxwell, here, right fond of them two. Uses the othern to dreen his rheumatiz, doesn't you, Mista Warren? Or mayhap this one. I kin never tell 'em," Redfield reinforced the owner.

Meg returned, dragging his brother with him. Roche knew that the unclothed twin had been the one that he had seen; otherwise they seemed alike. He summoned Alph toward him and felt in his mouth; then, without rising, he asked to have him stripped. His slave, at the master's behest, came from behind his chair to hold the boy for his inspection. He manipulated the

340

joints and felt the child over. At length he stood the twins together, and found no difference in them except a somewhat deeper navel on Alph and a freckle on his shoulder which Meg did not have. His examination of the second boy was more cursory than of the first, but he was satisfied.

"I will give seven thousand, Monsieur. That is my last offer, seven thousand. It is enough—all that two such are worth," Roche made a show of finality.

"They cheap at the price. I'd give it, an' if I had it, handy, in cash that is. Mista Maxwell wantin' cash." Redfield knew that Maxwell would be unable to resist such a sum of ready money.

"I tell you whut," Maxwell hesitated. "Make it five hunderd more, seven thousan' and five hunderd, an' we deal. You a-cravin' 'em so, I cain't afford to not 'commodate. But cash, mind. Seventy-five hunderd, an' not a dollar less."

"You are mine," Roche turned to the young slaves. "Mine, mine. Seventy-five hundred, it is little enough. I knew that I should buy them, after Mista Brownlee told me about them more than a year ago. He endeavoured to purchase them for me, you remember."

"Brownlee, that houn' dog. He wouldn't offer nothin'. Had to run him off the plantation. He a swindler and a nigger stealer. Low down, low down." Maxwell was not certain enough of Brownlee's part in the hold-up to include that in his accusation.

"They tellin' he die, that Dealer Brownlee," observed Redfield.

"I do not know about his death. I have not heard," Roche declared.

Hammond came. He kissed his father, greeted Redfield and surveyed the strange assemblage.

"This my son Hammon', suh. Gen'lman come from New Orleans," Maxwell made the introduction. "I sellin' the twins. Reckon you not a-goin' to care."

"Lucretia Borgia say?" asked Hammond.

"Seventy-five hunderd dollars," said the father. "She git over. We give her two dollars, one fer each one of 'em."

"Lucretia Borgia?" questioned Roche.

"That they mammy," Hammond explained. "We promised not to sell these bucks withoutn her say."

"Oh, then they have a mamma? I must buy her also," Roche said with surprise, as if he had believed the twins had arisen parthenogenetically. "We cannot take them away from her. They will need her. I shall buy."

"We cain't sell Lucretia Borgia," Hammond declared. "She our cook; beside she nursin' a sucker."

"I will buy her," affirmed the Frenchman. "I will give her to her boys, a present to them."

"But she our cook, an' she runs things, jist about. We ain't a-sellin' Lucretia Borgia," repeated Hammond.

"I will buy her," Roche repeated.

"She a thirty-five hunderd dollar wench, her an' her sucker," Maxwell volunteered.

"But they are three, four, or five suckers in her yet," Doc Redfield softened the price.

"No matter. I will buy her," said the stranger. "Jason, you and Albert bring in that iron strongbox. You know where it is, at my feet in the coach."

Hammond had paid but a glance to the slave behind the chair and had failed to recognize him. At the boy's name, he looked at him. "Jason!" he cried. "Is that you, you varmint?"

"Yes, suh, Masta Ham, suh. It is me. Didn't you know?" The boy came forward, fell at Hammond's feet, embraced his legs, and began to cry.

"Whut you run fer?" asked Hammond. "Whure you get this buck?" he turned to Roche.

"You meanin' they carved you up, made you a capon?" Maxwell chuckled in derision. "Servin' you right fer runnin'."

"Brownlee! He was stole, stole from right here at Falconhurst. He Papa's nigger," Hammond exclaimed. "Whut fer you want to go off with Masta Charles?" He turned to Jason.

"Masta Charles told me, Masta, suh. He said I his," Jason explained. "I never knew he would, he and Mista Brownlee, treat me like they did." He wept and sobbed, head bowed in contrition, still clinging to Hammond's legs.

"You meanin' how they carve you up, made you a capon?" Maxwell chuckled in derision. "Servin' you right fer runnin'."

"I never ran, please, suh, Masta. Don't believe I ran. I never knew," pleaded the boy, wiping his eye with his hand.

"Brownlee gave me a bill of sale," Roche sought to vindicate himself. "I do not have it with me, but I will send it to you."

"No matter," declared Hammond. "He stolen from us and I claimin' him back. I goin' to keep him."

"Won't have him, won't have him back," said his father with resolution.

"But Papa," Hammond protested. "Mista Wilson——"

342

"I sayin' I won't have him, an' I won't. Let the gen'leman keep him. He come by him honest."

"But I promise Mista Wilson."

"Nev' mind," said Maxwell, spitting toward the cold fireplace. "Your new masta good to you, I reckon? You seem fat," Hammond temporized with his promise to care for the boy.

"Yes, suh, Masta, he is good, that is he used to be when he first bought me. Now, though, since I gettin' big and growin' hair, he makes me his waitin' nigger, his body servant, and he is strict, slaps me and has me whipped whenever I get careless."

Roche was unable to stop Jason's outpouring. "That will do," he said sternly. "I told you that you and Albert should bring that strongbox. Did not you hear?"

Jason slunk from the room, aware that he had said too much.

"That spoiled nigger lies," Roche protested in his own defence. "He is indeed my servant. I keep him for that. Twice he cut my face while shaving me, and I had him corrected with the whip—once, only once. I shall have to do it again to stop his lying mouth."

"Time comes, you got to use the snake," agreed Maxwell.

"Nigger ain't no worth till he welted up some," Redfield opined.

"We goin' ridin' in your kerriage?" Meg asked his new owner.

"You mine now, you understand? You are going with me," his new master assured him.

The two slaves brought the heavy iron chest and set it at their master's feet. Roche drew a key from somewhere about him, inserted it into the lock, and threw back the lid. The box, Maxwell could see, held a treasure in gold coins, loose, uncounted; he was unable to estimate them. He was for an instant displeased with the bargain he had made; he might have extracted a larger price.

Roche moved his fingers and calculated under his breath. "Seven thousand and a half for the bucks, thirty-five for the wench; eighty-five, ninety-five, ten five, eleven. Eleven thousand. That's right, gentlemen?"

"That about even us," asserted Maxwell. "What we 'greed on."

"Then help me to count it out, please, sir," the buyer appealed to Hammond. "I make mistakes."

Reluctant to place his hands on another man's money, Hammond nevertheless consented. He got to the floor beside the chest, one leg straight, the other doubled under him. He knew there were fifty twenties in a thousand, and confined himself to coins of that denomination. Each thousand dollars, he placed in a pile by itself. He counted seven piles, while Roche, by no means certain of himself, counted four thousand dollars into a single lot. Redfield looked on, resentful of not being included in the invitation to count the money. Once he reached down and picked up a coin, which he bit to make sure it was gold that was being so carelessly handled.

Roche pushed the coins he had counted in Hammond's direction. "Better count them," he said. "I am never sure." He did not recount what Hammond had counted, and did not fear being cheated.

When Hammond had certified the sum as correct, Roche toppled the stacked coins together and pushed them across the floor towards where Maxwell sat.

"But you ain't even looked at Lucretia Borgia," Hammond objected.

"That is the wench?" asked Roche. "I shall see her. She is their mamma. It does not matter." Before he closed the box on the remaining coins, he selected two golden eagles and pressed one into the hand of each of the twins. "Keep it to buy you something when we get to the city," he told the boys.

The gesture took Redfield aback. He believed that money was demoralizing to slaves. What could they buy with it that their masters did not provide? Food, clothes for their nakedness, primitive shelter—such were all they needed, all they knew what to do with. The slaves knew nothing of values; the coins might as well have been pennies. Alph held his gold piece in his hand and looked at it; Meg, for safe keeping, placed his in his mouth.

Roche locked the chest, and told Jason and Albert to return it to the coach. He rose and bowed from the hips towards Redfield and Maxwell. Placing his hands upon the shoulders of the naked boys, he guided them toward the hall.

"You wantin' papers," Hammond protested. "I make 'em and Papa, here, he sign."

With a gesture, the buyer declined any formality. "I deal with gentlemen," he said.

Maxwell suggested dinner which would be ready soon. "Jist a small collation, but right stayin' in the stomick."

The guest's regrets appeared real enough, but he excused himself. He was in haste; he must go. "But the wench, sir. Please bring the wench."

Hammond went to the kitchen to inform Lucretia Borgia that she had been sold.

The woman opened her great legs and faced him. "I ain't a-goin'," she said. "Sold! Sold! Who you reckon goin' to cook your papa's dinner? Who goin' to drive them sewin' wenches? Who goin' to run things here? I ain't a-goin'."

"You goin'. You sol'," Hammond affirmed. "Git you ready an' your sucker. You goin'. Got a good new masta. Treat you good. Me an' Papa, we git alon'. Don't git to think Falconhurst blow 'way 'cause you ain't here." The young man's stern words hid his emotions of parting from the woman who he knew loved him, who had been his champion through his childhood and his adjutant in his maturity. "And come out soon as you ready," he told her and retreated to avoid a show of tears.

Maxwell and Redfield had followed Roche to the gallery, and all waited for Lucretia Borgia to arrive. Albert, at attention, held open the door of the coach, and Jason stood behind his master, whose hands rested on the shoulders of the twins on either side of him.

Hammond, coming through the sitting-room, picked up the garments the twins had shed and carried them to the gallery. "You ain't a-goin' to carry them bucks without no clothes on," he told Roche. "Here they trogs be. Ain't a-costin' you any extry."

"My slaves don't wear raiment like that," the buyer scoffed. "I shall dress them when we reach the city. It is that the day is hot and I prefer them nude."

"They too big to go nekid," Hammond argued.

"They are more beautiful so. It will offend none to see angels without clothes."

Lucretia Borgia came, her baby on one arm, a bundle of clothing in the other. Her eyes were red, but she had wiped away her tears. Roche, who had bought her unseen, looked at her casually and without interest, felt her biceps and ran his hands over her back and buttocks.

"She is the mamma?" he asked rhetorically. "It is strange, is it not so, that such a goose should hatch swans?"

Dropping the bundle and resting her baby on it, the woman embraced and kissed the Maxwells, first the father and then the son. "I ain't goin' to ever see you-all no more, I reckon, an' you've been so good to me," she said.

Her new owner broke off her lamentations with, "Get in the

coach, wench. Henceforth, you belong to these boys. Do what they tell you!"

The boys looked at each other and then at their new owner with surprised approval. With their minds upon the ride in the coach, they dispensed with farewells. They sensed indulgence from this strange little crooked man whom they were to call master.

Lucretia Borgia and her child were first stowed in the coach on the forward seat, the woman's back toward the horses. Next, Jason handed in his master who settled himself in the middle of the rear seat and reached to receive the twins; he placed Alph on one side of him and Meg on the other. Lastly, Jason got in and sat beside Lucretia Borgia. The coach was crowded with its six passengers. Albert closed the door sharply and clambered to his place beside the driver as the horses wheeled and the outrider fell into his place with the leaders. The coach swayed as the horses broke into a gallop and the Maxwells stood on the gallery with Redfield and watched it disappear down the lane.

Pleased but baffled, Maxwell breathed, "Whut you reckon?"

"Whut I reckon? Whut I reckon is that you could a got more," Redfield answered his host's question literally. "That hunchback ninny was set, dead set on them bucks. He had money left. Didn't you see? Could a-took it all."

"Mayhap could," Maxwell conceded. "Could a leastwise kept the wench's sucker, only would a-begot a carryin'-on. It old enough fer weaning an' the Frenchie never looked at it, never know whether she got it."

"Ain't you pilfered him enough?" demanded Hammond. "Eleven thousand dollars fer three niggers—two on'y jist saplin's and a wench comin' to the end of her breedin', three, that is, addin' the sucker."

"Whut you reckon he wantin' 'em fer?" pondered Redfield. "Whut he goin' to do with 'em?"

"Kin grin' 'em up fer sausage, he a-wantin'. We all gotten our money," said Hammond with a toughness he did not feel.

The party entered the house and Memnon brought them toddies. Blanche, sure that the stranger had gone, came down the stairs, ready for dinner.

"Glad we shet of 'em. They too smart-alecky, too big fer they britches," she declared of the twins.

Hammond sat on the floor and ran the gold lovingly between his fingers, recounted it and stacked it again.

346

DITE DID her best in the kitchen. Lucretia Borgia had taught her to cook, but the family food, while it was still plentiful and good, lacked the savour that was the result of Lucretia Borgia's skill. Dite was unable to undertake the other tasks that Lucretia Borgia had carried on without apparent effort, and Hammond was compelled to issue rations to the slaves and assume such other chores as the former cook had vacated. He soon learned how valuable the woman had been, how shrewdly she ruled her fellows, and of what a load she had relieved his busy shoulders. He missed her not only for the work she had done but also for her wisdom and character, her obsequious aggressiveness, her domination of her domain. She had managed things well, and always in the Maxwell interest.

The labour performed by the twins had been much less important and their functions were absorbed by others. Memnon was again called upon to stir the toddies, and while Maxwell complained that the drinks were not so good as those prepared for him by Meg, it was really the child's efforts to put on an adult role that the master missed. Ellen served as well as Meg had done in helping Hammond off and on with his boots, which was all the assistance he needed with his simple toilet. Hammond had never roused Meg in the night to call upon him for service, but he now realized that no slave slept outside his bedroom door if one should be wanted. He considered installing another boy, possibly Kitty, whom Lucretia Borgia had partly broken for house service, but postponed detailing him in the belief that no other's loyalty, amiability, and readiness would be as great as those he was used to. Meg's going produced a void, small and vague and undefined, in the white man's existence.

Maxwell was less happy in Black Willie, Alph's replacement, for Black Willie smelled. Maxwell sniffed at him every night as he went to bed with Willie at his feet and never failed to find him musky. Dido, by Maxwell's command, scoured Willie daily, but his master still said he stank. Alph's musk, such as it was, the old man had not found unpleasant. Willie was larger than Alph, even if no older, dark enough to call black, thicker-lipped, flat-nosed, with gross, broad feet. After Memnon had been called in

347

the middle of successive nights to apply the paddle to Willie, the boy learned to lie across the bed without turning and squirming, and Maxwell thought him as absorptive of his rheumatism as Alph had been, but Willie did not possess the imagination that had taught Alph to ape the old man's malady and limp and complain upon occasion.

Maxwell did not relish having Willie crawling at his feet and seldom in the daytime spread him out and utilized him as a reservoir of his pain. Nor did Willie drink out of his toddy goblet. Those thick, black lips would have contaminated the glass, as Alph's lips had not done. The employment of Willie was purely practical.

Of course, the addition of the money to the pot buried under the tree to some degree made up for the absence of Lucretia Borgia and her brood. Never did the Maxwells, either of them, express regret for making the sale, but the slaves were not forgotten. The fatuity of Roche, his moustache, his jewels, his coach, his wealth, and his motives were topics of unfailing interest when there was nothing better to talk about. But speculation was vain. Why he should have wanted the twins so much, and still more, why he should have insisted upon having their mother also, was incomprehensible.

The cotton ripened, what there was of it, and was ginned and sent to market. The corn was laid by. Hogs were killed and the meat smoked or salted. Two of the mature field hands were sold to a passing dealer, and the trip to New Orleans with a small coffle of slaves was postponed, much to Redfield's disappointment.

Blanche was again pregnant. She postponed the announcement until she was no longer able to conceal the fact. She was not sure who might be the father of the child she carried. She hoped, as she forced herself to believe, that it was Hammond, though she realized that it might be Mede, even less likely Meg. She tried to formulate excuses if the child should be black, but they were too late. If she had accused one of the Negroes of rape, Hammond would have killed him and the thing would be settled, but it was now too late. Blanche reverted to drinking more and more toddies, which her father-in-law encouraged as being good for her condition, but they did not increase her amiability. Hammond was elated, as was his father, at the likelihood this time of a male heir.

The arrival of Blanche's mother in November was unannounced and unlooked for. If her visit was inconvenient, it was concealed

348

from her. Blanche, at least at first, was delighted to see Beatrix, who would commiserate with her over her pregnancy.

Mrs Woodford brought tidings of the death of her husband, the Major, who had succumbed to starvation in the belief that his wife and son were poisoning his food. Dick had assumed sole possession of Crowfoot and from an easygoing, open-handed, indolent youth had turned to a cranky niggard, intent upon squeezing from the soil, the slaves, the draft-stock, and from himself the last iota of revenue possible. The Negroes had been placed upon shorter rations with longer hours, and Dick begrudged his mother and himself the food they ate. He rose at daybreak or before and toiled till dark, driving and coercing with whip and cudgel to glean the last boll of cotton, the last nubbin of corn. Only, so, he had assured his mother, should he be able to free the plantation from debt, to the glory of God and the salvation of his soul. He had abandoned his preaching—except the exhortation of the slaves on Sunday—but his religion had taken a turn to diligence coupled with stinginess.

Beatrix suffered Dick's quirks as long as she was able, but at length had packed her worn and scanty clothes, summoned Wash to hitch the carriage and driven to Falconhurst for at least a respite from her son. In her hollow, querulous voice, which she was unable to hear, she urged her son-in-law to claim Blanche's half of the inheritance (Charles being dead, as she believed) and to assume the management of Crowfoot.

"No. Let Dick have it, ma'am, you an' him," Hammond shouted into her ear-horn. She could not hear him, or pretended so.

"Time the debts off, ain't goin' to be nothin' left noway," he explained to his father, "unlessen the man they owin' never turn up. Don' want we should mix with Dick. He lunatic, seem like, bad as the old Major." Hammond needlessly lowered his voice, and Blanche evinced no concern about her share of the legacy. She had worries more urgent.

But Beatrix continued to discourse upon the Major's death and the estate he had left and insisted upon Hammond's claiming Blanche's share. Her empty, unpleasant voice was loud as if she believed the other to be as deaf as herself.

Hammond, unable to reply to her, turned to his father. "Cousin Beatrix tryin' to take her place back from Dick," he said. "She ain't carin' nothin' about me and Blanche and our part. Crowfoot, let Dick have it."

Beatrix continued to censure Dick without actually accusing him of any definite offence until she saw that her breath was being wasted. Thereafter, seeing that Hammond was indifferent to her plea, she turned on him.

"Men! Men!" she cried. "Men and their lusts. Ain't got no nigger wenches, seem like. You got to keep your wives always knocked up, always knocked, always in the family way. I tellin' you when you got married, she young and innocent, but you got to have a baby right away, and now another one comin'. Seem like you'd have some shame and give little Blanche here a rest between. Ain't no end to whut men does to women." Beatrix stopped to sigh.

"I was cravin' me a boy," Hammond called into the horn at her ear, unheard.

"We got to bear. It their duty, an' their men say. Cain't git away, got to have white babies!" Beatrix ranted. "Glad I through with it, the Major dead. Me, I wouldn't have the best man livin'. I wouldn't believe his say on the Bible. All a man wants is pesterin'. Cain't tell me nothin' about 'em. I knows. The Major!"

Hammond did not feel himself censurable, but was unable to refute the charges because he was unable to make himself heard.

Her mother's arrival put an abrupt end to Blanche's tippling and even Hammond confined his infrequent toddies to the kitchen where Beatrix would not see them. Maxwell, however, was obdurate in his refusal to give up his drinking or to go elsewhere for it. Rather, out of perversity, he drank more than before.

"My rheumatiz," he used as his excuse. "Oncet I let my rheumatiz git ahead of my drinkin', I'll never ketch up to it."

Beatrix shook her head, whether in implication of her failure to hear what was said or of her disapproval of Maxwell's medicament he did not know or care. Her failure to hear was often an unwillingness to consider, although her deafness was real enough.

To his visitor's insistence upon family prayers the morning after her arrival, Maxwell made the concession of getting out of the room to avoid participation. Hammond was out of the house, and Maxwell, who took no stock in religious observance, refused to permit the summoning of the household slaves, except Tense, who was Blanche's own to do with as she might choose. It was Maxwell's belief and experience that religious practices made his slaves, especially the younger ones, restive and dissatisfied with their state.

" 'Lessen you comes to Jesus an' kneel down at his feet, you goin' to the bad place, sure are a-goin' straight to the bad place, Cousin Warren, you and Hammond along with you," Beatrix threatened him. "I hates to think about settin' up there in heaven with Blanche and a-watchin' you all burn."

"I hope, ma'am, I hope." Maxwell did not say for what, but it made no difference for his guest failed to hear him.

When the prayer meeting was assembled—Beatrix, Blanche, Tense, and Old Wash, who had been summoned for the function —Maxwell took his goblet and went into the dining-room. He could hear Beatrix as she haltingly read aloud from the Bible, and later after she and the two slaves had knelt—Blanche being excused because of her pregnancy—the rise in her voice was superfluous as she prayed for his and Hammond's salvation. Indeed, she prayed long and passionately, with many sobs and sighs, for Charles, and Dick, and the Major, for Blanche and her children, born and unborn, for herself, and incidentally for the slaves. But it was on behalf of the Maxwells, father and son, that her suit was loudest.

The prayers concluded, Maxwell returned to the sitting-room and rather pointedly, it seemed to Beatrix, called for Memnon to bring him a toddy. Henceforth Beatrix found other places than the sitting-room for her meetings, and while Maxwell was always invited he was never urged to attend them. He cared not at all how much she prayed so long as he was not constrained to listen and so long as his slaves were not demoralized by her proselytizing.

The primary purpose of Beatrix's visit was to enlist Hammond to claim his wife's part in the Major's estate or at least to oust Dick from its management. Beatrix had not been aware that her daughter was pregnant again, but, when she found Hammond indifferent to the supposed legacy and Blanche so close to her lying-in, she resolved to wait to see her new grandchild. There was nothing to draw her home, and here she at least got enough to eat without Dick's grumbling. She believed that she was welcome at Falconhurst, as, indeed, she was; for, even if she had not been Blanche's mother, she was born a Hammond.

Blanche, when she was questioned, had no notion of the duration of her pregnancy or when it might be expected to terminate. She had lost track of time, and was reluctant to talk of the event. This her mother charged to female modesty. Beatrix had her first grandchild to admire and to dandle while she awaited the second.

351

Blanche, who was no longer able to get into her challis dress, gave it to her mother. Somewhat soiled but little worn, it heightened the leathery sallowness of the woman's lined face, and Hammond, who had been allured more by the dress than by the girl who wore it, speculated whether his wife might some day come to this sour favour. The worn, dark brown woollen in which he had always seen Beatrix was more befitting to her ochre skin and eyes and teeth.

Beatrix had been at Falconhurst about three weeks when another visitor arrived. The gentlemen were up early, eating their breakfasts of eggs, ham and red gravy. The food was noticeably better than usual, the ham more tender and better done, the gravy richer and redder.

"Dite, she learnin' how at last," commented the older man.

"Lucretia Borgia come back, suh, Masta, suh. That whut! Lucretia Borgia back," grinned Memnon, pouring coffee.

"Seem like; taste like. Reckon Dite goin' to soon learn," Maxwell replied to the servant.

"But she back, suh. Lucretia Borgia come last night on a mule," Memnon reiterated.

"Got to tear this nigger down agin, I reckon. Lyin' so. Got so as he cain't tell true," Hammond said. "Want I should shuck you down an' touch you up aroun' the edges, like the other time?"

"Naw, suh, please, suh, Masta, suh; naw, suh. I good, I tell true. I be good. I ain't lie to you, Masta, suh," the Negro pleaded.

"You lyin', you know you lyin', boy," Hammond said sternly. "Whut fer you want to lie like that?"

"Yas, suh, Masta, suh," Memnon admitted the accusation. "On'y she back, she here, Lucretia Borgia."

Hammond pushed back his chair. "You lyin', I goin' to hang you up this very mornin'. I goin' to take the skin off you agin," he said as he rose and went toward the kitchen.

Lucretia Borgia stood before the fire, giggling nervously.

"Lucretia Borgia!" Hammond exclaimed. "Whure you come from? Your masta knowin' you come back? He say? He lettin' you?"

"Masta Ham, suh, Masta Ham!" the woman cried, throwing her big arms around him.

"Whut you doin' here?" the master demanded.

"Cookin' you-all's breakfast'," she answered literally.

The young man was glad to see her, to have her back, whatever

352

might have brought her. "Come 'long with me. Papa is in the dinin' room. Come 'long and see him," Hammond pushed the woman before him.

If Lucretia Borgia had been white, Maxwell might have believed he was seeing a ghost, but there was no doubting the evidence of his own eyes. "Whure you come from?" he asked. "Lucretia Borgia, you know you sold! Whut fer you come back?"

"I come back from New Orleans, suh, please suh, Masta, suh," the woman replied. "I cou'n't stan' it."

"You never run away?" he asked in horror.

"Yas, suh, I reckon I did, suh," the woman said contritely. "I reckon that whut you goin' to call it, suh. On'y I ain't a-goin' back, I ain't. You goin' to whup me. I know you goin' to whup me. Goin' to hang me up an' snake me. You kin, Masta, suh, you kin tear all the skin offn me. On'y I ain't goin' back. I ain't."

"Oh, yes you is, Lucretia Borgia. You is too a-goin' back," Maxwell said quietly. "Correctin' you, we goin' to leave that to your masta when he come fer you, but you know whut runnin' means an' you know whut he goin' to do to you. You goin' back all right. You sure is!"

The woman broke into tears. "Please, Masta, suh, keep me here. This my home. Whup me, you wantin' to, Masta. Only let me stay with you," she sobbed.

"Dry up! Dry up!" the master commanded. "Cryin' ain't a-goin' to save you. Whut fer you run? You know it ain't right. Your new masta not good to you? He starve you or somethin'? You looks right good an' fat."

"Masta, he right good. Feeds good. White vittles," Lucretia Borgia specified.

"Then whut?" asked Hammond.

"It them two varmints. That whut it is, suh, them varmints. Alph and Meg."

"The twins?" asked Hammond. "How they ac'? Whut they do?"

"I theirn. My masta, he give me to 'em, fer theirn. I got to wait on 'em an' dress 'em, an' shuck 'em, an' wash 'em, an' do fer 'em, all the time," she explained.

" 'Tain't right," Hammond agreed, "givin' one nigger to another. 'Tain't right, only it the way they does in Louisianie."

"I reckon he never give you to them twins, Lucretia Borgia," the older man questioned her story. "On'y you their mammy an' he lettin' you take care of 'em fer him. Whut he wantin' of of you, whut he bought you fer? Don' seem he bein' hard on you."

"That ain't all," Lucretia Borgia countered. She was ill at ease, not knowing how her charge was to be received. "That ain't all. I got to call them varmints 'Masta, suh.' Yas, suh, Masta, suh, I got to say 'Masta suh' to them niggers. I ain't a-sayin' 'Masta, suh' to no nigger, least not to them two that I had my own se'f, an' raised up my own se'f, an' whupped into house niggers fer you-all."

The old man shook his head in disapproval, and Hammond said, "I reckon, if your masta, your white masta, say you name them li'l bucks 'Masta, suh,' they ain't no other way. They treats you good?"

"Yas, suh, Masta," Lucretia Borgia begrudged the necessity to reply. "They treats me good enough, I reckon. On'y they always sayin' they goin' to tear me down an' whup me good. Always sayin', threatin' like. They ain't done it yit, but they always sayin' an' laughin' 'bout how funny I'd look, dancin' nekid under their snake, an' how I squeal while they goin' to rub in the pepper."

"Your masta wouldn't let 'em, not 'lessen you do somethin'," Hammond said.

"How they come on, them twins of yourn?" Maxwell asked without much caring.

"They good, Masta, suh. On'y they mean; they awful mean, suh," the mother said. "Meaner, seem like, ever' minute."

"They new masta, he still likin' 'em?" the white man asked with greater concern for the answer.

"Yas, suh! He sure do," Lucretia Borgia chuckled in a kind of derision. "That whut makin' 'em so mean. He ain't whup 'em, neither one of 'em, not even oncet, nor even slap 'em or kick 'em. Leaves 'em carry on jest like they wants. Sure is awful. Don't have 'em do nothin', 'ceptin', that is, stan' by his place while he eatin' an' he feedin' 'em right offn his own plate, an' they drinkin' wine right outn his glass. Yas, suh. They drunken ever' night. Standin' nekid, plumb nekid, without a stitch on 'em, right by they masta's chair, savin' on'y their earbobs an' they finger rings with little white rocks a-twinklin', jest like that ring of Miz Blanche."

"Di'mon's!" Hammond guessed. "Di'mon's wasted on niggers, nigger bucks."

"Yas, suh, that right, Masta, suh. That whut they calls 'em. I got to say they purty, right purty, them little bucks, standin' there, them little rocks twinklin' in the can'lelight. Jason, he wait table on his masta, do ever'thin' fer him, wash him, undress him, put him to bed, take him up mornin's, put his clothes on, ever'thin'. An' masta, he not care whut them young bucks does to Jason. No, suh, don' care at all. He jest laugh when they pinches Jason, or slaps him, or makes him spill things."

"They out of han', I reckon," Hammond said. "Had ought to be hung up, hung up by they heels with a little snakin'."

"Yas, suh, Masta. Sure ought," the woman went on. "Course, they different when Masta takes 'em along out with him, to drive in his kerriage, or to show 'em to the gent'men down at Maspero's Exchange, or to Mass——"

"A Papist. Makin' them niggers Papists," Maxwell interrupted the tale in an aside to his son.

"Then they wears clothes," Lucretia Borgia said. "Fine clothes, all slick an' smooth an' sof', an' fine stockin's, an' shoes."

"Silk?" Hammond suggested.

"Yas, suh, that whut they calls it, somepin' like that. But gittin' 'em dress', gittin' they clothes on! Lord A'mighty! Me? Masta tell me wash 'em, wash 'em all over, an' dress 'em devils. They is devils, suh. They kick like young jackass, they scratches an' bites me an' slaps me hard, hard as they kin, won' hol' still or nothin' while I scrubbin' 'em. I tells Masta, on'y he laugh an' don' do nothin', say I theirn to do with how they likes. But when they dressed with clothes on, an' them earbobs an' rings a-twinklin', they good, they so good they won' melt butter, walks so proper that they like angels or kittens or molasses or somethin'. On'y when they comes home, an' I shucks 'em nekid agin' they worse than ever, jumpin', caperin', teasin', pesterin', hittin', hittin' ever'body, that is, 'ceptin' the masta. Never do nothin' to him, 'cept makin' him laugh or beggin' fer a bite offn his fork."

"Whut you reckon the fool mean, carryin' on like he do, like Lucretia Borgia say he do?" Maxwell turned to his son. "Seventy-five hundert dollars worth of good nigger meat, jest a-wastin'!"

"He do, he sure do, Masta. I ain't fib to you, ain't tol' you half. Why, Masta hire a white man, white, hire him an' pay him money, jest to come an' learn them bucks to talk that lingo like he talk. That white man crack the head of Alph 'cause he won' learn, an' Alph tell Masta. I don' know whut Masta say in his kin' of talk, but he mad, mad, an' white man say he not do it agin. He skeared of Masta, that white man is, an' I reckon that whut he say."

"Them bucks kin talk, talk good as you or me," Maxwell said to Hammond. "An' that man un'erstan's American talk. Don' need no learnin'. They niggers."

"That right, Masta, suh. Sure kin talk. They talks too much. An' Jason fetch 'em chocolate in bed ever' mornin' jest like they masta. Cain't pile out, cain't set foot on floor afore they have they chocolate."

"That enough. I don' want to hear no more, Lucretia Borgia," Maxwell silenced the woman.

"But you goin' back the way you come," said Hammond. "You hisn an' bought an' paid for. You goin' back."

Lucretia Borgia assumed her stubborn, wide stance and, arms akimbo, defied her former master. "No, suh, please, suh, Masta, suh, I ain't a-goin'. I got to stay right here."

"You a-goin'. You goin' to do whut you tol'," Hammond said firmly but without anger.

"I ain't," affirmed the woman.

"You know whut it mean an' ifn your masta got to come fer you, don' you? Mean you a runner, a ordinary runner, an' you know whut he goin' to do to you—hang you up upside down an' snake all the skin offn you, that whut. Ifn you go back your own se'f, mayhap he won' do nothin'," Hammond argued.

"I not a-goin' back an' call them niggers 'Masta, suh'. I ain't goin'," Lucretia Borgia maintained. "You kin drive me off, on'y I goin' to turn that ol' mule an' go the other way."

"What ol' mule? We ain't a-goin' to give you no mule," declared Maxwell.

"My mule," Lucretia Borgia explained. "My ol' crippled mule I brung from New Orleans."

"Whure you git any mule?" the old man demanded.

"I bought it, bought it with money I done took out of Meg's box, suh," Lucretia Borgia confessed candidly. "They, both of 'em, got lots of money they masta give 'em. An' I pay a yaller boy who kin write, a light yaller boy who usten to be Masta's pet afore he gotten them twins, to write me out a pass, suh, fer the patterolers."

"A real sure enough runner," Maxwell nodded. "You got to write a letter to that white son-of-a-bitch to come an' git her. I 'on't care whut he is or whut he do, he bought her an' pay fer her. An' you cain't trust her to go back alone by her own se'f, mule or no mule. She actin' like a mule."

There was no other honourable course. Lucretia Borgia was

dismissed to go back to the kitchen to resume her former duties until her owner should come or send for her.

Breakfast over, Hammond wrote the letter. It was a task, for he was unused to writing. The letters wouldn't come right, the ink spattered, and Hammond sharpened and resharpened the nib of his goose-quill. An hour's agony over the brief note and it was finished and ready for his father's approval.

"How am I goin' to back this letter?" he asked, "not a-knowin' his name? He never said."

"He said all right, time 'fore you come in, on'y I disremembers. Somethin' like Roach. He'll git it. Roach close enough," said his father. "First, ast Lucretia Borgia. She'll be knowin'."

Memnon was sent to bring the runaway into the sitting-room. When she came, Hammond said to her, "Whut the name of your new masta? Whut he call hisse'f?"

"Sometin' like Roach," the father suggested.

"Soun' like, somethin' like that," she agreed.

"You doesn't know how to spell it out?" Hammond asked hopefully.

"That be readin'. I don' know readin', Masta, suh. You knows that a'ready."

Stumped for the want of a first name for his correspondent, Hammond addressed the letter merely to 'Mister Roach, New Orleans.' He could not be sure it would be delivered; in fact, he would not admit to himself the hope that it might not. He had done his best and his conscience was salved. However, he would be reluctant to give the woman up again, despite that he saw no reason for her coming back.

"I goin' to sen' Mem to the Post Office with it," Hammond said to his father.

"That nigger cain't sen' no letter," the father replied. "I needin' him to stir my toddies. Wait till you goin' to Benson your own se'f. Ain't no press."

Hammond grasped the excuse for delay, but the following Saturday he went himself to Benson, mailed the letter, and went to the tavern for the fights. He could hardly expect a reply short of a week, but a week went by, two weeks, a month, and nothing came, and his letter was not returned to him. He assumed that it had been delivered. Lucretia Borgia went on working, fearful when her former owner went to town that he would get a reply to his letter. But none came. None ever came. Lucretia Borgia was again a Maxwell slave. She could not, of course, be sold, but

357

the Maxwells had no desire to sell her. She was her old self, obsequious to the whites, dictatorial to her fellow slaves, efficient, obliging, indispensable. Hammond was glad she was back, and dreaded the day when her owner might arrive to take her away. But he did not come.

CHAPTER TWENTY-SIX

For Blanche, childbed impended. She grew larger and larger, and her mother worried about the delay and about her own prolonged absence from home. Beatrix was accepted as a part of the Maxwell family, walking as if in a dream; unhearing, her hollow voice, if not unheard, was ignored.

In January, Blanche developed pains in her abdomen and it was believed that her time was upon her, but she recovered and nothing happened. She was content. Her breasts enlarged and she felt the baby, but a languor enveloped her. She watched her father-in-law drink his toddies and knew that, but for her mother's presence, she would drink with him.

Cotton planting time arrived and Hammond ploughed his fields and put in his crop. The Mandingo exercised and Lucy rubbed him with serpent oil; he ate and thrived. Hammond looked at him from time to time and considered that it was wasteful to maintain so futile a luxury, but the elder Maxwell insisted upon keeping him as a stallion. His progeny, as they were born, were stalwart and healthy.

Hammond had been tacitly impatient with Blanche's prolonged pregnancy, but his impatience ceased. The baby would come when it would come. He was vexed with her failure to reckon the date, but vexation was vain. He was happy with Ellen.

March, with its bluster, showers, and sunshine, with its dogwood and wild roses, came and went. The first of April, Blanche awoke in labour. The house was solemn. Lucretia Borgia was the only person of any use. Tense wished to help but knew not what to do. Beatrix went around asking questions to which she was unable to hear the answers. Maxwell swallowed impatient toddies. Hammond sent Memnon riding to Benson to summon Doctor Murrey, who although he would probably be drunk upon his arrival was the only physician in the community whose experience in such matters was great enough to enable him to deliver a child, drunk or sober.

Blanche's recurrent pains begot groans as she lay and waited for the doctor, but there were no such screams of terror as had heralded the birth of her former child. Her mother, who sat beside the bed and rocked in her anxiety, was unable to hear the groans of her daughter but in her sympathy suffered more than Blanche. Lucretia Borgia pattered back and forth between the kitchen and the bedroom, fetching hot pepper gruels to stimulate labour and stooping by the bedside to massage Blanche's abdomen. Tense hung over the foot of the bed in a futile desire to help, but was able to do nothing except to fetch such things as Lucretia Borgia required from other parts of the house.

Memnon was gone for hours, while Maxwell drank the toddies which Lucretia Borgia found time between her trips upstairs to prepare for him, and Hammond limped the floor and cursed Memnon for his delay. It was three o'clock before the clatter of mule-hoofs on the lane announced the messenger's return. Hammond met him at the door as he crawled from the mule's back.

"That Masta Docta, he cain't come. He down sick—got lung fever, Miz say," the Negro informed his master.

"Did he say? Did you talk to him? Did you tell him who a-wantin' he should come quick an' whut fer?" Hammond demanded.

"Naw, suh, Masta. I never seen him. Miz, she wouldn't leave me inside," Memnon explained. "But she done say."

"You damned triflin', slothy nigger. I had ought to know better than send you. Had ought to go my own se'f," Hammond muttered and went in to tell his father the tidings and to consult with him about what should be done.

"Lung fever? Liable, jest drunken!" was the older man's comment. "Well, I reckon the yarb woman, Doc Redfield's Widder, got to get her. Reckon she as good as any doctor anyways; has grannied enough women, white an' black, she had ought to know how to ketch a chil'."

Hammond sighed his acquiescence. "On'y whut Cousin Beatrix goin' to think? How I goin' to make her hear that there ain't no man doctor?"

"Don't try. Ain't no other way," said the father.

Hammond went upstairs to tell Blanche that Doctor Murrey was unavailable and that she should just have to suffer while he went himself to bring Redfield's wife. He would make all the haste that Eclipse was capable of, he promised her.

"Why ain't that other doctor come instead of Murrey?" Blanche asked.

"Whut othern?"

"That young doctor. Doctor Smith," said Blanche. "He real nice. Ruther him than Miz Redfield."

"That blackguard! That scoun'rel! That houn'!" ranted Hammond so loud that Beatrix's trumpet caught the sound and she directed it toward him. "He ain't no doctor man yet, that Willis Smith, an' ain't never goin' to be. Goin' aroun' spreadin' the clap through clean niggers, makin' more sickness than ever he cure up. I'd sooner have Mede, sooner have that Mandingo ketch a chil' as that Willis Smith."

A spasm of pain overtook Blanche and forestalled any argument. Her husband, ignoring her suffering in his indignation, stalked out of the room, down the stairs, and toward the stable.

Maxwell recognized the hoof-beats of Eclipse's canter as Hammond rode down the lane and knew his son had gone for Mrs Redfield. The house was quiet except for the creak of the stairs as Lucretia Borgia made her heavy way from Blanche's bed to the kitchen and back again and for the loud ticking of the crazy clock above the cold fireplace. Two toddies later he heard the crow-hop gait of Mrs Redfield's tired horse and the turning wheels of her vehicle, and he knew that the herb-woman had come. He rose stiffly, made his way to the window, and saw her crawl down from her lopsided seat, gather her paper bag of herbs, and stalk with brisk importance toward the house. Without waiting for the door to be opened for her, she entered, and Maxwell heard the stairs under her firm tread as she ascended. Maxwell felt easier, now that help had come.

Hammond, with Doc Redfield on his dun gelding, followed the woman down the lane a furlong behind her buggy. Redfield, with nothing else to do, had come along for a visit while his wife performed her professional duties. He was elated that his wife should be summoned on so notable a mission and sought to partake, however vicariously, of her distinction. Maxwell was glad of somebody to talk to through the vigil.

The random conversation touched on many subjects—the Mandingo, his condition and fitness for a fight, the size and vigour of his babies, cotton, the current market for slaves and the prices they brought, a suitable diet for young slaves, tribal differences, the virtues and dangers from infusions of white blood in Negroes, anything to avoid discussion of the weight upon all their minds. Hammond, between sips of his toddy, limped from window to window, looked at the landscape and assessed the weather. Not that he cared.

"Redfield! Redfield! Come up here! Hurry!" came his wife's loud voice from the upper hall. Mrs Redfield was a placid woman, not unused to emergencies and taking them in her stride, but to his amazement, Redfield detected an implication of terror in the summons.

He set down his toddy glass, rose, and went into the hall. "You callin' me? You wantin' me, Widder? Whut you reckon I kin do?" he asked as he made his way up the steps.

"Come up here!" the woman repeated. "Come quick!"

Redfield hastened as best he was able. "It come yit?" he demanded as he reached the head of the stairs.

"It come!" the midwife said in a loud whisper. "It come! Only it ain't white! It a—a nigger! Whut we goin' to do?"

The astounded man was taken aback. He did not believe her. "A nigger! You wrong; it ain't no nigger!" he contradicted.

"You sayin' I don' know a nigger, me who have ketched a hunerd black suckers in my time?" the woman said with indignation.

"Whure is it?"

"On the bed. I laid it on the bed till I could call you. Whut we goin' to do with it?"

"If it a nigger, like you sayin', we jest cut the cord short an' let it bleed. Mista Maxwell, he don' want no nigger chil', not his own, not from his wife, he don'." Redfield was resolute. By destroying the baby he calculated to save Hammond the necessity. As he followed his wife to the bedroom, Beatrix Woodford emerged from it, weeping, but her head high, her tread firm, and went into her own room.

Blanche lay exhausted, but calm and comfortable, relieved now of her long burden. Her baby was not beside her where the herb-woman had left it. Blanche opened her eyes at the turning of the door on its hinges.

"Whure is it? What you do with it, your chil'?" Mrs Redfield demanded.

"Mamma, she mad! She done took it an' squashed it agin the commode an' throwed it over there in the corner," Blanche answered unmoved. "She say it a nigger. I 'on't know how come."

361

The naked baby lay on the floor in the corner of the room under a window, its skull crushed. Mrs Redfield picked it up into her arms and held the warm body toward her husband.

Redfield looked at the beautifully formed little boy. "The Mandingo, Ham's Mandingo," he breathed. "Look jest like him; an' big must be fifteen pounds. Jest like the Mandingo."

"An' a boy," declared his wife. "They a-wantin' a boy."

"But not a nigger boy," said Redfield. "Ham's mother-in-law, her a-doin' it save me from gotten to do it. Me, I'd haten to got to kill it—it so big an' purty an' soun' like."

"Is it a nigger, sure 'nough?" Blanche asked but was indifferent to the reply.

Redfield sighed as he went down the stairs, trying to make up his mind what to tell the Maxwells.

As he entered the sitting-room, Hammond looked at him, expectant, and the older man asked, "Well?"

"It dead. Come dead, I reckon," said Redfield.

"Dead," sighed Hammond. "A boy?"

"A boy. Made purty like," Redfield answered.

"How Blanche? Kin I go up now? All over?" Ham asked.

"She all right. That is, she goin' to be," said Redfield. "But no, no! Don' go up. You don' want to see it. Purty bad messed up. You don't want to see it. Let the niggers bury it. Whure that cook-wench, that Lucretia Borgia? She bury it."

"I cravin' I should see him. A boy! Dead!" declared Hammond, starting toward the stairs.

"Not yit, not yit!" Redfield grasped his arm in an effort to detain him, but the young man eluded him.

In the emotional turmoil, the Woodford surrey with old Wash in the front seat and Beatrix in the rear was hardly noticed as it went past the windows and down the lane. Beatrix had done her duty as a Hammond and would not stay for questioning. Later, Blanche's challis dress, which she had given her mother, was found on Beatrix's bed.

Redfield stood by the door until Hammond was half way up the stairs, after which he turned and walked towards the elder Maxwell. "Nigger!" he said in a tragic whisper. "The chil' a nigger!"

"Whut you mean? Nigger?" Maxwell failed to comprehend.

"It a nigger, I tell you. The Mandingo, jest like him. A nigger!"

"No! No! It can't be!"

"It is!"

"A white lady have a nigger? Blanche, she white, she Ham's

wife! It his chil'. Ifn any buck rape her, she'd say, she'd tell. No, no! You wrong!" Maxwell set aside his toddy glass which had suddenly turned bitter. "Not the Mandingo?"

"You reckon I don' know a nigger?" Redfield asked rhetorically, expecting no answer. "I tried to keep Ham from goin' up; that why. Ain't no use in him seein' an' knowin'.'"

"An' you killed it? That whut the Widder wantin', that whut she call you fer, to kill the nigger?" Maxwell had no doubt. "You done right, right."

"Miz Woodford, afore I got there, she done bashed its head. I would of, would of cut the cord an' let it bleed. I tol' the Widder so, but I never needed. Miz Woodford," Redfield explained.

Hammond returned, his face bloodless, his limp hardly noticeable, his step resolute. He sank into a chair and stared, wide-eyed, at nothing. "Doc Redfield," he said, "that powder? That pizen powder? The kin' you used on an old, blin' one of Widder Johnson's, 'fore you married? You said if ever I needin' it. You got some left?"

"I reckon so; they's some in my saddlebag," the doctor nodded. 'On'y it too good fer him. You had ought to burn him."

"Mede, you meanin'? My Mandingo?" Hammond inquired, dazed.

"It was him all right. Sure was. It look jest like him," testified Redfield.

"The powder not fer him. I got another I got to do fer. I goin' to take care the Mandingo my own se'f. I take care of him. Don' you fret," Hammond promised.

Mrs Redfield came heavily down the stairs and across the hall. "I reckon she be all right now," she said, framed in the sitting-room door. "That big wench, she kin do fer her good as me. She know how."

The lack of concern with which Hammond answered "I reckon" told Redfield for whom the poison was intended.

"You kin go along home, Widder," Redfield told his wife. "I'll come, soon as I kin git somethin' out of the saddlebag fer Hammond, here. I'll ketch you up afore you git there."

The woman adjusted the bonnet on her head and her husband followed to help her into her buggy, after which he turned to his own horse, opened the saddlebag and delved among the powders and pills and bottles. At length he found the poison, wrapped in a soiled paper, unlabelled. He divided the contents and placed a

363

quantity in a scrap of paper torn from the larger piece. After restoring the miscellaneous contents of the saddlebag, he re-entered the house with the small packet.

The Maxwells had not moved. They had hardly spoken in his absence.

"Here it be," the doctor said. "It ain't got no taste to it. Jest you stir it up in coffee or a toddy, an' have her drink it down. She won' feel nothin' but jest go to sleep an' stiffen out. It sovereign, sure sovereign."

"Jest put it there on the mantel, please suh," Hammond managed to say. There was resonance in his voice.

Redfield did as he was bidden and took his departure without any farewell. Sensing the young man's agony, he knew that no civilities were indicated.

When the doctor had gone, Hammond struggled to his feet and went into the kitchen. He soon returned with a toddy into which he poured the contents of the small paper on the mantel.

"Goin' to give it?" asked his father.

"I got to. There ain't no other way," said the son, stalking down the hall.

Maxwell heard him as he went up the stairs. Memnon brought him a toddy which he tasted but did not drink. His knees ached and he rubbed the joints but failed to relieve the pain.

Hammond went into the room where Blanche lay on the bed. The girl was awake, and Tense, who sat on the foot of the bed, arose. Hammond carried the goblet of toddy and sat in the chair beside the bed where Beatrix had sat.

"Rouse you up an' swaller this. It a-makin' you feel better," he said with no evidence of rancour. "Help her to set up, Tense."

The odour of the potion was alluring to the girl and she reached for it. Hammond sat and watched while she sipped it slowly as Tense supported her.

"I didn' mean no harm, Hammond," Blanche declared weakly. "I didn't mean no harm. Only you an' that Ellen—you didn't pay me no mind, no min' at all, an' I reckoned—I never knowed the baby goin' to come a nigger."

Hammond was silent.

"That good. It taste real good," Blanche said between swallows of the toddy. "It right stren'thenin'. On'y somethin' in it, somethin' in the bottom, white-like."

"That medicine Doc Redfield left fer you. It make you sleep quiet," said her husband.

Blanche drained the goblet and Hammond took it from her hand. Tense eased her mistress back upon her pillows. Hammond sat quietly a few minutes, after which he got up from his chair and, taking the empty glass with him, went downstairs and into the kitchen where he rinsed the glass and set it aside to be washed.

He made his way, dazed but resolute, across the area to Lucy's cabin, which he entered without knocking. "Mede here?" he demanded.

The Mandingo rose from the bed where he lay.

"You know that big hog kettle," the master told the slave. "Well, you fill it up with water, an' strike a fire under it, an' heat it up hot. Bring fire from the kitchen to light it with. We goin' to brine you agin, brine you good."

Being steeped in hot brine was not a pleasant experience, Mede knew, but there was no way to evade the master's purpose. He knew better than to protest. Hammond appeared grim and determined, but betrayed no anger. The slave wondered, however, at his failure to examine him and criticize his condition, as was Ham's custom.

Mede left the cabin and went to the end of the gallery where the vatlike kettle sat, saw that it was raised from the ground with blocks of wood. Then he began carrying more wood from the stacked pile and arranged the pieces around and under the kettle to heat the contents quickly. Next, he went to the kitchen for a brand with which to ignite the wood. He saw to it that the dry wood was burning well all around the kettle before he went to the well for water to fill it. He attached the bucket to the well-sweep and placed his weight against the pole, bringing the water to the surface. He poured the water into two buckets which he carried to the kettle. When the first of the water touched the bottom of the kettle, it hissed into steam which soon subsided with the addition of more water. Again and again he went to the well until the kettle was well filled. He shivered at the thought of getting into the hot brine and remaining there until it should toughen his skin. Why should his master undertake this process just at nightfall? There was no accounting for a white man's whims. Mede knew nothing of what had occurred inside the house that day, and, if he had known, would not have associated it with his salting.

After Mede left the cabin, Hammond turned to Lucy and told her, "You goin' to tote the wood to keep that fire, after Mede git in that water." As he went toward the house, he paused to see that Mede was preparing his bath.

Accompanying his father to the dining-room, Hammond could eat no supper, and the older man, sensing the anguish of his son, did not urge him to talk nor offer him counsel. He knew that the boy had poisoned Blanche, but could conceive no other course. He was, rather, grateful for the young man's restraint, the absence of violence. He knew, of course, the need to destroy the Mandingo, but left the time and manner to his son. Hammond did not divulge his plans. Maxwell would have liked to have a few more women pregnant to the Negro stallion before his demise, but had misgivings about saying so. Indeed, he feared that the youth might undertake to exterminate the babies Mede had already gotten.

Supper over, Hammond went upstairs to make sure the poison had done its work. Blanche was not dead. She lay on the bed, her breathing shallow with a detectable heart-beat. Her husband was impatient for the end, but saw that the woman could not long survive.

Outside, the night was black, with only the stars for light, only the stars and the embers that sparkled beneath the hog kettle. Mede had gone. Hammond felt the water, which was hot but not boiling, then he limped toward the stable where he got a rusty pitchfork. As he came toward the house, he saw Mede replenishing the fire. The water had begun to bubble. He entered the house and went to the sitting-room where his father was drinking a toddy.

"Throw the blue coverlid aroun' your shoulders. The nighttime is cool-like. Don' want you should catch anythin'. But come," said the boy. "I cravin' you should see."

"Whutever you goin' to do, Son, it all right," declared the father. "I ain't a-needin' I should watch."

"Come," urged the son, adjusting the shawl to Maxwell's shoulders.

The old man rose stiffly, and Hammond took his arm to guide his steps. He went no further than the gallery, from which he watched.

The water in the kettle was turbulent with heat. The fire around it was brilliant in the dark, crackling and emitting sparks as the wood burned and fell apart.

"Shuck down now," Ham ordered the slave, who kicked himself out of his garments and stood naked.

366

The coppery skin reflected the fire's glow as the Negro stood with unconsidered dignity before his owner. Ham ran his hand over the youth's flank, valuing the property which pride and duty prompted him to destroy. He took a firm hold on the pitchfork.

"Git you in," he ordered.

"It hot. It bilin'," objected Mede.

"I didn't ast you was it hot. I sayin' git in," said Hammond.

The Negro stepped toward the kettle and tested the heat of the water with his hand. "I cain't," he argued. "Please, suh, Masta, suh, that water burn me. I cain't."

"Never min' burnin', I say," Hammond commanded. The Mandingo knew that the instruction was not to be gainsaid. He swung one leg into the cauldron but the water was unbearably hot and he withdrew it.

"God-damn, git in there," said the master.

The Negro replaced the leg in the pot, grasped the iron edge to support himself while he hoisted the other leg, and burned the palm of his hand. He stood in the bubbling water deep as his knees, treading the bottom of the hot kettle, lifting one foot and then the other to keep from burning them.

"Stop that bouncin' an' set you down," commanded his master. "Set right down, I sayin'."

"I—I cain't," said the Negro, beginning to weep.

Hammond stepped forward, raised the pitchfork, and drove it into the Negro's abdomen. The water muffled the boy's screams of rage and anguish, so long as they lasted, but at length he ceased to struggle.

Hammond stood a long while over the cauldron, the fire-shine in his face, until he was sure the slave was dead.

The moon appeared on the horizon and illumined the black night.

Hammond called to Lucy and told her to replenish the fire and to keep it going throughout the night.

"Masta, Masta!" the woman wept, wringing her hands. "You done kill Mede, done kill him. He ain't done nothin'. Whut fer you kill him, Masta, suh? Whut fer you kill him?"

She expected no answer, but Hammond said, "Serve him right."

Maxwell, when it was apparent that the Mandingo was finished, turned toward the door, but before he reached it his son joined him and grasped his arm.

"You got to look about now, I reckon; buy you another fightin' buck," said the father. "Ain't apt to find you anothern like that

367

Mandingo. Mighty purty boy," he sighed as he entered the house.

"Not reckon I git me any othern. Ain't no point in fightin' 'em," the boy replied. "A good one, an' you cain't fin' nobody wantin' to fight him, an' a bad one al'ays gittin' whupped. Cain't trus' no fighter, noways."

Hammond lay alone that night. When Ellen came to remove his boots for him, he sent her away. He lay alone but did not sleep. He lay and looked through the window into the moonlight. He heard Lucy throwing fresh wood upon the fire, and occasionally he saw the sparks that flew upward from the embers and went out. He felt his face redden with shame, not for what he himself had done, which was only his duty, but shame for his wife, a white woman and a Hammond, who had brought forth a Negro child.

At the first hint of dawn he rose, got into his clothes, struggled to put on his boots without aid, and made his way to the room in which Blanche lay. He stepped over the body of Tense, sleeping on the floor of the hall outside her mistress's door, but did not rouse her. The room had been his mother's, and Hammond felt that it had been desecrated by the birth in it of the Negro child and, perhaps, by the assignation here at which it was begotten. He stepped to the bedside and laid his hand upon Blanche's brow. It was cold. She was indeed dead. He made an effort to adjust the position of an upturned arm but found it rigid. She must have died early last night. The face was peaceful and there was no indication that she had struggled with death.

He went out, closed the door, stepped again over the sleeping Tense, and went down the stairs.

It was early, but the Negroes were beginning to stir. He encountered two stout youths, Brutus, shortened to Brute, and Treasure, whom he commanded to bring shovels and to follow him. He walked ahead while the boys went to get their shovels, but they soon came up with their master. He walked through the now brightening day, the two slaves at his heels, across the row of burgeoning cotton toward the worm-fenced, weedgrown enclosure set aside to serve as a family burial ground. Instead of going to the entrance gate, he climbed the fence and his slaves threw their shovels across and followed him. He paused before the wooden slabs that bore the half-effaced names of the members of his family buried beneath them, and stooped to pull the tallest of the weeds and grass from his mother's grave. The family was huddled side by side in death in the very middle of the broad

368

expanse, broad enough to accommodate ten numerous generations. Traversing the burial ground was another fence, beyond
which there was a host of unmarked mounds beneath each of
which rested the body of a dead Negro. Hammond remembered
some of these servants and knew just where they lay. It was a
quiet, peaceful stretch of high ground with a group of large elms,
the young leaves of which were just turning from yellow-green
to the deeper green of summer. Seldom disturbed by humans and
never shot over, the area was a refuge for bob-whites and jays
and cardinals which sensed their safety within its confines. Garter
snakes bred here unmolested, and other small things scurried
through the weeds at human approach.

Hammond surveyed the scene while the slaves waited to be
told what to do. Brute leaned on his shovel, while Treasure threw
himself on a grass clearing among the weeds. The customary
course was to bury members of the family, as they died, in a line,
the last to die alongside the last-made previous grave, but Hammond, choosing a resting-place for his wife, felt the profanation
of placing her beside his mother. That spot, he reasoned, should
be reserved for his father. He went to the division fence and
looked across into the Negro burial grounds, moved to inter his
wife there. After all, had she not had a Negro child, and was it
not to be buried with her? But he could not bring himself to do
such a thing to a white woman, however culpable.

At length he chose a spot on the white side of the fence, but
hard against it, well away from the white dead, with them but
not among them. He paced the space with his feet, length and
breadth, and ordered the Negroes to dig the grave, cautioning
them to conserve the soil and to pile it against the fence. He
waited while they removed the surface with its weeds from the
plot, seeing to it that the corners were square.

"Now, dig it on down, straight and clean an' deep," he told the
boys. "We wanting to bury 'em nice."

Seeing the grave well begun, Hammond left the Negroes at
their task and walked toward the house. He paused by the side
of the barn and chose one of a suitable size from the assortment
of crudely carpentered coffins stacked there weathering while they
awaited tenants. The Maxwells buried their dead slaves in coffins
instead of merely wrapping them in blankets and tumbling them
into graves, and there was always an assortment of coffins of
various lengths made in anticipation of the deaths which were
happily infrequent occurrences among the plantation population.

Having made his selection of the soundest and most neatly fashioned of these boxes, Hammond looked about him for two strong boys to carry it for him to the house. This they did by grasping the handles of rope passed through holes in the sides of the coffin and knotted inside it. He had the bearers set the coffin down on the end of the gallery and then dismissed them.

Entering the house, Hammond found his father at breakfast and joined him, eating heartily, having foregone supper the previous night.

"Reckon it needful, you a-carryin' on," sighed the elder man regretfully.

"Ain't no other way. I wouldn't feel right inside without I do it," Hammond said. "I not a-likin' to do it, no more than you, on'y you knowin', your own se'f, that no gen'leman kin have a woman whut carry on like that—you know—with no nigger buck. Ain't no other way."

"Kind of break up our Mandingos, seem like. Coursen, we got them two suckers, Lucy's wench an' that Ol' Masta Wilson buck outn Big Pearl. Glad we saved somethin' from Mede, but they take a long time to grow." Maxwell appeared to deplore the Mandingo more than Blanche.

"Him! Whut I done is too good fer him. I not a-cravin' more Mandingos. They treach'ous!"

"Not treach'ous an' they watched, no more treach'ous than any nigger buck. Cain't turn your back on any of 'em, any buck, aroun' white ladies. They all lustylike," opined the elder. "Made that way. I ain't a-blamin' 'em. Ain't no call to behave, savin' you make 'em."

Hammond pushed back his chair and rose. He summoned Lucretia Borgia and Tense to help him, and together they wrapped the bodies of Blanche and her baby in a quilt, carried them through the hall, down the stairs, and across the gallery, where they laid them in the open coffin. Only Tense wept, not because she had loved her mistress or had been well used by her, but out of self-pity and doubt about her own future. Hammond was grim and determined to carry out the duty he had set for himself. He had loved the girl, he thought, whom he had killed for her own honour and for his, and, despite her shortcomings as his wife, had protected her and treated her well, but he had no tears to shed for such a woman. He knelt by the coffin and nailed the lid securely in place.

Hammond limped back up the knoll to the burial grounds to

assess the progress Treasure and Brute were making in the digging of the grave. He had not expected them to work rapidly and was pleased that they had done so much. The sides of the hole were not quite plumb, and he cautioned the boys to straighten them. Then he stood by and watched them throwing the dirt from the pit, the task progressing more rapidly under the master's surveillance. At length, he tired of watching the slaves and wandered over to the cotton field and finally back to the house. Except for the boys who dug the grave and another boy assigned to keeping the fire going around the kettle, work on the plantation was suspended, and the slaves, all of whom knew about Mede's martyrdom but not the reason for it, kept to their cabins, not knowing which of them might be the next victim. Terrified as they were, none questioned their owner's authority to do what he had done to Mede or to dispose of any of them as he should wish. Hammond climbed the stairs and threw himself upon the bed, but, despite his sleepless night, he was unable to sleep now. He was obsessed. All of his imaginings turned upon visions of his white wife in the bestial arms of the Mandingo. His vengeance had been prompt, but it did not suffice. No vengeance would suffice. He pondered what he might do to make it more terrible and more just.

Hours he lay there, wide-eyed and pondering. Then he arose. The grave must now be finished. He walked mechanically down the stairs, across the areaway, to the meeting-house barracks. He called upon two stout boys, the first he encountered, and took them with him to the gallery, where he told them to wait for him. He went into the house and along the hall to the sitting-room, where his father's chair was drawn up beside the window. The old man had drunk more than his usual number of toddies in an effort to quell his perturbation over the anguish he knew his son to be suffering and which he knew not how to allay.

"We're goin' now," the young man announced. "Crave to come along?"

"Whure to you goin'?" asked the father.

"To bury her, her an' her chil'," Hammond said, with an air of false casualness. "Reckon you kin come? You relished her right well; that is beforehan' you did."

"You knowin' I cain't walk so fur."

"Well, we'll rig up that hammock I brung you from Natchez. ꞌ knowed it would come handy someday," Hammond proposed.

"ꞌI'll not ride in that contraption," the old man refused. "It would seem like you totin' me out to dump me in the grave, my own se'f."

He got to his feet, however, and followed his son to the gallery where he stood and watched as the two slaves, one on either side of the coffin, lifted it by its hempen handles and started with it toward the burial ground, followed by his son. He remembered that it had been he who suggested Blanche Woodford as a consort for Hammond and he blamed himself for what had occurred. If he had been more vigilant during his son's absence, the assignation would have been impossible. He assumed that the Mandingo had waylaid the girl and raped her, but deemed her at least as culpable for her failure to tell of the assault as was Mede for committing it. All knew the lust of black men for white women, which it was the white man's duty to thwart more than to censure. Maxwell stood and watched. He saw the slaves set the coffin on the ground and change sides, each transferring the weight to the opposite arm. Then he saw them lift their burden again and disappear around the corner of the meeting-house barracks, where he lost sight of them.

Arrived at the worm-fence, Hammond called to Brutus and Treasure to take down a panel of it that the coffin might pass. They had finished their digging, but the bottom of the grave was not level, and Hammond ordered the two slaves to set the coffin on the ground while the two others scraped the grave and levelled it. When it was ready, he had Treasure remain in the hole to receive the coffin, which the other slaves eased down to him. In the process, the box turned on its side and fell upon Treasure's foot, at which he cried out and complained so much that his master ordered him to the surface and delegated Brute to descend into the grave and right the coffin. When it was placed to the master's satisfaction, Brutus climbed out of the hole and Hammond, grasping the loose, dank earth, pelted the coffin with clods. He then ordered Brutus to shovel back into the grave the dirt that lay beside it, while he, himself, knelt on the ground to manipulate Treasure's foot to make sure it was not broken.

He did not wait until the grave was filled, but, instructing Brutus how he wished it to be banked, dismissed the slaves and walked slowly back toward the house.

Supper over, Hammond sat with his father, who drank his toddy. Hammond drank nothing. When Memnon came to refill the old man's goblet, Hammond said to the slave, "That Lucretia Borgia, tell her she should come here."

Memnon marked the stern and peremptory tone, and soon Lucretia Borgia, smoothing her apron, stood before the master in the twilight.

"Lucretia Borgia!" Hammond began.

"Yas, Masta, suh," she said.

"Lucretia Borgia, you knowin'—you knowin' 'bout this?" the master charged rather than asked.

"Knowin'? Knowin' whut, suh?" the woman countered for time, aware what he meant.

" 'Bout Miz Blanche an' that Mandingo. You knowin'," he said.

Lucretia Borgia hesitated, not sure whether it was more discreet to admit or to deny the accusation, doubtful that denial would be believed. At length, with a hint of a giggle in her voice, she acknowledged in part that she knew. "I knowin' Mede come in the house an' up the stairs. Tense say Mist'ess sen' fer him," she said. "I not knowin' whut he do."

"Lucretia Borgia not here that time. She in New Orleans that time," the father sought to defend the woman.

"That time? While I gone up in Tennessee? That afore she sold," replied the son.

"Yas, suh, Masta; that the time, while you gone," admitted the cook.

"Whyn't you say? Whyn't you tell me? Whyn't you call Papa, here? You knowin' Mede got no hold in the house, no business here," the young man upbraided her.

"Tense say——" Lucretia Borgia retorted.

"Nev' min' whut Tense say," said Hammond.

"Tense say Miz Blanche, she sen', suh," went on the woman. "Say Miz Blanche say tell that Mede to come here. Tense, she cry. All time cry."

"Nev' min' Tense, I tellin' you. Whyn't you tell Papa, your own se'f?" the boy interrogated. "Whyn't you look after things, like you supposed?"

"It white doin's," Lucretia Boriga shrugged. "I not never mess in white folk's doin's. You tol' me, you own se'f, Masta, suh, white doin's is white doin's, an' me, I ain't no call to mess."

"I reckon I did. But lettin' a nigger buck to a white lady. You know it ain't safe, ain't never safe."

"If'n white lady wantin' that ol' hog boar of yourn, I ain't a-goin' to put in," Lucretia Borgia shrugged again. "White lady know whut she crave."

373

"She, Miz Blanche, never crave that black ape. You know she never. She sen' to give him them red ear-drops, that all, an' he rape her," Hammond rationalized.

"Whut fer she sen' the second time and the third time then?" rebutted the woman.

"More than once? It ain't true," declared Hammond.

"Four days in all, while you away, suh," Lucretia Borgia held up her fingers. She had tolerated rather than liked Blanche and was pleased that she was able to indict her. "That Mede, he right temptatious to a woman. You-all done seen him nekid."

"To a nigger wench. Not to no white lady."

"I not a-knowin' 'bout no white lady, suh," sighed the Negro.

"I got me a right good notion to gather you up an' carry you back to that white gen'leman in New Orleans whut bought you," Hammond threatened.

"Yas, suh, Masta, suh, I a-hearin'," the woman answered.

"As you goin' out, sen' me in Tense. Hear?" he dismissed her, baffled by her taciturnity. He limped the floor impatiently until Hortense arrived.

When at length she came, he hardly knew what he wanted to ask of her. "Tense," he stated rather than questioned, "you Miz Blanche's nigger, takin' care an' doin' fer her?"

"Yas, suh, Masta," Tense whispered her reply and shivered in her fear of him.

"You a-knowin' that Mandingo rape your mist'ess?"

"Mede, suh. Yas, suh, I a-knowin' it."

"Whyn't you say? Whyn't you tell me?" he demanded. "You a-knowin' I kill him."

"Yas, suh, Masta, only Miz say I mus'n't tell. She say she mad at you, say she goin' to pay you back. I a-tellin' her—much as I could—she hadn't ought to, you be mad," the girl absolved herself. "She say fetch him."

"An' you do it? You fetch him? Then whut?"

"I 'on't know, suh, Masta, suh. I 'on't know. I 'on't know nothin'," Tense broke into frightened tears.

"Whut you do while—while he in there, while he in there with your mist'ess?" the master inquired.

"I set outside on the stair steps—jest set."

"Didn' say nothin'? Didn' tell your ol' masta?"

"Naw, suh. I jest set an' cried. I tol' Miz Lucretia Borgia—afterwards."

374

"She knowin' all the time whut a-goin' on?" Hammond sought to incriminate somebody.

"She know. Ever'body know. All the niggers know," she admitted. Tense raised her skirt to dry her eyes.

"The house niggers or all of 'em?"

"Leasewise the house niggers, 'ceptin' Ellen. She away with you that time. Nobody ever tell Miz Ellen. They afeared to."

"How many times? How many times you fetch that ape in fer Miz Blanche?"

"You meanin' Mede?" Tense asked. She counted on her fingers and held up her hand with the thumb concealed in the palm. "That many," she said, unable to count to four. "That many, I reckon."

"All you niggers knowin' an' none of 'em ever sayin'—none of 'em tellin' me?" Hammond shook his head in disbelief.

"Them twins, that you done sol', one of 'em, I 'on't know which one, I couldn't tell 'em one from the other, one of 'em was a-goin' to tell, said he would, 'lessen Miz Blanche—'lessen Miz Blanche——" Tense could not bring herself to go on.

"Unlessen Miz Blanche do whut?" the master prompted.

" 'Lessen she pleasure him too, like she done with Mede," she said.

Hammond, pacing the floor, turned on the standing girl, raised his arm and brought his palm across her cheek with a slap that staggered her. "That a lie, a damn lie! You dirty, lyin' skunk of a nigger!" he exclaimed.

The elder Maxwell, who had so far been silent, murmured, "Nigger talk. You know that ain't true, Son. Them twins wasn't big enough."

The son doubted the validity of the objection. "They big as I was the first time, the time you give me that li'l yaller wench." He knew that Tense told the truth. "That Meg, leastwise, was."

"Too late, too late now. You cain't do nothin', Ham, even an' if she tellin' true," said the elder man, draining his goblet.

Hammond shrugged. "How many times? How many times that Meg rape your mistress? How many times?"

Tense stood sullen and did not answer.

"How many times, I askin' you, nigger?" Hammond demanded.

"I 'on't know, suh, please, suh, Masta, suh," at length she replied. Then she added, "Mos' ever'day, I reckon, afore you went an' sol' them twins. Mos' ever'day, when he could sneak out an' upstairs, an' sometimes at night when you asleep with Miz Ellen."

"Then it was Meg, 'cause Alph always sleepin' with you, Papa," Hammond reasoned.

"Sometimes both of 'em, in the daytime, one after the othern," Tense said. "But jest one said he'd tell."

Hammond was revolted, desolated, impotent to revenge himself upon the twins. "That enough," he said, dismissing Tense.

Mede's body was removed from the cauldron and buried with scant respect.

Days passed. The cotton grew in the mild spring weather, and the hands, under Hammond's supervision, kept the weeds in check. A Negro boy went down with persistent pains in his lower abdomen, but was purged and there was no alarm. Two women bore children the same night, both without serious difficulty. Hammond told his father briefly of the occurrences on the plantation, but there was little discussion of them. The whole house was quiet. The houseslaves spoke among themselves in subdued voices. Maxwell was aware that Hammond seethed with unvoiced emotions.

Blanche had been buried nine days. Supper was finished and Maxwell sipped his toddy. Hammond's sat on the floor at his side, untasted.

"Well," said the younger man, "I reckon I goin', goin' 'bout tomorrer."

"Goin'? Goin' whure to?" asked the father placidly, with no show of the alarm which he felt.

"Jest a-goin'," replied the son. "First off to New Orleans. I got to kill me them two twins."

"You cain't; cain't do that," objected Maxwell. "They ain't yourn."

"I'll pay for 'em. Won't be much, two triflin' saplin's. If need, I give it all back, the money we sol' 'em fer. Won't need though." Hammond's blue eyes were focused as in a dream. "No jedge goin' to assess me more than they worth, leastwise, when he hear why I done it."

"You ain't got no proof," the older man protested.

"You hear whut Tense say? Tense ain't tellin' no lies. Whut she sayin' 'bout Blanche don' count, but a nigger kin say agin a nigger an' that the truth," Hammond said with finality.

"Mayhap be," the father admitted. "Only——"

"Shoot down that Meg and that Alph is the only way to clear

out my head. I know it is. Things jest keep goin' 'roun' an' 'roun' inside of me. Cain't sleep, cain't eat, cain't pleasure, cain't think, cain't do nothin' so long as they a-livin'. Gittin' shet of her an' the Mandingo don' count none, now that Tense say 'bout them twins." Hammond spoke slowly with apparent deliberation. He paused only to sigh.

"They dead, you goin' to be satisfy, you reckon?" Maxwell asked doubtfully.

"I 'on't know," admitted Hammond. "After that, mayhap I goin' to saunter on west, mayhap clean to the Texies, fin' some good groun' to grow cotton on, whure I kin look a white man in the face without he sayin' to hisse'f, 'There go Hammond Maxwell, whose white wife pleasured with niggers'."

"Nobody don' know that," argued Maxwell.

"Savin' I knows it, an' you knows it, an' Redfield knows it, and his Widder. An' who know how many more?"

"Well, you growed up now, an' you knows how you feel inside. I cain't hold you from goin'," Maxwell conceded. "Take along the gold, whutever you want of it, an' the niggers, many as you need. Falconhurst is here fer you to come back to."

"I'll come back an' git you, soon as I settle, you an' li'l Sophy. Take care of her."

"Lucretia Borgia an' Big Pearl, they'll min' her good until you ready fer her. Only me, I reckon I ain't goin'. Come back an' git niggers, all you craves of 'em. They yourn. Only let me stay, me an' Memnon an' Lucretia Borgia, an' the Mandingos, what's lef' of 'em."

"Papa! Papa!" Hammond threw himself at his father's feet and embraced his legs. " 'Tain't a-goin' to be right—me in the Texies an' you here."

"Falconhurst always here fer you to come back," the father said. He paused before he went on. "Me? I belong here, seem like. My bones an' the meat on 'em are made of Falconhurst dirt. Born here, growed here, lived here all my life a-knowin' ever'-body. Reckon it's fittin' I die here an' rot back into the groun' I come from, rest me alongside your mamma on the hill. You gone, Son, I got to throw to one side this rheumatiz, I reckon, an' take aholt."

George MacDonald Fraser

FLASHMAN 35p

This racy instalment of the Flashman papers solves the mystery of what happened to Harry Flashman – the cad-bully from 'Tom Brown's Schooldays' – after he was expelled.

ROYAL FLASH 35p

The second part of the now celebrated Flashman Papers ... While the destiny of a continent waits, our hero takes the place of his spitting image, a young Danish prince, at a royal wedding, enjoys the unsuspecting bride and plans to steal the Crown Jewels ...

FLASH FOR FREEDOM 35p

The third outrageous instalment of the immortal Flashman Papers, plunges our hero, all unwillingly, into the West African slave trade. Both the fighting and the wenching are fast and furious as Flashy goes from bed to bed and from fix to tighter fix – saved only by the skin of his chattering teeth.

'Breathless adventures, pretty continuous lechery' – THE TIMES LITERARY SUPPLEMENT

Wilbur Smith

SHOUT AT THE DEVIL   40p
'For those who like their violence in large doses, this book gives tremendous value' – OXFORD MAIL

WHEN THE LION FEEDS   40p
'Wilbur Smith has built up his wide-screen story with energy and shrewdness' – SUNDAY TELEGRAPH

THE SOUND OF THUNDER   40p
The sequel to *When The Lion Feeds*. 'A violent saga-type novel set in Boer War South Africa, told with vigour and enthusiasm' – EVENING STANDARD.

THE DARK OF THE SUN   35p
'Bloodthirsty, blood-stained excitement of white mercenaries in the Congo ... it's impossible to put down' – SUNDAY EXPRESS.

GOLD MINE   35p
'Set in Africa today, a brutal tale of violence, greed, chicanery, and lust amid the gold dust ... packed with action and excitement, it surges along in crisp style' – SUNDAY EXPRESS

THE DIAMOND HUNTERS   35p
Wilbur Smith brings a nerve-stretching tension to this spacious, virile and compellingly readable story as two men battle for supremacy in the Van Der Byl Diamond Company.

Eric Corder

Ruthlessly exposes the violence, horror and passion behind the traffic in human flesh.

SLAVE   35p

A scorching, savage novel of life on a pre-Civil War cotton plantation. Trapped in a violent world where men and women suffered a brutal discipline, where young girls were raped and male slaves tortured, Jud lived only for freedom and revenge ...

SLAVE SHIP   35p

Hot blood and dark passions crowd the pages as three men find their destiny linked: Adoko, proud Ashanti warrior, Captain Horneby, lustful renegade, and Dunbar, the young journalist who loathes this degrading trade in human lives, yet becomes the owner of a beautiful slave ... 'The most infamous black market of all brilliantly described in this gory novel of slaves and slavers'

— MANCHESTER EVENING NEWS

Harold Underhill

JAMAICA WHITE   40p

Jamaica in the early 1830s. James Arthur came
fresh from Manchester's squalor to be book-
keeper on the island's largest plantation.
Young and squeamish, his education is completed by:

BRODERICK – the lustful overseer who ruled by
whip and fear,

MARY LOU – sex gave her all the satisfaction
and sensation she wanted.

ANNIE PALMER – beautiful White Witch of
Rose Hall. Cruel beyond belief, an eager bedmate for her slaves, guilty of murder and to
torture. This was the woman who taught
James the meaning of love – and death.

'Powerful and compelling ... savage and
exciting' – OLDHAM EVENING CHRONICLE

In the robust tradition of the Falconhurst saga
– 'The action is skilfully handled, the story
gripping' – BBC

David Morrell

FIRST BLOOD   40p

Bare-bottomed naked, Rambo roared out of
Madison on a stolen motorcycle – leaving a
trigger-happy cop spilling his guts on the cell
floor ...
Be-medalled Green Beret, Rambo had survived
captivity and torture in Vietnam. He was an
expert in death.
If Police Chief Teasle kept on pushing, Rambo
would give him a fight to remember. Sonofa-
bitch ...
'The most chilling story of a man-hunt I have
ever read ... ends in massive violence' –
DAILY EXPRESS